# Journey to Freedom

# Journey to Freedom

Klaudia Zec Djuranic

| | | |
|---|---|---|
| Library of Congress Control Number: | | 2011962536 |
| ISBN: | Hardcover | 978-1-4691-3641-7 |
| | Softcover | 978-1-4691-3640-0 |
| | Ebook | 978-1-4653-0614-2 |



This book was printed in the United States of America.

**To order additional copies of this book, contact:**
Xlibris Corporation
1-888-795-4274
www.Xlibris.com
Orders@Xlibris.com
106630

# CHAPTER 1

"San Sabba Refugee Camp!" the bus driver exclaimed, glancing in Katarina's direction. She rose from her seat and walked to the front of the bus and looked at the driver.

"Thank you," she replied. Her long brown hair bounced as she stepped off the bus. Suddenly she froze. The access to the refugee camp was right in front of her. Her greenish-brown eyes fixed on the sign that hung over the cobbled gate with iron bars: "SAN SABBA, CAMPO DE REFUGEE." It read in Italian. Her body stiffened. "What am I doing here?" she muttered to herself, after everything she had gone through.

During the last twenty-four hours, Katarina had taken a train to the Italian border, slipped through Yugoslav border police, and crossed the mountain on foot to arrive in Trieste, Italy. All the afternoon, she wandered through the street, trying to find her way to the refugee camp, and now that she finally stood in the front of the entrance, she felt eerie.

The camp looked like an ancient fortress from the days of the Austro-Hungarian or maybe even Roman Empire. It was securely enclosed with a ten-foot brick wall, and an Italian carabineer stood alert at the attached guardhouse. His hands clutched the strap of his rifle, which was slung across his back. His eyes were watching her.

Skeptically, she began to move toward the gate. "This looks more like a prison than a refugee camp. If I go in, I might never get out," she said under her breath, and Katarina's mind spun full of questions and reflections. Her wonder was intruded by loud voices of laughter drifting across the street. She stopped, and her eyes darted toward the noise to see a restaurant packed with people enjoying their coffee on the veranda. The late afternoon light shimmering golden attribute gilded the city with the special quality that could be seen only around the Mediterranean Sea.

"Oh, how I wish I could join them," Katarina grumbled, knowing it wasn't possible. Before she could catch herself, she was musing, fantasizing, seeing herself and Leo sitting on the veranda together, having a romantic night out, his hand reaching for hers across the table.

"Oh, stop it!" she ordered herself, almost in a rage, and refocused on the refuge gate. "I hate those Communists for forcing me to leave my own country." Sad tears began rolling down her cheeks, her heart wilted under the heavy burden she carried, but she knew what she had to do. Katarina bowed her head, wiped her tears, and continued on her way. She was startled by the ringing of a nearby church clock striking the time. "It's four o'clock," she noted, glancing around as she shuffled forward. But she couldn't see the clock or the church.

As Katarina approached the entrance of the camp, she hesitated and cast a glance at the carabiniere whose eyes were still following her. She still had unanswered questions spinning in her head, even though she had charted her course. Instead of entering the camp office, Katarina leaned against the gate.

She peered through the steel bars and saw a courtyard swarming with carabiniere. The panicky butterflies in her stomach were on the wing, battering her brain with doubts and buffeting her heart with indecision that came too late. "Have I chosen wrong?" she asked herself. *Maybe I should turn back*? she mused, but only for a second or two, realizing she would be thrown in jail, harassed, and treated like a common criminal if she returned. "I certainly would never be allowed to work my trade, even though the nursing skills are desperately needed," she muttered to herself. Swallowing hard, she sighed deeply and whispered, "In any case, my whole life would be ruined. I have no choice but to follow my plan and go forward. There are many in the position as I. I will be fine, and I'll be free." She assured herself, but still continued to lean against the bars, her mind twirling. Katarina was not in a rush to make the final step.

The carabineer, still keeping eyes on her, began to wonder what she was doing there and walked over to her.

"Is there anything I can do for you, young lady?" he asked, from one hundred meters away. She was wrapped deeply in her thought and didn't hear him. The carabineer moved closer and placed his hand on her shoulder from behind her. "Can I help you, young lady?" he asked again.

Startled by his touch, Katarina stiffened and paused. For a split second, she was paralyzed and slowly turned to see the carabineer towering over her, but had no idea what to say.

He looked at her mud-spattered clothes and the bag in her hand. "Are you looking for refuge?" he asked with an authoritative voice, glaring down at her.

She lifted her long brown hair from her face and met his eyes. "Yes. Yes, I am," she answered in a frightened tone of voice, thankful that his rifle was still on his shoulder.

"Do you want to come in?" the carabiniere asked, still gazing at her.

"Yes," she replied apprehensively.

"Then come along with me," he said and walked through a small gateway he unlocked.

Katarina stared at the carabineer for a few seconds, then hurried after him. When she passed, the gate slammed shut and her body trembled. *There's no turning back now,* her inner voice warned as she continued to follow him down the pathway into an old building and down the corridor.

The carabineer stopped in front of an open door and knocked. "Go on," he encouraged her and turned to walk back to his post.

She paused and glanced after him. Then without a word, she entered the door and walked slowly toward the officer who sat behind a desk. His head was buried in a stack of papers. As soon as she approached the desk, the officer offered, "Sit down, please," pointing to the chair opposite without even lifting his head. It was rude of him, but then she was used to the cold-shoulder treatment from the Communists at home and didn't pay much attention. She was exhausted.

"Thanks," she replied dazed and sank into the chair. The enormity of her decision and the journey over the mountains almost overcame her. She was glad she could finally get some rest, but soon fear wrapped around her heart as she realized she could never go back. Katarina stiffened and stared at the man at the desk, anxiously waiting for what would come next.

"What's your name?" the officer asked finally, still shuffling through the papers on his desk.

"My name is Katarina Sarrac," she replied in a barely audible voice.

"Where are you coming from?"

"I came from Yugoslavia," she answered. "Right across the Italian border. Croatian Republic, Istrian Peninsula, that is."

The carabineer lifted his head and looked at her with a smile. "I can see why you would speak Italian so well. That territory was under Italian control until 1945."

"That's right. It was seized from Croatia by Italy during the First World War. After the Second World War, it was returned to Yugoslavia," Katarina explained, lifting her long brown hair from her face.

"You seem to know your history well," he commented. "But let's go back to my questions. What made you decide to make such a big change in your young life? What was the problem?" the officer quizzed as he returned to staring at his papers.

"I am afraid, being a Catholic and a Croat in Yugoslavia is a sin," Katarina sighed. "Being both was a big problem." She shifted uncomfortably in the chair.

"Oh!" he smirked under his eyebrows and asked, "And to where would you like to emigrate, Ms. Sarrac?"

"I don't know. I never thought about it. Do I have to decide now?"

"No. Not this minute, but we really need to know soon. Here is the list of countries that are accepting refugees," he said, handing her two long sheets of paper.

"Thank you," Katarina replied and took the list. As she read the names of the countries, she recognized one name that was often whispered in her homeland. "Yes, Canada!" she voiced aloud.

"What was that?" the carabiniere asked, lifting his head from behind the pile of papers.

"I'll go to Canada. That's where I will go. I heard it's a good country," she replied, returning the list to him.

"Canada is a great country, but there, it's very cold," the carabiniere warned as he took the list back.

"It's all right. I still want to go," Katarina stood firm on her decision.

"Then, can I have your ID papers and passport, please?" he requested.

"Why?" Katarina asked, panic creeping into her voice. Her face became beet-red. "I don't have a passport," she stuttered. "I came over the mountains and sneaked into your country. You are not going to send me back, are you?"

"No. No, don't worry," he smiled. "You are not the first or the last without any papers," he acknowledged. "You'll be given a new set of Italian papers and a passport when it comes time for you to leave Italy."

Assured, Katarina replied, "If that's the case," and surrendered the papers she had.

"Thank you, Ms. Sarrac," the officer said, looking over the papers. Suddenly he lifted his head and asked, "I need you to give me your little Red Book too."

"I don't have one, and I never had it. There are still those in Yugoslavia who don't belong to the Communist Party, you know. Maybe if I had become a member and had accepted its rules, they would treat me better. I might not be here today. Or maybe they would have found another reason to drive me out of my homeland?" Katarina murmured.

"I believe you," the carabiniere agreed. "One last thing," he added, "You'll have to spend twenty-one days in quarantine as a precautionary measure against communicable diseases. The first twenty-four hours you'll be totally confined. Now, go into the waiting room," he said, pointing to it. "Someone will soon come to escort you to the quarantine."

"All right. Thank you," Katarina said and strolled into the waiting room with her little bag in hand. Overwhelmed by the travel and the tensions of the day, she collapsed in the soft chair, drained of energy. After waiting for a while, her head began to ache; she laid her head against the back of the chair and closed her eyes to relax a little.

A short while later, loud voices made her open her eyes. Two carabineers had entered the waiting room through the back door and were walking toward her, chatting and laughing. One looked much older than the other. The older had thinning gray hair, was somewhat chubby, and wore a name tag inscribed with "Bruno." As he walked by her into the office, he smiled at her without saying a word. The other, younger and taller, came over to her, finger-brushing his short dark hair. His name tag identified him as Dino. He picked up her bag and prepared to leave. "Are you ready to go, Ms. Sarrac?" he asked and turned to walk toward the door with her belongings.

"Yes, of course," Katarina replied and rose from the chair, but instead of moving, she just stared at him, dazed.

Carabineer Bruno came out of the office with some papers in his hand and glanced at her. "Come with us, little lady. Don't just stand there," he commanded with a smirk on his face. Without any further comment, the carabineers strode ahead and out the door as if they were in a hurry.

"I'm coming," Katarina replied and followed them out into the courtyard. They stood in front of a long five-story building, waiting.

*What is going to happen to me?* she wondered.

They were standing in front of a long building. Her eyes drifted away from them and fixed on an old church on their left side. She paused and glanced at the big church clock. "This must be the clock I heard before," she said and walked over to them.

"Probably," Carabineer Dino replied.

Her eyes drifted toward the building again. "Is the camp in there?" Katarina asked, quickly surveying it, anxious to find out as much as she could about the camp.

"No. This is the administration building," Carabineer Dino answered, placing himself on her right side as they walked, and added. "Every time you'll have something to sign or things like that, this is the place to come."

"The camp is behind it," Carabineer Bruno interrupted, answering her question as he fell in on her left.

Katarina glanced first at one, then the other, and continued to walk between the two carabineers.

They walked to the side of the building and passed under a vaulted dome into a passage that led to a compound. "That's the camp," Carabineer Bruno said as they entered. Katarina gazed at the eight-foot-high brick wall that surrounded it, making escape by even a mouse impossible.

"This is the camp? Now I feel like a hardened criminal with no escape," she smirked as they were crossing the yard.

"You are too beautiful to look like a criminal," Officer Dino noted and chuckled. "Besides, you don't have to worry. You can leave any time you want."

"Are you sure about that?" Katarina quizzed as her eyes were preoccupied looking at the refugees peeking from the windows of the crumbling building.

As they walked, Carabineer Bruno noticed her stare. "They do that every time new people come in. Everyone wants to know who's coming to the camp," he explained.

"Oh?" Katarina replied and continued to observe. One wall and most of another had fallen from one of the buildings. The doors were missing and the windows had lost their glass. The roof was barely supported by old pillars. She paused, her eyes fixed on an indent under the windows that was six feet high and three wide. The water was dribbling out from the top of the pipe. "What are those things?" she asked, pointing at it.

"Medieval torture chambers," Carabineer Bruno replied with a chuckle.

"What?"

"Well, now they don't look like the torture chambers, the doors are missing and other things. Anyway, the soldiers would place the prisoners inside, and open water pipes to drip over their heads. They had to stand upright all the time as there was no room to lie down," the carabineer tried to explain.

Her heart sunk. She could feel cold sweat crawling up her spine. "What kind of camp is this?" she asked with a look of worry.

"This is a refugee camp," Officer Bruno said quickly and cheerfully.

"It looks more like a postwar zone than a refugee camp," Katarina replied, with wide eyes.

"No, but close," the carabineer agreed. "It's an old, old army prison. A few buildings are fixed for the refugees, the others are left. After all, this is a historic site."

"Yes, I can see. From the old Roman Empire, no doubt," she smirked and continued to walk, still glaring at the destruction.

"Oh, it isn't that bad, Katarina," Carabineer Dino tried to assure her. Just then, they were faced with another high brick wall and another door. She felt as if they were walking through a maze.

"I only joked before, but now I really do feel like a criminal who has been led to the deepest dungeon," she sighed, her eyes wandering.

Carabiniere Dino looked at her and laughed, pointing at the entrance. "Behind this door is the quarantine area. I can assure you, it's not a dungeon," he explained and handed her her bag.

"Thank you," she replied as she took it. Carabineer Dino knocked on the quarantine door then strode off, leaving her with Carabineer Bruno.

As she waited with him for the door to open, Katarina's eyes continued to wander, interested in what the camp was all about. Fear began to creep into her heart. Were they going to send her back? Her stare fixed on a chimney spewing foul exhaust as she noticed from the corner of her eyes that Carabiniere Bruno was surveying her from head to toe.

"The kitchen is under that chimney," he volunteered.

She glanced at him, forcing a smile, and replied, "That's nice to know. Thank you for the information."

The door finally opened. A wrinkled faced carabiniere presented himself at the door.

"Bone sierra," he greeted them, staring at Katarina from under his thick glasses. "You must be our new guest," he chortled, holding on to the door with his shaking hands.

"Yes, I guess I am," She agreed but didn't know if she should worry or be happy. She wasn't even sure she was in the right place.

"Bona sierra, Giuseppe," Officer Bruno acknowledged and turned to Katarina. "Giuseppe is one of our oldest and dearest officers still working, but only nights, I'm afraid," he commented and added, "He is always early for his shift," and walked through the door into quarantine.

"This is very early. When does the night shift start?" Katarina asked, looking at old Giuseppe.

"Six o'clock. But today, I did a favor to my friend and came two hours earlier so he can go home to his family," the Carabineer explained.

"That was very nice of you."

"Let's go, little lady," Carabineer Bruno called out to Katarina.

"I am coming." Katarina threw a smile at old Giuseppe and followed Carabineer Bruno, paying no attention to her surroundings. As she walked a few steps away from the door, her foot sank deeply into the mud. "Oh no!" she exclaimed.

"What's wrong?" the carabineer asked without turning his head.

"My foot is stuck in the mud," she replied anxiously and lifted her head.

The carabineer said nothing and didn't stop until he reached the wooden door of a small shack located not far from the entrance. He placed a key into the keyhole and then paused, glancing up at the sky. "We had a week of rain here," he chuckled. "Today is the first sunny day. Isn't that lovely?" Then he suggested. "There are cement tiles over the mud, use them."

"What tiles?" Katarina shouted, struggling to pull out her foot. "I don't see any!" In the yard, a few male refugees sat on the stone benches, just ahead, staring at her. As she extracted her foot, they chuckled and clapped.

*It's not funny,* she mused, deciding where to place her foot next. "Where are those tiles?" she muttered. The tiles were submerged in mud so she couldn't see them, but by the time the carabineer unlocked the door, she managed to get herself out of the mud and was standing beside him. "Twenty-four-hour confinement room, I presume?" she chortled, leaning against the outside wall of the shack.

"Yes, and it's all yours, little lady," Carabineer Bruno smirked as he pushed open the door. As it swung inward, he quickly stepped back.

*What a moron,* she thought, glancing at him as she entered the empty three-meter square room. The stench inside filled her nostrils and took her breath away. "Phew!" she shouted, quickly covering her nose and turning toward him. "Now I can see why you stepped behind the door swiftly!" she exclaimed, trying to exit.

The carabineer blocked her path with his body and said, "I can't let you go out."

"The room stinks! I can barely breathe!"

"You're actually a really lucky lady," Officer Bruno tried to convince her, grinning widely and taunting her.

"And why is that?" Katarina asked as she studied his face.

"Because that room is for ten women, not for one," he chortled. Then he closed the door in front of her face, locked it, and left.

"I feel like a bird caught in a cage," Katarina muttered, glaring at the closed door.

With gritted teeth and plugged nose, she turned to survey the dim room with one huge bed that took up half of the space. Katarina tried to envision ten women locked in the room. "I guess I'm lucky if I survive this stench," she said under her breath. There weren't any chairs or tables to place her bag on, so she threw it on the bed and began searching for the source of the terrible odor. She found the toilet soiled with feces and her stomach retched. "There you are!" she exclaimed under her breath. With both of her hands covering her mouth, she hurried to the sink to get some water to throw into the toilet. She lifted the dust-covered sink top located under a small window and turned on the faucet. Just a few drops of water trickled out. "No water! That's just great!" she yelled and threw herself on the bed. Katarina buried her face into the army blankets that were piled in one corner of the bed. Tears of frustration prickled at her eyes. "Why hadn't I turned back while I had a chance?" she chastised herself and shuddered to think what was waiting ahead for her.

Carabineer Bruno interrupted her sad and dreary thoughts by entering the room with a tray of food. "Hello, little lady, I brought your supper. I thought you might be hungry," he informed her and placed a tray on the bed.

The stench in the room was making her feel sick to her stomach. Even though she wasn't sure if she would be able to eat, she decided not to complain. She lifted her head from the blankets, glanced at him, and said guardedly, "Thank you. But I would like some water first. There's none in the sink."

"I'm sorry," the carabineer replied. "I should have turned it on as soon as you arrived. Forgive me. You see, we turn the water off when there is no one here, although that doesn't happen too often," he chuckled. "It will be fixed immediately." He turned and rushed out.

Katarina ran to the sink, opened the top, and waited, anxiously. It wasn't long before the sink filled with water. Gladly, she picked up the bucket that stood under the sink and threw some water into the toilet. "Now, that's better," she sighed in relief and washed her hands. Then she climbed onto the bed and ate everything on her tray despite the stench.

After eating, she crawled under an army blanket, folded another one for a pillow, and lay down. She quickly drifted off to sleep.

In the night, a noise rattled through her dreams and awoke her. "What's that?" she asked herself, startled. Katarina lifted her head, supported it on her left elbow, listened, and looked. It was quiet and pitch-dark inside. She couldn't see a thing. Then she heard the door unlocking. *Oh my god! Someone is coming in,* she thought and lowered her head back down, pretending to be asleep. A person entered the room and flipped the light on. Katarina peeked through her fingers to see it was only the older carabineer, Bruno. Seeing him at the door, she breathed a sigh of relief and promptly sat in bed. "What are you doing in here?" she asked, staring at him.

Instead, he asked, "Did you eat all your supper, little lady?"

"Yes, thank you," she replied and slid the tray to the side of the bed. "Here," she said, thinking he came to pick it up.

Carabineer Bruno came close to the bed, leaned against it, then pushed the tray farther down the bed, and ignored it. "Did you get any sleep?" he asked, staring intensely and surveying her from head to toe, taking his jacket off.

"Some," Katarina replied, watching him with wide eyes. When she saw he had no intention of leaving, her eyebrows lifted. *There is nothing to worry about,* her inner voice tried to calm her. *Of course, there isn't. He's an older man, he wouldn't do anything to hurt me,* she agreed inwardly while waiting anxiously for him to leave. Silently, he reached for her and gently began stroking her hair and her body with his hands.

"What do you think you're doing?" Katarina asked and pushed his hands away.

"You are such a lovely woman!" he complimented with a smile and tried to stroke her again.

"Get away from me!" Katarina yelled and instantly pulled back on her bed.

"Oh, come on, I know you like it," he said and suddenly grabbed her with both of his arms, trying to hug and kiss her. It was only then that she caught a whiff of alcohol on his breath. Horrid and twisted thoughts began to whirl in Katarina's mind as she realized what he was after. Cold sweat washed over her face. Her body stiffened, and her heart began to pound so hard she was sure it would jump out of her chest. "Oh no! Oh god, no! Don't!" she shouted as she struggled to jump off the bed.

"Don't make it harder on yourself, little lady. There's no place to run," he snorted, yanked Katarina by her shoulders, and threw her back on the bed. The gentleness and smile disappeared from his face; his eyes were now as cold as ice.

"For God's sake, let me go!" she shouted and fought him as he tried to secure his grip on her.

"Settle down!" the carabiniere yelled, grabbing her legs when she tried to kick him as he climbed up on the bed. He pinned Katarina under his obese body and began stripping her clothes off her savagely, ripping her sleeve.

"Don't touch me! Let me go!" she cried, beating on him with her free hands.

"You can shout as much as your little heart desires. Nobody will hear you," he smirked and grabbed her hands. He pinned them down hard and added, "If you hit me one more time, I'll choke you!" Suddenly, he drew back and then rammed himself full-length into her tight virginal passage vengefully.

Searing pain ripped through her, like someone cut her with a knife. "Oh no!" she screamed, and her body collapsed in pain. She couldn't do much except cry, shout, and call for help, but no one came.

Dejected, exhausted, and in severe pain, she considered giving up, but the anger about what he had done to her helped her to continue the struggle. "Why are you doing this to me? You old pig!" she screamed at the top of her lungs. Somehow, she freed one of her hands, punched his face with her fist, and scratched him with her nails.

"Oh! You're a little tiger, aren't you? I like that," Carabiniere Bruno laughed, taunting her. "Women like you ask for it and then cry wolf later."

"I didn't ask for it! You bastard!" She slapped him hard across the face. "You know how dirty you make me feel? You're a disgusting dirty old man, old enough to be my father!" Katarina shrieked and spat in his face.

Instantly, his expression sobered and his color faded. "What did you say?" he asked, angrily grabbing her free hand and pressing her down even harder. His voice was like steel. However, Katarina didn't let him scare her.

"You heard me! Let me go!" she screamed. The tears continued to stream down her cheeks.

But Carabiniere Bruno didn't let her go. He kept raping her, ignoring every word of her plea. Then suddenly it was over for him. He jumped to his feet, put on his carabiniere jacket, and zipped up his pants. Katarina crouched into a corner of her bed, trembling like a leaf on a tree branch, ashamed and scared.

Before the carabiniere left, he turned to her and warned, "If you ever breathe a word to anyone about what just happened, you'll be sent back to your country in a flash. I'll make sure of that." He dared her. "By the way, no one would believe you anyway." He cackled.

Anger exploded in her chest. "Son of a bitch! Get out of here!" Katarina screamed in fury and threw her shoe at him as he disappeared through the door into the dark night, snorting. As soon as he was gone, she threw herself across the bed and sobbed uncontrollably. Then unable to stand the filth he cast upon her body, she crawled off the bed to wash. A warm fluid trickled down her legs. What's this? Katarina wondered and glanced at it. "Oh no! It's blood," she voiced and wiped it off with the lower part of her nightgown. She then rushed to the sink. "Thank God, Mama isn't here. She would never have understood it wasn't my fault and blame me. 'No man would want you after this,' Mama would say and she would probably be right," Katarina mumbled and turned the water on. While waiting for the sink to be filled, she tore off the bloody part of the nightgown and threw it into the water. She used the rag to scrub her private parts. As she washed with cold water as there was no hot, her tears poured into the sink and mixed with water.

After a while, she didn't know if she was scrubbing herself with water or with her tears. Even so, she continued to feel dirty and couldn't get herself to stop. It was almost dawn when she crawled back into bed, half-frozen. She couldn't sleep. For hours, she sobbed, unable to settle herself. Exhaustion finally took hold, and she dozed off, only to wake a few hours later. She found herself lying in a fetal position; her face was crusted with tears. There was fresh blood on her underwear and she felt a sharp pain in her abdomen. "What had he done to me?" she muttered, cursing him.

Resignedly, Katarina got up and scrubbed herself again, but still she felt dirty. "I should report him," she voiced, anger blazing in her eyes.

"But to whom?" Her body shivered just at the thought of being sent back to her country. "My best bet is to go on with my plans and not look back," she said, still scrubbing herself. But she didn't know if she could survive another night like the last one.

Her wrath toward the man that violated her body was interrupted by the key turning in the door, just as she finished changing into clean clothes. "Oh no, he's coming back," she whispered and quickly bundled her dirty, bloody clothes, tossed them into her bag, and rushed to bed. She managed to pull the blanket over her head just as a carabiniere entered her room.

"Hello, Katarina," he greeted her. It was Dino.

A sigh of relief passed through her body as she realized it wasn't Carabiniere Bruno's voice. "Hi," she replied, barely audible, peeking from under her blanket.

"Here, I bought your lunch tray," Carabiniere Dino announced.

"Lunch already? What happened to breakfast?" she asked, puzzled.

"Bruno said you wouldn't need breakfast because you had something earlier."

"Oh, that bastard," Katarina muttered.

"What did you say?"

"Nothing, nothing. Put the tray down at the foot of the bed," she told him without lifting her head off the pillow.

"All right, but you better eat soon, otherwise it's going to get cold," he warned and laid the tray down, turned, and walked out.+

"I will," Katarina promised, but she was too tired and upset to eat. She grabbed a cup with coffee and ignored the rest of the food. Sipping on the cup, painful memories of last night continued to swirl through her head, racking her body with tears.

Outside her window, she could hear children's voices laughing and playing. They were too loud for her to sleep, not that she would have been able to anyway. She spent most of the day in bed trying to sleep the ordeal away, waiting anxiously to get out of this infested rat hole.

Finally, the old church clock struck five, signaling the end of her twenty-four-hour total confinement. Relief and fear washed over her body. She crawled off the bed, straightened her clothes, and kneeled beside the bed. "Please, God, don't let that ugly animal who had raped me savagely be my escort," she quickly said. But that was too much to ask. Carabiniere Bruno was already at the door.

"Hello, little lady!" he bellowed as he entered with a smirk on his face.

"What are you doing here?" Katarina shouted boldly, her fists ready to lunge at him.

"Now hold on," he rumbled and walked over to her. "Remember what I said? I want you to forget last night!" he demanded, waving a threatening finger at her.

"How can I ever forget what you did to me, you pig! she yelled even when her instinct warned her to keep quiet or be severely punished. Slowly, she began collecting her things into her bag.

"Let's go. Hurry up," he commanded, nudging her with his elbow. His breath still smelled of alcohol, and that made the blood boil in her veins.

"Oh my god, if you don't move away, I'm going to hit you," she warned, clenching her fists. But then, she grabbed her belongings and swiftly walked out the door.

The carabiniere hurried after her and grabbed her bag. "Let me carry it," he said.

Katarina was in a fury; she wouldn't let him have the satisfaction. They struggled for a little while, but both of them kept holding the bag tightly in their hands.

"Here," she said finally and let him have the bag, not wanting any trouble.

He took the bag and accompanied her to the next building where he said she would spend twenty more days of quarantine. She walked beside him quietly. As they were climbing the stone stairs, he teased, "Why that long and sad-looking face, Katarina? Give me a big smile."

"Just leave me alone!" she replied defiantly.

"You have to be good to me, otherwise you can be in trouble," he boasted and continued to climb. They reached the second level of the building, and Carabiniere Bruno knocked on the first door off the steps. "Here we are!" he spat, looking at her. "This is your room. You'll share it with six other girls."

"Good! At least I won't be alone," she glowered and waited for the door to open.

Two girls came to the door and chanted, "Hello, Officer Bruno!"

"You two look beautiful as always," he answered with a smile. "This is your new roommate," he announced, pointing to Katarina. "She's assigned to the empty bed beside the window."

"Thanks," Katarina replied and briskly walked past him to the bed, paying no attention to the girls at the door or the others lying in their beds. She threw her belongings on the bottom of her bed and glanced toward the door.

The girls were still chatting and snickering with the carabiniere. One of the girls looked at her and said, "What a snob."

"Give her time, she'll be just as mellow as you two," Bruno replied, pinching the girl's cheek, and left chortling. The girls laughed as they closed the door.

His words angered Katarina. She lay down, turned her head toward the window, and stared out, wondering what did he mean by that.

"My name is Silvia," the girl on the bed next to her announced. Katarina turned, but didn't answer. Her ears were tuned toward the other girls snuggled on one of their beds. They began to whisper, throwing glances toward her and giggling as if they knew what had happened to her. Katarina became distraught and felt self-conscious, but said nothing, just glared at them.

"Don't mind them. They chuckle for every little thing," Silvia informed, looking crossly at the girls.

"Hello," Katarina replied finally, in a low tone, without looking at her.

Katarina was suddenly filled with shame as though it had been her fault that she had been raped. A terrible feeling of emptiness consumed her heart, and she didn't know how to deal with it. She wished that she never ran away from her home.

The food wagon arrived shortly after. "What's for supper tonight?" one of the girls exclaimed, leaping off her bed to pick up her tray.

"What else, spaghetti, of course," Silvia said sarcastically, strolling to the wagon. The loud voices and smell of food brought Katarina back to reality. She followed Silvia silently to get her portion. As Katarina turned to walk back with her tray, one of the girls stepped in front of her.

"What's your problem?" the girl taunted, rolling her eyes, glancing at the others, giggling.

"I have no problem, and you should mind your own business!" Katarina shouted and pushed the girl away, then continued toward her bed. But then, another girl interfered.

"Why won't you answer a simple question?" she asked, coming behind her.

Katarina turned in one swift motion and screamed, "Listen! I don't have any problems, and I don't have to answer your questions or anyone else's. Got that?" She sat on her bed and tried to eat her supper, but the girls continued provoking her.

Silvia settled on her bed and began to eat her supper. She didn't interfere at first. But after a while of their yelling and screaming at each other, she had enough. "Cut it out, girls!" she shouted finally. "Let her eat in peace, for God's sake!"

Katarina said nothing, but sat in silence and continued to eat her spaghetti. Feeling heavy with a burden of shame she carried, she was too rattled to confront them.

The girls pulled back to their beds. There was a silence, but only for a while. As soon as Katarina had finished her supper and took the tray back to the wagon, the girls were up giggling, rolling their eyes, and throwing glances of insults toward her again.

It was more than she could bear. "Oh god, life's getting dreary," she said, glaring at them, barely able to disguise the scorn that had crept into her voice.

"Oh really! For whom?" they responded in unison, looking at each other.

"There's no point talking to them," she muttered to herself, not that she felt like it anyway, and lay down on her bed. Her eyes drifted toward the window and stared out at the stars in the sky. She hoped her privacy would be respected, but that wasn't so.

Suddenly, Silvia's tall, slender body bounced onto Katarina's bed. She peered out the window at the sky. "Isn't it a lovely spring night?"

she commented in a calm soft voice, twiddling with her long blond hair. "The sky is full of amazing beauty, I love that. Don't you?"

Katarina glared at her briefly before turning her head back toward the sky. They both watched the sky fill with twinkling stars in silence.

"What happened to you?" Silvia asked in a serene voice, breaking the silence.

"Listen! I don't need a psychiatrist," Katarina replied angrily.

"I'm not a psychiatrist. I'm a friend," Silvia said and placed her hand on Katarina's shoulder. "I can see you're hurting terribly. Something horrible must have had happened to you."

Katarina turned and looked at Silvia, sadness overwhelming her. "I've lost everything and everyone I love," she sighed heavily and tried not to cry. "I feel as though I've been sentenced to death," she paused. "And for what?" she asked. No longer able to control herself, she placed her hands over her face and burst into tears. "Leave me alone!" she yelled and turned her head to stare out the window.

"All right, but I know you are still keeping something from me. Though I don't know what, I do know that kind of attitude will get you nowhere in here," Silvia warned and walked to her bed.

Katarina sighed deeply and ignored Silvia's question. Her soul drifted away into the sky, and her thoughts took her deep into her subconscious mind and reflected on the day she left her country, her family, and her boyfriend. It was hard to believe that only a day earlier, Katarina had been with her family and Leo, excited by her plans of escape that she and her friend, Ana-Maria, had cooked up.

*Oh, Leo, my love,* she thought with heartache. She could still see his tall, slender body standing at the train station and his blond hair tussling in the wind. The sad look on his face as the train began rolling forward would never leave her heart.

# CHAPTER 2

At twenty years of age, Katarina was brimming with dreams of the future, but these had been destroyed when she was blackballed by the Communist government: she knew she was about to lose her job, and she would never get another anywhere in the homeland. So in the spring of 1961, she left her homeland to find freedom and hope for a better life.

"Some life this is turning out to be! Oh, how I wish I'm back home," Katarina muttered from her refugee bed, still staring at the sky. Her memories spun backward in her mind like a roll of film, recalling every detail of the day:

She arrived at Pula train station just before 2100h in the evening and walked toward the ticket counter. She stopped and looked around, but she didn't see her boyfriend, Leo. He was supposed to meet her there as she asked him. While she waited, she debated: should she tell him her plan that she was leaving the country or not? She hadn't even told her parents for a fear the Communist authorities would find out. A telling Leo would be even more dangerous as he was a member of the police department. Could she trust him not to send them after her? she wondered. After all, she hadn't known Leo that long. They'd been seeing each other for only a few months. She didn't think Leo would turn her in, but he was a policeman and a member of the Communist Party. He carried the membership card, Red Book, in his pocket. Like a wind, her thoughts rushed through her head. Finally, she concluded it would be safer not to tell him.

"Hello," Leo said as he approached. She looked up. As their eyes met, her heart skipped a beat and her stomach fluttered. He startled. His tall handsome body stood in front of her dressed in black flannel pants and a light-blue blazer with a knitted shirt under it and black shoes.

"Hello, my love," finally she responded in an upbeat voice and quickly turned her head away.

Leo wasn't taken in by her tone. He planted his hands on his hips and demanded, "What is going on? Why did you want to meet me here of all places?" Before Katarina could respond, his impatience began to gnaw at his gut and his expression changed. "Oh no. No," he said sharply, throwing his arms up in despair. "Don't tell me you're leaving the country!" Then in a low tone, he asked, "Does that include me too?"

"But I'm not leaving you or the country," Katarina replied calmly. "Where did you get such an idea?"

"Where? You ask me where? Look around you, darling. Most of your friends and mine are gone," Leo whispered tensely. "Especially our Croat friends who are disappearing, either across the border or to prison." She waited nervously while his big blue eyes studied her before he continued. His eyes filled with tears. "Will you leave too? Please tell me, Katarina, if you are?"

"Well," she replied, "Yes, if you must know.

"I knew it!" He jumped right in.

"Hold it," she yelled, staring straight into his eyes. "I'm going to Slovenia, to Sezana to be exact, to buy a few things for my older sister, but I'll be back tomorrow. Is that all right?"

"I'm sorry that I got so upset. For a minute there, you scared me," he admitted, relaxing his shoulders. "You should have told me that right away."

"I should have, but I wanted to surprise you," she replied mischievously.

"You surprised me all right. You scared me to death!" Leo responded and wrapped his arms around her waist to kiss her.

"Oh, wow! Now I know that you really do love me," she teased and rejoiced.

When Leo let her go, a small red book fell out of his shirt pocket. Katarina bend down and picked it up. It was the Communist membership he had been carrying around. "Here, this must be yours," she said and handed it to him. Leo took it and placed it back in his pocket without a word to her.

Katarina looked at him, but said nothing, pretending she didn't know what the red book stood for.

Leo's eyes drifted to the big bag she held in her hand. Pointing at it, he asked, "What's with this?"

"This is a bag with my clothes in it," she said.

" Isn't this multicolored pleated skirt and lovely fascia blouse you're wearing good enough for an overnight stay?" he asked.

"Of course, but I do need some other clothing," Katarina replied, lifting the bag. "In here, I only have my sweater, nightgown, and a few other things. I know the bag is big, but I'll need it to bring home the things I'll buy for my sister," she answered nonchalantly.

Leo paused and turned his head away. He still hadn't reconciled with her explanation. He suspected that she wasn't telling him the truth. Nevertheless, his eyes pinned Katarina with a mellow gaze and tried to discourage her from leaving. "It's your first trip to Slovenia," Leo hinted. "And they speak a different language there. How are you going to manage?"

She looked at him and smirked. "Since when did Sezana become a foreign country?" she asked. "Just because it lies on the border of Italy doesn't make it a foreign country. Everyone knows it is part of Slovenia."

"And Slovenia is part of Yugoslavia, I know," Leo replied and pointed out in no uncertain terms. "You're too young to travel by yourself."

Katarina's blood pressure rose, "There you go again, trying to tell me what I should or shouldn't do. For God's sake, I'm almost twenty years old. I can go anywhere I please," she fumed. "Your concern warms my heart, but I resent the implication that I need your permission to go."

"That's because I love you," Leo demurred shocked at her answer; he didn't know what else to say.

"I love you too, but there's no need for such concern. I'll be back tomorrow," Katarina lied.

"The reason I don't want you to go is because I have this feeling I might not ever see you again," he persisted, gazing at her with a wounded look.

"Don't be silly," Katarina assured him and quickly turned away toward the ticket window as she felt her heart sinking.

Almost like she arranged it, the man at ticket shelter yelled, "Next!"

"Thank God! I'm saved," Katarina muttered.

"What did you say?" he asked.

"I'd better go and get my ticket before the man closes the window I said," she replied and rushed toward it.

"You're up to something, Katarina," Leo said under his breath, his eyes following her. "I can feel it in my gut."

She paused just before arriving to the window and glanced back. Noting his intense gaze, she realized it would be hard to convince him. "Ana-Maria, where are you when I need you?" she muttered under her breath. Then she remembered the tricks her friend taught her when she coached her how to slip by the authorities.

"Where to, young lady?" the man asked.

"To Sezana. Return ticket! Please," Katarina asked loud enough for Leo to hear.

"Three hundred dinars," the shelter man said and handed her the ticket.

She took the ticket and said, "Thank you." Upon her return, she flicked the ticket in front of her boyfriend. "See, return tickets. Are you satisfied?" Katarina chirped. He sighed in relief and in her benefit said, "Yes." But Leo's suspicion lingered at the back of his head; he just couldn't shake it. His experience told him a return ticket would prevent authorities from questioning the trip, but he didn't want to push his luck as he had no evidence. So he said nothing further.

Katarina thought her trick worked; she turned her head and whispered, "Thanks, my friend." After she put the ticket in her purse, they walked, hands entwined, onto the platform where the train stood, ready to leave.

"The train to Sezana will be leaving in five minutes. This is the last call!" a male voice droned through the loudspeaker.

Leo wrapped his arms around Katarina's petite body, and drew her closer. "I love you," he whispered in her ear and ran his fingers through her long brown hair, kissing her tenderly and repeatedly. The passing crowd, striding toward the train, didn't bother him. He held her as if he was afraid that if he let her go, he would never see her again.

"I love you too," Katarina said, sliding out of his tight embrace. "I have to go now, my love." And she rushed toward the train.

Leo stood there motionless. "Good-bye, my darling," he replied, barely above the whisper. "See you tomorrow," he added as if to convince himself that the words were true, even though his heart was telling him differently.

Katarina paused on the train steps before going inside to take one last look at her love. His eyes looked enormous and sad. "Oh, how I love you," she whispered and smiled at him. "I wish you could come with me," even though, she knew that was not possible. Leo had sworn his allegiance to the Communist Party and was devoted to it. She had seen the Communist membership many times, the Red Book as they called it. He carried it so proudly around in his pocket. It was like a Bible to him, it seems. Katarina knew that if she'd stayed, things wouldn't work out between them anyway. He would never give up the Red Book. She could never accept the Communists, and that would keep them apart, she feared.

A huge lump filled her throat while she reflected, looking at him. "Good-bye, my love," she yelled and rushed inside the train. The tears that had been welling up in her eyes abruptly burst free as she strode to her designated cabin. Katarina wiped the tears from her eyes, threw her bag on the seat, and quickly pulled the window up, thrusting her head through to see if Leo was still there. He was. His tall, slender body stood planted on the platform, his blond hair tussled in the cool evening breeze as his eyes searched the windows for her face.

"Good-bye, my love," she yelled and waved as the train started forward. His hand reached high up in the air as he noticed her.

"Bye, darling," she heard his faint voice and saw his hand waving.

Katarina stared at him and waved until she could no longer see him. Her heart wilted when he disappeared from her sight as she realized she would never see him again. Her body remained frozen leaning out the window, and her eyes stared at the empty space. She felt bad, even though, it was her choice to leave.

As the train picked up speed, the sound of the clattering wagon wheels passing over the cobbled tracks grew louder with each revolution, and soon, the noise deafened her thoughts. She could no longer hear herself think. Her eyes began to wander; she wanted desperately to absorb and carve each passing scene into her memory forever. A tremor ran through her body as the train roared along the beautiful coast of the Adriatic Sea. It was only spring and still early to swim, but there were many people seen over the beaches walking, some even swimming. "Oh god, how I'm going to miss you," she muttered to herself, knowing the Communists would never allow her to return. A stream of tears flowed down her cheeks as the train left the coast and rolled west. Katarina didn't move, even though the wind became stronger and colder. Black exhaust fumes from the train blew past her face, filling her lungs and choking her, finally forced her to retreat back inside. She pulled the window down and sank into her seat. Still staring out, a mix of emotions washed over her as pictures of her parents and Leo flashed in front of her eyes.

"Mama and Papa, please forgive me," she muttered under her breath with an ache in her heart. She just couldn't trust anyone because if they reported her to the authorities, she would spend the rest of her life in jail. She shivered at the image, picturing herself as an old gray-haired woman mopping the prison floors. She couldn't risk that and destroying the lives of her girlfriend, Ana-Maria, and Dario, her boyfriend. They were helping her in her escape over the border to Italy and freedom.

"Ana-Maria! Oh my god!" she voiced and jumped from her seat. Suddenly, she realized that her friend hadn't found her yet.

"Are you all right, young lady?" a voice within the cabin startled her.

Katarina turned her gaze away from the window toward the voice. She was surprised to see a couple sitting across from her. They had been so quiet she hadn't realized they were there. The lady was reading a book and the man was dozing off.

"Yes, I'm all right, thank you," she finally replied sheepishly.

"I couldn't help but notice that you look troubled," the woman said.

"Oh, it's nothing. I'm fine," Katarina responded, "I'm just a little worried though. A friend of mine should have been here by now. We have supposed to travel together and she's not here."

"I'm sorry," the woman said and turned to her book while her companion still dozing.

"Not as much as I am," Katarina muttered and turned back to stare out the closed window, and her mind began racing. *Ana-Maria should have been here by now*, she thought.

It was part of their escape plan, and if Ana-Maria didn't show up, everything would be messed up. Cold sweat washed over her face. "Dario and I never met. What am I going to do if she isn't here?" she heard herself saying. Katarina worried how they would recognize each other.

"Hello, my friend!" Ana-Maria greeted suddenly from the cabin doorway.

The familiar voice made Katarina turn quickly toward it. She couldn't believe it. Her friend was standing in front of her. Sigh of relief washed over her. "Where have you been?" she asked anxiously.

Ana-Maria walked to the seat and sat beside her. "Sorry if I made you worry. I was in the next cabin talking to a friend of mine," Ana-Maria explained and wrapped her arms around her shoulders. "Don't worry, I know what I'm doing," she whispered in her ear.

"How could I not? I was scared you were caught or something," Katarina replied in a low tone.

"Relax. We won't get caught unless you blow it. Get some sleep or something," Ana-Maria ordered, upset with her behavior. She pulled a small blanket that was folded on the seat and leaned her head against the side of her seat, covering herself with it.

"Fine," Katarina grumbled and turned to stare out the closed window, not very pleased with the tone of her friend's voice. After tussling with her thoughts for a while, she acknowledged Dario and Ana-Maria were experienced in their work. They had been smuggling people over the border for years. At least, that was what she told her. Still, Katarina couldn't help but worry; her body trembled as she continued to stare out the window.

As the darkness of the night blanketed the countryside, she could see nothing but the occasional dim light in the distance. The passengers in the seat across from them were sound asleep together with her friend, Ana-Maria. Katarina pulled down the window blind and wanted to forget everything and get some sleep too, but every time she closed her eyes, she envisioned the dangerous and unknown road ahead. *Who am I fooling?* she finally admitted. *I can't sleep.* She rested her head against the window and let her mind loose. Exhaustion finally got the upper hand, and before she knew it, she had drifted off to sleep.

Katarina had no idea how long she slept. The light of dawn was piercing through the window blind when she awoke. Her eyes darted toward the couple and Ana-Maria. All of them were still asleep, but there was no more sleeping for her. Five hours on the train was like an eternity to her. She stood up and opened the window to a loud whistling sound, awaking them.

"Close that window!" Ana-Maria shouted, turning her head to the other side.

"Where are we?" the lady asked, extending her neck from the seat out without turning.

"The sign says Ljubljana," Katarina said and thrusted her head out without turning.

"Then, we must be pulling into the Ljubljana station. One more stop," she announced and relaxed on her seat.

Katarina leaned out the window, her eyes drifted toward the bright clear sky as she inhaled clean sharp mountain air. "Look, Ana-Maria, it's going to be a beautiful spring day," she called. Her eyes wandered over the people rushing in and out the train as she enjoyed a fresh cool breeze that gently ruffled her hair.

Ana-Maria mumbled something incoherently and pulled the blanket over her head. Katarina ignored her and continued to scan through the crowd on the platform. Suddenly, she saw the Yugoslav border patrol board the train. Every muscle in her body tightened.

"Oh no, what are they doing in here?" she exclaimed, and quickly pulled back inside. She grabbed her purse and frantically rummaged through it to find her train ticket and other papers.

"Is there something wrong?" her friend asked and leaned closer to her.

"The border patrol stepped onto the train," Katarina said in a low tone, anxiously.

"Relax and don't talk too much," Ana-Maria warned with a stern voice.

"I'm calm. I'm merely surprised as I thought you told me they were supposed to come on the train at Sezana, not Ljubljana," Katarina said with her voice elevated.

"The border guard. Oh, no, dear!" the lady on the seat across intruded. "They board here in Ljubljana, and they go through the train checking everyone's papers until Sezana. It's been that way as long as I can remember. But don't worry," she added. "They're very nice."

Oh, I'm not worried," Katarina forced a smile as she finally pulled out her ticket, grasping it tightly in her hand. Ana-Maria cast a disappointed look at Katarina.

Suddenly, the cabin door flew open and a border guard stood there. He planted his hands on his hips, and a sharp, cold smile of self-righteousness carved itself on his stone face. "Tickets and ID cards or passports," he commanded, chewing his tobacco slowly and deliberately as he began checking their papers.

Katarina felt his sharp eyes on her from the moment he entered, which made her even more nervous. She feared she might have given herself away. Panic boiled inside and she blushed.

"Is there something wrong?" the border guard asked, glaring at her face. Before she could answer, Ana-Maria peeked from under the blanket and cast a stern look at her as if to say, you better keep cool.

"No. No, nothing is wrong," Katarina quickly replied.

After the guard checked the other passengers' tickets and ID papers, he turned to Katarina. "Can I see yours?" he demanded with his hand extended.

Nervously, she forced herself to look him straight in the eyes. "Sure. Here," she said, and handed her ticket and ID card to him with both hands to prevent her hands from trembling. As the guard flipped through her papers, he occasionally glanced at her from under his eyebrows.

*What now,* she mused and asked, "My papers. They are all in order, right?" Her eyes didn't even flinch.

"Yes," the border guard replied. "But what's a young girl like you doing alone this far from home?" he quizzed, with a suspicious look.

Katarina swallowed hard and gave him the coldest stare she could muster. "I'm not that young," she complained. "I'll be twenty soon."

The border guard returned her ticket and ID card with a chuckle, spun on his heels, and left. After he had gone, the lady sitting across glanced at her male companion and laughed, "What! He thinks only older people have the right to travel alone these days."

"I guess," Katarina smirked, forcing a smile.

Once the train pulled out of Ljubljana station, she collapsed farther into her seat beside her friend, deeply relieved, knowing that she was safe. "Wow!" she whispered into Ana-Maria's ear. "That was close."

"We are still not out of the woods, there's one more hurdle to overcome," her friend warned in a low tone. "Then we'll be completely safe."

"Yes, I know," Katarina replied, subdued, any comfort she had felt erased. Soon she would be completely alone and in a strange land. She would never see her family and her boyfriend again. Her tired eyes flooded with tears. "Everything I had, I've lost," she muttered, thinking about her parents and Leo.

"What's wrong, dear?" the lady passenger inquired.

"I just broke up with my boyfriend," Katarina quickly replied.

"Oh, I'm sorry," she replied and glanced at her companion as if she didn't believe the story. Katarina felt uncomfortable, but the lady persisted, "What happened?"

"I really don't want to talk about it. It's too painful," Katarina replied, trying to wipe her tears off her face, but they wouldn't stop coming.

Ana-Maria embraced her and said, "Now, now, everything will be all right. You'll find another love. Just be careful next time, my friend," she warned, giving her a hint: she had to behave.

"That woman, why doesn't she mind her own business?" Katarina replied barely above the whisper.

As the train continued on its way, she turned to stare out the open window. Outside the sky was clear, except for a few small puffy clouds. The robins and the sparrows flitted from tree to tree, twittering happily as if they were excited by the prospect of a sunny day ahead. The forest was in full blossom and greenery blanketed most of the mountainous area. The signs of winter were visible only at the top of Alps, and she knew the snow would began to melt there soon too. "Hot summer days are not far behind," she said under her breath.

Suddenly, they were plunged into darkness as the train sped through a tunnel. When they emerged, the lady announced, "We're now entering the city of Sezana. It's the last stop on this side of the border."

"Oh, then we'll be pulling into the station soon?" Katarina asked anxiously.

"Yes, and here we are, Sezana station," the lady exclaimed as the train slowed down and came to a complete stop. The couple immediately rose, gathered their bags, and started toward the door.

Katarina sat frozen in her seat; she felt her body shivering. The images of her family, friends, and Leo flashed before her eyes, making her hesitate. The butterflies in her stomach were working overtime. The tears in her eyes welled up, but she was determined not to let them out.

Ana-Maria saw Katarina's face and quickly wrapped her arms around her shoulders. "There, there. Don't be sad, there's still a lot more fish in the sea," she teased aloud.

The lady turned toward them from the doorway.

"Aren't you girls coming?" she asked before they stepped out into the hallway of the train.

Katarina mustered enough strength to reply, "Yes, of course! We'll be right behind you." She stood up and picked up her bag.

Ana-Maria nuzzled close to her and warned, "Be careful. You never know who's watching and listening. Even these two old people could be spies!"

"Is my freedom worth the sacrifices I'm about to make?" Katarina questioned aloud as if she hadn't heard a word that Ana-Maria said.

"Yes, it is! You are young, beautiful, and smart," Ana-Maria reassured her.

Katarina's excitement and sadness were so tightly bundled up inside her that it took Ana-Maria awhile to convince her that her life was worth fighting for.

The train was about to leave the Sezana station toward the Italy border and the girls were still in their cabin. "Come on, hurry! Don't just stand there," Ana-Maria said with a high-pitched voice and turned to walk out.

Finally, Katarina's doubts were erased and a new determination sprung inside her. "You are right, my friend. Fate has placed these ever-present mountains in my path. I can't give up now. They took everything from me, but they can't take my soul. This is it," she said and, with her bag in hand, dashed off the train before Ana-Maria.

"That's the spirit," Ana-Maria cheered as she followed her.

# CHAPTER 3

Katarina and Ana-Maria rushed through the station. Ana-Maria's eyes wandered over the crowd searching for Dario. Finally, she spotted him on the far side of the platform and let out a sigh. "There he is."

"Who?" Katarina asked as she had no idea that Dario would be waiting for them on the train station.

"The love of my life!" she yelled and hurried through the crowded station to him.

"Wait for me," Katarina shouted and began to run after her.

"Hello, sweetheart!" Ana-Maria said as they came close.

"Hello, girls," Dario greeted them and hugged Ana-Maria with one hand; in the other one, he held a knapsack. "I'm glad you're here."

"Is there anything wrong?" Ana-Maria asked as she noticed that Dario was very tense and reserve.

"No. Did you have any trouble on the way?" he quizzed, looking worried, his eyes scanning around constantly.

"No. No," the girls answered in unison, glancing at each other.

"Why are you asking?" Ana-Maria questioned, staring at him.

"The train was a little late. I was concerned about you two, that's all," he replied and handed his hand to Katarina. "It's very nice to meet you finally," he said.

"It's nice to meet you too," she replied and took her hand back. He wrapped his arm around Ana-Maria's shoulders, handed her a key, and kissed her while whispering something into her ear.

Katarina laid her bag to the ground and asked, "Now what?"

Dario said nothing. Ana-Maria embraced her friend and said, "Good-bye and good luck, Katarina. I hope things go well for you."

"Bye and thanks," Katarina replied, realizing that this was the end of the road for Ana-Maria and didn't question, but watched her friend stride out of her life. "Pick up your bag, Katarina, and come with me," Dario ordered her with an authoritative voice. Anxiety showed on his face almost immediately.

Startled by his strong voice, she turned and looked at him. "Where are we going?" she asked as she picked up her bag.

"You ask too many questions!" Dario thundered and continued to walk. After a long walk down the street, he abruptly turned toward an old dilapidated building.

"Why are we turning here?" she asked, anxiety creeping under her skin. She just couldn't keep her mouth shut and continued. "These are probably ruins from the World War II and never rebuilt," she said just above a whisper.

"The less you know, the better it is for you," Dario hissed through his teeth and said nothing more as he strode into the ruins. She stopped and glared after him, observing his every move. "Is this the same man Ana-Maria told me about?" she muttered to herself, unable to express her feeling about his attitude toward her.

Suddenly, he dragged out a motorcycle and immediately started the motor. The sweat rolled down his pale face and his hands were shaking as he mounted it. "Come on, Katarina! The time is running out. Don't just stand there!" Dario shouted, his voice trembling. Anger and fear shone in his eyes.

Katarina couldn't move; it was as if she was nailed to the ground, her eyes kept staring at him. Panic began to boil inside her, and her heartbeat increased as she walked toward him. She knew that her plan was a dangerous one, but she never realized how much until then.

"Hurry, jump up behind," he urged her.

"What's going on?" she asked as she climbed on the backseat of the motorcycle. Dario ignored her question and revved the engine. As soon as she was seated, he sped off like a madman down the street that led away from the city. "Hold on!" she shouted and quickly wrapped her arms around his waist for safety.

Dario continued to speed ahead in silence, without any sign of acknowledgment, as if he wanted her to be aware of the danger. His body shook and his shirt was soaked with sweat, even though the wind blew strong and cool. The farther they got away from the city and into the deserted forest and mountainous area, the stronger the wind got.

Katarina's body began to shiver. "Why didn't I put my sweater on," she muttered, realizing there wasn't any point in asking Dario to stop as he would probably just get angry at her, so she said nothing.

He turned on a dirt-ragged road that led farther up the mountain and continued to speed wildly. She held tightly to Dario as they drove along the dirty, stony path that twisted and zigzagged higher up the mountainside, leaving clouds of dust behind. *Where is he taking me?* Katarina wondered as she nuzzled against Dario's back to protect herself from the strong wind and her eyes and mouth from the dust and insects that were carried by the wind.

Suddenly, Dario stopped the motorcycle high in the thick forested part of the mountain. "Get off, Katarina," he ordered, still sitting on the motorcycle.

"Here?" she asked, choking on the dust and shivering.

"Yes! Here! Hurry up!" His voice was hard and sharp.

Without a word, Katarina slid off the motorcycle, pulled her sweater out of her bag, still hanging at the side of the motorcycle, and quickly put it on before she froze to death.

"You should have done that before, the sweater didn't do you much good in the bag," Dario commented, smirking.

"I should have, but I didn't know it would be this cold," she replied. "Where are we?" she asked with concern.

"In the Julian Alps," Dario replied less anxiously. "Get your bag off the motorcycle."

She removed the bag from the motorbike and turned to stare at the thick bushes and weeds that lay around and ahead of them. "Thank God, we got the motorcycle," she said and turned to Dario to see he and the motorbike weren't there anymore. "Where are you?" she called anxiously.

"Here," he answered in a low tone.

"Wait for me," Katarina shouted and rushed toward the voice. She found him in front of a small cave, covering the entrance with thick green branches. "Where is your motorcycle?"

"Inside the cave," he answered and returned back to the place where they had stopped.

The wind blew fiercely at this altitude and sliced through the sweater Katarina wore. Her body shivered, even though the day was sunny. Swirling dust and wind were stinging her eyes, and she could barely see.

"Now what?" she asked. Her body stiffened and her heart pounded, anxiety building up inside her. "The mountains are too high, I'll never make it over!" she exclaimed as she stared up at the peaks with fear in her eyes.

Dario looked at her and chortled. "We have to go," he replied and grasped Katarina's hand. He began walking swiftly in front of her deeper into the thicker part of the mountain.

"Who are we running from?" Katarina asked, struggling to keep up through the craggy terrain. Like many other times, he didn't answer, but kept his pace.

Just as Katarina thought she was going to survive the tussle, her feet tangled in some knee-high weeds. "Oh my god, what have I got myself into?" she yelled, unable to move.

Dario let go of her hand so she could free herself easier and thundered, "Watch where you are stepping next time!"

"All right, all right," she replied and bent down to free herself from the attackers. Pulling the weeds off her feet and legs, she wondered, would they succeed in getting out of this jungle? Would she ever see Italy?

She could see herself caught, brought back to her city, and spending the rest of her life in jail. What kind of life would that be for her? Her body shivered just at the thought of it. "I should have stayed home," Katarina said under her breath.

"Stop daydreaming, Katarina, and hurry, pull those weeds off your legs and feet," Dario yelled, his patience running out.

"I'm finished," she replied and strode toward him.

"It's about time!" he thundered and rushed ahead. After a few more steps, Dario disappeared through the thick weeds and greenery.

"Where are you?" Katarina called as she followed his path, but he didn't answer. Suddenly, she found herself in a dark hollow space. Blinded by the darkness, she stopped. "Are you in here?"

"Yes, come forward," he replied.

The fluttering of the bats scurrying for cover and the sound of continuous water dripping gave her a creepy feeling. Katarina trembled, her heart seized and leapt into her throat. She felt her blood leave her face and a sick, slick sweat oozed from her pores. Where are we?" she asked, with a barely audible voice.

"In a cave under the Alps," Dario replied and continued to walk.

"In a cave! What are we doing in a cave?" she asked, surprised.

"Come on, keep walking, and don't ask questions!" he retorted and kept his pace. She could hear the earth beneath his feet swishing as he padded farther away from her, deeper into the cave.

"Wait! I can't move, it's dark," she yelled, with a growing sense of horror.

Dario pulled a flashlight from his pack and shone it at her feet. "Walk toward my voice. Hurry, I don't have all day," he called, lighting her path.

"All right! All right!" she muttered as she didn't know what else to say.

"Here, give me your hand. Now, follow me," he instructed and stuck the flashlight back in his pack.

"What are you doing? Get that flashlight out," Katarina hissed angrily. "I can't walk in the dark."

"No. I don't want anyone to see the light from outside," Dario explained and continued walking, holding on to her hand tightly.

Following him, Katarina rattled, "Of course, you don't need the flashlight because you know the way, but I feel like a blind bat."

After a long walk through the dark, water-dripping, and muddy cave, Dario stopped and announced, "Here we are."

Katarina couldn't believe it, "Here! Where's here?" She glanced around. "I don't see anything."

"Look here," Dario said once again and pointed the flashlight at a wall in front of them.

Each hair on her body bristled as Katarina found herself looking at a solid brick wall. "What in heaven's name is this? Where is the exit?" she yelled panic-stricken and slapped him across his shoulder.

"Settle down! Don't worry. You'll see the exit soon. Here," Dario handed her the flashlight. "Keep it pointed at my hands," he instructed and began pulling rock after rock from the wall.

Katarina held the flashlight pointed at the solid wall steady as she could and glared at it with suspicion. "You really think I can get out through this?" she quizzed, her voice was shaky.

"Yes I do," Dario said and continued his work.

After Katarina calmed down a little, she said, "I'm sorry I slapped you. But you scared me half to death."

"It's all right, I understand. You didn't hurt me," he said calmly, glancing at her frightened face.

"Why all this secrecy?" she asked.

The fear in Katarina's voice compelled him to give her an explanation. "Well, you see," Dario began. "The city is swarming with UDBA agents in plainclothes. You never know who's watching you or listening to you. In my job, you can never be too careful. I have to be vigilant at all times. You understand, I have to protect myself and my secret. You know, don't you? If I get caught, I'll be killed by the secret service," Dario explained with fear in his eyes.

"No! I didn't know that, but I've heard stories," Katarina looked at him dismayed. "I know the Communists are dangerous, but I didn't know they would kill their own people in cold blood, would they?" she asked naively.

"Believe me, they would and they do. There is no place to hide. The Communists have killed many Croats around the world and would have no problems making me disappear without a trace," Dario replied, wiping sweat off his face.

Katarina stared at him in disbelief. "Really" was the only thing she could muster.

"This passage in the cave is a secret," Dario continued. "Only two of us know about it. That's me and one other person, and it's not Ana-Maria."

"Why? Because Ana-Maria is a woman, and you think she can keep a secret. How about the thousands of people you've helped pass here over the border to the other side, including me?" Katarina asked, trying to get her composure back.

"Now, you don't think I'm a chauvinist pig, do you?"

Katarina pointed the flashlight at his face and said, "The only thing I want to know is: when are we going to reach the other side of the border?"

"Not we. You, Katarina. I'm not going any farther," Dario said, "But before I pull out this last layer of rocks. I'm going to say something and you listen very carefully." He took her hand, reached into his pack, and pulled out a small paper and placed it in her hand. "Here, this is your ticket for the train that will take you directly to the Trieste station."

"Thank you," she said, putting the ticket in her purse. "My hope was you would be going with me to Trieste," she added, with sadness on her face.

"That's not possible," Dario replied and continued. "You'll have to find the way to the refugee camp on your own. When you leave this cave, you'll be on Italian soil, so stop worrying. The train station is not far from the cave exit, just over a small hill. Look around to make sure no one is watching you. To answer your previous question, once you've passed through this secret passage, you're no longer a threat to me. Though I must say that you are one of the most chatty people I have ever helped through here," he chuckled.

"Oh, I see, thank you. I think," she smiled.

Dario took the last layer of the rocks out of the wall. "Here is your exit. Good luck, Katarina," he said and hugged her.

She took a deep breath in a sigh of relief. "Please forgive I doubted you."

"Don't worry about it."

Katarina walked close to the exit and turned to Dario. "What are you going to do after I'm gone?" she asked, trying to make a conversation, scared to death of the unknown ahead.

"I'll stay here until you've passed safely through," he replied. "Then I'll put the rocks back to close the passage and return to Ana-Maria in Sezana. In a few days, we'll take a train to Trieste."

"Clever plan. Just don't ever get caught." Katarina pulled an envelope out of her purse. "Here it's your money," she said and handed it to Dario. "Two thousand lira as we agreed."

"Great. Thanks. Did you leave some money for yourself?" he asked as he folded the money and stuffed it in his pocket.

"Yes, but not much. It will have to do until I reach the camp." She didn't really want him to know that she has barely left for a few bus tickets, a cup of tea, and maybe a sandwich or two.

"One more thing," Dario said. "You do speak Italian, don't you?"

Yes, I do."

"Use it, at least until you get to the camp," he suggested. "Spies are everywhere. Be careful, you don't want to be caught and sent back."

"Of course not!" She hugged him and turned toward the windowlike opening on the wall. "Oh, God, please watch over me," she muttered.

"Katarina," Dario called, just seconds before she was to crawl out. "Here, you'll need this," he said and handed her a bottle.

She took the bottle and put it into her bag. "Thanks for the water," she replied and squeezed through the opening, leaving Dario behind in the cave.

Katarina got through to the other side, but she found herself in an area that was part cave and part swamp. The light was coming in from outside. There was a manurelike odor throughout the area, and she could barely breath. "Oh, that SOB, he never said anything about this. I wonder what else he forgot to tell me?" she muttered and turned to look back. To her dismay, the windowlike opening was gone. She could only hear the revel the rocks were making as Dario was mounting them back.

"Great! There's no going back, and I don't see the way forward," Katarina said to herself under her breath and began to walk along the man-made narrow rugged path. The ground beneath her feet swished and crunched with each step she took, sending flocks of frightened birds flitting for cover in all directions and scaring Katarina out of her skin. *At least I can see where I'm stepping,* she mused, glancing up at the sunlight that was filtering through the thick green branches, lighting her path.

After what seemed like hours of scouring, she finally stopped and sat on a rock. "Now what? Where's the exit?" she asked herself, staring angrily at the branches and thick thorny weeds entangled tightly together, all around her. "I feel like a bird in a cage," she pondered. Her fear grew bigger, wondering how or if she ever would get out of here. Suddenly, a big hare went hopping by. "How did you get in here?" she asked and leapt to her feet, quickly followed the hare behind a huge rock to see her get out. The hare passed to the other side through a passage not much bigger than the hare.

Katarina glared at it, "Great! You passed, but how on earth am I going to get out through this?" The hare said nothing, but hopped away. Katarina stared after the hare. She didn't worry about being alone; she was used to being in the forest and strolling through the woods. Her parents lived on a farm far away from the cities and towns. But she feared being trapped in here.

"Damn you, Dario! If I ever see you again, I'll strangle you." She spat and kicked the huge rock several times in anger before she knelt down and began creeping through on her hands and knees.

The tight passage gave Katarina a lot of grief. Her hands were both scratched from the thorny weeds she pushed aside to make more room for her passage. Her dress had been smeared with mud. She crawled out and emerged onto a small meadow of thick green grass filled with beautiful violets and yellow roses. The sunlight beamed through the thick green tree branches, giving the grass and the flowers a golden sheen.

Katarina inspected the area and concluded the only voices she could hear were those of the birds singing. The exit was well hidden from the outside world by the thick bushes and big trees so no one could see her there.

Happy to be safely in Italy, Katarina took a deep breath of the fresh mountain air tinged with the scent of flowers and stretched on the green grass. She took a sip of water from the bottle that Dario had given to her and watched as a gentle breeze set the blue and yellow flowers nodding a greeting on their slender stems.

"Oh, wow! They are so beautiful, and they smell heavenly," she said under her breath. Wrapped in their scent, the fresh air, the singing of the swallows and sparrows, she relaxed a little too much and dozed off, but only for a minute or so. As she opened her eyes, she shuddered, thinking about the next step. She rose to her feet and cleaned the mud off her shoes, but she couldn't remove the mud stains on the dress.

"I'd better get going," she ordered herself. "If I don't, I'll miss the train." Katarina glanced around. Again, she heard and saw no one. With her bag in her hand, she slowly began her descent down the steep zigzagged path through the thick bushes and around the big rocks, fighting off masses of bloodsucking insects.

Upon reaching the end of the path, she was greeted by a steep hill. Her knees buckled under her when she glanced up toward the top of the hill. "Just over a small hill, ha, Dario? Oh! This is another of your big lies!" she shouted and kicked the ground. It seemed to be a long way up and she felt too tired to tackle it, but she began to climb anyway. Halfway up, she was forced to stop and catch her breath. "I'll never make it to the top," she sighed with fear in her heart and threw herself down on the ground. She rested a few minutes, then rose and looked up toward the top of the hill. "I hope this is the last one to tackle," she muttered under her breath and continued her trek. Katarina literally crawled the last few meters to the top, her energy was totally gone. "Thank God, it wasn't any higher. Not far, hmm, Dario? I wonder if he ever passed through here?" she grumbled, wiping the sweat running down her face.

Her thoughts were interrupted by a large shadow passing overhead. "What's that?" she asked and glanced up at the sky. A huge hawk was soaring above in ever-widening circles, making no sound. It seemed as he was preparing himself to have lunch. "Oh, go away! I'm still alive!" Katarina yelled to the bird, annoyed. "Let me rest a few minutes in peace. I'm exhausted!" She lay on the ground unable to move. Every muscle in her body ached, but even so, she rested only for a short while; there was no time to rest more.

*You wouldn't want to miss the train, would you, Katarina*, she mused and mustered enough energy to force her body to its feet and drained the last drop of water from the bottle that Dario had given her. Her eyes peered down from the hill, searching for the train station below. It was hard to see because the area was wrapped in a blanket of greenery, big bushes, and tall trees, but the train station was not in sight.

Finally, she noticed a house a few hundred meters from where she was standing. The house was glittering in the sun. "It must be the train station!" she cried in delight, briskly walking toward it. The piercing whistle of a train approaching the station cut through the air, confirming it. "Just in time!" she shouted and began running. The train roared into the station just as Katarina stepped onto the platform. She boarded and quickly settled in the seat beside the door. *I have to be careful. I don't want to be discovered as being in the country illegally,* she reflected and hid the mud-smeared dress with her bag.

"Ticket please," the conductor demanded, looking at her messy clothes, but saying nothing.

As she pulled the ticket out of her purse, she remembered Dario's suggestion to use her Italian. "Echo la qui," she replied and handed the ticket to him.

When the conductor returned her ticket, she sighed in relief. *So far, so good,* she mused and turned to stare out the window. The tall trees and small villages flashed by as the train rolled down toward the coast, leaving behind the Julian Alps. "Good-bye, mountains," she muttered to herself, resting her head against the window.

A half hour later, the conductor yelled, "Trieste station next!"

*Yes! I made it!* Katarina mused. *I can almost smell the freedom!* A surge of excitement swept over her, even as her inner instinct warned her it was too early to celebrate. Her eyes peered toward the front and, in anticipation, waited for the train to pull into the station.

Katarina stepped off the train and walked up the main boulevard right in the heart of Trieste. With her eyes dazed, she continued to walk. The city was bustling, rowdy, and throbbing with cars and buses crowding the downtown streets. Vendors were hawking and shopkeepers were putting out their wares for display. Small grocery stores took up corners, and everywhere there were Vespa scooters, people, and pigeons a lot of them. Restaurants and coffee shops were numerous, set in rows stretching down the boulevard as far as her eyes could see. Their stone terrace fronts were graced by palm trees, and overhead, there was latticework with vines crawling across the wooden slots providing shade in the midday heat. The terrace chairs and tables were decked with blue-and-white checkered tablecloths. They were crowded with people enjoying the beautiful sunny spring day with Turkish coffee after their lunch.

Katarina continued down the boulevard, remnants of its old Roman and Austro-Hungarian occupation surrounded her. She had never visited such a big city before and was awestruck. Exhausted and thirsty, Katarina crossed the street and vended her way into a coffee shop. Lunch was nearly over, and the shop was quickly emptying. Her eyes searched around for an empty table and the veranda was still full of customers. She sat at the first empty table she saw inside and drank down two small glasses of water from the jug that was on the table.

A waiter came striding from the terrace over to her table. "What can I get you?" he asked and pulled a small notepad from the pocket of the black apron tied around his waist.

"Tea con lemone, prego."

"Something else," he asked, staring at her.

Katarina paused and thought for second, listening to her stomach rumble. "Si, uno piccolo mortadela sandwich," she ordered.

The waiter rushed away and almost immediately returned back with a cup of tea and sandwich. "Here is your order," he said and placed the cup of hot tea and the sandwich in front of her.

"Gracie," she said and paid. The waiter strode to the next table where a few new customers had arrived.

After she ate her sandwich, Katarina sat and sipped on her cup of tea looking at her shaky hands. She chuckled, "A stiff drink would be better to settle my nerves."

She wasn't sure how long she stayed, drinking tea, but she knew she felt tired to go on. Yet she had no choice so she forced herself to resume her trek down the boulevard, which was buzzing with people. Her eyes scanned every building for a sign indicating where the refugee camp was, and she faced almost every passerby and constantly questioned, "Please could you tell me how to get to the refugee camp?"

"I don't know." It was all she heard.

After several hours of walking, asking, and looking, she still didn't know where the camp was and she was getting even more tired. She stopped and leaned against a big tree, her eyes scanning. "If I didn't know better, I'd think that the camp didn't exist," she whispered to herself.

Then it suddenly hit her. "Carabineers," she voiced. "I'm sure they would know." With a smile on her face, Katarina rushed down the boulevard in search for a carabineer. Birds flitted overhead from tree to tree singing, and pigeons strolled proudly over the plazas and park grounds. The sidewalk was full of them. The pigeons were constantly under Katarina's feet. However, they got her attention; she stopped and admired them. They were so friendly, they let her touch them; she could have caught one if she had wanted.

A few minutes later, Katarina was on her way again. As she passed through a long tunnel of dark greenery, she noted that the birds had fallen perfectly silent. "It's so strange," she said to herself. "It is almost as if they want to warn me about something." As she emerged out the other end, two young carabineers were leaning against a post office building, chatting.

She paused and stared at them, wondering, *What if they ask to see my papers*? Suddenly she could hear Dario's voice, "Use your Italian language."

"Yes, that might work," she said under her breath and walked over to them. "Can you help me, please?" she asked in Italian, in a shy voice.

"What can we do for you, signorina?" They stared, grinning.

"Can you please direct me to the refugee camp?"

"Oh, you're not one of those, are you?" They burst into loud laughter, and both took a sip of something from small bottles they held close to their jackets.

Katarina didn't find her request funny. Their laughter humiliated and shamed her, but she realized they had been drinking. Her inner voice raged, but her instinct warned her to keep quiet. Holding her anger in check, she replied, "No. I'm not one of those. I'm visiting someone."

Feeling like a fool, she rushed away without waiting for an answer. Katarina stopped farther down the street and glanced back at them, fighting the tears that threatened to burst forth. They were still laughing.

"No doubt on my account," she muttered to herself, glaring at them and then dismissed the two carabineers as cretins and continued on her way. The air, which was fragrant with the scent of daffodils and tulips that filled her nostrils, helped her forget the two carabineers. *What lovely flowers,* Katarina reflected, stopping to admire them. Her reverie ended abruptly as a strong wind began to blow and a dark ominous cloud suddenly obscured the clear sky. A big storm threatened the perfectly lovely spring day.

"I better keep going," she reminded herself and scurried across a bridge spanning an inlet of the Adriatic Sea. Seagulls and pigeons flew overhead, hectoring and wheeling, frantically seeking shelter. Katarina knew that the spring shower was approaching, and she had to hurry.

At the end of the bridge was a man watching the boats gliding along the water's surface. She walked toward him with hesitation and, in her best Italian, said, "Excuse me, sir."

He swung around to face her. "Yes," he replied. "Can I help you?" His tanned face broke into a smile.

Katarina's pulse raced. She paused and surveyed him from head to toe. "Can you please tell me the way to the refugee camp?" she asked, hoping he wasn't as ignorant as the two carabineers.

"But of course," he replied, without asking her any questions. "That's easy. Just take the bus number 4. It will take you directly to the camp gate. You can't miss it."

"Thank you for being so kind," Katarina said and was on her way. She was happy that she had enough courage to ask him and even happier that he hadn't asked any questions. Wrapped in her thoughts, she passed right by the bus sign and kept going.

"Miss," the man yelled after her. "You just passed the stop for your bus," and pointed toward the sign.

Katarina turned and replied, "Thank you," and backtracked a few hundred meters. The bus was approaching just as she arrived to the bus stop. The bus door opened and she hopped in. "Can you please let me know when we arrive to the refugee camp?" she asked the driver, handing him the bus fare.

"All right, signorina," he replied, placed the money into his black bag, and drove off. She sat on the opposite seat, leaning her head against the window glass. Those ominous clouds she encountered at the other side of the bridge were now dangling over the bus. "Oh no!" she muttered, her eyes darted toward them. *You can get me in here,* she mused as the bus rode toward the refugee camp.

# CHAPTER 4

Wrapped deeply in memories of the family and the love she had left behind, Katarina didn't hear Silvia calling her name. "Katarina! Katarina!" Finally the voice broke through Katarina's daydream and pulled her back to earth with a thud. She turned toward Silvia.

"What do you want?" Katarina shouted impatiently as reality set in. "What! Why are you looking at me like that?"

"You look like you're somewhere else. Are you all right?" Silvia asked, staring at her neighbor with a concerned look on her face.

"Of course I am! What's the matter with you?" Katarina frowned, using all her energy to hold back her tears.

"I have been talking to you. You haven't heard a word I said, have you?" Silvia replied, staring at her askance.

Seeing Silvia's concern, Katarina mellowed. "I'm sorry. My mind wandered. Tell me again, Silvia, what did you say? I promise, I'll listen this time."

"I said, 'We've all lost everything. All of us here were subjects of the silent ethnic intimidations by Communists. I left my family behind too. I'm not even sure if my parents know where I am.'" Her eyes were filled with tears. "But we all have to go on, no matter what!" she added, wiping the tears from her face.

"I'm sorry," Katarina apologized and turned back to the window. "My life is gone, that's all I know. Just like that shooting star," she said, pointing toward the falling star across the sky. "It shines in the sky one minute and disappears the next."

"Would you like to talk about it?" Silvia asked.

"No, I really don't feel like talking about anything tonight," Katarina replied and continued to admire the stars.

"Fine! Fine, we'll talk tomorrow, that kind of attitude will get you nowhere in here. Let's get some sleep now," Silvia said and crept to her bed, disappointed.

"Yes! That's a very good idea!" the other girls shouted in unison and then chuckled.

Though Katarina wanted to scream at them for bullying Silvia, she decided against it. Instead, in a low tone of voice, she said, "She wasn't talking to you, she was talking to me." She slid under the blanket and pulled it over her head.

Katarina liked Silvia instinctively. There was something remarkably candid and appealing about her. She was easy to talk to and wanted to help everyone. Katarina needed a friend and was hoping she'd find it in her, but tonight she wasn't in the mood to talk. Trying to accept what happened to her was more then she could bear.

The other girls continued to giggle and talk late into the night. Katarina and Silvia fell off to sleep.

The next morning, Katarina slept in late and crawled out of bed only when the breakfast wagon arrived, not because she was hungry, but because she had to.

"Good morning, Katarina," Silvia chanted, walking back with her tray.

Katarina said nothing, but walked by her to pick up her tray with a sad face and a broken spirit. Her eyes were sunken deep in their sockets and she looked ragged.

"There goes Ms. Prim and Proper," one of the same girls that teased her yesterday said while the other stared at her from under their eyebrows and chuckled.

Katarina threw a stern glance at them, but didn't have the energy to respond.

"Girls, girls, give her a chance. She's new here," Silvia begged in her defense.

Katarina's energy burst forth and she replied, annoyed,

"Thanks! Silvia, I can fight my own battles."

"Well, all right, but you should stop giving the girls ammunition to tease you," Silvia warned and said nothing further.

Katarina took her tray and returned to her bed. She sat down and ate her breakfast in silence, but the food did nothing to still the anger that was eating her inside. She had no friends to talk to, at least not the kind she could trust. Anxiety was building up inside her. She glanced at Silvia and wondered, *Could I dare tell her about the rape?* But the fear of not knowing if Silvia was trustworthy kept Katarina from telling her her secret that she never wanted to come out. "Just because she had stood up for me with the other girls, that didn't prove much," Katarina whispered to herself and returned her tray to the wagon.

The following week, Katarina spent moping around the room, taking daily abuses from the other girls, and stopped standing up for herself. She didn't care about anything anymore.

Silvia didn't bother Katarina for almost a week, but one evening, she noticed that Katarina was sinking deeper into depression. Silvia felt obliged to intervene. She sat on her bedside and, in a low tone of voice, said, "Katarina, you have to fight for yourself." Silvia encouraged her. "It's not good for you to stay inside and not talk to anyone."

"Mind your own business!" Katarina thundered and turned to stare out the window.

"That kind of attitude will get you nowhere here," Silvia said and settled in her own bed without any further word to her.

Katarina didn't respond, but continued to observe the sky. That evening as she lay on the bed, Silvia's words, "That kind of attitude will get you nowhere here," grew louder and finally sank into her mind. She realized she had to change her demeanor if she wanted to survive in this camp and started to make plans in her head.

*The first thing I have to do is try to accept the things I can't change and then forget them, like rape. Second, I have to stop moping around. I'm not very good in defending myself and I don't want any questions about what had happened to me,* Katarina thought, and with that, she fell asleep.

The next morning, Katarina awoke and decided to put her plans to the test. "Good morning, everyone," she forced a smile and looked out the window. "What a beautiful day. The sky is clear blue with not even a cloud," she chanted, with more optimism than usual.

"Good morning to you too, Katarina, you look and sound better this morning," Silvia commented and embraced her. "It's nice to see you like this." The other girls said nothing but smirked and turned away.

"I had a beautiful dream. Do you believe in dreams, Silvia?" Katarina asked, giving her a signal she could be her friend.

"Yes, of course, I do."

Katarina sat on the bed with her legs folded under her. Silvia leapt excitedly beside her. "Let's hear it."

"I dreamed about a man," Katarina began. "He looked like an angel dressed all in white, and he had a white crown on his head with a golden halo."

"Ha! Ha! Ha! Of course, he did and gave the golden crown to you," one of the girls said cynically, then huge laughter followed.

"Just ignore them," Silvia said.

Determined, Katarina didn't let anyone spoil her plans. Without a word, she continued, "The man turned toward me, looked straight into my eyes, and in a low calm voice said, 'Never give up on your dreams, fight for them.' The man repeated it twice and then disappeared."

"That's a lovely dream. What does it mean?" Silvia asked.

"Well, I think God doesn't want me to give up on my life. God sent me a message through my dream to be strong and fight for it. I believe in God. That's exactly what I'm going to do, fight for myself."

"Good for you!" Silvia replied and embraced her. "I'm glad to see you happy and smiling." Katarina didn't feel that much better, but she used the dream to force herself; she wanted Silvia's friendship.

After breakfast, the morning passed quickly. Sunrays peered brightly through the window on the beds, encouraging the girls to do their morning chores. They were excited and thankful for the prospect of a sunny, warm day ahead. They made their beds and cleaned the room with supreme efficiency.

"It's all done!" Silvia shouted and signaled Katarina to get ready. "Let's go!" and they ran outside first. The other girls ran after them.

In the yard, all the benches were occupied except one. Katarina and Silvia dove for it. They made themselves comfortable and relaxed. Silvia threw her head back and looked up at the sky. "The air is marvelous," she remarked as she took a deep breath.

"Yes, it's truly a wonderful spring day," Katarina agreed, deeply inhaling the fresh air. They both giggled in delight as they watched the other girls standing.

While Silvia and Katarina were having fun, Carabineer Bruno stood behind them, unnoticed. "Are you enjoying the lovely sunny day, girls?" he finally said, chortling. His voice startled them. Silvia turned toward the voice but not Katarina. She never wanted to see his face again, much less hear his voice.

"Katarina, I have something for you," he called, with a smile.

"Yes, Officer," she answered in a low tone and slowly turned toward him. She hated that ugly smirk and wished she could wipe it off his face.

"Here," he handed a letter to her. "It's from the immigration department office. You are asked to answer it promptly," he said.

"From the immigration office?" Katarina jumped to her feet, puzzled. "Why would they send me a letter?" As she hurried to open the letter, her hands trembled. "What now?" she asked, glaring at the carabineer, fearful that he might have something to do with it. "I hope they're not sending me back!" She gulped and threw an angry look at the carabineer.

"I guess you better go and find out," the carabineer replied and strode away with a smirk.

She unfolded the letter and began to read. "Your presence is required in the office as soon as possible. That's it!" Katarina shouted nervously.

"Katarina! What is it!?" Silvia asked, staring at her pale and frightened face.

"I don't know." Her tone sharpened with alarm. "It doesn't say. I'm going there right now." She folded the letter in her hand and rushed toward the quarantine gate.

"Wait, I'm going with you," Silvia said and leapt to her feet. But by the time, Katarina was almost at the gate.

"Can you please let me out," she asked the carabineer sitting on a chair beside the gate.

"You haven't been cleared yet," he said, "You still have a few more days before you can go out, Katarina."

"Here," she handed him the letter. "Maybe this will clear me." The stern expression on her face meant business.

"Why didn't you say so? In that case, you can go," the carabineer said and looked at Silvia, who was by then standing by Katarina's side and ready to step out of the quarantine. "Where do you think you are going?"

"She is coming with me, if that's all right," Katarina replied promptly.

"Fine, go," the officer said and unlocked the gate.

"Thank you," they both yelled and hurried through the gate, across the yard, and passed under the dome finally entering the carabineers' courtyard and into the building.

Fear rose in Katarina's heart. "I hope they don't send me back home," she whispered and threw a sad glance at Silvia as they sped up the steps to the third level.

"I'm sure they are not going to send you back," Silvia tried to calm her friend.

As they arrived to the third level and stopped in front of the office, Katarina trembled and voiced concern. "If they decided to send me back, I'll be thrown in jail by the Communists at home. What am I going to do?"

"Just be calm, everything will be fine," Silvia replied.

Katarina looked at her and felt Silvia was the only one who really cared whether Katarina stayed or went. "You're right," she acknowledged and tried to relax, but she couldn't stop shaking. Katarina took a deep breath and checked herself. Finger-combed her hair and straightened her dress, hoping that wasn't too wrinkled before she reluctantly knocked.

"Come in." She heard the husky voice from within. Katarina cast an alarming look at Silvia as she grasped the doorknob.

"Go on! Don't be afraid," her friend cheered. "I'll be here when you return." Encouraged by her words, Katarina opened the door and slowly walked in, closing the door behind. The room was huge, dim, and cold; it sent a shiver down her spine. The clouds of cigarette smoke floated around the room, causing her to sneeze. "Excuse me!" she said in a low tone.

"Come forward, Ms. Sarrac. I've been expecting you," demanded the man behind the desk with his head buried in a stack of papers. Katarina walked in silence over to the desk and stared at him; she was afraid to speak.

"Sit down please," he ordered without looking at her.

She sat on the opposite chair and waited for what seemed a long time before the man spoke again. He glanced at her a few times from behind the pile of papers, but said nothing. Outside the door, Silvia paced the hallway wondering what was taking so long.

Finally, the man spoke. "Ms. Sarrac, you finished four years of nursing school in your country, right?" he said from behind the pile of papers.

His high-pitched voice made Katarina jump. "That's correct," she acknowledged with a shaky voice.

"I also see here that you speak Italian."

"Yes, I do, but not as well as I would like to. I read Italian newspapers daily," she quickly added.

"Well, that's promising," he chuckled as he finally lifted his head and looked at her. "I need someone to help in the infirmary: assisting the nurses, translating, and doing any other work they might require. You have the qualifications for all of these. If you want work, the job is yours," he said bluntly.

"Yes! Of course, I want to work!" Katarina agreed, wiping sweat from her forehead, relieved that it wasn't what she thought it might be.

"Great. Report tomorrow morning to Matron Tonina at the infirmary. And don't be late. Good-bye," he added with a smile. Then he stuck his head back into his papers.

"Good-bye and thank you," Katarina replied and rose from her chair, delighted with the outcome.

Exhilarated, Katarina wrapped her arms around Silvia's shoulders and yelled, "I'm not going back! I got a job instead!"

"I'm so glad you are staying," Silvia replied as they ran down the steps giggling.

"Let's not tell the other girls what happened, at least not right away," Katarina said, looking at her friend mischievously. Her feet barely touched the ground as they walked back to the yard. By then, it was close to lunch, and everyone returned to their rooms.

At the door, the girls greeted Katarina and Silvia with loads of questions. Before she could answer any of girls' questions, the food wagon arrived.

"What's for lunch?" Katarina asked, with a straight long face.

"Minestrone soup. I can smell it," Silvia replied, staring at her, barely able to contain herself from bursting into laughter.

"Thank God. I was getting tired of spaghetti every day," Katarina replied and walked to get her food.

"Don't worry, it'll be on the menu tomorrow," Silvia commented, following her to the wagon.

"Well! What happened?" the girls insisted, leaning against the wagon as they surveyed Katarina's and Silvia's faces.

"What happened, what?" Silvia asked. She took her tray and started to eat her lunch as if nothing happened. Katarina did the same.

"Aha, don't tell us that you'll be leaving soon," the girls said, chuckling at the prospect of her being sent back to Yugoslavia.

Katarina glanced at the girls from under her eyebrows. "You would like that, wouldn't you?" she said defiantly. They said nothing, but talked among themselves.

Katarina finished her lunch and took her tray back. Then she turned toward them and smiled. 'Well, guess what, girls? I'm not going back. Instead, I got a job in the infirmary. So there, now you can laugh as much as you want."

"And I'm so happy for her! Bravo! Katarina!" Silvia clapped and asked, "When do you start working?"

"Tomorrow!" Katarina chanted as she whirled in front of the girls' noses.

The next morning, Katarina awoke early. Her excitement burst free as she shouted from the bottom of her lungs. "Good morning, world! I had the best sleep since the day I arrived."

"It's nice to see you cheerful," Silvia said and stared at her. She could see signs of happiness spread across her face for the first time since Katarina came. Her brown eyes danced with laughter full of hope as she dressed and strode to work.

At the gate, the old carabineer Giuseppe sat guarding it, just as he did every morning. Everyone knew him. He was nice to the refugees.

"It's a lovely spring morning, isn't it, Officer Giuseppe?" Katarina chirped as she approached him.

"It sure is, signorina," he replied, half-asleep as he toddled to the gate and let her pass.

The infirmary entrance was outside just off the quarantine door on the left side. When Katarina entered, an Italian nurse at the desk working on some papers asked, "Can I help you?"

"Yes, please."

"What can I do for you?"

"I'm looking for Matron Tonina," Katarina replied, wringing her hands intensely. Tension was creeping into her body. *It doesn't seem real, maybe this is a cruel game,* she thought.

The nurse smiled, "You must be the help we requested for."

"I hope so. My name is Katarina Sarrac."

"And mine is Olivia, nice to meet you. Sit down please. The matron should be here any minute," the nurse pleasantly explained and turned back to her work on the desk.

"Thanks," Katarina replied and sat on the bench in front of the desk. While she waited, she let her eyes wander around the room. In front of her was an examining table. Opposite the nursing station stood a big cabinet filled with medicine. Through the glass door, she could see a lot of small bottles of antibiotics and vials of other medicine, including capsules and tablets. On the right wall, there were wooden drawers. *Probably for other supplies,* she thought. Her eyes fixed on a closed door at end of the infirmary. "That must be the matron's office," she commented, glancing at the nurse.

"Yes, but she's not there. Like I said, she'll be here soon."

"All right," Katarina replied and muttered, "Who knows how long I have to wait until she comes?" She was anxious as she had being waiting for a while. Her thoughts were interrupted when a middle-aged woman hustled through the infirmary door like a desert dust storm.

"You must be the help I asked for, follow me into my office," she ordered, motioning Katarina with her hand as she strode by her.

Katarina was startled by her abruptness and barely opened her mouth. The matron had walked so quickly that she was already at her office door by the time Katarina had leapt to her feet. Puzzled, she looked at Nurse Olivia.

"Go! Go on!" the nurse urged from the desk and gestured Katarina to follow the woman.

The matron didn't ask her any questions. She just said in one breath, "All right, Katarina. For the first few days, you'll be responsible, among other things, for the upstairs emergency room. I want the floor sparkling clean and the beds neatly made at all times. That's all. You can go now." She then turned her attention to the files on the desk.

"Thank you," Katarina said and returned to the nursing station. Then another nurse came around the desk and walked up to her.

"My name is Gabriella, but you can call me Gabby," she said, extending her hand.

"Nice to meet you, Gabby," Katarina acknowledged.

"Come with me," the nurse said and led the way up six stone steps.

She opened the door to a large room, saying, "Here. This is it. You'll scrub this wooden floor and make these beds whenever necessary. We use them for emergency cases. As you can see, we don't have any patients at this moment."

"Great. It's not going to be hard," Katarina replied, staring at the empty bed.

Katarina mused, *I don't mind doing that for a few days, but I wonder when I begin to do my real nursing job.* However, it wasn't going to be as simple as she thought.

Her job in the infirmary remained the same. Eventually, she realized the real nurse duties were out of her reach. She was disappointed.

Soon the twenty-one-day quarantine time had elapsed, and the girls who had been in the room when Katarina first arrived were to be released, including her friend Silvia.

The evening just before the girls left, Katarina lay on her bed and stared out the window subdued. Suddenly, she felt a strong bounce on her bed. It was Silvia. She placed her hand on her shoulder and said, "Isn't it a beautiful spring night?"

Katarina looked at her and added, "The sky is full of twinkling stars. I love that. Don't you?" It was just like the evening when they first met.

"You remembered!" Silvia replied, surprised, and gave a hug to her friend.

"Of course, I do. I only wish I could turn the clock back," Katarina affirmed, with a few tears running down her cheeks.

"What's wrong?" Silvia asked.

"Oh, nothing, except that I'm not getting to do any nursing at my job and now you are leaving. It makes sad," Katarina lied. She was crushed; losing a friend wasn't what she needed at this moment. A knock on the door interrupted their thoughts.

"I have to go," Silvia said and rose to her feet. "Don't worry, Katarina. I'm sure we'll see each other around when you get out of here," Silvia added as they walked to the door.

"Yeah. I am sure. But in here, it's not going to be the same without you," Katarina said, less enthusiastic.

At the door, they were faced with a new bunch of girls arriving to take their beds. Silvia looked at them laughingly and commented, "Wow! That was quick. The beds are still warm." Silvia and Katarina said their good-byes at the door, and her friend walked out of her life, at least that was what Katarina believed.

Defeated once again, she walked back to her bed and threw herself on it without paying any attention to the new crowd that just arrived. Her watery eyes darted toward the sky.

Suddenly, she heard a familiar strong bounce of Silvia's bed and turned her head quickly, thinking it was Silvia. Instead, she met with a new face.

"My name is Angelina," the new girl chirped as she settled in bed.

"Hello," Katarina replied uninterested and turned back to stare out the window.

Angelina was nice enough, but Katarina didn't look for any friends among the new girls since there were only a few days left in her stay in the quarantine. Besides, no one could replace Silvia in Katarina's eyes.

The night before Katarina was to be released from the quarantine, she lay on her bed and reflected on the nights she had spent with Silvia. Katarina wondered what had happened to her. There had been no word from her since she left. However, she had heard that two of the girls were sent back to Yugoslavia.

Later, she found out that both of the deported girls were of Serbian nationality. This puzzled her because if anyone was to be returned she thought it would be one of the Croatian girls.

"Can I get your bed after you leave tomorrow?" Angelina's voice suddenly broke through Katarina's dreams.

"I guess you can. I don't really know. Goodnight, girls," Katarina said and settled herself under the blanket to sleep.

As always, before falling asleep, she looked for Mama and Papa's reflection in the clear sky, especially when she felt alone, but they were not there. When Katarina thought about them, her heart ached.

She also had been having dreams about being with Leo and that she would be seeing him soon. She knew that was impossible, but she couldn't get it out of her mind.

"I better get some sleep. After tomorrow, I'll be free to go anywhere. I hope I'll see you again, Silvia," Katarina whispered into her blanket and pillow and shut her eyes.

# CHAPTER 5

The following morning, Katarina got up very early while the girls were still asleep, gathered her things, and left.

The old Giuseppe opened the gate and said, "Bye, Katarina, see you around."

"Same here," she replied and walked through anxiously.

A camp worker was waiting for her outside the gate. "Hello, Katarina, I'm Paula," she said. "I'll take you to your new sleeping quarters. Follow me."

"Where are we going?" Katarina asked.

"To the supply room first, you'll need some things," Paula said as they walked.

"Oh," Katarina replied and followed Paula inside, hoping to get some real supplies, not army stuff. But when Paula opened the door, Katarina was shocked to see the room filled with green military blankets, mess tins, and other army supplies.

Paula pulled out a bundle and placed it on the desk beside the door, then announced, "This is for you."

Katarina glared at Paula, then at the bundle, with her mouth wide open. "Army things again?"

"Is there something wrong with that?" Paula asked with piercing eyes.

"No, no," Katarina replied, shaking her head. She picked up her bundle and walked out the door.

Paula locked the supply room and said, "Let go," as she stormed ahead. Katarina followed her to the second floor of the building. Paula stopped at a door on the left and knocked. There wasn't any answer, so she just walked in.

Surprised, Katarina asked, "What? No locks on the door?"

"No locks," she replied. "All the doors in the camp are to be unlocked at all times."

"Why is that?" Katarina asked, with a concerned look.

"The officers make their rounds constantly," Paula tried to assure her. "There's no need to worry."

"That's what you think," Katarina muttered, chills shooting through her body as she remembered her first night in the quarantine.

"What's that you said?"

"Great! That's great, I said," Katarina explained quickly.

"Your bed is there," Paula pointed to the bed beside the window.

Katarina forced a chuckle, "Oh, how lovely. I've been lucky enough to have a bed beside a window each time I've changed rooms."

Paula glanced at her, smiled, and continued. She placed her hands on the two beds on the left side and said, "Two of the girls that these beds belong to work in the city. They are waiting for their papers from the Italian department of immigration to stay in Italy. They seldom come here, even though they're allowed to stay in the camp until then. We are to respect their wishes and their things." She turned to walk away, then paused. "Oh, by the way, the other girl is here somewhere. I saw her an hour ago." But Paula left without mentioning the girl's name.

Katarina threw her things on her bed and rushed to her job. She continued to work hard in hopes to get promoted to the nursing position.

At the end of the shift, she noticed some empty boxes in the infirmary. Looking at them, she recalled that there wasn't a dresser or shelves in her new room. "Olivia, can I have these boxes?" she asked the Italian nurse that worked with her.

"Sure," Olivia replied, chuckling. "What are you going to do with them? Pack and send yourself home?"

"Ha, ha. These boxes will come handy for my things, thanks." Katarina smiled, grabbed them, and walked out. Katarina was so glad to finally be out of quarantine that she sang as she placed the boxes beside her bed and neatly folded her clothes and belongings into them. She liked to keep her things in order.

An hour later, the door swung open and Silvia entered. Katarina was so stunned, she was momentarily immobilized.

Then they both shouted in unison, "Wow! What a lovely surprise!" and ran into each other's embrace.

"Oh god, am I glad you're here!" Katarina yelled. "When you left quarantine, I thought I'd never see you again."

"Same here, my friend."

"Why didn't you visit me in the infirmary where I work?" Katarina asked.

Silvia looked at her and reminded her, "You know we are not allowed to frolic with quarantine people."

"Yes, I know unless you're sick, but I thought since I'm working there it would be all right."

"No, silly. It's not."

They sat on the floor beside Katarina's bed and chatted for hours. As the sun dipped behind the horizon and their conversation slowed, Katarina exclaimed, "Look! They gave me army supplies."

Silvia laughed, "What do you think I have?"

Katarina pulled an aluminum bowl out of a small box. "Did you get one of these?" she asked, dangling it from her hand. "But it's only one?"

"It could be worse," Silvia sighed. "At least we have something to put our food in."

"What? The cook puts all your food in this one aluminum bowl?" Katarina asked, her eyes widened.

"Well, yes, something like that. I'll show you later when we go to supper," Silvia promised.

"Great, thanks."

Their conversation was interrupted by the other two girls who arrived from the city. Chatting with each other in Italian, they paid no attention to Silvia or Katarina.

Katarina glanced at Silvia. "What's with those two?"

Silvia made a sarcastic gesture with her hands and whispered, "They are showing off. Besides, they are not interested in us, villagers."

"And why not?" Katarina asked with barely audible voice, throwing occasional glances at them. "Just today, Paula told me they don't come here very often."

Looking at the girls from under her eyebrows, Silvia replied, "I'll explain later." And she changed the subject. "Did you know that I met a young man? His name is Rino," she said, her face beamed with happiness.

"That's lovely! Congratulations! I'm happy for you. Is it serious?"

"I think so," Silvia replied, a little unsure of herself, but her eyes twinkled as she mentioned his name.

Katarina could see Silvia loved Rino, and a sudden sadness washed over her as she thought about Leo. "I wish my boyfriend was here," she blurted.

"You have a boyfriend too? Why didn't you tell me that before?"

"Well, I'm telling you now."

"Is he also coming here?"

"I'm afraid not. As far as I know, he won't be coming, but you never know," Katarina smiled.

"What do you mean by that?" her friend asked.

"Oh, just that I've been having these dreams where he tells me, 'See you soon, darling.' And I believe in them."

Silvia gazed at her. "That would be wonderful if he comes, wouldn't it? Oops, it's time to go for supper. Don't forget your mess tin."

"Mine, what?" Katarina asked wide-eyed.

"Your aluminum bowl. It's called a mess tin," Silvia explained from the door.

"Oh, all right." She grabbed her bowl and rushed after Silvia. As they entered the cafeteria, Katarina asked, "What are we having? I'm hungry."

"What else!" Silvia replied as they lined up for their supper. "As always, spaghetti with as little meat as possible topped with a green garden salad."

"This is the cafeteria?" Katarina asked, looking around at the wooden picnic benches set on a stone floor under an open cement roof. Straight ahead was the kitchen where two women served the meal from behind a wooden counter.

"Hello, Ana, this is my friend Katarina," Silvia introduced her to the plump young woman wearing a white apron and hat.

"Nice to meet you," Ana smiled, continuously brushing a few long black hairs from her face that dangled from beneath her white hat. They handed Ana their mess tins, and she filled them with spaghetti, topping the sticky mess with green salad.

Scooping out the food, she glanced at Katarina. "You must be new?"

"Yes, I am," she replied, moving on as the refugees were pushing ahead.

Silvia led the way to the table. "We can sit and eat here," she suggested. Katarina didn't mind. As soon as they sat down on the bench, Katarina dug into her bowl and began to eat.

After her first spoonful, Katarina jerked her head up. "Oh god! What's this?" staring at the garden bugs crawling around in her mess tin.

"That's your protein!" an unfamiliar voice said from behind looking into her bowl. She turned her head and saw a young man standing with his full mess tin in his hands.

"I'm sorry," Silvia interrupted. "This is Rino, the man I told you about." Her face flashed red when she introduced him.

"You call this protein for human consumption?" Katarina showed them the bowl full of green bugs. Watching them crawl made her stomach churn. "I won't eat this!" she shouted, grabbing the bowl and throwing everything into the garbage, except the mess tin.

"I never imagined things could be this bad here. The food's terrible. The least they could have done was wash the lettuce. Good God, there's no hot water, no chairs, and no table in the rooms. The beds are covered with green army blankets and there are no pillows or sheets."

"What did you expect, hotel service?" Silvia chuckled and glanced at her boyfriend.

"It's not funny," Katarina replied. "I didn't expect hotel service, but I certainly didn't expect this, especially since the International Red Cross and Americans are involved."

"You are right, Katarina," Rino admitted. "The Americans are giving the camp seven dollars a day for each of us. That should pay for better and cleaner shelters than this old dilapidated prison they stick us in. And the food should be more varied. Not spaghetti without meat and enough sauce!" Rino added, his face flashing with anger.

"If that is true, we should have better food," Katarina agreed.

"How do you know that they get that much money from the Americans?" Silvia asked, wondering.

"I hear things around the camp, people talk. According to my information, the camp only spends fifty cents per day per person," Rino added without further comments.

"Really!" Katarina said in disbelief. "You seem to know a lot. Why don't you tell us more about our homeland, what's really happening there? At home, my parents always whisper, even if no one is around, and never give me a straight answer. 'We can't talk about that now,' they say. Tell me more," she asked.

There were many things she didn't know. She had her own experiences and a lot of suspicions and whispered stories, but that was all she knew about what was really happening to her people in Yugoslavia, to Croatians, that is.

"Next time," Rino said and began to eat, bugs and all.

Katarina's stomach rumbled and made her nervous. "I can't believe," she thundered, staring at both of them. "Everyone is still afraid to talk about things. Aren't we free now?"

"In a way, yes and no, the camp is infiltrated with Communist spies," he warned. "Be careful who your friends are."

"Thanks for warning me. I won't say anything unless I'm sure the person is trustworthy, like Silvia and you," Katarina chuckled, not realizing how much danger she could be in. She picked up her mess tin and stood up to leave.

Rino grabbed her hand and pulled her down toward him. "I'm serious! I'm trying to help you," he whispered, looking anxiously at her. "Be careful."

"All right! I will!" She turned to go.

"Where do you think you're going?" Silvia interrupted.

"I'm leaving so you two lovebirds can have some privacy. Besides, I'm very tired," Katarina said as she walked back to her room and went to bed.

The next morning dawned bright and hot. Katarina didn't care. It was her day off from work and she was going to sleep in. She had just drifted off when she was jarred awake by Silvia. "Rise and shine!" Silvia yelled, pulling the cover from Katarina's body and plummeted herself beside her on the bed. "What are you doing with yourself today?"

"I don't really know, probably wash some of my clothes," Katarina replied, grabbing the cover, "and get some extra sleep if you let me." She needed to have some time off. She had been working since the day she got the job.

"Or you could come with Rino and me after supper to the outside coffee bar. We'll have real coffee, not the chicory that they serve us in here," Silvia suggested.

"Well, all right. I was planning to sleep a few more hours, but I guess I have to get up. If I finish doing my laundry in time, I'll come. It's not like I have tons of clothes to wash, but there's no hot water and hardly any soap, so I have to scrub them with a brush, one by one, and that takes time. I hate that. I'll try to meet you there after supper. You and Rino go ahead. I'll see you later," Katarina said and went to the laundry to wash.

As she washed her clothes at the sink, memories of Leo and her family constantly nudged themselves to the forefront of her thoughts. A dark sense of dread descended over her with each passing minute. Katarina wondered how she could manage the rest of her life without them. "Stop dwelling on this I can never go home," she ordered herself and shook the maddening thoughts from her head. She picked up her wet clothes, rushed to her room, and hung them over the back of her bed to dry. Then Katarina hurried toward the coffee bar; she didn't want to be alone.

Her favorite song, "Tequila" was playing loudly on the jukebox when she arrived. The music raised her spirit. She looked around for her friends, but the bar was so crowded, it was hard to see them. Finally, she spotted Silvia meandering toward her.

"Hello, Katarina, I'm glad you could come."

"You did this, didn't you?" Katarina asked, her eyes piercing Silvia.

"Did what?" Silvia acted surprised.

"Oh, come on. You selected "Tequila" from the jukebox when you saw me coming, didn't you? How did you know it was my favorite song?" Katarina asked, taking Silvia's hand as they pushed through the crowd toward the table where Rino was sitting.

"It's nice to see you again," Rino said, standing to shake her hand.

"Thanks to both of you for inviting me," Katarina said. "It's very nice in here." As soon as she sat, the waiter approached the table.

"What can I get you?" he asked, smiling at her.

"Cappuccino, please."

The waiter took the order and returned with her cappuccino in a flash, placing the cup on the table with the bill.

"Wow! That was quick, thanks."

Rino grabbed the bill. "This is on me," he said and handed it with the money to the waiter.

"That's nice, thanks," Katarina smiled and sipped on the cappuccino. "It tastes more delicious than I remembered."

They all laughed aloud. The three of them chatted and danced the evening away. The outing and the music raised Katarina's spirit. It was the first time she had enjoyed herself since she had left her homeland.

# CHAPTER 6

Days passed and Katarina was kept busy at the infirmary with new refugees streaming into the camp daily. The border crossings increased during the spring and summer months as it was easier for refugees to cross when there wasn't any snow, less cold winds, or much rain to battle through.

Among the new refugees was a young man named Ivan, who collapsed as he entered into the camp. He was brought into the infirmary by two carabineers to be checked. Katarina stared at him with wide eyes. Ivan could barely walk; his tall, slender body was weak and shivering. He was burning up with fever and choking with a harsh cough. He looked tired and was unshaven. The shirt sleeves hung down at his side, torn, wet, and muddy. His naked knees showed through the holes in his wet pants that clung to his skin. She could hardly see the blond hair straggling over his flushed and muddy face. Katarina grabbed a blanket and wrapped it around Ivan's shoulders and handed him dry clothes. "You can take your wet clothes off now," she suggested, but Ivan was too weak, he couldn't do it. His body shivered, slouched, and began sliding. Katarina grabbed him, but she couldn't hold him, they both went down to the floor. "Oh no!" she yelled in panic. "Help!"

The two officers, who were on their way out, rushed to Katarina. "Let us do it," they said in unison and had Ivan on his feet in no time.

"Now hold him so I can pull his wet clothes off," she ordered.

"Sure," they replied. She quickly peeled off his wet clothes and replaced it. The officers helped her settle him on the examining table under the blankets and they left.

While she waited with him for the nurse and the doctor to come, Katarina took a wet cloth, washed his face, and asked, "What happened to you?" trying to see a glimmer of life in his racoonlike eyes, sunk deep in their sockets.

"I spent too many days in the Alps without food," Ivan gasped. "In the pouring rain. I was waiting for a chance to sneak by the carabineers and cross the border hills to Italy. I'd have rather died than go back," he whispered, hardly audible and broken by severe coughing spells.

Their conversation was brought to the end when Nurse Gabby entered. "Katarina, get some water for the doctor to wash his hands," she ordered as she stuck a thermometer into Ivan's mouth and proceeded to take his blood pressure.

"All right," she replied and rushed for it. She filled the basin with warm water and pulled out a special towel for the doctor, then she was on her way out when the doctor arrived.

"Don't go, Katarina. I need you here to translate for Ivan and me," the doctor requested as he walked to wash his hands.

"Yes, Doctor," she acknowledged and returned to the patient's side as the doctor examined Ivan and found him dehydrated and suffering from pneumonia. "You'll need to spend a few days here with us, Ivan. We'll be giving you daily injections of antibiotics for the next five to seven days. We need to observe you for the next couple of days until your fever and pneumonia subside. Katarina, get the bed ready for him. Ivan will be our guest for a while," the doctor directed.

"Right away, Doctor," she replied and scurried off. By the time she had finished, Nurse Gabby had given Ivan his first injection of antibiotics and a few aspirins for the fever. Gabby and Katarina took him upstairs and helped him settle in bed. Then she sponged his body with alcohol and tepid water. His skin trembled at her touch.

"When will this medicine help?" Ivan asked between his chattering teeth.

"It will take a day or two," Katarina explained, repeating the doctor's words. She stayed at the infirmary an extra hour that day to check on him. The medicine Ivan took began to work, and he was drifting off to sleep. When she could stay no longer, she leaned over him and said in a reassuring voice, "Ivan, get some rest, and I'll see you tomorrow."

Despite her many hours of work, Katarina couldn't sleep that night. She lay awake in her bed for hours. Her mind struggled to forget her first night in the camp and the rape. Memories of home flooded her mind. Ivan reminded her just how much she missed her family. Then there were memories of Leo, too.

No matter how hard she tried, his image was still clear in her mind. It was as if she had left him standing on the platform only yesterday.

"Stupid fool, Katarina. Stop thinking about him. You're supposed to forget him," she scolded herself, striking her blanket pillow a few times.

"Stop muttering, Katarina! Go to sleep!" Silvia shouted angrily from her bed. Katarina didn't answer, but shut her eyes sheepishly.

That night, she fretted in and out of sleep, restless, tormented by the dream of Leo. He was telling her the same thing. "I'll see you soon, my darling."

The next morning, she felt helpless, angry, and frustrated. 'Why do I keep dreaming the same thing over and over again?" she asked, staring at Silvia.

"I don't know, I wish I could put your mind at ease."

"I'm sorry, Silvia, I know you don't. Just that I'm tired of being tormented by this dreams night after night!" Katarina thundered and stormed to work.

At the infirmary, the night nurse Olivia was getting ready to go home. As soon as Katrina entered, the nurse grabbed her purse and said, "Ivan's fever is down and he feels much better. Good-bye!"

"That's great! I'm glad he is better. Have a good day, Olivia," Katarina replied and walked upstairs. Before she even entered the room, she heard a voice calling.

"Good morning, Katarina!"

"Good morning to you too, Ivan. I can see that you feel much better already. But you need to take it easy," she warned.

"Yes, thanks to your care. No more fever or cough. So tell me, Katarina, what's a young girl like you doing in a place like this?" Ivan asked, chuckling. His charm was showing. There was a glint of humor in his eyes.

"Oh, that's really funny, coming from the man who almost died in the mountains to get here," she teased him.

"Well, I do have my reason," Ivan replied. He turned his head to hide the sadness in his eyes.

We all have our reasons, otherwise, none of us would be here," Katarina reminded him and looked at him with a quizzical expression on her face. "Why don't you tell me yours first?"

Ivan glanced at her and paused as he surveyed her face. "All right, you win!" His eyes darted toward the window. "I finished shipbuilding school, but when I tried to get a job in the Rijeka shipyard. I couldn't. Each time I came to apply for a job, the manager would say, 'I'm sorry, there aren't any openings for your trade yet. But you could take a laborer's job. When a position comes up you can just transfer.'

"I got tired of waiting and did just that. I took the labor job the manager offered me in hopes that I would have a better chance when a position came up." Ivan paused, his face flashed red. "Two years! Two years! Katarina, I waited to get my position. Each time it came up, the manager again kept saying, 'I'm sorry, but we gave it to someone more qualified than you.' My skin crawled every time I heard that," Ivan explained through his teeth. "Months later, I found out that the manager had been bringing men over from his hometown in Serbia to fill the positions in Croatia Republic.

"It is not only the position these people were getting, apartments, too, but what made me angrier was that those men knew nothing about the job they got. It was a political fill, like everything else in our country. These people barely finished fifth grade."

"But they were Serbian," Katarina interrupted. "Exactly, there were getting jobs just because they were Serbian. When I complained about it, the manager fired me. I realized then, that because I'm Croatian, I wouldn't get any position, even though I finished school and had a diploma. Isn't that sickening?" Ivan asked, with a tear-stained face.

"Why are the Serbians doing this to us?" Katarina asked. "What happened to the brotherhood that they have been so faithfully proclaiming?"

"Haha, what brotherhood?" Ivan laughed cynically. "The Serbians are the bosses in all the republics of Yugoslavia. Brotherhood is just a mask. It works with them only if you are Serb. They do whatever they feel like, and no one would dare question them or their motives." Ivan grinded his teeth on the words.

Katarina's eyes flashed, remembering her own problems with Serbs. "Oh, yes! You don't dare question Serbs if you know what's good for you." She knew that very well, for she had worked with many of them.

"What's the point of going to school when I can't get the position I'm trained for?" Ivan asked, exasperated. "I'm very tired." He lay back on his bed and turned away to hide his teary eyes.

"Or when you do have a position," Katarina frowned. "They do everything they can to push you out of it!" In anger, she turned away, leaving Ivan to get his rest. She stomped downstairs.

The following two days Katarina had off and enjoyed every second. The evening before she had to go back to work, she found herself wondering about Ivan. Would he still be there? She looked at her friend Silvia lying on her bed and said, "Poor Ivan, he's very sad and torn."

"Who's Ivan? And why is he torn?" Silvia asked, puzzled.

"He's a newcomer and a patient at the infirmary. He got sick in the mountains and collapsed at the entrance of the camp the day he came. He feels bad that he left his country. But I think he did the right thing, just like you and I did. We both know there wasn't any life for us there, right?"

"Yes, we do. Now tell me what's the deal with this Ivan and you. It looks like you are beginning to like him," Silvia asked.

"No! I don't. I'll never love anyone but Leo," Katarina stressed, turned her head away, and waited for sleep.

When she returned to work the next morning, she found Ivan's bed empty. He was gone. *Just as well,* she thought.

Katarina never had a chance see him again. She wondered about him most of the day, but never found out what happened or where he ended up going.

That day, Silvia surprised Katarina in front of the infirmary. She grabbed Katarina's hand as she emerged through the door and yelled, "Come with me!" pulling her as they walked. "Hurry!" Silvia shouted, panic-stricken. Her hands were shaking and her eyes were red and teary.

"What's wrong?" Katarina asked, barely able to keep up. But Silvia wouldn't explain. The only thing she kept saying over and over was "Come with me. Hurry."

"Wait a minute!" she shouted, and dug her heels. "Tell me at least where we are going?" Katarina knew there was something very wrong because Silvia would have never acted like this.

After a short while, Silvia finally, through her tears, said, "To the coffee bar, come quickly!" and kept tugging on her hand.

"All right! All right. I'm coming, just calm down," Katarina said and ran along.

As they entered, Katarina saw Rino. He sat at the table with his head bowed, his face pale. The possibility of them going back was the first thing Katarina thought. Silvia rushed ahead and sat beside him, placing her arm around his shoulders.

"Hello, Rino," Katarina said and sat on the chair opposite them. Rino looked at her with a blank stare and didn't answer; he was too distraught. She gazed at his sad face and glanced at Silvia. Tears rolled down her cheeks. "What's going on with you two?" Silvia literally dragged me here without any explanation. You are both acting weird that chills my bones, and you are frightening me."

They didn't answer, but just looked at each other sadly.

"Silvia, you are my best friend. Don't you think I should know what happened?" Katarina asked again. Her widened brown eyes stared at them, puzzled.

Silvia wiped her face and began. "A few of Rino's friends and his cousin came here. We were all to emigrate together to the USA."

"I didn't know you have a brother in here," Katarina interrupted, looking at Rino.

"Yes," Rino replied and took a deep breath then continued the story. "During the night, the carabineers tiptoed into our room while we were asleep. Then, in complete silence, they rounded up at least ten of the men of Serbian nationality and my cousin. The carabineers glanced at me and thought I was asleep, but I wasn't." Rino explained, adding, "I saw them very quietly go to one of the sleeping men and tap him on his shoulder. When the man awoke, the carabineer motioned with his finger to come with him with the other hand on the gun. I kept still, afraid that if they noticed I was awake they would take me too. My cousin took a step toward me, but one of the carabineers grabbed him by his shoulder and pulled him back. Bastards! They wouldn't let him say good-bye to me!" Rino said through his clenched teeth, covering his face with both of his hands.

"Oh my god! That was close," Katarina commented and hugged him. "I'm sorry for your cousin. But you should thank your lucky stars the officers didn't take you too."

Silvia's anger rose. "They're like brothers as Rino has no brother. Now his cousin will never be able to come over. He'll spend the rest of his life in prison, he is a militia man. I feel like giving the carabineers a piece of my mind." Her body trembled.

"Don't be a fool, Silvia. Keep your mouth shut," Katarina advised with a stern voice.

"Why?" Silvia shouted back with fury in her eyes. "Aren't we free? You are the one who said that, remember?"

"Think about it, Silvia," Katarina stared at her fearfully. "Wasn't it you who told me that acting stupid wouldn't get me anywhere? And besides, you wouldn't want to find yourself standing on the other side of the border one morning, would you?" She stressed her point.

Rino lifted his head and looked at Silvia, "She's right, you know," and hugged her. "I don't want you to be deported. Besides, I saw my cousin this morning as they were escorting them into a carabineer's van. Through the iron bars, I handed him a cigarette and said good-bye before they drove them over the border to Yugoslavia. I may never see my cousin again, but I'll do everything not to lose you too. But thanks for trying to help me ease the pain." Rino sighed and embraced Silvia.

"Fine," Silvia exhaled deeply and calmed down a little. "You're probably right, both of you."

"Well, good. I'm happy because I'm not prepared to give up my best friend," Katarina replied. "What puzzles me though is that the majority of refugees sent back are of Serbian nationalities. I wonder why that is?" she mused, hoping to change the subject, but her comment seemed to make things worse.

Anger flashed in Rino's eyes. "I will tell you why! The story is that there seems to be an agreement between Belgrade and Rome to send Serbian people back when they arrived in the camp. They were marked under specific refugees."

"Is that possible?" Katarina frowned.

"Yeah and there's more," Rino said. "If you wonder where these people go when they are sent back, don't anymore. You see, Serbians that were sent back with my cousin will not end up in jail. They'll be settled right across the border in the Istrian Peninsula in the province of Croatia, with nice apartments and good jobs. My cousin, who is a Croat, will go to jail."

"Why would they do that?" Katarina questioned.

"In a word, ethnic cleansing. Belgrade wants to clean the Croats people from the province of Croatia on the border with Italy and replaced them with Serbs. Belgrade hopes one day to have all of Croatia including her Adriatic Coast for themselves. They have a plan to create Greater Serbia from part of the territories of Croatia and Bosnia and Herzegovina for a long time. But in 1918, the silent genocidal cleansing of Croatian people of their land intensified. Belgrade hopes that one day there will be enough Serbian people to claim Croat land as theirs. And then they can say, 'The Croatian people never lived here.'"

"Why don't the Croatian people fight this?" Katarina asked.

"How can they?" Rino answered. "Serbian people hold all the high-level jobs in the Communist government: police, army, news media. All the top managers of every company were Serbian, and some maybe Montenegrian, Slovenian, or Muslim from Bosnia and Herzegovina, but never Croatian. The same was in the embassies around the world.

"Croatian and other non-Serb people are deprived of human rights. They have no rights to a professional job, to speak their own language, to sing their national song, to do anything. This way they force the Croats and other non-Serbs to leave their country. That has been their silent plan all along: to ethnically cleanse the province of Croatia of its people."

"Are you sure Croatians can't do something?" Silvia finally spoke.

"Croats and other non-Serbs can't do anything. Most of them know what's going on but are afraid to speak up. They must keep quiet or run. But I tell you, they will have a hell of time pushing out five million Croats from the Republic of Croatia plus almost a one million Croats from Bosnia and Herzegovina," he spoke with a stern expression on his face and fire in his eyes.

"Wow! That's some story!" Katarina said and rose from the chair, agitated, walked to the window, and looked out, then returned back. "So you are telling me that Croatian people are being pushed out so the Serbians get their homes and their jobs. This is the way our people are being forced to wander throughout the world as refugees, begging strangers for a piece of bread and wondering where they can spend the next night. Who would believe it?"

"No one! Unless you know it and lived through it, like we do," Silvia put her two cents in.

"That's brotherhood to the Serbs, that I know it!" Katarina commented.

"Yugoslavian secret police, UDBA, are swarming around the camp, trying to stop as many of us as possible from entering the free world. Many Croats have gone missing from here," Rino warned. "So you girls have to be careful to whom you can trust."

"What do you think happened to those people?" Katarina asked with wide eyes. She was deeply bothered by what Rino had said. The words made her furious and scared; she needed to leave.

"I'm going to sleep," she announced as she stood up and stormed away.

Katarina was still fuming when two beautiful snow-white pigeons suddenly landed in front of her and strolled proudly side by side next to her. They made her forget the anger as she imagined Leo and herself as the pigeons. Somehow, he always managed to disturb her thoughts, no matter what.

"Oh, Leo, I wonder how it would be if you'd really come here," she whispered, following the pigeons as they wobbled forward. "What's wrong with me?" she muttered in disgust. Katarina loves Leo, but after the rape, she hated the thought of any man touching her, so her emotions were mixed. Besides, she was sure it would never happen, even if her dreams were telling her it would. "Leo will never come. I have to forget him," she ordered herself. She was angry all over again and walked briskly to the cafeteria. There she grabbed a cup of coffee to take to her room.

# CHAPTER 7

A week later, Silvia and Rino received their transfers to another camp in southern Italy. When Silvia told her, Katarina hugged her and said, "I'm missing you already. When are you two leaving?"

"I don't know. In a day or two. Once the papers are signed, they'll tell us," Silvia explained. That was when Katarina learned that the camp in Trieste was only transitional and that she would also be leaving one day. On their final night, Rino invited both girls for cappuccinos at the coffee bar. All three sat on the bar terrace sipping on their drinks and chatting, Rino and Silvia excited, Katarina sad.

"It's a lovely day today," Katarina noted, her eyes drifting.

"It's not lovely, it's hot and stifling," Rino replied and looked up at the sky, wiping the sweat from his face. "I hope it rains." As if to agree with his thought, the weather began to change rapidly.

Katarina gazed at the flickering light in the distance that zigzagged through the darkening sky. "You just might get your wish, Rino, and soon, by the looks of it," she smirked.

They stared upward, captivated by the clouds that were hurrying in from the north. Suddenly the clouds shifted direction, unveiling a surprise summer storm in front of their own eyes. At first, everyone's spirits were lifted. They enjoyed the fresh breeze brought by the beginning of the storm. And then just as suddenly, the trees in the surrounding forest began to sway. The alarmed birds took flight, screeching as they flew for cover.

"Look, Katarina. Did you see those birds?" Silvia yelled, pointing a finger toward the forest.

"Yes, I saw them. It's going to rain!" Katarina shouted, running into the bar for cover. Rino and Silvia followed. No sooner had she spoke than lightning, thunder, and wind heralded a fierce rain that came down with a tremendous force. The terrace was quickly deserted as everyone fled to sanctuary inside. When the madness of the storm had passed and the rain had stopped, the waiters swarmed busily over the terrace, wiping the tables and chairs and taking new orders. After all, the guests strolled onto the terrace again. They reclaimed their tables and seats and enjoyed the cool, fresh breeze.

"There, Rino, just as you ordered. The air is fresh and cool, not stifling," Katarina teased.

Rino glanced at her and smiled. "Two cappuccinos and a beer," he called to the nearby waiter.

"Wow! Look at that!" Silvia pointed. Her eyes widened as she stared at the green lawn and gardens littered with broken twigs and fallen leaves.

"Oh my god! Look there!" Katarina shouted, indicating the flower beds where hundreds of lashed flowers were strewn, their windblown petals covering the ground.

After they finished commenting on the destruction caused by the storm, Katarina turned to her friend. "Well, tell me, Silvia, where have you two been transferred to?"

"To the Latina Camp, it said on our papers."

"Where is Latina?"

"Somewhere south, close to Rome, I believe."

Before Katarina could say anything, Rino placed his arm around Silvia's shoulders and announced. "We'll get married there."

"Congratulations!" Katarina exclaimed. "You are getting married! That's wonderful news. Oh, I wish I could be there for your wedding day." Disappointment showing on her face.

"Me too, you would have been my maid of honor," Silvia replied, looking unhappily at her friend.

Rino looked at his watch. "Goodness, look at the time. We have to get packing." He rose quickly.

Katarina got to her feet, hugged him, and said, "Good-bye, Rino. I won't be able to see you two off tomorrow. I'll be working. Take good care of my friend, all right." She remarked, tapping Silvia on her shoulder.

Rino smiled. "Don't worry. I'll take care of her. Good-bye Katarina. Who knows? We might meet again some day."

"You never know," she replied and sat back down to finish her cappuccino.

"Katarina, I'll see you later in the room," Silvia said as she accompanied her boyfriend out of the coffee bar.

Watching them leave, Katarina's heart saddened. "I can't believe I'm losing the only two friends I have here." She stayed for a little while, sipping on her drink and feeling sorry for herself before returning to her room.

Later, Katarina and Silvia chatted long into the night; before she fell asleep, Silvia said, "After tomorrow, when I'm gone, you're going to be alone in this room. I heard today, those two girls found an apartment for themselves in the city, so they won't be coming into camp anymore, except to collect their things."

"That is a nice thought!" Katarina smiled. "But you really believe that the beds will stay empty for long. I don't. I'm sure someone will come as soon as you are out of it. I heard the beds here never get cold. But no one will be as nice as you."

The next morning, Katarina awoke earlier than usual so she could spent a few minutes with her friend Silvia. Before Katarina left for work, she gave Silvia a big hug, "Thank you for everything. I'll never forget you. Good-bye, and good luck with Rino."

"Good-bye, Katarina," Silvia replied and squeezed her tightly. "Take good care of yourself too."

"I will. Good-bye, my friend," Katarina said and ran down the stairs, fighting the tears that threatened to burst forth.

At the infirmary entrance, the carabineer guarding the quarantine door gazed at her and asked, "What's wrong with you?"

"Nothing. I have something in my eye," Katarina said and disappeared inside. The departure of her friend clouded her whole day. She couldn't be more pleased when the shift finished. On the way to her room ,she was preoccupied by her thoughts about Silvia and Rino, and sadness filled her heart. As she paused in front of the door, she muttered, "It would be nice to be alone just for a little while." Katarina expected to find the room empty, but when she opened the door, she was greeted by a woman and two of her sleeping children. They occupied all the empty beds except hers.

Katarina froze. "Who are you?"

"My name is Manda and these are my little ones," the woman replied, pointing to the children who were already asleep in the next beds.

Katarina murmured. "I told you, Silvia. I knew the beds wouldn't get cold," as she strolled to her own bed.

"What was that you said?" Manda asked puzzled.

Katarina threw herself on her bed. "Oh, it's a private joke between me and my friend who just was transferred to another camp this morning. The bed you're sitting on was hers. By the way, I'm Katarina. Where are you coming from?" she asked immediately.

"From Germany. My husband is in Australia for a year now. He wants the children and me to join him there. But as you know, it's not easy to get out of Yugoslavia. So I escaped with my children into Germany, but when I got there, I realized it would take forever to get the necessary papers to emigrate to Australia. I learned that the waiting period is much shorter if I'm in the refugee camp. Germany doesn't have refugee camp, so I decided to come to Italy, and here I am."

"Isn't Australia on the other side of the world?"

"Well, yes, it is. But my husband is already there and I have no choice but to follow him."

"How old are the children?"

"My little girl, Josipa, will be five soon. Franko, my boy, just turned two," she smiled, gazing at them.

"You look young to have children," Katarina commented.

"I was married very young," Manda chuckled. "How about you, Katarina? You're not married, are you?"

"No, I'm not."

"Where are you emigrating?"

"I'm going to Canada," Katarina answered proudly.

"Are you? Isn't Canada just as far?"

"Probably, but I don't care. I heard the life is good there." She peeked at her watch. "Goodness, it's supper time," Katarina said and leapt from her bed. "Manda, would you like to come with me? I'll show you where the cafeteria is."

"My children are sleeping. Do you think I could get supper later?"

"I don't know about that. They have very strict rules. You must have been told that there's only one hour to come eat or pick up your portion. Children or no children, after that you won't get any food. The cafeteria is closed, and your children will go hungry until tomorrow," Katarina explained.

"Yes, yes, I've been given instructions, but I haven't read them. All right, let's go then while my children are asleep. I'll bring the food back."

"Will the children be alright alone?" Katarina asked on the way to cafeteria.

"Yes, I'll be coming right back." Just as she said that, she noticed a long lineup in the front of the cafeteria. "Oh no! It will take forever. I can't wait that long. My children will be awake soon," she panicked and turned to walk back.

Katarina walked toward the cafeteria counter.

"Get back in the line!" a voice from the line shouted.

But she paid no attention. "Hello, Ana, is there any way to get some food without waiting in the line?" Katarina asked. "There's a woman here who just arrived into my room with two small children."

"Where are the children?" Ana asked loudly.

"They're in the room, sleeping at the moment, I hope. But we don't know for how long."

"All right, I'll give her the food, but only for this time. She has to bring the children with her to get quick service," Ana said, glancing around as if she was expecting disapproval, but there was none.

"Thank you!" Katarina said and signaled Manda to come forward. After Ana filled Manda's mess tins with food, she rushed back to her children. Katarina waited in the line for her own portion and returned to the room after she ate her supper.

Even though Manda had been very friendly to her, Katarina wasn't keen to begin a new friendship. She had just lost Silvia and that was difficult for Katarina. But it was more than that; she felt she wouldn't be here much longer.

# CHAPTER 8

A few days later, a tall, young carabineer with curly brown hair walked into the infirmary and handed Katarina a letter. "What's this?" she asked, noting the left upper corner said Department of Immigration.

"I believe it's a transfer notification, Ms. Sarrac," the officer replied as he left.

"I hope the transfer is to Latina," Katarina muttered as she hurried to open it. "Oh no! To a convent! Why are they sending me there?"

The Matron Tonina looked at her frowning face and replied, "You are going there because you're a single girl and a Catholic. All girls like you are sent to the convent. From there, you can emigrate anywhere you want. The nuns take good care of the girls. You should be grateful. The food and beds are much better and cleaner there than here." She took the letter from Katarina's hand and quickly read it. "Look here, it says, you get to keep your job in the infirmary. You're lucky. The nuns will be expecting you the day after tomorrow."

"Thanks for letting me know about the job, I mean." Matron Tonina handed the letter back to her and strolled to her office.

Nurse Olivia looked at Katarina's unhappy face and agreed with matron. "You have nothing to lose."

"I guess. Better food and clean white sheets, that sounds good to me," Katarina mused.

The next morning, the day before her transfer, Katarina awoke early to gather her things before she went to work. As she closed her two small boxes with her belongings, her face was covered with sadness. She had no idea that this would be the happiest day of her life.

"I'll be sorry to see you go. When will you be leaving?" Manda asked before Katarina ran out the door.

"After work. At four o'clock, the bus will pick us up at the gate. There are a few other girls going. I guess we all have to get used to these quick changes," Katarina commented and ran to work as she was already late.

Sometime in the middle of the morning while Katarina was busy making beds in the room upstairs, she heard her name being called from downstairs and recognized the voice as being that of the carabineer Bruno, who had raped her, so she didn't answer. But he kept calling. Anger and fear grew inside each time he called her name. She continued to ignore him, hoping he'd go away.

"Katarina! I know you are there," he yelled again, coming up the steps.

"One good thing about going to a convent is that I won't have to deal with Carabineer Bruno, anymore," she muttered, walking down to meet him. "Yes, Officer," she said without looking at him.

The gray-haired officer chuckled, "Come with me," and turned to walk out.

*Oh, I hate his ugly face. I wish I didn't have to obey him*, Katarina mused, angrily following him. As they stepped out the door, she asked, "Where are you taking me?"

"Just out here," he smirked, pointing at the quarantine door and walked over to knock on it.

"Why? I've done my twenty-one-day!" Katarina, fearing the worse, froze on the spot as if she was rooted to the ground. She stared at him waiting for an answer, but he didn't give her one.

The door opened, and the officer took Katarina by her shoulder. "Let's go," he said. His face was serious as he led her through the gate.

Petrified, she looked at him.

Apprehensive that something terribly wrong was going to happen to her, she walked over a step slowly into the quarantine yard, hesitating.

He locked the door behind and leaned on it.

As she stood there, she didn't know what to expect from the man that raped her. The threats after he raped her came to her mind. Blood drained from her face and her body quivered, "What's going on? Why did you bring me to the quarantine?"

Officer Bruno said nothing, but turned toward a tall young man with short blond hair who stood beside the gate with his back turned. Suddenly, the carabineer announced, "Your fiancé!"

Speechless and unable to move, Katarina covered her mouth with both hands. She couldn't believe her eyes, even though she was standing only a meter or so from her boyfriend. He was dressed in the same clothes he wore the last time she saw him: black flannel pants and a blue blazer with a knitted shirt under it. And he had black shoes on his feet.

Heat flamed in her cheeks, and her heart fluttered. *Oh my god! It is Leo. It is really Leo,* her brain shrieked, unable to say a word, all the while staring at the man. *What is he doing here? Is it possible he forgave me for leaving him stranded and lying to him?* The thoughts were flying through her mind as Leo strode toward her.

"Hello, darling," Leo greeted her warmly.

She nodded and smiled, but could find no words to express her feelings.

Her wide-open eyes remained on him as he studied her face. Then his lips parted again to speak as he moved closer to her. "I love you, darling," he announced, embracing her and pulling her tightly against his body. He gave her a long passionate kiss.

Surprised, Katarina paused almost out of breath and abruptly stepped back, remembering the word *fiancé*. "Now stop teasing me. Fiancé? Is that some kind of cruel joke?" she asked, her voice highly charged, her body trembled. She studied him with suspicion, but still could barely speak.

"I hope not," Leo replied, with a twinkle in his blue eyes and the sweat dripping from his face. His crooked smile showed as he appraised her from head to toe. A thought of distrust crossed her mind.

"What are you really doing here? Did you come to take me back?" Katarina asked point-blank. "After all, I was the one who left you. Why would you come here and tell me that you love me? It doesn't make sense, does it?"

"It makes sense, if you love someone," Leo said. "I can see, you have the reason to mistrust me, but I can assure you, I'm not here to take you back. I'm here because I want to be with you if you will have me." He took her right hand and kissed it, then knelt down in front of her. His knees twitched in the dirt, but he didn't move until he asked, "Katarina, will you marry me?" The refugees sitting on the stone benches in the yard swiveled to stare at them.

Katarina listened to Leo with tremendous uneasiness while all kind of thoughts and worries ran through her head. Suddenly, she asked, "Are you serious?"

"Yes! Of course! That's the reason I'm here," he replied, gazing into her glimmering brown eyes.

Caught up in the excitement, Katarina shouted, "Yes! Yes! I will marry you, my love!" pulling him to his feet. The tears clouded her eyes, so she barely saw his face when she leapt into his arms. "How could I not love you?" As he wrapped his arms around her body, the rape scene flashed in her eyes and she winced. It took all of her energy to keep it under control. A man's embrace brought back the horror of that night. She stepped back and gave the officer an iced grin, wondering if the love she had for Leo would be enough to overcome the fear in her.

"All right! All right," the officer said. "It's time for you, Katarina, to go back to work."

"Yes, Officer, you're right." Thankful for his good timing, Katarina said, "I have to go, my love. I'll see you soon." She gave Leo a quick kiss and ran out through the small gate, elated.

She paused and squinted at the quarantine gate that separated them, and muttered, "Thank God, I'm not alone anymore." Katarina's delight shone on her face, and her eyes sparkled. She was grinning from ear to ear when she returned to the infirmary. Everyone soon knew that her boyfriend, Leo, had followed her from their country and had asked her to marry him.

Matron Tonina stared at Katarina's beaming flushed face. "You're not pregnant, are you?" she asked point-blank.

"Of course not! I have plenty of time for that later," Katarina replied, offended that anyone would even suggest something like that, and turned away. Besides, she didn't want a big family like hers had been. She remembered only too well how hard it was being in a family of ten children.

"Matron didn't mean anything bad by it," Nurse Gabby said, placing her hand on Katarina's shoulder.

"I know, but I'm not! It couldn't be!" Then suddenly, a frightened thought ran through her head. Her face drained of blood and her body shivered as she remembered the terror of rape. "What if I got pregnant that night?" she heard herself asking, "No! No! That just isn't possible," and rushed upstairs to work so no one would notice the sudden fear on her face. Then she remembered she just had her monthly and relaxed.

Leo's arrival put Katarina's mind in a tailspin for most of the day. She rushed into Matron's office and asked, "Would I still be going into the convent today?"

"Let me make a call to the emigration office and I will let you know what they are planning to do," Matron Tonina said.

"Great, thank you." Katarina returned back to her work, but it wasn't easy. Her mind was preoccupied most of the day. She never wanted Leo to learn about the rape. There's no way she could tell him she was raped, knowing how he would react. Even if she had to lie to him, she would keep the secret. Katarina didn't like the idea, but she felt she had no choice. She knew he wouldn't understand and would blame her, just like her mama would. But the most important thing to her was he would never marry her if he knew.

When the clock struck three, Katarina sighed, *Finally*. She thought the day would never end.

"Katarina, where are you?" Matron called from the office door.

"I'm coming." Katarina ran into her office as she wanted to know what to do today.

"All right, the situation is like this. You are to wait here in the camp until further notice," Matron explained.

"Wonderful!" Katarina was delighted with the outcome. "See you tomorrow," she said and ran out the door.

On the way to her room, she thought about Leo and their future together. Now that Leo was here, she had many things to sort out, and the rape was one thing she'd rather not deal with. She pushed the thoughts about it to the back of her mind and walked into her room.

Ignoring her roommate, she threw herself on the bed and laughed with joy. Hope and happiness flamed across her face. Manda sat on the opposite side and stared at her red face quizzically. "Only a short while ago you looked like you were going to a funeral, and now you're bursting with joy and have a twinkle in your eye. Are you suddenly that happy to leave from here? Or something happened."

"Manda, if I told you what happened today, you wouldn't believe me. Heck, I wouldn't believe me either," Katarina chirped, light-headed at the thought.

"I still have no idea what you're talking about," Manda replied, scrutinizing her face. "Please tell me. I'm dying to know what put you in this elated mood. Aren't you supposed be leaving this afternoon?"

"Yes, but," Katarina took a deep breath, "one of my dreams just became reality. My boyfriend, Leo, has arrived here from home. He's in the quarantine. Today he asked me to marry him, and I said yes! Isn't that wonderful?" She said breathlessly, "Especially since I didn't expect him to come. Oh, Manda, I'm so happy." She hugged her new roommate.

Manda laughed. "That's splendid! I'm very happy for you. Does that mean you won't be going to the convent today?"

"Yes, that's exactly what it means. My transfer has been cancelled at least for today." Katarina bubbled with excitement. "Silvia teased me many times about my dreams. I wish she was here so she could see for herself that dreams do come true."

"You're talking about the girl that occupied this bed before me?" Manda asked. "She must have left a big impact on you."

"Yes!" Katarina said and returned to her daydream.

That night, Katarina couldn't fall asleep. Thoughts of Leo and happiness he brought her, a happiness she thought she would never have.

The memory of the day she left without saying good-bye to her mama and papa and the things she went through brought her back to reality.

Many bothersome questions rushed through her head about Leo's sudden appearance in the camp. Was he still a Communist sent to spy on the refugees? He had probably guessed where she was and could be using her to get to know the other refugees. And why was it so important that he ask her to get married, the minute they met? Couldn't he wait until he got out of the quarantine, at least? He told the carabineers he was her fiancé without having even asked her. Why? Had that helped him get into the camp? Was this marriage just a ruse? These thoughts were casting shadow over her happiness, but she couldn't rid herself of them.

One night, as she sat wrapped in these thoughts, Manda joined her, put her arm around her, and asked, "What is wrong, Katarina? We all miss our families, but Leo will be out of quarantine soon, and you should be looking forward to that."

"Yes, I miss my family, but that isn't what is bothering me the most now. It is Leo. I didn't think he would ever leave his country and he had a good job with the police department there, so I'm surprised he came here. It worries me a little. That's all," Katarina explained.

Manda moved away from her a little and, with wide open eyes, asked, "You mean he is a member of the Communist Party?"

"Was," Katarina replied.

Katarina was only able to speak with Leo through the upstairs infirmary window that overlooked the quarantine during his quarantine time. She had many questions for him. "Have you seen my parents? Were they very upset that I fled Yugoslavia?"

"Yes, your papa is still very angry that you fled the country. He's worried about you, and your mama, too. They are sad that you couldn't trust them enough to say good-bye to them. But they're both well."

"I'm glad. I hope they don't hate me," Katarina replied. Choking on her tears, she retreated inside and sobbed. She missed her parents very much and couldn't wait for Leo to be free so he could tell her more about her family.

Each day, when the refugees came out into the yard, Katarina would find an excuse to go upstairs and then, leaning over the windowsill, talk to her boyfriend. The days were going by slowly. The twenty-one days seemed like an eternity to Katarina, but they did give her time to work out some of her concerns.

She remembered the conversation she had with Rino about the spies.

On the morning of the twentieth day, Katarina awoke in a jubilant mood, ready to celebrate. "Finally!" she exclaimed as she leapt off the bed.

"What do you mean?" Manda asked, combing her daughter's hair.

"One more day, then Leo will be out!" Katarina smiled and whisked to work.

"That's great. I can't wait to meet the man who makes you this happy. I presume that you came with the terms with those problems about Leo," Manda said.

"Yeah, I think he's here for real," Katarina replied. "He could have kept me home if he wanted to before I left. Thinking back, I'm sure he knew I'm not coming back, but he did nothing to stop me. So I believe him when he said he loves me," she chirped; without waiting for Manda's reply, she ran down the steps to work.

The day's work in the infirmary seemed to last forever. Katarina was too excited to stay away from the window, and she continually talked to Leo. Toward the end of the day, she asked, "Were my parents made to suffer because I defected?"

But before Leo answered, another voice shrieked into her ear. "What are you doing at the window?" Startled, she turned and saw Matron Tonina standing in front of her. Katarina soon realized she had been found out. "You should have been working, Katarina, not hanging over the window!" Matron shouted again. Her face was red with disgust.

"I'm sorry. It won't happen again," she apologized, bowing her head, knowing her job was on the line.

"Make sure it doesn't. Now, do those beds and scrub the floor," the Matron ordered, the hatred audible in her voice.

Katarina had finished those jobs already, but how she could tell that to the angry matron now. She had no choice but to do them all over again. She scolded herself, "How could I've been so stupid to let myself get caught red-handed?" She wallowed in self-recrimination while scrubbing the floor, which kept her at work past quitting time. When she finally finished, she moved slowly holding her hand on her back as she walked back to her room.

"What's wrong with you?" Manda asked, looking at her with a smirk.

"Haha. You can laugh as much as you want. I'm sore all over! I can't believe that Matron ordered me to do the work all over again, just because I looked through the window," Katarina replied angrily.

"Just for looking through the window?" Manda quizzed.

"No. I spoke to Leo. I wanted to ask him more questions about my papa and mama. Besides, the beds were made and the floor was scrubbed already."

"You could have waited until tomorrow with the questions. Leo will be out by then."

Yes, you're probably right, but I didn't. Now I might lose my job," Katarina sighed, barely able to drag herself to her bed.

The next morning, Katarina's body still ached from having scrubbed the floor and made the beds twice. Still, she left for work as usual. She couldn't afford to get the matron even more angry at her then she already has.

Then she noticed Leo standing beside the infirmary entrance leaning against the door and a sudden burst of energy shot through her body.

As she dashed toward him, her aches disappeared. “Wow! What are you doing in here so early?” she asked, surprised to see him. “I didn’t expect you until the middle of the morning.”

Leo wrapped his arms around her waist and kissed her. “I missed you so much. I couldn’t wait to see you again,” he said between kisses.

Katarina recoiled. “I’m longing for you too. I wish I could stay in your arms, but I have to go to work,” she admitted with a smile, glancing over at the officer sitting beside the quarantine door, and slid out of his embrace. But he held on to her hand.

“When will I see you again? We have a lot to discuss. Hurry back,” Leo said as he let her go.

“Yes. We need to talk,” she agreed and suggested. “After I get off work, we can go to the coffee bar just outside the camp. We can talk there.”

“That’s a great idea. I’ll meet you in front of the cafeteria.”

“Great! I’ll see you there,” Katarina smiled and strode inside.

Another slow-motion day ensued. Her emotions flew high; everything else seemed to stay still. The day was going on and on, and she couldn’t wait for her shift to end.

“Katarina, calm down,” the Italian nurse Olivia cautioned her. “You’re going to wear out the steps, running up and down, looking at the clock.”

“I just wanted to see the time,” Katarina replied sheepishly and walked to the door.

“Well, you still have a few more minutes before the clock strikes 1600 hours. Then you can go meet your fiancé,” the nurse Olivia laughed and turned But, no one was there to hear her.

Already, Katarina ran out the door seconds before the clock strike the time and rushed to meet her boyfriend. Leo waited by the cafeteria as he said he would. “Hello, darling,” Leo said as she approached him.

“Hello to you too,” she chirped and hugged him. He gave her a kiss and then they walked into cafeteria for supper.

Later, Katarina and Leo sauntered over to the coffee bar.

“Goodness. I didn’t think it would be so crowded,” Katarina remarked, staring at the mob inside. After waiting for a while, they found two empty chairs on the terrace.

“It’s lovely here,” Leo commented, looking at the four trees occupying each corner of the terrace. Then his eyes shifted to Katarina. “Do you come here often?”

"Yes. The sun shines on the terrace until it drowns in the sea, and the service is excellent," Katarina chuckled. "Just like this lovely evening, with a fresh breeze bringing the sea smell in," she said and sat down.

Before Leo had a chance to respond, a waiter approached the two of them with a notepad in his hands, almost as soon as they sat down. "What can I get you?"

"Beer for me," Leo ordered. "How about you, darling?"

"Cappuccino, please." Looking at Leo, she said, "I don't like beer that much. But I do like wine once in a while."

Leo looked at her, "Would you like a glass of wine instead?" His hand was up and ready to call the waiter back.

"No, not now. Cappuccino is just fine."

Leo didn't waste any time. He went right to the heart of the matter. "Now, I wonder why you didn't have enough trust in me to share your going-away secret?" Leo asked, staring straight into her dark-brown eyes.

She hesitated, staring back at his big blues. She had hoped to tell him more about the family before discussing anything else. Struggling for words, Katarina replied, "There were so many things that you didn't know about my situation, especially at work."

Leo took her hand, "Well, why don't you tell me now, darling?"

Katarina pulled her hand back. "What's the big rush anyway?" she sounded calm enough, but her brain was racing. It was hard for her to bring up those painful memories.

"I'm sorry if it seems like I'm rushing you, but I would like to know the whole story," Leo smiled and broke off as the waiter came back; coffee and beer were served and the waiter left. He continued, "I was told that we have to get married as soon as possible because the marriage document is needed to finish our papers for a transfer from here."

Katarina took her cup into her hands and stared at him. "Fine. I'll tell. After my graduation from nursing school, I started to work in the children's department as a staff nurse. A few weeks later, I received a call from the personnel office to come and sign some papers. I didn't recall all of them, but I do remember a little red book.

"After I signed all of the papers, the secretary pushed the red book under my pen without explanation. I hesitated for a second or two because I didn't like the way she threw it to me. I felt it was underhanded. I picked up the book and asked, 'What is this?'

"The secretary snatched the red book out of my hand and hissed, 'So you don't want to become a member of the Communist Party?' collected the rest of the papers, and stormed away before I could say anything." Katarina paused.

"Knowing you. Your answer would have been, 'No thanks,'" Leo chuckled.

"I guess I was little irresponsible."

"Then what happened next?"

"On the way back to the floor, I wondered what had happened. Why was the secretary so angry with me? What had I done? But I could not come up even with one answer. As the days went by, I forgot all about it.

"Then unusual things started happening. For example, one day a three-year-old boy walked out of the children's floor, hours after I left, but I was blamed for it. I made the boy follow me by becoming too friendly, the chief of pediatrics said.

"I wanted to respond that I spend equal time with all of my little patients, but I kept quiet. Then I noticed I was being forced to work overtime almost every day while the other nurses weren't. When I complained, I was told to quit if I couldn't handle the job.

"Not long after that, I was transferred from the children's floor to stomatology clinic with the title of dental assistant. I was told that was a promotion, but in actuality, the hospital authorities had demoted me from a staff nurse to a non-diploma dental position. I became simply a laborer. When I asked why they were transferring me, the chief of pediatrics said that I was too small to work with children. What a joke!"

"I began to get the picture," Leo intercepted, but didn't comment.

Katarina glanced at him and continued. "It wasn't just that. While working in dentistry clinic, I was exposed to severe abuse by the office staff. Every Friday, routinely, I was called in and harassed, humiliated, with words like 'You're lazy and dirty. Your work is a mess. Your pay will get cut in half, you're not keeping up with your work.' The attacks were coming from all sides. I was afraid to say anything. I sobbed until they let me go.

"Then one Friday, when the secretary started with her usual attack on me and the others' eyes pointed at mine just waiting for their turns, something snapped inside. I just stood there and took all the garbage they threw at me calmly. I could see fire growing in the secretary's eyes, her face was turning red and her anger was showing. She grabbed my shoulders and shook me hard, shouting, 'What's going on with you? The dentist isn't happy with your performance. He complained again that you're slipping and that you're never on time. What do you have to say about that?' she said and sat down.

"Before I let anyone else speak to me like that, I decided to defend myself, no matter the consequences. 'That's not true!' Suddenly I protested, calmly. 'In the whole year, I have been late twice.'

"That made the secretary who was leading this parade angrier. 'Shut up!' she yelled, jolting me to attention. 'I don't want to hear another word out of your filthy mouth, understood!' As she continued her rant, I winced at the words, 'Messy, stupid, good-for-nothing!'

"Even though, feeling less than the dirt that had come from the bottom of my shoes, I stood in front of her calmly and didn't let go of one tear. This kind of abuse went on from the day I was transferred there, and there were many, many more." Katarina's cheeks flooded with tears of sadness as she told her story.

Leo passed her a tissue and said, "I'm very sorry that they put you through that terrible ordeal."

"Are you?" Katarina said, glancing at him.

"Yes, I wish I could have been there for you," he replied and took her hand.

"Well, I didn't want to get you in trouble because of me. A week before I left, the secretary called me in the office and gave an ultimatum: 'Either quit or be fired, but do not come to work.'

"I did neither."

Leo looked at her and said, "Oh, I remember. That was the week you're sick."

"Yes, only I wasn't sick. I was too upset and scared for my life and that of my family's and even yours, my love, to tell anyone what had happened to me. Besides, I needed the time to think things through to what to do next."

Leo's blue eyes turned serious. His eyebrows shot up, "Those bastards! You should have told me. Especially when you decided and made the plan to run," he said, grinding his teeth.

"Only, I haven't had the faintest glimmering of an idea what to do until I met my friend Ana-Maria, and that was a few days before I left. She said not to tell anyone. Besides, what would you have done if I had told you?" she asked, wiping the tears that were still coming down her face.

"I would have talked to my boss."

"Ha, talked to your boss?" Katarina said, sardonically. "You've got to be kidding! You would have lost your job and just knowing that I was planning to escape would have gotten you life in prison or worse."

Leo gazed into her eyes. "You know, darling, you did the right thing. I know I was pigheaded a little. I should have realized a long time ago, and maybe on some level, I knew that things are not as they seem to be. But I ignored it until you left. As I realized you're not coming back, I began to look into things that we as Croatian officers were not privy to and the things that were deliberately kept from us. I listened more closely and watched what's happening around me, especially things that concerned our people."

"What did you find out?" Katarina asked.

"You wouldn't believe," Leo whispered. "The kinds of things are going on in our country. I was shocked to find so many human rights abuses, silent ethnic cleansing, and pressuring mostly on Croats and non-Serbs to leave the country."

"Did you find out why this is happening?"

"My theory is the Serbs are doing that because they are trying to populate our area with Serbian people in hope to claim it one day as their own."

"That's what I heard too," Katarina agreed.

"But what really convinced me was when one evening I was standing in front of a restaurant with my friends. One of them was celebrating his birthday, and during the party, he began to sing a Croatian national song. In the middle of the song, police came and arrested him.

"The next day, when they let him out of prison, I went to visit him at his home. When I saw him, I shivered. Both his eyes were black and swollen and there were bruises all over his arms and legs.

"'Get the hell out of here!' he shouted, barely able to move around. 'Don't ever come back.'

"I stood there, too shocked to speak. He wouldn't talk to me, but he didn't have to. I had seen enough to draw my own conclusion. I glanced at him once more before I left and thought, *If that is the kind of punishment you get for just singing a song, what would happen if you really did something wrong*? I don't know if I want to stay here either. That's when I decided to follow your footsteps."

"Oh, I thought you came because you love me," Katarina glanced at him coyly.

Leo's face flushed. "Oh, of course, I did. You gave me that little extra push I needed to find the courage to leave." He smiled and hugged her.

"I'm sorry, it must have been awful for you to see your friend beat up like that from your working buddies," Katarina said and warned. "Now, you need to be careful in here. So you don't end up like your friend or worse."

"Why? Aren't we free?"

"That's exactly what I said when I was warned," Katarina chuckled. "The danger is coming from the secret Yugoslav police (UDBA). I heard there are many spies hiding among us in the camp. Several people have disappeared and nobody has heard anything about them since."

"Are you sure?" he asked, calmly sipping on his beer.

"Well, yes, fairly sure. It happened before. This isn't the only time."

"Don't worry about me, darling," he assured her. "Let's talk about our wedding. We only have a week to get all the papers together and get legally married, otherwise, they'll send you to the convent, and I'll go forward alone, I was told. That's not what I want."

"I don't want that either," Katarina smiled and cuddled closer to him, her eyes drifted across the sea. The sun sank in splendid coloring behind the horizon and a cold wind began to blow in. Her body shivered. "I should have brought my sweater."

"I guess we better get going then," Leo replied and rose.

"Yes. Let's go. I'm cold," Katarina said, took his hand, and cuddled close to his body as they sauntered toward the door.

As they walked out the door, Leo said, "When you get off work tomorrow, we can meet in the cafeteria and discuss our wedding and the documents we still need to gather for it."

"Oh, we can meet tomorrow for breakfast. I'm off for the next two days."

"Well, I'll see you in the morning then," Leo said and sent her off with a kiss.

"I'll see you in the morning," Katarina echoed as she walked back to her room.

"You are back!" Manda chuckled. "I thought you and Leo eloped."

"No! No! There's no need. Thank you. I've been rushed enough by Leo. Don't you even try," Katarina replied with a smile and jumped on her bed.

"So what did you learn about Leo this evening?" Manda quizzed her.

"The way he talked and things he told me about the Communist and Serbs, it convinced me that he's telling the truth."

"What is the big rush for the wedding anyway?" Manda sounded calm enough, but her brain was racing. She was worried about the spies and UDBA police too and wanted to know if Leo was one of them.

"Leo didn't tell me who, but someone told him, if we don't get married in a week's time, the Department of Immigration will send me to the convent, and he doesn't want me to end up in there."

"Well, I don't know. But I will tell you one thing, Leo seems to know a lot of what's happening around you," Manda replied and walked to the children's beds to cover her children up and settle to sleep.

Katarina didn't respond; at this moment, she was more confused about things than ever. Although she appeared to accept Leo's words at face value, there was still a glitter of suspicion in her eyes. She learned how to trust nobody.

The following day, Katarina began on her two days off and was to meet Leo at cafeteria for breakfast. They reserved the day to collect the necessary papers to be married.

At the cafeteria's door, Leo spotted his wife-to-be and walked over to her. "Hello, darling," he said and gave her a kiss.

"Hello, yourself," she managed to say before he sealed her lips with a big kiss. Breakfast was a cup of coffee and a small piece of a days' old strudel. After they ate, they went about their business.

They hadn't had much trouble; they both had all the papers they needed in their possession.

A few days later, they made an appointment to get married in the Trieste community office.

It was Monday. Leo had spoken with a priest of the camp and asked if he would marry them this coming Saturday. The priest agreed.

That night, while Katarina and Manda sat on their beds chatting across in the dark, Katarina asked, "Manda, would you please be my maid of honor?"

"Of course, I will! I'd be honored!" she accepted joyfully. Katarina could almost hear the smile in her voice.

"Thank you, Manda." Katarina spoke through unwelcome tears that poured down her cheeks when she realized no family member would be present at her wedding.

"Hey, hey, what are those tears for?" Manda asked as she walked over to her. She sat on the bed beside her and lay her hand on Katarina's shoulder. "You know your mama would be here if she could," she whispered as if she read Katarina's mind.

"I know. I'm not blaming her. I'm blaming those bastard Communists who forced me out of my country!" Katarina shouted and jumped to her feet. "I need Mama now and she isn't here for me. It's my fault, I should have stayed home," she said and embraced her roommate.

"There, there, don't cry," Manda consoled, wiping the tears from Katarina's face. "A wedding should be the happiest day in a girl's life."

"Oh, Manda, I am happy. I'm sorry, I didn't mean to become emotional like this," Katarina apologized. "I don't know what came over me. It's just that I've always wanted to be married in a long white gown and have my family around. Instead, I'm getting married in a burgundy suit, the color of the Communist Party, and no family will be present. I hate it," Katarina cried on Manda's shoulder.

"Oh, my dear, the dress doesn't matter. Your love for each other is what matters."

"The dress matters to me a great deal! And in times like this, I miss my family," Katarina said, lifted her head from Manda's shoulder, and wiped her face.

"Everything will be all right, Katarina," Manda replied. It was exactly what she needed to hear at that moment.

After Manda calmed her down, they both returned to their beds. Katarina lay awake in her bed for hours. She couldn't stop thinking how happy she'd be if her parents could attend her wedding even though she knew that was impossible.

It was almost midnight and Katarina was still awake. It didn't help that the night was hot and downright stuffy. In frustration, she left her bed and walked outside. She sat down at the top of the stone stairs and tried to bring order to her chaotic and suspicious mind. Instead, she managed to create more chaos as new questions nudged in her brain.

Why had Leo left the country? That was something she thought he would never do. And why had he chosen the same camp as she had?

No, she decided to dismiss them. She loved him too much to let them worry her. He was here and she wasn't about to let him go.

Suddenly, Katarina felt a hand on her shoulder and jumped. It was Manda. "What are you doing here?"

"It's a gorgeous night," Katarina replied and pointed at the North Star. "Look at those bright twinkling stars in the sky. See how beautiful they are!"

"But that's not why you're here, is it, Katarina?"

She stared at Manda. She didn't want to share with her the suspicions she had about Leo. Finally, she said, "It's my dress. It still bothers me. How can I marry Leo in burgundy?"

Manda's fingers clasped Katarina's chin and she gently tilted her head toward hers. "Listen to me. You're going to look lovely no matter what you wear."

There was an awkward pause while Katarina wished that she could postpone the whole thing, but she knew she couldn't. If they didn't get married now, Leo was right, they would be separated. Who knows whether they would ever see each other again? She would probably be sent to the convent and Leo who knows where.

"Are you all right?" Manda asked with a worried look.

Katarina glanced at her, stood abruptly, and walked back to her bed without a word to her roommate.

# CHAPTER 9

In the days which followed, Katarina struggled to find more control over the situation. She was disgusted with herself for having lost her control in front of Manda the previous night. Whenever she began to dwell on the burgundy dress, she closed her eyes in an attempt to block out the vision of it and said to herself, "Stop it."

The night before the wedding, she lay on her bed with pre-wedding jitters, unable to sleep. Katarina tossed and turned, worried how she would react to Leo's touch. *Will I cringe and withdraw? If I do, will he just think I'm shy or will he ask me why? Even if I convince Leo that my withdrawal from him sexually is shyness, he will not believe it forever. Will I even be able to enjoy sex with Leo or has the rape ruined that forever?* she wondered. *I wish I could tell him, but I know he will not understand—and I love him too much to risk losing him.* "Oh, why did this happen," she groaned.

"What did you say?" Manda asked, from across the room, half-asleep.

"Nothing, nothing."

Then get some sleep, Katarina. Your wedding is tomorrow," Manda whispered and turned to the other side.

"You're right," she replied, but sleep still refused to come. Her fear about the rape and her suspicions about Leo's sudden desertion of the police kept it away until fatigue closed her eyes and sleep finally ensued.

The morning of August 25, Katarina was awakened by the glaring sun shining through the window onto her sagging bed. "Great! It's going to be nice day," she jumped from the bed with a burst of energy and looked out at the clear blue sky. "Today is my wedding day! I will be

Mrs. Leo Lisic," Katarina chirped and leaned out the window, grinning from ear to ear. Her heart was filled with a joy and happiness, but also sadness she had never felt before.

"Yes, I know," Manda smiled back. "But you better go and get dressed." She and her two children were up for a while and they were all ready to go.

"Why did you have to remind me about the dress? You spoiled my mood." Katarina moved toward the dress and began to dress herself.

"Katarina, I don't think anybody could spoil your mood. You're positively glowing this morning."

Minutes later, Manda's daughter Josipa ran into the room with a bunch of yellow dandelions. "Katarina, these are for your wedding," the girl said and handed the flowers to her. She took the bouquet and threw a smile at the girl.

"Oh, how appropriate," she said and placed them against her dress. "They will go well with my burgundy attire. Thank you."

Manda chuckled and glanced at her watch. "You'd better hurry," she reminded her. "We're already running late."

"I'm dressed. Let's go." She grabbed her little purse and the flowers in the other hand. They rushed out and ran to get to the church.

As they were climbing the church steps, Katarina noticed Leo and the priest walking out of the church. She stopped dead in her tracks and broke into a cold sweat. "Oh no. I'm late to my wedding," she squeezed the words through her teeth, staring at them with a panic-stricken face.

"Just one minute," Manda said and walked toward the priest and Leo strode over to Katarina.

Manda handed her hand to the priest and said, "I'm Katarina's maid of honor. I apologize for the both of us. I'm very sorry that we are late. Please don't go. They need the marriage certificate for their documents. I know you're in a hurry, but please, a few minutes won't make that much of a difference."

Leo was infuriated with his bride-to-be, but kept his anger under control. The priest looked at Leo's and Katarina's disappointed face and smiled, "All right, come, my children." He turned and walked back into the church.

They rushed after him, and Leo said, "Thank you, Father!"

They all took their places at the altar. Leo reached for Katarina's hands and brought them up to their waists as they said their vows, and the ceremony was over. "We' re so grateful to you, Father," Leo said and shook the priest's hand. "Thanks, once more."

Manda also felt badly about making the priest wait that long, so she pulled the wine that she brought for Leo's and Katarina's wedding reception from her bag. "Thank you for being so kind, Father," she said and gave the bottle to him.

The priest took the bottle and smiled. As they walked out of the church, Mr. and Mrs. Lisic, euphoric and full of energy, all three strolled out of the camp toward the coffee bar.

At the door of the coffee bar terrace, Manda looked at Leo. "Now, we only need wine. Well, at least I still have the sandwiches from the camp cafeteria," she announced. The sunlight touched her blond hair. It glowed.

"That's great, Manda. Thanks!" Katarina replied as they sat at the table.

The waiter breezed by almost immediately. "What can I get you?" he asked, armed with a pen and a notepad.

"Three glasses of red wine," Leo ordered.

"I see, you still drink red wine," Katarina commented.

"But of course. The red wine is the best," he proudly announced.

"You never did like to drink the white wine, and you got angry with me if I did," Katarina commented, as she remembered the terrible headache she used to get after drinking the red wine, just to please him. And she was doing it again. *The day was too special to ruin it,* she mused.

Manda spread the sandwiches on the table, and they waited for the wine.

Leo looked at Manda and asked, "The coffee bar people won't get upset if we eat our sandwiches in their bar?"

"No. In here, the costumers are mostly refugees," Manda explained, just as the waiter arrived with their wine. The wine was served and the waiter wished them all the best and left.

Manda picked up her glass of wine and said, "Congratulations, Mr. and Mrs. Lisic!"

"Thank you, Manda," they said in unison and sipped on the wine. The three of them slowly picked on sandwiches and sipped on the wine until everything was gone.

"When are you two going to move into your new room?" Manda asked.

"Tomorrow," Leo said, with finality. "Paula couldn't get one ready for us today."

"It's going to be lovely having a room to ourselves," Katarina admitted, beaming at him.

"Yes, it's going to be nice," Leo agreed, sipping his glass of wine. Then he cleared his throat, turned to face Katarina, and added, "I know that the wedding wasn't to your liking. You wanted to get married in a long white gown. I wish I could have given you that. But I do give you my solemn promise that when we get to Canada, I'll give you a wedding you won't ever forget."

"That's very nice. But I was only upset because of my dress," Katarina replied and gave Manda an iced grin, which meant to keep her nose out of her business. "I wish that the dress was white or cream, instead of burgundy, but this is the only nice dress I had. I hesitated to put it on, that's why we were not on time at the church. I'm sorry. A mere promise from you means so much to me. Thank you, my love." She smiled and wrapped her arms around Leo's shoulders and added, "Will you ever forgive me for being late for our wedding?"

"Oh, let me think!" He looked at her with his crooked smile.

"Come on, will you?"

Leo leaned toward her. His fingers clasped her chin and gently tilted her head toward his, pressing her body against his, slowly. Katarina wasn't sure whether it was thunder she was hearing or the pounding of her own heart. Firm, soft lips met hers and were pressed together for a long moment before Leo pulled away. "Of course, I forgive you," he finally said with a smile.

As Manda watched them cuddle, she knew the wedding celebration was over for the three of them, and it was time for her to leave. "This's my cue to leave," she said with a smile and stood up.

"You don't have leave yet. Would you two like a coffee?" Leo offered. Katarina said nothing.

"No, no. You probably spent all your money on those few glasses of wine, Leo. It's very expensive. Besides, I have to pick up my children and take them for supper. Maybe I shouldn't have given the bottle to the priest," Manda chuckled.

"Oh no. That was a good gesture you did. Don't worry, we'll survive," Leo said and lit a cigarette.

"Thank you, Manda, for standing up for me at our wedding. I really appreciate it." Katarina gave her a hug.

"Well, see you later then." Manda strode away.

Leo put his arms around Katarina's waist and squeezed her close. "How about you? Would you like a coffee, darling?"

"No! It's too hot as it is."

"Let's go for a walk," he suggested, looking toward the small woods, just in front of them. "We might find a cooling breeze over there."

"That's excellent idea," Katarina agreed and stood up.

There was still about an hour of sunlight left. In love, on their wedding day, arm in arm, Leo and Katarina strolled through the woods, chatting, kissing, and teasing their way following the train tracks as their orienteers.

"If we were home, things would be different," Katarina said out of nowhere. "Our wedding would be better. There would be a lot of people, food, drinks, your and my friends. Then, of course, my family!" Katarina chirped. As soon as she finished, she realized she shouldn't have brought it up and raced ahead along the tracks through the high green grass, full of familiar scents. Lilacs and lilies of the valley were everywhere and they were her favorites.

She didn't wait for his answer that was why, she didn't wait for it. But, more than that, the rape nudged itself to the forefront of her brain.

She stopped and smelled her favorite flowers as she picked them.

Leo caught up to her. His bright blue eyes fixed its gaze beadily on her. "Are you trying to run away from me?"

"No! Here," she said and handed the flowers to him.

His eyes were still on hers. "I love you very much, darling," he said as he took the flowers and squeezed Katarina tightly against him with an abruptness that took her breath away. The flowers scattered all over the ground. She didn't manage to answer him. He pulled her down into the green grass with him, kissing her with a ferocity that she couldn't resist. His hands were pressing them closer and closer. His lips were warm and demanding on hers. As they made love, she felt dizzy as a wave of sensations swept through her body and emotions tumbled about inside her. On the end, she was lost in a world she had never known for a moment. The smell of lilacs and fresh green grass made her thoughts groggy and slow. She didn't realize what was happening until after they made love.

When Leo finally released her, they rolled into the grass.

"I love you too," she finally said and thanked her lucky star, things went just the way she hoped it would. Katarina rose to her feet, shook the grass off her clothing, and lay beside him, softly placing her head against his chest as he lay stretched in the grass in his joyous contentment and peace.

As she lay in Leo's embrace and enjoyed the evening, her breath came in deep sighs as she fought against the tears of bliss threatening to burst. Her husband reached her lips to kiss her once more, but her tears came forth like a river from a broken dam, wetting his shirt. Leo lifted his head and asked, "Darling, what's wrong?" He gently wiped her tears away with his fingers.

Katarina raised her shining brown eyes filled with tears to his. "There's nothing wrong, my love. It's just that I'm so happy. These are the tears of joy, not sorrow," She smiled and lay her head back on his chest, not sure herself why the tears. Stretched in the grass, they both stared at the sky in silence and enjoyed the lovely evening with a fresh breeze bringing the sea smell over to them. By then, the daylight was long gone and the moon was smiling high in the sky as millions of twinkling bright stars looked down upon them.

Suddenly, Leo said, "Did you know I've always dreamt of making love to my wife under a beautiful moon and bright stars on our wedding night?"

"Yeah, yeah. I'm sure you did. You also wanted to have the wedding like this one we had, right?" They both chuckled.

Katarina shivered and cuddled closer to his body.

"Cold?" Leo asked, with a grin, looking at her.

"A little," she answered.

"We'd better go back. It's late," Leo said and stood up. He gave Katarina his hand and pulled her up. He squeezed her tightly against his body and kissed her once again before they sauntered back.

They hit the camp around ten o'clock. He accompanied Katarina to the door of the building she stayed and then went to his room. Manda and the children were asleep when she entered. Katarina hurried to her bed and covered herself with the blanket as she was cold.

The next morning, Leo and Katarina were to meet with Paula, the camp worker, in the cafeteria to get the new room.

"Rise and shine!" Manda yelled and pulled the cover off Katarina. "You have to go meet your hubby," she reminded her.

"Oh no! What time is it?" Katarina asked and began dressing in a hurry.

"It's still early. Slow down," Manda urged her.

"No, I can't. I'll be late." Katarina rushed out the room like a storm.

When she arrived, Leo was already in front of the cafeteria. "Hello, my husband!" Her face beamed with joy as she said it. "The night was so lonely, I can't wait to be alone with you in our new room."

"It's lovely to see you too, darling," he greeted her, showering her with hugs and kisses. They picked up their breakfast, coffee and sweet rolls, and ate in the cafeteria.

Just as they finished, Paula walked in. "Oh, there you are, you two. Congratulations on your marriage."

"Thank you," they said in unison.

"All right, let's get you those supplies and your room," Paula said and walked out toward the supply storage. Ecstatic, Leo and Katarina followed her. From the supply, they both knew what they were getting, army things, but the room was a mystery.

"In which building is our room?" Leo asked after Paula piled up their arms with army blankets and few other things.

"Come with me. You'll see," she said and walked toward a building, but instead of up the stairs, they went down the stairs. When she opened the small door, Katarina and Leo were dumbfounded. Instead of a small private room, it was a gigantic warehouse filled with rows and rows of tents fashioned from blankets where young couples live. When they heard voices, the refugees stuck their heads out to see what was happening.

"What's this?" Leo and Katarina shrieked, staring at it with wide eyes.

Paula looked at them, her eyebrows lifted. "I'm sorry, but we have no more empty rooms left for couples without children. I have to settle you here, just like these other people. You'll have to make do until the next transport of refugees leaves the camp."

"These are not rooms, but only beds sheltered by blankets," Katarina said, disappointment showing on her face. "That's the best I can do!" Paula replied angrily. "There's a river of refugees coming in the camp every day. We can't accommodate everyone as they wish. Your bed is number fifty-five." Paula handed some papers to Leo, pointed the way to the number, and then walked out.

"I wondered why that many blankets," Leo commented as they slowly moved down the rows in the direction Paula pointed, squeezing the supplies in their arms.

"This is terrible," Katarina said and continued to walk, staring at the rows of blanket-made tents.

It was early in the morning; most of the refugees were still asleep or were going to work. Some of them peeked out of their tents and others came out. "Hello," they said as Katarina and Leo passed by en route to their bed. The refugees followed them.

"There!" Leo pointed to an empty army bed with the number they were looking for written on a piece of paper tied to the bed.

The refugees stayed aside and watched, but started to clap to give them courage when Leo and Katarina walked over to their bed. They threw the blankets on the bed. She couldn't take her eyes off it. "This is it? One naked bed, with one lightbulb hanging from the ceiling attached to a string that served as the switch? This is our room?" She felt her body shrivel.

Leo glanced at her, his lips arching into the kind of thin smile that fails to make you smile in return. "I'm afraid so, darling."

Katarina slid to the dusty cement floor beside their assigned bed and grumbled, "This is horrible."

Leo gave her his hand and pulled her up. "Come on, darling, we can do this." He embraced her and gave her a kiss. Then he began to build their new room following the design of others around them.

When the refugees saw Leo struggling with the blankets, they came over. "Hello, it looks like you might need some help there, young man," one of the older men said.

"Yes, please. I would appreciate any help I can get. Thanks. My name is Leo Lisic and this is my wife, Katarina." He glanced at her as he extended his hand to the men. Some men helped while others just gave advice. Katarina threw an occasional glance toward the bed in disbelief as she paced back and forth. The second happiest day of their lives had suddenly turned into a nightmare they would never forget. A few women came to support her. Soon the area around them buzzed with people's voices.

A young blond woman turned to Katarina and took her aside. "I understand you are having a hard time accepting this kind of arrangement." She chuckled.

"I can't believe it," Katarina replied. "A tent for a room?"

"We've been here two weeks already. Of course, there are no solid walls, but it's not that bad. Besides, it isn't like we'll be here forever." The woman smiled and patted her on the shoulder.

"I know, but we just got married yesterday." Katarina's face flushed red, "I wanted a real room to give us privacy."

"I understand. We were newlyweds too when we arrived. It'll be all right," the young lady said.

"I don't know if it will. The only thing I know is this is worse than what we had before." Katarina still struggled to accept what had happened.

"Yes, but you two were apart," the lady replied. Katarina was spared the need to answer by her husband's voice.

"You can make the bed now, darling!" Leo chanted as they finished, offering a cigarette to the men that helped him get the tent off the ground.

"Come, Katarina, we'll help you," the blond woman said. She and her friend started toward the tent. Katarina said nothing, but followed them inside.

After they made the bed, Katarina sat on it and said, "Thanks, you have been a big help to me. I'm sorry I acted stupidly."

"No problem. If you need anything else, come and call on us. We'll be glad to help you," the blond woman said before returning to their tents. Katarina remained sitting on her bed, her eyes wandering around. Suddenly, something reminded her of that horrid night when she was raped. Her body shivered just as her husband entered.

"There you are," he said and sat beside her. Without another word, he tilted her chin toward him, drew his finger down the side of her neck. His mouth came down on hers, parting her lips in a deep, languorous kiss as his hands began boldly to explore her body.

Katarina tried to kiss him back with all the love and emotion in her aching heart, but she jerked away as if she had been scorched. "Let's go pick up our things," she said quickly.

"Is there something wrong, darling?"

"No, nothing is wrong. I need clean clothes."

"Yeah, sure. Let's go then." Leo noticed the tension in his wife but dismissed it as by-product of the situation they were in. They both left to pick up their things from their previous rooms.

On the way, Katarina's mind was tormented. She just couldn't get comfortable and relaxed with her husband in the tent as she had in the woods. For a moment, she thought she would suffocate as the rape scene kept flashing in front of her eyes. It began to worry her, and she feared, she wouldn't be able to make love to her husband in the tent as she had outside in the grass.

When Katarina entered the old room, seeing unhappiness on her face, Manda shouted, "What's wrong with you?"

"Nothing!" Katarina snapped back and sat hard on her old bed.

Manda's eyes widened. "Ouch!" She paused and stared at her. "Did something happen, or shouldn't I ask?"

"Oh hell! What should have been one of the happiest days of my life turned out to be the worst nightmare I ever had. There's no room for us. I have to share my honeymoon with hundreds of other people. It's terrible. There's no privacy for us to make love. Every move we make can be heard by our neighbors."

"It can't be that bad. Where's this place you're settled in?"

"Paula took us in a huge warehouse filled with small tents built of blankets," Katarina sighed and hugged Manda with tears in her eyes. "Our room is made of blankets, if you can believe that."

"I'm sorry! I know how much you were looking forward to your privacy," Manda replied.

"You'll never know how much," Katarina muttered as she released Manda from her embrace. "I'm glad you're still here. At least, I don't have to say good-bye to you too. I would have hated to do that."

"It's good to know I have a good friend in you. Can I help you with something?" Manda asked.

"No, thanks."

After Katarina blew some steam off, she gathered her things and returned to the place where her new husband waited for her. Leo was already in their tent when she appeared, carrying her things. "Do you need a hand, darling?" he asked, coming toward her.

"No, thank you. I can do it." She dropped her things on her side of the bed. "See, there's nothing to it."

"Are you hungry? Do you want me to go and pick up lunch?" Leo wanted to do something nice for his wife to cheer her up as their morning didn't go the way they planned.

"Yes. Sure. Go and get it."

After he left, she sat down on the floor beside her things. While she was sorting it, the love scene in the woods was on her mind, so grateful that the rape hadn't interfered in their lovemaking. She hoped it would happen again in here, but after what happened today, she feared it won't.

"Here I am, darling. Did you miss me?" Leo quizzed as he returned with lunch.

Startled, Katarina lifted her head and smiled, "Of course, I did."

"Great!" He spread a blanket on the floor beside her and then placed their food upon a tea towel. "Let's eat." He managed to say before he dug into his portion of dry spaghetti.

She took her portion, glancing at him as he gobbled down his food and laughingly said, "Wow. It must be good." But she wasn't as enthusiastic as he was to dig in; she looked and carefully picked only the spaghetti that was covered with sauce, and there was not a lot of it.

Busy stuffing his face, Leo didn't have time to say anything, but when they finished, he asked, "Darling, would you like to go for a walk with me?"

"I'll be delighted! You owe me a few questions, which I've been meaning to ask you for a while, but never had a chance."

"About what?"

"My parents. I would like to know if they were made to suffer because I defected?"

"Sure. Why don't we discuss right now?" Leo suggested.

"In here? So everyone can hear what we are talking about. No thanks," she replied with simple candor, rose to her feet, and gave him her hand. "Let's go out!"

With hands entwined, they walked out into the camp yard crowded with refugees. Everyone was enjoying the beautiful sunny day.

"So what do you want to say, my love?" Katarina asked as they strolled around in the yard.

"About your parents?"

"Yes." Katarina's eyes pierced his.

"Everyone suffered in the hands of the Communists when someone you know leaves the country, you know that. And it happened to your parents and me."

"You? Why you?"

"You were my girlfriend. The chief of police wanted to know if I knew you're leaving, and what did I know? But your parents and your siblings were dribbled with questions for weeks."

"Oh no. My poor family, what did I put them through? The decision I made not to tell you and them about my plan for leaving, it haunted me for a long time. I felt bad because I didn't say good-bye to my parents. But I can see now, I did the right thing."

"Yes, you did," Leo said. "If you told us and the police found out about it, your parents could be sitting in jail right now and probably me too."

"Hello, you two lovebirds," said a voice from behind. Katarina turned her head and saw Manda and her children rushing to catch up to them.

They stopped and waited. "What are you up to?" Katarina asked, looking at Manda as they approached.

"I thought my children and I can take a short walk before supper. Then I saw you and wanted to know how are things going?"

"Oh, it will be all right," Katarina said.

Leo laughed. "Everything is fine. Katarina needs to get used to the blanket tent and probably me too."

"Of course. Would you like to spend supper with us?" Manda suggested.

"Why not? Is it that time already?" Leo asked.

"Yes," Manda said and turned toward the cafeteria.

For supper, they get bean soup and bread. After they ate, Leo and Katarina returned into the warehouse. As they walked down the pathway, they could hear voices coming from both sides of the aisle and what the refugees were talking about was clear.

"See, that's what I'm worried about," Katarina commented as she entered into their tent and threw herself on the bed, dressed. She stared at the ceiling, preoccupied in her thoughts.

Leo lay down beside her in his underwear only. He didn't give much time to her meddling thoughts. Without a word, he tilted her chin toward him and drew his fingertip down the side of her neck. His mouth came down on hers, parting her lips in a deep, languorous kiss as his hands began boldly to explore her body.

"Let me take my clothes off," she said, leapt off the bed, and began undressing herself slowly.

As she reached for her nightgown, Leo said, "Keep it off, darling," and slid under the blanket, lowering his boxers to the floor on his side of the bed.

She flashed a shy look at him. "All right," Katarina replied in a low tone. Desperate to hide her nakedness, she crawled to bed and quickly pulled the blanket up to her chin.

Leo greeted her with a quick kiss. "Don't cover yourself from me, darling. You're very lovely," he proclaimed and began stroking her hair with one hand and slid the other down over her throat to her breasts, circling the pink crests with his thumb until they stood up proudly. "I love you so much," he mumbled, crushing her breasts against him and covering her body with his own as he kissed her with deep and tender reverence.

Katarina shivered with delight as she felt flames racing uncontrollably through her veins. As she started to fit herself to his hardened length, a thousand of her nerve endings cried out for more.

"Oh, darling," Leo groaned. His husky voice was muffled as he snuggled against her naked flesh, his arms holding her tightly and pressing closer to his body. He made her forget everything around them. She didn't care anymore if someone was listening or not. The only sound she heard was their deep irregular breathing.

Later, when Leo let her go, he stretched on his side of the bed, happy and contented. She grabbed her nightgown and quickly pulled it over her nakedness, then quietly lay down beside him with her back turned. He turned facing her back, wrapped his arms around her body and said, "Love you. Goodnight, darling," kissing her on the back of the head.

"I love you too. Goodnight." She was tired and needed to get some sleep. The three days off that was given to her to get married were gone, and she had to report to the infirmary in the morning.

The next day, while Katarina worked, Leo handed their marriage document to the immigration department to be processed for their next move.

After that, there was nothing else for them to do but to wait until they were transferred out of the transitional Trieste camp.

xxxxxxxx

It was hard for Katarina to adapt to the marriage, especially the sex part. But as the days passed, it became easier. Leo was loving, caring, and fun to be with. That helped her get through the ordeal, at least for the moment.

Xxxxxx

After Leo and Katarina handed all their documents in to the immigration department, there was nothing else for them to do but to wait until they were transferred out of the camp.

Xxxxxx

When they were not happily surrendering to their passions and she wasn't working, they spent time with Manda and children and in the coffee bar listening to their favorite music on the jukebox as they anxiously waited for the day.

xxxxxx

After all of the preparation for immigrating was done, papers signed, medical tests preformed, the refugees waited in Trieste camp until the quota was filled for transfer.

XXX

While other refugees waited a long time for transport, Leo and Katarina were lucky. Only a week after their marriage, the lists of refugees to be transferred were announced, and Mr. and Mrs. Lisic were on one of the lists.

A few days later, Leo and Katarina received a written confirmation of their departure and two small ID cards to be used to travel. They were to leave Trieste camp for dusty climates of southern Italy, somewhere between the cities of Rome and Naples on September 1.

XXXXXXXXXXXXXXXXXXXXXXXXXX

XXXXXXXXXXXXXX

Torn between her love for her family and anger for the Communists, who had compelled her to leave her country, she almost wished she had gone to the convent and been able to stay in Trieste. "Wait one minute!" Katarina shouted and started walking.

XXXXXXXXXXXXX

# CHAPTER 10

For a while, Trieste had been a lifeline attaching Katarina to her family and country. Now she was leaving its safety, and she suddenly realized she had been so busy with her work that she hadn't given a second thought to leaving.

As Katarina and Leo packed their belongings and prepared to leave the camp in Trieste, her heart started to thud like a drum, and she choked on her tears. To her, it meant much more than merely leaving a city: it meant breaking ties with everything and everyone she held dear and moving farther away. Realizing she might never be able to come back, at that moment she almost wished she had gone to the convent and stayed in Trieste.

"What have I done to deserve this?" Katarina asked after a long silence. The tears clouded her vision; she could barely see the things she was packing.

"Nothing. You have done nothing wrong," her husband assured.

"I'm sorry, my love. I've been silly. Could you please go find Manda and the children and ask them to come here?" Katarina told her husband, not wanting him to see her teary eyes. "I would like to say good-bye to them properly rather than on the run."

"Sure, darling, but we don't have much time. Hurry packing," Leo replied and ran out to look for them.

She was alone and outwardly quiet, every single muscle in her body fought to be strong and not to let her tears out, but despair still weighed against her relief at leaving Trieste. The images of her family members being punished by the Communists for what she had done spun around in her head. Each of them left a deep sorrow on her heart.

She tried to stop the tears, but couldn't: the sadness was too great, they came pouring down her cheeks, just as her husband returned. "Don't cry, darling," he said and wiped her tears with his fingers.

Still no more at ease, she walked her room as if she were in a cage. "You know that we might never be able to come back and see our families and country again. Oh god! Am I strong enough to withstand all this?" Katarina cried out.

"Of course, you are! You have to be!" Leo exclaimed and wrapped his arms around her shoulder, kissing her nose to reassure her. "Darling, it's going to be all right. One day when things change at home, we'll come for a visit."

Katarina went to finish her packing and glanced at her husband. "I'm not sure about that. Canada is far away. I have a horrid feeling that once we leave here, it will be forever."

"Are you telling me, you believe the Communists will govern our country forever?" Leo quizzed. "Nonetheless, we can't go back now."

"Yes, I know we can't go back. And the way things are now, I wouldn't want to. I'm afraid the Communists will be there forever!" Katarina admitted sadly.

"Well, I don't know about that," Leo disagreed. "I do know, there's nothing we can do except go forward."

"Oh, where's Manda? Didn't you find her?"

"No, I didn't. Don't worry, she'll probably be at the gate. Listen! There's the bus horn. Hurry, we have to go," Leo said as he headed for the bags.

"All right! All right! I guess we'll see Manda at the gate." Katarina wiped the tears from her face and threw the last few pieces into her travel bag. "Let's go before I change my mind."

Leo picked up their bags and walked out. She glanced around one more time. She was happy she didn't have to stay here any longer, yet she was sad to be leaving. She grabbed her purse and followed him outside.

It was a morning of bleached light, the sky hanging above Trieste, and the sea, silver gray like the inside of an oyster shell. But, the sun hidden behind the clouds was sending warm rays to the ground. Still, she left out her sweater, just in case the weather worsened. When she caught up to her husband, he put his arm around her shoulders and smiled. "We will be fine. We have each other."

"Thank God for that."

They continued to stride toward the big iron gate where the buses waited for the refugees to board and take them to the train station.

On the way, Leo and Katarina were so engrossed in their thoughts that they forgot about Manda and her children.

"Katarina! Katarina!" a voice thundered from the noisy crowd around the buses. She looked and noticed Manda and the children struggling through the crowd to come over to them.

"Manda!" Katarina called and hurried to meet them. "Where have you been? Leo looked everywhere for you and the kids. I wondered if my maid of honor would make it on time to see us off."

Manda glanced at him suspiciously. "You looked for us?"

"Yes, I did. I looked everywhere," Leo confirmed.

"You really think I would miss my last chance to see you two and to say good-bye?" Manda quizzed.

"I'm glad you didn't because you couldn't rely on me to do anything. My mind is all over the place this morning. I'm not sure if I'm coming or going," Katarina responded. "Good-bye, my friend, and good luck to you and your children in Australia."

"Thank you. Same to you in Canada," Manda smiled and glanced at Leo. "Take good care of my friend Katarina and watch for each other. I see there are six workers going with the transport. You'll be in good hands on the way to Rome. I'm glad." Manda held on to her children's hands as they shouted in unison. "Good-bye to both of you."

"Good-bye." Katarina barely got the words out before she rushed ahead, choking on her tears.

Leo said a quick good-bye to Manda and the children, then ran after his wife, seizing her hand. "Wait for me, darling!"

Katarina kept up the pace, sniffling. "Manda is another good friend I'm losing since I got here."

"I understand, but we both know that's not why you are crying." She glanced at her husband as they got close to the buses, but didn't answer.

Surrounded by the noisy crowd, thoughts of her family crammed her mind and the reality hit her again. Her stomach fluttered. "Oh no. This is it! I will never see my papa and mama again," she groaned and put her hand across her abdomen, missing them more that day than at any other time, even more than on her wedding day.

"Are you all right, darling?" Leo asked, looking at her pale face.

"Yes, I think so," she answered. "I just had this empty feeling that started in my abdomen and spread all over my body. It was horrible!"

"It's probably your nerve," Leo replied nonchalantly as they mingled through the crowd to take their places.

"It likely is, but it made me feel like a shadow of myself." She glanced at Leo, but he didn't hear her. His mind and ears were on alert for their names to be called as they settled in the line and waited.

About ten minutes later, there was stillness everywhere as a clock in the camp church struck eight, and the officials began to call the refugees' names. The silence didn't last long, however, for the shouting and shaving began again soon.

"Mr. and Mrs. Lisic" finally echoed through the crowd.

"It's about time," Katarina muttered as they began moving toward the bus where they had been called. An official stood in front of each bus door to make sure no one went in without ID.

"ID please," the official requested as Leo and Katarina reached the official.

"Here," Leo replied and handed her both ID cards.

The official checked it against her papers and gave them instructions. "You're to stay close to the officials and not to go or do anything without their knowledge, do you understand?"

"Yes, we do," Leo answered for both of them.

"You can board now," the official ordered as she handed the ID papers back to Leo and yelled. "Next!"

Katarina climbed the steps and, just before she entered the bus, glanced up at the sky to see that the sun had peeked from behind a passing dark cloud. "Let's hope it doesn't rain," she commented, throwing a glance at her husband following behind her.

"I wouldn't mind a little rain," Leo teased. "I love rain, especially when I travel. It puts me to sleep."

She gazed back at him sharply. "What? Does that mean you'll be sleeping all the way to Rome?"

He chuckled and shrugged his shoulders, pointing. "Look, there are two empty seats, darling."

"Lovely. I enjoy looking out the window when I travel," Katarina said and took the seat beside the window.

The noise level crescendoed as more refugees pushed and clambered down the aisle to get seats, but not everyone found one. Some of the refugees had to stand. There were only two buses for more than three hundred people.

"Thank God, we came a little early, otherwise, we'd be standing," Katarina commented, looking up the crowded, chatty aisle, which resembled a farmer's market.

"What did you say, darling?" Leo asked as he couldn't hear her. Katarina motioned with her hands not to worry and turned to gaze out the window.

The officials boarded the bus, just to give the driver a signal to drive off, then they stepped down and climbed into private transportation.

The buses pulled forward, and the standing refugees went scrambling for any kind of grip to keep them from falling. "Hold on!" they shouted as the buses went out through San Sabba iron gate unimpeded and sped on their way.

"Why didn't the camp use more buses so we wouldn't have to stand?" someone from the aisle yelled, but no one from the authority was there to respond.

XXXXXXXXXXXXXXXXXXXXXXXXXXX

Before the bus turned the corner, Katarina threw a glance out the window. The last thing she saw was Manda and her children, still standing at the San Sabba camp gate, waving. Katarina grabbed her husband's hand and pointed to them as she waved. "Look, Leo, they are still there. Good-bye, my friends," she whispered, waving back at them, even though they no longer could see her.

Her husband nudged her shoulder and said, "You'll find another good friend, I'm sure of it."

"I suppose I'll have to," Katarina whispered and continued to watch the scenery: lovely plazas, colorful pigeons with their wings outspread as they flitted from tree to tree, and ancient buildings flashed in front of her eyes as the bus rolled through the city.

After about a thirty-minute drive, the buses stopped in front of a building, and the refugees raucously disembarked into the train station.

At the station, they were, again, given instructions. One of the officials accompanying them on their journey to Rome climbed on one of the stone benches in the train station and yelled, "Everyone, calm down! Nobody is to move from here without our knowledge. If you do, you'll be left behind. One more thing, when boarding begins, the regular passengers go first. Understand!"

"Yes. We understand," they grumbled back and look for something to do in the station to pass the time.

"She's ordering us around like a sergeant mayor," Katarina commented.

"What would you know about that?" Leo chuckled and went around to observe the pictures hanging on the walls.

Katarina smirked and sat on the bench beside the window to stare at the mountains towering over the city like a gigantic bear. They reminded her of the trip she took through them not long ago. "I wonder what Dario and Ana-Maria are doing now?" she said under her breath. "I hope they got out of there safely."

As soon as memories of her family began nudging forth in her mind, she stood up and strolled back and forth to shake them off.

"All aboard!" a conductor yelled as he walked from one side of the train to the other, swinging the red lamp in his hand, shaking Katarina out of her daydream.

Xx

The doorway of the train station was instantly flooded with the passengers.

XXX

Instantly, the train station doorway was flooded with passengers, pushing and shoving to get through first.

As soon as the commotion started, Leo came rushing to his wife's side. Through the window, they watched the regular passengers push through the doorway and hurry to seats, like herds of sheep. It took fifteen minutes for the regular passengers to get into the train.

The same official was again standing on the bench and commanded, "Now, the refugees can proceed. Everyone move toward car-wagon number 30 and begin to board. No pushing and shoving please!"

Another struggle for seats ensued as the refugees began to board the southbound train to Rome. Leo and Katarina were near the doorway, and they easily slid into the first line to board after the regulars. As the doors opened, refugees proceeded toward the car number 30.

Leo decided he'd race his wife for the window seat. "Let's see who will find the window seat first," he announced and rushed ahead.

"You're going to lose," Katarina grumbled and followed him through the shoving and pushing crowd. She squeezed through where he couldn't, so when Leo appeared in the car, his wife grinned from ear to ear. "I told you so," she chirped, settling in the seat beside the window.

Leo sat beside her and sheepishly said, "Oh, darling! I let you win. I know how much you enjoy it."

"Sure you did," Katarina scowled as she tried to find a comfortable spot in the wooden seat.

No sooner had the refugees settled in their hard wooden seats then the train began to leave the station. Katarina and Leo looked into each other's eyes and read each other's mind. A sad feeling came over both of them, knowing they might never be able to come back.

"Don't worry, darling, everything will be fine," Leo assured her. They both had mixed emotions leaving Trieste. He tried to hide them, but Katarina could hear the pain in the tone of his throaty voice.

After a moment's thought, she answered, "Are you sure about that, my love?" The strain of leaving Trieste made her so tense that she had a wild urge to jump out of the train and run home. Instead, Katarina leaned her head on her husband's shoulder and listened to the clattering noise of the train wheels passing over the cobbled tracks, carrying them farther away with each revolution. The sound also brought back memories of the train ride she had taken the day she left her country and poured forth inside her head like a roll of film. "Here we go again," she whispered to herself.

Suddenly, the rumbling of the train became more pronounced as it sped toward Rome. "Hold on to your hat! It's going to be a bumpy ride!" Leo exclaimed and reached for his wife's hand.

"Oh, yeah. Aren't you a funny comedian? Have you ever been in Rome?" she asked finally and leaned against his shoulder.

"No, but I read about it," Leo scoffed, trying to defend himself.

Again, it became too noisy for conversation as the refugees sang and chatted and the children fought and cried. Leo closed his eyes and, in the middle of it all, fell asleep. She pulled away from him to stare out the window.

They had left the Alps behind and passed through the ship building and industrial town of Manfalcone on the shores of the Gulf of Panzano, an inlet at the head of the Gulf of Trieste. In front of her eyes was an endless flatness through which the irrigation ditches stretched away to what seemed like infinity between the high embankments. The farmhouses and villages stood like islands isolated in seas of ripening corn and grapes.

The farmers in their wide-brimmed straw hats were calmly engaged in sales on the outskirt's roads of the villages, even though the weather seemed to be worsening. Katarina opened the window, and the strong chilly air of the first touch of autumn rushed in, ruffling Leo's blond hair. Her body swung right around in her wooden seat to see his head looked like a porcupine's back.

She giggled and quickly closed the window. Leo awoke seconds later. "I'm sorry, my love. Did the cold wind wake you?" She flashed a mischievous look at him, hardly able to contain her chuckle.

"Not really," he finally muttered in a groggy voice. Katarina could barely hear him above the din. Instead of talking, they decided to join the others in singing.

Sometime after 1400 hours, the camp workers accompanying the transport finally showed their faces. "Bravo!" the refugees yelled and clapped as two officials entered, carrying sandwiches and water for the refugees and milk for the children.

"You must be hungry?" they said, serving the food.

"Yes, we are!" the answer came from all sides.

As soon as they served the food to everyone, they shouted, "See you later," and were gone.

Leo turned to his wife and whispered in her ear. "They are rushing to their soft seats. I'm sure their seats are not hard and wooden like ours."

"They are probably in the first-class wagon," Katarina agreed as she took a bite of her sandwich.

During the next hour after they finished their food, they all joined in a general chat. Everyone participated, back and forth, exchanging thoughts and ideas as to the future that lay ahead of them, just to pass the time. Politics was not mentioned as everyone was afraid of Communist spies among themselves.

"I'll be back with a Rolls Royce to visit my parents," Katarina blurted suddenly.

Everyone burst into laughter. Leo almost leapt out of his seat, choking on his water, and glared at her. "Wow! Rolls Royce? You have a big appetite, darling. You are kidding, right?"

"If I make enough to eat good and have a place to stay, I'll be more than happy," one of the refugees replied.

"But I say, if we work hard, why not? I heard Canada is a rich country," Katarina persisted.

They all chuckled again. Everyone thought it was an absurd idea. Katarina did too, but she was offended anyway. "Nobody offered any better one," she retorted and turned her head to stare out the window. She let her reflection take over, which was soon joined by the faces of her family. She knew she could no longer dwell on them that much; she had to be strong and concentrate on her husband as he was her family now.

It was some minutes later when she realized the train had left behind the flat land and was now moving up the hill through a forest. The wind was severely swaying the big treetops from side to side; dark ominous clouds were growing in the sky. The sun would occasionally peek from beneath the clouds and send shadows scattering through the woods along the way, but making some of the branches glitter like twinkling stars in the sky.

"What a beautiful sight!" Katarina commented and glanced back at her husband.

Leo moved closer and peered over her shoulders. "Yeah. Look at the beautiful rainbow over the darkened sky. It means the rain is near."

"No, no! It signifies the end of the rain."

"No. You're wrong," he muttered and sat back on his seat. Katarina glowered at him and remained leaning against the window, staring enchanted by the colorful forest until she eventually fell asleep.

She awakened a little after five in the afternoon and noted the sun's glint had been replaced by the pitter-patter of rain on the window and the roof of the train. "I guess you were right, my love. Your wish has come true. It's pouring outside," Katarina remarked, holding her stiff neck as she turned to him.

"Yes, I know. It has being raining hard for about an hour or so. And it's wonderful!" Leo chuckled and asked. "Have you got a good sleep?"

"Yeah, I did. Have they brought supper?"

"Not yet. But it should be soon," Leo replied and glanced at the entrance door. "There, someone is coming now." He was right.

As the officials entered with another around of sandwiches, applause was heard. "Bravo!" the hungry refugees yelled.

"Listen up, everyone!" one of the officials exclaimed from the door. "Slowly and orderly come over and get your portion! Adults have choice today, coffee or tea, courtesy of the train."

"Thanks to the train!" the refugees shouted in unison as they slowly walked to the door to pick up supper and their hot beverage. Katarina and Leo both chose coffee.

Later, they stood up to stretch their legs, strolling up and down the car aisle. Leo pulled out a cigarette and they walked to the end of the car close to the window. The last four seats were occupied by four male refugees who were smoking and talking. "Need a light, buddy?" one of them asked, looking at Leo.

"Sure! Thanks," he said and leaned over to get it, then slanted against the window and began puffing.

XXXXXXXXXXXXXXXXXXXXXXXXX

While Leo was smoking, Katarina stared out into the darkness that enveloped them even though it was still some hours before the nightfall. The rain was coming down hard; she could hear it against the window and the top of the rough. It was depressing.

"I'm going to my seat," she told Leo and strolled back. He stayed behind to finish his cigarette. The noise in the car settled somewhat as most of the children fell asleep and the adults rested with their eyes closed. She wrapped her sweater around her shoulders and settled on the seat with her head leaning against the window. When Leo returned, he found his wife sound asleep.

The next morning, the sun shining upon Katarina's face woke her. The car was quiet as most of the refugees were still sleeping. It took her a few seconds to orient herself to where she was.

"Good morning, sleepyhead." Leo's face stared at hers.

"Hi, where are we?" she asked, stretching her back, which was stiffened from the hard wooden seat, her eyes drifting around.

"In your Rolls Royce," her husband teased.

It didn't bother her; Katarina threw at him a mischievous look and replied, "Haha, who appointed you the comedian?"

"How should I know where we are?" he defended himself.

"Can you tell me the time, at least?"

"It's ten o'clock. None of the camp workers have come yet and I'm starving," he replied angrily.

"They are probably still sleeping in their soft beds," she remarked cynically, holding her sore back with one hand and opened the window with the other. Chilly air burst in and brushed against her cheeks.

"Close that damn window, it's cold!" someone shouted from the back of the car-wagon.

"All right! All right!" she shouted back and quickly shut the window. Leo peered over her shoulders out the window, but before he could say anything. Katarina announced, "It's going to be a beautiful day. So don't jinx it."

"I wouldn't dream of it!" he exclaimed. He reached up with his right hand and brushed the hair from her neck, then leaned over and kissed it. "I hope someone brings some food soon. I'm famished," he whispered.

"You are always hungry," she scoffed.

"Oh, give me a break. I haven't eaten since yesterday. I'm still a growing boy, you know," he retorted and nibbled at Katarina's ear.

"Sorry, but my ears are not on the breakfast menu, my love," she informed him and pulled away.

"Aren't you hungry?"

"Yes, but it's still early. I'm sure they'll bring something soon."

"Ten o'clock is early for your breakfast!" Leo cried and settled back on his seat.

As the minutes stroked away and the hours passed, the children began to cry and begged for food. "Give me milk! Give me bread! Mama, I'm hungry!" they yelled and screamed.

In dismay, Katarina listened to the children and watched the mothers as they struggled to keep the little ones calm while frustrated fathers marched up and down the aisle cursing. It baffled her.

"What's keeping them?" she asked, looking at her husband.

"I don't know!" He stood up and joined the fathers in the walk.

It was past midday before any nutrition was brought to the refugees and then it was only a small cheese-spread sandwich and water. As soon as they entered the door, they shouted, "Keep the noise down! Stop the children from crying."

One of the fathers was so angry that he was ready to lunge at them, but the quick reaction of Leo and the other men kept him from making a big mistake of his life.

"Are you crazy? Even small anger shown toward them could keep you and your family behind for years," Leo whispered into his ear. "If you touch any of them, they can throw you in jail and you're finished. Then what?"

The father shook his head and said, "It drives me bananas. When I know they are having fun in their soft first-class wagon while our children are starving in here. I'm not worried about myself. It's already lunch and the children didn't even have their breakfast yet."

"I understand, but you can't threaten those people no matter what. You know what's going to happen if you do," Leo explained.

"You're right. I know," the father admitted. They both walked to their seats to have their lunch such as it was.

Soon the car became totally silent. The children, somewhat satisfied with the food they had, fell asleep one by one. The adults stared into a blank space, subdued, deep in thought with signs of frustration wearing on everyone's long unhappy face. Leo, on the other hand, dozed off to sleep. He would have been able to fall asleep anywhere and anytime, even on the rocks, as long as his belly was full. Katarina, as usual, watched the scenery through the window, occupied by her own thoughts, so her sleep didn't come that easily.

The refugee's unpleasant thoughts were interrupted by a loud whistling sound as the train entered into the city line of Rome. The refugees jumped to the windows. "Rome!" someone yelled, just as the big coliseum presented itself in front of Katarina's eyes. "Wow! It's beautiful!"

"What is?" Leo asked and looked over her shoulders.

"The coliseum. But it isn't as beautiful as ours in Pula," she chirped.

"You are right it isn't," he agreed. "But the city of Rome is beautiful."

The second whistling sound went off before the train entered the station and came to a halt. It was a little after three o'clock in the afternoon when they arrived in Rome.

"Finally!" Katarina exclaimed, stretching her sore muscles, still viewing the scenery through the window. People rushed in and out of the train cars.

"We are here, darling," Leo informed his wife as the train came to a halt, and he reached for their bags.

"Yeah, I know, but we have to wait for the officials, don't we?" she said without turning her head.

"Yes, and they just arrived. They are standing at the door." Leo picked up their bags and turned to her. "So let's go."

"I'm coming," she replied, grabbing her sweater from the seat. They followed the others down the aisle. The refugees stepped off the train, and the officials hurried them through the station out to the other side where two buses were waiting for them. No sooner had they disembarked from the train then they boarded buses again.

"Here we go again. Another hour or two of a bumpy bus ride and yet another camp," Katarina muttered to herself, frustrated. Leo glared at her as he noticed she hasn't taken the water that was offered to each of them as they stepped onto the bus. He grabbed two bottles and handed one to his wife, but said nothing. They were both hot and tired from the long train ride.

Katarina settled into the seat, crossing her arms across her chest, looking worried. Leo sat beside her and asked, "Are you all right, darling?"

"Yes. I'm only tired and the heat is suffocating," she replied, and leaned her head against the window, hoping to get fresh air.

As soon as all of the refugees boarded, the buses began rolling toward a city called Latina.

Typical southern autumn weather followed them all the way. One minute it was sunny and warm, and the next, rain, thunder, and cool air blew from the sea.

The bus was crowded and stuffy. Everyone was tired and frustrated, especially the children. They fought and cried and the noise was high.

Later, from the back of the bus, Katarina heard tiny voices calling out, "Mama, I'm hungry."

"Food will be served at the camp on arrival in Latina," one of the camp workers repeated calmly in response to those mothers who asked for food for their little ones.

"Those poor children. How do they think the children can be convinced to wait until they come to Latina? It's beyond me," Katarina said and cuddled against her husband.

"I think they should have given extra food for the children. Cookies or something to keep them busy during the travel," Leo replied.

"You're right," she agreed and listened to the hungry little souls and thanked her lucky star she wasn't a mother at this point in her life. "How long do you think this ride will last?" she asked, frustrated.

Leo, squeezed her close and said, "I don't know, but it shouldn't be long."

Suddenly, the buses began to slow down. Katarina sighed and glanced at her husband, "It looks like we have arrived!"

XXXXXXXXXXXXXXXXXXXXXXXXXXXXXXXXXX

"It looks that way. Let me see," he replied and rose to his feet. Looking out the window, he saw the buses drive slowly through the gate into Camp Latina. Leo dabbed her on the shoulder. "Yes, we are here, look." The buses were besieged by a huge waiting crowd when they came to a stop.

She peered out. "Wow! So many people. It must be a big camp," she said and prepared to leave. As they inched toward the bus exit, Katarina and Leo had to shout to hear each other over the noise. "I'm so glad the ride is finally over," Katarina said as they stepped off the bus.

"I don't know if you going to feel the same after we pass through this," Leo yelled, looking at the crowd besieging the buses. It was noisy: people were yelling, shouting, singing, and calling names, probably waiting for friends or family members. "Let's go pick up our belongings," Leo said and took hold of his wife's hand.

They pushed through the crowd around the buses to the other side where the drivers had thrown everyone's bags. Leo and Katarina picked up their bags from the pile and proceeded to follow others along the pathway that led to the cafeteria.

"I wish that we could have continued on, directly to Canada," she commented, wondering what was waiting for them here.

"Wouldn't that be nice?" Leo smiled, looking at his wife.

"Yes. That would have been splendid indeed, wouldn't it?" Katarina's eyebrows lifted. "Here, the camp is huge, and being buried in the middle of the small woods makes it a little scary."

"Don't worry, darling. I'll protect you," Leo promised, extending his strong arm in front of her eyes.

"Oh, my hero! Thank you, thank you," she giggled and marched ahead with her chin up and her eyes wandering.

When they reached the cafeteria, there was a long lineup for food as it was supper time. The refugees here were more aggressive: everyone pushed and shoved throughout the line. "This is going to be a long wait," Katarina noted, her body hunched under the weight of her bag.

"Give me your bag, darling. I'm going to put our things over there," Leo pointed to the pile behind the cafeteria door. "You wait in the line for the food. I'll go and get our supplies and the number of the room assigned to us."

"Fine," she said. He kissed her on the forehead and strode away.

Almost two hours later and hundreds of refugees after, Katarina finally reached the cafeteria counter. A tall skinny man with a bushy mustache asked, "Your name and ID please?"

"Mrs. Leo Lisic," Katarina replied and handed him their IDs.

"Are you one of the new arrivals?"

"Yes."

The man took two mess tins from under the counter and filled them with food. "Here, Mrs. Lisic," he said and handed two bottles of water and the mess tins to her.

"Thank you," Katarina said, took the food, and moved away from the counter. With two mess tins in her hands, she walked slowly down the cafeteria aisle, her eyes scanning the area for an empty picnic table, but they were all occupied. "Now what?" she muttered and walked up to their bag, leaned against the wall, waited, and watched for whichever come first, her husband or an empty table.

Leo soon returned with the blankets under his arms and other supplies. "What're you doing, here?" he asked, surprised she was still waiting.

"There is no place to sit down, all the tables are occupied."

"Oh yeah." Leo stretched his neck and looked over the tables to see people preparing to leave the table in the corner of the cafeteria. He flew over there and was able to secure it for them.

Katarina followed him. "I was getting tired of holding this," she said as she placed the food on the table.

"This is heavy too," her husband replied and dropped the blankets on the ground beside him. "I'm starving," he said, pulling his mess tin in front of him. "What is it?"

"What else. Macaroni," she replied.

That's what he was afraid of. Leo was tired of eating pasta every day. He wanted meat. "Macaroni? This looks like spaghetti to me," he teased to hide his disappointment.

"I know that! But down here they call it macaroni," she grinned, looking at him.

Her husband dug into his mess tin like he hadn't eaten for days; he had no other choice, his stomach demanded food. "Slow down, my love, don't eat that fast. You're going to get a stomachache," Katarina warned.

Leo glanced at her with a serious face and continued eating. She let him finish the food before she asked the burning question in her mind.

"What kind of room did we get this time?" she finally asked, just as he was about to finish his supper. He lifted his head and looked at her.

"I don't know. It is number 6, but I haven't seen it yet. Let's go and find out."

"Yes. Let's." They rose from their chairs; he picked up the army blankets from the ground, and they walked to their bags.

"I can see that nothing has changed. Army supplies again," she frowned with a disappointed voice. She had hoped that things would change for the better as time passed; instead, they were getting worse.

"Things can only get worse, but never better," Leo commented.

"I suppose," Katarina said. They picked up their bags and climbed two flights of stairs to the third floor of building that towered over the cafeteria and went along the corridor checking the numbers on each door. When they finally found door number 6, Katarina exclaimed, "Hurry, open the door!" anxious to get inside.

"Hold your horses," her husband replied, placed the key in the keyhole, and unlocked it. "Here you go, darling," he said and pushed the door open.

Her eyes widened. She walked in, slowly squeezing the bag against her chest. "Wow! It's a real room, made of brick, too. And it's ours, alone!" she shouted and whirled around the floor with the bag in her hands as happy as if she had won the lottery.

The room was small, with only two single naked beds pushed together, but she was delighted. Privacy was her first priority. Leo closed the door and leaned against it as he watched his wife dancing and was pleased to see a happy expression on her face.

"Where did you get the energy?" Leo asked, throwing his belongings in the corner and diving into bed. She followed him.

"I get it from you, my love."

Leo wrapped his arms around his wife and thought they would just rest a little, but they immediately fell asleep, still in their clothes; they were so exhausted from the journey. xxxxxxxx

The following morning, they both awoke to the church bells. xxxxxx

They changed their clothes and made their bed with the blankets they got from the camp.

Katarina was soon on the move. "I'm going to find out where the bathrooms, laundry room, and showers are, if there are any," and she rushed out.

"Don't take too long and meet me in the cafeteria for breakfast," Leo yelled after her.

"Fine," she acknowledged and skipped down the steps. The morning air was cool, and a chilly wind blew, brushing against her face. As she walked through the stretch of woods between the buildings and the barracks, the frost-covered earth crunched beneath her feet telling her that autumn has already taken hold. Katarina buttoned her sweater as the wind was piercing through her clothes and making her shiver. But nothing was going to stop her from finding out where the laundry room was located as her clothes needed to be washed.

The camp ground was crowded with refugees, and once again, she was shocked to see so many people. *It seems as if there's half of Europe here,* she mused as she briskly moved from building to building.

"There is the sign. Right in front of my nose," she said under her breath as she entered the building next to theirs. She checked to see if everything they needed was there: showers, toilets, and lines to spread clothes to dry. Last, she went to the sink to check for hot water when she noticed a huge map spread and pasted to the wall beside it. *What's this?* she wondered and took a peek. "Wow! Just as I thought," she sighed. "There are thousands of refugees here." She turned the sink tap on. "Oh no. There is no hot water here either." Disappointed, she rushed to meet her husband in the cafeteria.

There was a big crowd waiting to get in, so she tried to push through to search for Leo, but the refugees wouldn't let her. "You have to wait your turn!" they shouted and pushed her back.

From inside, Leo heard the crowd's noise and saw Katarina. He walked to the door and asked, "What's the commotion?" Then he extended his hand to her and said, "You're here, darling. Come." As they walked to the table, he asked, "Did you find everything we need?"

"Yes, I did," she said and sat beside him on the bench. "All the utilities are in the building next to ours, even the latrine, so that makes me happy. Everything is close by, but there's no hot water, even in the showers," she replied, somewhat preoccupied.

"What is it? Did something happen?" Leo asked, noticing her distant stare. "You're worried about something?"

"Oh no! No! Nothing happened. It's just that this camp is so huge, and there are kilometers of woods all around us. I think it would be easy for the Communists spies to make us disappear," she whispered into her husband's ear and began to eat her sweet roll.

"Now, we don't know that for a fact, and you shouldn't preoccupy yourself with that," Leo replied, not wanting his wife worried.

"Yes, I do know! My best friends in Trieste were taken," she exclaimed, with a mouth full of food, swallowing hard to push it down.

"But you didn't see them nor did anyone confirm it. You can't go around accusing, if you don't know. That's all I'm saying."

Katarina looked at Leo and said, "Let's change the subject. Did you know that there are thousands of refugees in here and they're separated into categories?"

"Oh, really? How do you know that?"

"In the laundry room, there is a map of the camp for everyone to read. It's written on it," she explained. "There are families with children, couples without children, single men, and single women. Each has its own area. The single men's barracks are the farthest of them all."

"That's good to know," Leo said, sipping on his coffee.

"Yes!"

"Oh, by the way, darling," Leo exclaimed. "A lady from the Red Cross came to the door after you left and invited us to come down to the office to look around. We might find some clothes to wear or something else we need."

"Sure, let's go," Katarina said. They both rose to their feet and strolled to the Red Cross office. From the cafeteria, they crossed over to the main building where all the government offices were.

"Look over there, darling," Katarina pointed to the infirmary cross.

"You might work there one of these days," Leo said and they walked into the building.

"One of these days, sure," she agreed, walking beside him. The office they were looking for was located on the first floor.

As they entered the office, Leo said, "Hi. My name is Mr. Lisic and this is my wife Katarina. A lady came to us and said to come here."

"Yes, come with me," one of the ladies said as they walked down the corridor. "You are one of the newcomers. Each time a transport with new refugees comes, we call on them to come here and look around. They might find something they need to wear or to use in the room to make it more homey."

"That's really nice," Katarina said as they watched her open this huge room full of goods.

"Here, you can look and check any boxes you want. If you need some help, call me. I'll be in my office across the hall," she said and left.

After about three hours of digging and checking almost every box there, Leo and Katarina had enough. They found a lot of good clothes for both of them and a beautiful soft pink blanket and a lovely checkered tablecloth. Katarina folded the things they found and placed them into plastic bags provided for them and walked next door to thank the lady.

"Did you find something?" she asked immediately.

"Yes, we did. Thank you," they chirped and were on their way back to their new room.

The next two days, Leo and Katarina spent making the room look homey. He went on a scavenger hunt, but so many refugees were doing it, there wasn't much left to find. He did, however, find a few cardboard boxes.

"What are you going to do with these boxes?" Katarina asked, glaring at them, thinking, perhaps, she could use them. Her brain was already cooking up her own plans for the boxes.

"We can use them as a table. They are strong and won't be buckling," Leo said and began to work on getting them ready.

"Are you going to use them both?"

"Yes," he chuckled. "I'll get another for your things."

She smiled and got busy with the bed. "Too bad, we didn't find any real bedsheets," Katarina commented as she finished making the bed.

XXX

"There, I'm finished too," Leo said and pulled out a cigarette than walked to the window. By then, it was 1500 hours.

As a final touch, Katarina spread the beautiful soft pink blanket over the bed and with the lovely checkered tablecloth covered the cardboard-table. Proud of her achievement, Katarina stepped back and exclaimed, "Now, that looks better!"

"Listen, darling!" Leo suddenly interrupted her reverie. They're calling your name."

"You must have heard wrong. Why would they call me?" Katarina paused and listened. Sure enough, her name was being paged through the loudspeaker to report to the infirmary as soon as possible. "I wonder what they want with me?" she voiced, a little alarmed.

"Isn't it obvious why they want you?" her husband said. "They have a job for you."

"That would be nice, but it's too early for that. We just got here. I hope they didn't find something bad on my medical tests that I had done in the Trieste camp," she said and ran to find out.

She introduced herself to the older woman leaning against the infirmary door and smoking. "I'm Katarina Sarrac-Lisic, I was called to come in."

Yes, I know. I'm Matron Rosetta," the woman said, dropped the cigarette on the floor and ground it out with her shoes, then extended her hand. "I've been waiting for you. Come with me."

They walked into her office and Matron Rosetta took a seat behind the desk. "I read your file that came from Trieste. You worked in the infirmary there, didn't you?"

"Yes, I did," she answered cautiously.

"Well, if you like to work, I have a job for you."

Stunned by the offer, Katarina paused. "Thank you. That's wonderful, I love to work. I accept!"

"Great! You can start tomorrow. Maria!" Matron Rosetta called, "Come and meet your new coworker." A young woman came toward her. "Maria has been with me over two years. She's waiting for Italian papers to stay here, and she's studying for her Italian nursing exams," Matron added.

"That's fantastic!" Katarina exclaimed and surveyed the nurse approaching, wondering if she was getting a job as a nurse or if she would just be cleaning as in the Trieste camp. She rose from the chair and extended her hand to the nurse. "Hello, Maria, it's nice to meet you. My name is Katarina, Katarina Sarrac-Lisic."

"I'm pleased to meet you too." Maria shook her hand and sat on the chair beside her.

"Now, Maria, you'll give your new coworker the rest of the details about the work since you two will be working together. And you, Katarina, I'll see you in the morning," Matron said as she turned her attention to the papers on her desk.

"All right, let's get started. Katarina, come with me," Maria suggested, and they walked out of the office.

Katarina took a deep breath as she made a few steps around the infirmary. "This infirmary is much bigger than the one at Trieste," she said.

"What did you do there?" Maria pried while preparing to give her the details about the work in the infirmary.

"Mostly washing floors and making beds, sometimes I did the translating, but that was seldom. You see, I don't have a permit to work in Italy so I really can't do much," Katarina frowned.

Maria glanced at her and said, "I don't have one either, and I'm working. Here we do just about everything. We give medications, injections, and take care of patients, including night or day visits to the barracks. But we have to be very careful. Especially when the call comes from single men's barracks, it can be dangerous."

"Why?" Katarina interrupted with a worried look in her eyes.

"Here are crowds of people all nationalities, all shades from pimps, drunks, drug abusers, and yeah, possibly criminals, you name it. Many refugees have been in here for years. No country wants to take those who are sick, alcoholics, or drug abusers. And we have to deal with all of them. If you ask me, Italian nurses don't want to have anything to do with those kinds," Maria whispered.

"That's wonderful!" Katarina smiled at her. "Nursing, it is exactly what I was hoping for. To be able to use my nursing skills, it means so much to me."

"I'm glad you are happy," Maria replied and went on to explain a few other things to her and showed her where to be located. "Well, that is it. Unless you have any questions."

"No. All my questions have been answered. Thank you. See you in the morning," Katarina smiled, walking toward the entrance.

"Yes. At six o'clock sharp!" Maria reminded and returned to her work.

Katarina glanced back, smiled, and strolled away happy as a clown. She couldn't believe they gave her the job only a few days after she arrived. *Oh, wow, my husband will be so proud of me,* she mused, just before she entered her room.

Leo was waiting at home for her, anxious to know what had happened. When the door opened, he rushed to her. "Is everything all right, darling?" he asked with a worried look on his face.

"No. It's better than all right. I got the job in the infirmary!" she chirped and ran into his embrace.

"That's great! I'm so proud of you!" he shrieked and squeezed her tightly against his body. They were both excited things were going well for them.

"Let's go out! We have supper, and after, we go for a walk along the path through the woods and get some fresh air."

"Sure. We'll take advantage of these few warm days still left of this year. But we're not going to wander too far into the woods. All right!"

Leo chuckled and took her hand as they strolled to the cafeteria to eat their supper. After that, Katarina and Leo went on exploration of the camp. They took a paved pathway down and between the barracks. They passed by all of them, even the men's, and now they were making their way into the deep woods.

"It's good to know where things are," she commented, looking around. "Especially to me as a nurse. It will come handy one day."

"Why?" her husband asked.

"I told you I got the job, but what I didn't tell, I'll be doing my nursing job in here. And as a nurse I would be duty-bound to go check things out if someone calls even in the middle of the night."

"I'm happy, but only for your nursing job," Leo said as they continued down the pathway. She glanced at him, but said nothing.

XXXX

Amazingly, the conversation and the walk reminded Katarina about the Communists, and she couldn't shake them of her mind. With each step deeper into the woods, the realization of danger flashed stronger through her mind. Suddenly, she stopped and said, "Let's not go any farther!" and rushed backward into the thick woods, thick with tall trees. At the same moment, there was a rustle of leaves and two birds flew up with swift flapping feathers from a tree behind them.

"Wait! You're scaring the birds," her husband yelled and rushed after her.

"Catch me if you can!" Katarina yelled and continued to run between the trees. Somewhere on the way, small sharp twigs caught her hair and scratched her legs as she pushed through the bushes and then stumbled over the great tree roots making her fall. "Oh no!" she shouted, looking at her sores.

"Great!" Leo muttered to himself and ran to her. "What happened now?" He ran and had stepped to a shallow pool of muddy water thick with the scum of rotting weeds and splashed over his pantaloons just as he came upon her. "Look, what you make me do." He pointed and sat down on the ground beside her. "Let me help you."

"Do what? I'm all right." Katarina giggled, stood up, and slowly began walking back to the pathway, feeling a little embarrassed, but she didn't let on why she ran. The trees were tick where they now walked and they were heavily shadowed; a chilly wind blew and made her shiver.

Leo wrapped his arm around her shoulder, concerned about her, he asked, "Are you sure you're all right?"

"Yes! I'm fine!" she answered with a smile while her feet rustled last year's leaves; her mind could not free itself from the fear of the communist spies. She wanted to discuss it with her husband but she just couldn't. Why did the fear come to her now? She didn't have the answer. Was it possible because of so many refugees in here? Or deep down, she didn't quite accept her husband's explanation for coming in here. For that reason, she might have been afraid of bringing up the Communists in their conversations, fearing his reaction.

In minutes, they were on the pathway and walking in the direction of their building. On their way, mostly they talked about general things. By then, the sun disappeared in splendid coloring.

After the flaming sunset across the town of Latina, the twilight came gently and darkness was complete by the time they arrived back home. In their room, there was no more talk of anything as she had to work in the morning.

XXXX

Lying that night in the bed, she heard the church clock strike one. Sleep seemed a long way off. No matter how hard she tried, she was too excited and couldn't fall asleep.

xxxxxxxxx

The following morning, the church bells rang with contempt, awakening Katarina unrefreshed and dazed.

XXX

She turned to the other side; it didn't even dawn on her she had to go to work, not aware that her husband was awake, and planned to snooze off. It completely slipped her mind that she had to go to work.

XXXX

Leo put his arm on her shoulder. "Aren't you going to work, darling?" he reminded her.

"Oh no!" she shouted, leapt out of bed, and dressed speedily.

Leo got out of bed and dressed himself. "Don't rush. There's a lot of time," he said and kissed his wife.

"You don't have to be up, it's still too early," she said as she walked toward the door. But before she left, she announced, "Leo, this will be our last camp and room before we leave for Canada. I'm convinced of that."

"I hope so, darling," he said, noticing his wife's imaginative mind working ahead of itself, and added. "But you know how it is. They choose the refugees for transfer at random. No one seems to know who'll be next, so don't get your hopes up too high. You never know what's going to happen."

Katarina ignored him because she believed in her gut instinct. As usual, she was convinced she was right. "See you later, my love."

She was about to walk out the door when her husband announced, “I’ll be going to look for work today too.”

“Fantastic!” she exclaimed and strode to work with a smile on her face, more convinced than ever things will be fine.

When she stepped outside, crisp morning and chilly air brushed against her cheeks as she walked, her eyes drifted to the sky. It was clear blue, no cloud in the sky.

“Good morning, Maria,” Katarina chirped, entering into the infirmary. She took her sweater off and hanged it up behind the door.

“Right on time! I like that,” Maria smiled, busy doing something already.

“Now, what?” Katarina asked, gravitating toward Maria, full of rejuvenated energy.

Maria reached into a closet behind her and pulled out a nursing uniform. “Here, put this on first. It might be a little too big for you, but if you like it, you can fix that.”

“Nursing uniform? That’s fantastic!” Katarina chuckled and her face beamed of exhilaration. “It has been a while since I had the uniform on.”

“Here, I have a job for you,” Maria turned Katarina’s attention to the work needed to be done. “You’ll sterilize these needles and these instruments here. After that, I have a lot more for you to do. By the way, breakfast and lunch will be brought in from the cafeteria for us, so you don’t have to worry about food. As for coffee, we get it here. Italian nurses were nice enough to let us have it, their own, free of charge.”

“Good,” Katarina replied and began her first day of work in the infirmary, so proud to wear the nursing uniform again.

Leo left a few minutes after she did and walked to the gate, hoping he’d get picked by the farmers to work. On the way there, he wondered if refugees went missing here like in Trieste. As he approached the gate, the huge crowd made him forget the thoughts about the spies, but only for a minute or two.

There were many men anxiously waiting on the walk-in path for the Italian farmers to come and offer them a job. They were the biggest suppliers of work for the refugees in this small dusty southern town. But Leo knew it also presented the biggest danger for the refugees of being picked up by the secret police and taken back to their native country. If that was what was happening in the camps. Leo didn’t know what to believe, so he decided to be vigilant as he joined the men, just to be on the safe side.

Not even ten minutes later, a farmer's truck approached and stopped in front of the crowd in which Leo stood, and a farmer with a big straw hat stepped out. "You, you, and you jump in," he said pointing his finger toward each of the man he wanted and returned behind the wheel. One of his fingers had pointed toward Leo.

"Yes, sir!" they all said and quickly leapt into the back of his truck.

"I'm Leo," he said, after they sat on the truck bed for a short while in silence, surveying each other.

"I'm Vladislav, and this is my good friend Karlo," one of them said.

After that, they only scrutinized each other's faces, but there was no more talk about anything. It was obvious they all knew how to play the game.

Leo realized they can't work together the whole day and not talk so he decided to initiate a small talk. "Cigarettes anyone?" he asked, extending the box with the cigarettes, first to Vladislav and then to Karlo, breaking the silence for the second time. All three smoked and talk, but only general things.

Each of them was careful in selecting their words. No one wanted to say something that would give himself up just in case there was a spy among them.

"I wonder what we are going to do first," Karlo mused, staring at the sea of corn, vineyards, and olive trees, just as the truck came to a stop.

"My guess is, we're going to find out soon," Leo replied, watching the farmer come out the truck.

"Let's go, boys, we'll harvest corn first," he ordered and threw three reaping hooks and three coveralls in front of them. "Put your cigarettes out so it won't cause fire," he warned and strode toward the field.

They picked them up and strode after him. "We need to work hard and fast," the Bulgaria-born Vladislav said in a low tone. "If we are going to be picked up tomorrow again."

The huge crowd of men waiting in front of the camp flashed in front of Leo's eyes. "You are right, we have so much competition. We better work hard," Leo agreed. Vladislav and Leo fastened their paces.

"When you are right, you are right," Karlo chuckled and rushed to keep up with them.

After a hard day of work at the infirmary, Katarina returned home and expected to find Leo there. But when she opened the door, the room was empty. Leo wasn't there. "I wonder where is my husband?" she muttered, taking her sweater off. So tired from her first day of work, she lay on the bed over the soft pink blanket and drifted off to sleep.

She awoke two hours later, her husband still wasn't home. An alarm went off in her head. A fear stirred inside her like a coil of ice unwinding and spreading throughout her body. "Where is he?" she said aloud, jumping off the bed. She glanced at her watch and noted it was supper time. "I go for supper and he'll be home by then. I'm sure," she whispered to herself and raced to the cafeteria with her two mess tins.

The men including Leo worked very hard that day and the farmer brought them back to the camp just after sunset.

Katarina returned in fifteen minutes. To her relief, Leo was home by then. "I'm so glad you are here!" she cried out as she entered the room. "I was worried sick about you. Where have you been?" she asked, placing the supper on the table before she ran into his arms.

Leo hugged his wife and exclaimed, "I worked all day!"

"You did?"

"Like I told you this morning. I went to the gate, and as soon as I got there, a farmer picked me and two other men, Vladislav and Karlo are their names, and took us to his farm."

"What did you men do there?"

"We harvested corn," Leo said and pulled the money he got paid from his pocket. "Here, darling. You buy what we need." He handed the money to Katarina and they had their supper.

"Wow! That's great. I get the money!" Katarina exclaimed, taking the money from him. "You get paid every day and I get paid every month."

"Darling, the work we do is private. The farmers have to pay us on the daily basis."

"I understand."

Since the harvesting season was in a full swing, Leo and his two buddies didn't have trouble finding work as the same farmer picked them up every morning at the gate.

Leo and Katarina were happy. The way their schedules were, they had a lot of time left to spend together. They had money coming in to purchase extra food, their own room, and he had made two friends.

But a week later, some of the nurses were transferred, leaving Matron Rosetta shorthanded. One afternoon, she came to Katarina, laid her hand on Katarina's shoulder, and said, "I need someone to work overtime. I wonder if you would consider taking a few shifts off my hands. Could you, please, just until I get someone else?"

Katarina found herself in a dilemma. She knew Leo didn't want her to work extra, and he'll be furious with her, but she didn't have the heart to say no to Matron. "Well, all right," she agreed and hoped that her husband would understand. "I'll do it, but only for a while."

"Thank you. I'll get someone else soon," Matron promised.

# CHAPTER 11

Summer was over. The autumn's chilly wind and rain raged through the camp almost daily, leaving behind mud and sickness. The flu season had just begun, and the infirmary was swamped with sick refugees. Many had colds and bronchitis; others, including babies and small children, suffered from dysentery and yellow fever.

Day in and day out, Katarina was forced to work hard long hours as Matron Rossetta still hadn't hired anyone to help as she had promised. Tired of the long hours, one afternoon, Katarina asked, "Maria, do you think we'll soon get some help?"

"Yes, but I don't know when," she replied anxiously. "But she'll have to do something soon. There are more refugees sick this year than even before. Much of the sickness is caused by dirty water, poor hygiene, and lack of nutrition, which we can't do anything about at the infirmary, but there are other problems that we do need to worry about."

"Like what?" Katarina asked, puzzled.

"Oh, like infections of muscles at injection sites from reusing needles," Maria said. Before she could continue, a young woman limped into the infirmary and Katarina soon found out for herself what Maria meant.

"Nurse, I'm here for my injection," the woman announced in a barely audible voice. There was sadness and pain on her agonized face.

"What's your name?" Katarina asked.

"Mrs. Vretic," replied the pale-faced woman.

After checking her name, antibiotics, and the dose, Katarina got the injection ready and turned to her. "Mrs. Vretic, would you please expose your buttock for the injection?" she requested in a calming tone of voice. When the woman lifted her skirt, Katarina was shocked. "What's this?

Your whole buttock is red, swollen, and infected. What happened?" she asked loudly.

"That's what I was talking about," Maria said calmly.

Mrs. Vretic said nothing until Katarina had finished with the needle. The woman pulled down her skirt and turned to Katarina. "This is from the penicillin injections I get for my pneumonia," she said shyly.

Katarina put her arm around Mrs. Vretic's shoulders and walked her to the door. "I'm so sorry you have to suffer this way," she said, consoling her. The woman shrugged her shoulders and tears poured silently down her cheeks as she walked out.

After the woman left, Katarina returned and faced Maria. "Is there anything we can do for her?"

"Not more than we are doing now, which isn't much. The camp has to do something more to make sure the refugees are healthy."

"And what are we doing now?" Katarina wanted to know.

"Well," Maria said. "We teach the patients to keep the area clean. Wash their hands and the sore area with a soap and warm water few times per day. Here, the needles are cooked twice, but nothing seems to help, there still have been new cases discovered."

Frustration washed over Katarina's face as she realized there was nothing she could do to help the poor woman or anyone else whose infection resulted from reuse of needles. "I wish they could give us more medical supplies including needles!" she suddenly thundered.

"Me too!" Maria agreed. "But for now, we don't have a choice. Needles have to be reused again and again."

Lately, Katarina devoted more hours to her daily work schedule. Between Leo's work and Katarina's constant filling in for someone's shift at work, there was no time or energy left for her marriage.

At first, Leo pretended that everything was fine, but she knew better. Their marriage suffered. Yet she couldn't bring herself to leave the poor sick children. Besides, she loved and enjoyed her nursing job too much to think of quitting. As Katarina became busier with work, Leo found himself more resentful because he wanted to spend that time with his wife. Tensions began to build between them.

One morning, anger flushed Leo's face. "Why do you have to work so much?" he shouted. "You said it would only be for a little while. What happened to that?"

Katarina looked at him. "I don't know. Matron Rosetta didn't find anyone yet. Why you are shouting? You should be thankful I'm working.

You know we need as much money as we can get and your job will stop soon. The food they give us isn't enough nor is it nutritious. We need the money to buy extra food. Can you see that we're both losing weight, especially you?"

"I know! But damn it, you're working all the time," Leo replied angrily. The small arguments between them continued almost daily.

Still, Leo joined his buddies for harvesting work. But it was beginning to slow down; most of the crops were already harvested. The only work left was olive harvesting, which Leo hated. He had to stay in the olive grove for hours while the chilly wind bit his body and ruffled his hair. His naked fingers froze as he gathered olives, one by one, that were dropped into a bag that hung around his neck. When the bag filled up, he would empty it into a barrel that stood on the wagon between the olive trees. Then he climbed back up the tree, repeating the procedure until the trees were free of olives.

About a week later, Matron Rosetta finally hired two new nurses to work in the infirmary. She knew this news would make her husband happy. Katarina was so excited, she practically ran home after her shift to tell him she wouldn't have to work overtime anymore. Then she remembered that he would still be out in the fields, working. "I tell him tonight when he gets home," she chirped as she entered their room.

To her surprise, Leo was home and staring out the window. "What are you doing home already? Is there something wrong?" she asked, puzzled.

He was silent.

Katarina approached him and noticed fear in his eyes and that his face was drained of blood. "What's wrong, my love?" she asked in a panic tone of voice as she placed their supper on the table.

After a short silence, he shrieked at her. "Nothing! There's nothing wrong! Except everything!" His eyes looked like steel. "We barely say two words to each other anymore!" Leo spoke through his clenched teeth.

Katarina backed away from him. "I really don't know how to answer words like these," she retorted.

Leo continued to charge. "It seems to me you're always doing things for everyone else but us!" Torment was showing in his eyes.

Katarina stood in front of him, not knowing how to respond. Things were bad between them, but she was unable to comprehend this kind of outburst. Not understanding the expression on his face, she had no words to convey her feelings. She trembled. There was an awkward pause.

Afraid that she might say something she would regret later, Katarina bit down on her lower lip and shook her head in frustration. She cast an angry glance at her husband, grabbed her sweater, and stormed out, slamming the door behind. She forgot all about the news she wanted to tell him. "Just as well, he wouldn't want to hear it anyway," she muttered, rushing down the steps.

Leo ran to the door. "I'm sorry," he whispered, but it was too late, she was out of the building.

As she walked briskly through the woods over the camp ground, the chilly wind pierced her shivering body. "I must be a weak-minded fool. Who does he think he is, treating me like that?" she grumbled, bundling herself in the sweater, and bitterly stormed ahead until the strong wind forced her to turn back.

Katarina returned to the room and found her husband staring out the window again. He glanced at her with a sigh of relief. It was obvious he had been worried about her. Without looking at him, she made her way to the bed, threw the sweater at the foot of it, and heavily sat on the bed.

It was their first big fight; she didn't know what to do or say, so she said nothing. There was a long silent pause between them. Then Leo came over and sat beside her. "Don't ever do that to me again," he spoke in a slow tone of voice.

"Do what?" she shrugged her shoulders, casting a quick glance at him.

"Walk out without a word, the way you did." He placed his arm around her shoulders. "I'm sorry. I didn't mean to yell at you. Please forgive me, darling."

She ignored him and looked away. He pulled a cigarette out of a box, then abruptly rose from the bed and walked toward the window. As he tried to light the cigarette, he burned his fingers. "Oh damn!" he yelled, shaking his hand.

Katarina lifted her head and noticed the burning match flying across the room. Her eyes darted toward him. Seeing how distraught and shaky he was, she realized that something terrible must have happened and walked to him. "What's wrong? Tell me please. No matter what it is."

Leo took a deep breath and stepped back as if he wanted to collect his thoughts first. After a minute of careful thought, he said, "Something happened today. I thought I could keep it away from you because I didn't want to upset you. But the way I went about, it made you more upset and angry. I should have told you the truth immediately. You know Vladislav and Karlo, they were with me harvesting olives today."

"Yeah, I know them. They work with you every day, don't they?"

"Yes, they did, but after today, I won't see them." he continued, puffing on his cigarette like a chimney. "They were both taken away in a black limousine right in front of my eyes. Two men in black suits came after me too, but I was deeper in the orchard and was able to escape with everyone else there," he explained.

His wife stared at him speechless for a second or two. "What! Oh no! Do you know who took them?" Katarina asked, worry creeping into her eyes as she remembered those who disappeared in Trieste camp and were never found.

"Who else could it be but UDBA? The Yugoslav secret police have access, through Interpol, to anyone in the world. They can go to almost any country, take or kill whomever they want, and get out without any questions being asked," he explained, his body shivering.

"So it is true! UDBA could pick up any of us any time it wants."

"Yes, I'm afraid so," Leo confirmed. His face turned pale and tears were in his eyes as he spoke. "I'll probably be next if I step outside this camp."

His tears and pained tone of his throaty voice filled her with pity. "No. We can't let that happen!" Katarina hugged her husband and forgave him as she had never seen him so horrified and upset before.

"What can we do?"

"Well, as for me, you'll not be going to work outside the camp anymore," Katarina suggested.

"You're probably right," Leo agreed it wasn't safe.

She rested her head on his shoulder and asked, "Why didn't you tell me that before, my love?"

"I'm sorry, darling. I wanted to spare you the agony, but it looks like I made things worse," he apologized. Katarina pulled away from him with alarm, trying to figure out for what reason UDBA would be after him.

"Are they after you because you were in the Communist Party? Do they think you know too much?" she bombarded him with questions.

"I don't know," he said with dread in his eyes. "It's possible, but I know nothing more than anyone else who has the Red Book. The Red Book is nothing more than a membership's card in the Communist Party. It doesn't give you automatic entrance into things."

"Except that you were a police officer," Katarina reminded him and began pacing the floor, anxiety spreading throughout her body. "It's possible they might think that you know more."

"Like I said, I have no clue why UDBA would be after me."

"That's just great! I told you to be careful!" she roared.

"Oh, now you think it's my fault, is that it?" he shouted and turned toward the window. Katarina came over to him and grabbed his hand.

"No! No. That's not what I meant. In no way is it your fault, I'm just scared and upset."

"Of course, you didn't. I'm sorry, I shouldn't have reacted the way I did. I'm worried too," Leo said, hand in hand they moved to their bed and Katarina continued with the conversation.

10XXXXXXXXXXXXXXXXXXXXXXXXXXXXXXXXX

"Nobody knows who the UDBA officers are looking for and who they are." She shivered. It gave her chills knowing that refugees had disappeared from the camp. "Now that they managed to force us out the country, why don't they leave us alone?" she snapped and turned her back to Leo. "When I came here, I thought I was free of them, but it looks like they are still in charge of my life. Why are they doing that to us?"

Leo wrapped her arms around her waist and replied, "The Communists don't want their dirty things being told outside the country. In that matter, it isn't only people from Yugoslavia taken. There are refugees from other Eastern European Communists countries who disappeared the same way, I was told. And Vladislav is Bulgarian."

"Then that means it wasn't UDBA but the Bulgarian secret police," Katarina quickly figured, happy that her husband finally was talking to her about the Communists.

"Maybe, but we don't know that, Karlo was Croatian. The only thing I know, one of the men must have been a collateral victim."

His wife continued on. "But the worst part is, we don't know the UDBA's spies amid us. Who they are and where they are. That makes it even scarier to make any friends among the refugees or to go anywhere outside the camp," Katarina voiced, but she didn't get an answer. Her husband fell asleep.

XXX

She closed her eyes, but her mind was occupied by thoughts that kept her awake long after Leo fell asleep. Now that he opened up and talked to her about the Communists. There was no doubt in her mind, she could crush her suspicion now and let her mind freely circle around her husband who excited and amazed her.

XXXXXXXXXXXXXXXXXXXXXXXXXXXXXXXXXX

The next morning, they awoke. Katarina leapt out of bed and realized they didn't have their supper.

XXXXXXXXXXXXXXXXXXXXXXXXXXXXXXXXXXXX

After that day, Leo and Katarina kept close to the camp. Leo held odd jobs in the camp while Katarina continued nursing in the camp infirmary. She only worked her regular hours now, occasionally taking an extra shift or two in an emergency. They were settling back into their marriage, and things were beginning to go well for them.

XXXXXxxxxxxxxxxxxxxxxx

As autumn advanced into winter, the weather worsened. Rains and strong winds from the sea increased in ferocity. Every day was dreary. Rain lashed against their window, driven by the fierce wind, blurring the view. The sameness of the days was also making the weeks blur. Sometimes Katarina wondered if this was all her new life would ever be, a dreary existence in a dreary camp.

Carrying supper in his hands, Leo opened the door quietly, thinking Katarina was still sleeping since she was working the night shift. "You're awake!" he said, surprised, finding her sitting in the bed. He placed the food on their cupboard box table and called, "Come. We can eat. I'm starving."

All right," Katarina agreed, took the cover off, and leapt off the bed. "Spaghetti! Again! Is that the only thing the Italian people eat? Oh god, I sound like a broken record."

"This is not spaghetti, darling, it's macaroni," Leo teased. He tried to brighten her face a little.

"Spaghetti, macaroni, what's the difference? It looks the same to me!"

"Isn't that what I said the first day when we arrived here from Trieste?" Leo smiled.

"I know what you're trying to do, but I'm tired of dry pasta. I would gladly call it both spaghetti and macaroni, if there was just a small piece of meat hidden somewhere between all this sticky white dry mass or even sauce. A small spoonful of olive oil is not enough," Katarina frowned.

"Of course not," Leo replied. "That's why I've lost ten kilos already."

"Then why are you complaining if I sometimes work overtime?" she asked. "Here take these few liras and buy some extra food tomorrow." Katrina handed the money to her husband and gave him a kiss. "See you in the morning, my love," and hurried to work through the dark and rainy night.

# CHAPTER 12

Katarina bustled through the infirmary door, running from the sudden downpour of rain. "Wow!" she exclaimed as she entered almost out of breath. "Hello, Maria. Have you been here long? How are things?" she asked, taking off her raincoat.

"I just got here. It seems to be quiet," Maria replied, sorting out the instruments for sterilization in front of the window.

"Good. You must have just missed the big splash. It's coming down in sheets," Katarina said as she walked to the coffeepot.

"Yes, I can see that," Maria replied, continuing her work. Katarina poured herself a cup of coffee and began to prepare medication for the midnight patients. Also, there was work to be done that was left from the evening shift.

XXXXXXXXXXXXXXXXXXXXXXXXXXXX

They have to deal with that every night.

Every night, there was extra work for them to be done. The day shift would leave the things they couldn't finish.

Xxxxxxx

"How much extra work do we have tonight?" Katarina asked.

The day shift always left extra work for the night shift.

The night shift had to do the work that the day shift had no time to finish. xxxxxxx

Things were quiet until one o'clock. Maria poured herself a cup of coffee. "I'm going to take a small break," she informed her coworker and walked into the small back room when a young panic-stricken man came running into the infirmary.

"A man in barracks number 5 is groaning like a bear! He's very sick. He needs a nurse!" the young man shouted repeatedly, then ran out.

"Wait! Wait!" Katarina called and rushed after him to ask him his name, but before she could, he disappeared into the dark muddy night. She returned to the infirmary, put on her raincoat, grabbed the emergency bag and a flashlight.

Maria came out of the small room to see what the disturbance was about. Standing at the door, curious, Maria asked, "Who was that?"

"I don't know," Katarina shrugged her shoulders, "But someone there seems to be in trouble. I'm going to check things out." She rushed out the door with the medical bag in one hand and the flashlight in the other.

Maria came running after and just outside the door caught up with her. "Wait! Let me go. I know my way around the camp better than you. I have been here longer."

"No, Maria." Katarina was determined to show that she was just as good a nurse as anyone else. "It's all right, but thanks. It wouldn't be fair to you if you went again tonight after having gone out several times last night. Besides, tonight, Matron put me in charge of outside calls. It's my responsibility on this shift. I need to know if someone is sick there."

"Don't go. It could be a trick," Maria warned.

"There is no trick. The young man was sincere."

"But you don't even know the name of the sick man," Maria desperately tried to stop her from going as she felt that something wasn't quite right.

But stubborn Katarina wouldn't listen. "I guess the barrack's number will have to do," she replied, and strode into the dark, cold, and rainy night.

"Stubborn you!" exasperated Maria shouted and slammed the door as Katarina disappeared into the night.

The incessant rain slowed down to a drizzle, but the ground was soaked turning it into mud. The camp was poorly lighted and visibility was almost zero. The flashlight hardly lit her pathway. Her feet kept sinking ankle-deep into the mud. It was impossible for her to move any faster than a porcupine. "Oh god, this is awful. I should have listened to Maria. Maybe she was right," Katarina admitted to herself. Yet she continued her trek. She had to show she was capable of doing her job, no matter what. However, she had no idea how dangerous it could be to wander around the camp, especially at night.

After all the trouble she had on the way: she was spooked by the birds, slipped a few times, and ran into a wet tree a few times, Katarina finally arrived. Breathing hard, she stopped in front of men's barrack number 5 and knocked on the door, but no one came out. She put her ear to the door. "I don't hear anything," she whispered to herself and tried the door. It was unlocked. She placed her flashlight into the medical bag and opened. "Is anyone here?" she called out.

There was no answer and no light inside. Cold shivers went up and down her spine, *Maybe it's a trick,* she thought, remembering what Maria told her just before Katarina rushed out of the infirmary.

Then suddenly she heard a groan. "This must be the right place," she told herself and rushed into the barrack unwarily. The room was dark. She palpated the switch light on the right side of the door and flipped it on. Although it was dim, she was able to make out the figure of a man curled up on the bed, bundled in a blanket. His face was turned away. "Are you all right, mister?" she called out to him.

He continued to groan, but didn't respond. Katarina reached down and touched his shoulder. The man turned with unexpected quickness and grabbed her by her long hair. Holding her tightly by the hair, he jumped to his feet and stuck a knife under her throat and warned, "Don't you dare scream!"

Katarina was shocked. Blood froze in her veins, and her heart's pounding amplified. Oh god! What had she walked into? She wondered and at the same time wanted to strike him with her medical bag, but his stranglehold was too tight for her to swing around. Finally, she shouted, "I came to help. I was told you were sick! I can see you're not. So what do you want from me?"

"Stop screaming!" he growled. "If you don't—"

"If I don't, you going to do what?" Katarina interrupted his sentence.

"I'll have to kill you!" he yelled.

"You've got that right because I won't let myself be taken alive," she said, knowing she was in grave danger.

"Wow, missy! You speak like you're the one holding the knife," he laughed. In the next instant, he pulled and tightened his hold on her, then slashed her uniform under her throat. That sent shivers up and down her spine, but she didn't give up.

"What are you doing to me?" she asked, persisted. "Why did you lure me here?"

"You think you're very clever, don't you?" he shouted acidly. "If you really want to know, I'll show you. For this!" he chuckled hysterically as he grabbed the medical bag from her hand and pushed her aside, commanding, "You stay there and be quiet!"

Katarina shivered in the corner, staring at his ruthless face while he ransacked the medical bag like a caged animal. Her fear became greater when she realized the man must be a drug addict. *God! Help*! she pleaded and prayed in her mind to calm herself down so she could find the way out of this mess she got herself in. Her heart continued to drum and her mouth went dry, but there was no time to think or argue or ask questions.

"Oh god, what am I going to do?" Katarina whispered against her fist and an idea dashed through her brain. She began to work out a plan of escape in her head. Her body trembled, but she stayed calm. "Please let me go. I mean you no harm. You can have all the painkillers inside the bag," she begged and pleaded, hoping he might let her go. But that wasn't what he had in mind.

"Keep your mouth shut or else you're dead!" the man shouted, pointing the knife at her.

Her fear grew even greater then because she realized he had no intention of letting her go. The male barracks were too far apart for anyone to hear if she shouted, so she would have to come up with a plan to distract him so she could make a run for it.

Then, all of a sudden, he put the knife down on his bed to fill a syringe with some kind of medicine. She couldn't see what it was, but she knew this was her chance. If she didn't take it now, God help her when the drug he takes began to work. Staring at the knife, cold sweat broke through her body and her heart drummed so fast as Katarina slowly moved toward the door, keeping a careful eye on the man. She was able to get as far as the door unnoticed. And then, just as she was about to dash out, he grabbed her by the hair.

"Where do you think you're going, missy? What's your rush? We're going to have some fun first?" the man chuckled. He pulled her back, crushed her body against his, and forced a kiss upon her lips, his eyes already shining from the drugs.

Katarina's blood boiled inside her, and she could feel the heat rising in her cheeks. "Oh no. You won't be having any fun with me!" she shouted, struggling. She had been raped once and had no intention of allowing it to happen again. "Let me go! You bastard!" She pushed and kicked him in the groin as hard as she could.

"Oh nooo!" the man growled and let go of her hair to grab himself, bellowing in pain. "Bitch! You'll pay for this!" Frantic, Katarina dashed out the door and disappeared into the dark night. It was still drizzling, but she managed to hide behind the bushes.

He came running out, swearing and holding his groin with his hand. "I'll get you for this," he yelled again. He looked around for her for a while but finally gave up and went back inside.

She wanted to recover her medical bag. She didn't want to go back without it. As she was pondering ways to retrieve the bag, the man came out again. She quickly ducked behind a bush and peeked through it quietly. The man was standing on the threshold, looking around and listening, still holding his groin. He stood there for a few minutes, then walked a short distance from his barrack and tossed something away.

She hoped that was the medical bag. When he returned to his barrack, Katarina slowly crawled on her hands and knees searching the ground around the spot and found the bag. She opened it and checked for the flashlight. "Thank God, it's still here," she muttered and pulled it out, grabbed the bag, and hurried in the direction of the infirmary, worried that the man could be looking for her.

Rushing through the woods, scared half to death, she stumbled and fell into a puddle of mud. "Ouch! Damn!" she grumbled. Quickly, she got to her feet and tried to run, but the ground was sinking beneath her feet and slowed down her pace. With mud dripping from her clothes, she struggled through the muddy woods. Her heart thud like a drum.

When she finally arrived in front of the infirmary, she could barely breathe and was wet and cold, her body shivered, but instead of rushing inside, she paused. "How am I going to explain the missing medicine and these torn, muddy, and wet clothes without telling Maria the truth?" she asked herself. There was no way she could hide them. "I can't tell her what happened. Maria would say I told you so. I'd be the laughing jingle of the infirmary. Besides, Matron would punish me for not listening to Maria. Oh no. What am I going to do?" she whispered, trembling. She had to find some kind of explanation to give to Maria for her appearance. Katarina was ashamed and didn't want anyone to know what kind of fool she was not to listen to Maria. Even though it was only an attack, to her, it was as if she had been raped again.

As soon as Katarina entered the infirmary, Maria's wide eyes darted toward her clothes. "Look at you!" she exclaimed. "You are dripping wet! What happened?"

"Hah! I thought you wouldn't notice!" Katarina cried out cynically and added. "Well, Maria, it's a long and muddy walk to the men's barracks and the rain keeps coming down."

"I realized, that's why I'm asking," Maria replied. "I'm glad you're not hurt in any way. But you do look awful messy."

"If you really want to know the truth, I stumbled and fell into a muddy puddle, all right," Katarina said shyly. "The medical bag flew into a thick bush. I probably lost some of the medicine. By the way, Maria, is there a way you can replace any of the drugs that were lost and keep it between us, please?"

"I am glad you didn't lose the bag. Matron Rosetta certainly wouldn't like that," Maria smirked.

"I know and I don't want her to know. I'm afraid she might fire me. So will you replace the missing medications?"

"Well, the medical bag is here so that's not a problem. But how did you tear your uniform?" Maria wasn't going to let her off the hook easily.

"What do you think?" Katarina flashed a mischievous smile. "I made passionate love in the mud with a tall, dark, and handsome man." She turned away so Maria couldn't see the fear and the lie in her eyes.

"All right, all right. No more questions," Maria replied. "But you could have been hurt badly on a terrible night like this. You should have let me go," she emphasized. "Go on and change your clothes before you catch a cold."

"I guess I should be thankful Matron cares more for the bag than the drugs," Katarina replied and went to change without further comments.

Maria chuckled and returned to her work.

While Katarina was changing into a dry uniform, she muttered to herself, "Yes, Maria, you're right. I could have been killed." Upon returning from the small room, Katarina rushed to do her work, which had backed up while she was gone.

A couple of hours later, Maria made a fresh pot of coffee and brought her a cup. "Let's take a small break," she suggested.

Katarina took the cup and said, "Thanks."

They both sat down at the table and sipped on their coffee. "So how was the patient?" Maria asked.

"Patient? What patient?"

Maria came face-to-face with her and glared into her eyes. "The man who was dying? Remember?"

"Oh, that patient, right," Katarina said. "I couldn't find him. It was too dark and muddy. I searched for a long time, then I turned back." Her body shivered as the scene played out in front of her eyes.

"After you tumbled," Maria quizzed, staring into her face suspiciously.

"Yes! After I tumbled," Katarina replied anxiously and then both returned to their jobs, chuckling.

The morning came too quickly for Katarina. She paused at the door and looked out.

XXXXXX

Going home to her husband wasn't going to be easy. The attack had opened up an old wound that she thought had healed. The terrible memories of the rape in Trieste camp poured forth as if it had happened yesterday.

Katarina tiptoed into the room, Leo was still sound asleep. Worried that she wouldn't be able to stand her husband's touch, she slipped carefully under the blanket beside him, hoping she wouldn't wake him. Just as she settled on the edge of the bed with her back against his, he rolled over and wrapped his arms around her. She stiffened with fear and pretended to be asleep as she choked back her tears. Thank heavens, he fell back asleep. One thing she didn't need at this time was a barrage of questions from her husband. Exhausted, she soon drifted off to sleep.

It was six in the afternoon when Katarina awoke. The first thing she saw when she opened her eyes was her husband's face staring down at her. "Did you have a good sleep, darling?" he asked and planted a kiss on her lips.

"Yes, I did," Katarina replied and tried to get out of the bed, but before she could, Leo rolled onto the bed, wrapped his arms around her body, and pulled her down with him.

"Where do you think you're going?" he asked playfully and snuggled close to her. His words sent a shiver down Katarina's spine as they reminded her of the rapist, and his face flashed in front of her eyes.

She pulled back and looked confused and frightened.

"Is there something wrong, darling?" he asked, alarmed.

"No, nothing is wrong. I'm just tired and still half-asleep. The night was very busy," she answered with a forced smile and buried her face in the blanket. She wouldn't dare tell him what had happened to her last night for fear of losing him forever.

Leo threw the covers off her and covered her body with his. "Are you sure you are still sleepy?" he asked, staring down at her face with deep affection. She knew then, she had to do something, as she didn't want him to crowd her at this moment.

She glanced at her watch. "Oh no, look at the time, I have to go," she replied, pushed him off her, and leapt out of bed.

"Do you really have to, darling?" Leo asked, stretching in bed, like a big old cat.

"Yes. I have to be at work early today for a meeting." She flashed a dazzling smile, and her dark-brown eyes assumed a tender expression, trying to show everything was fine. Katarina wasn't about to stay home and face her husband's barrage of questions, questions that she wasn't ready to answer. "I'm sorry, my love, but I really have to go," she explained as she hurriedly dressed.

"That's a lame excuse," Leo said, looking at her with a quizzical twinkle in his eyes.

"No, really, I do have a meeting," Katarina reaffirmed, looking directly into his eyes. She would have fooled anyone who didn't know her, but Leo wasn't fooled.

As she walked out the door, suspicion began to invade Leo's mind. He knew that she was clearly hiding something from him. "Why is she pushing me away? Why is she afraid of being touched? Is there someone else?" he half-whispered and felt perspiration breaking out on his forehead. "She isn't having an affair, is she?"

His heart pounded just at the thought of it and his mind filled with more questions. Frustrated, he rose to his feet and reached to his jacket pocket for a cigarette. "No, she wouldn't do that. Then what? There is definitely something bothering her," he grumbled, striking a match.

At the infirmary, the nurses were wrapping up the day shift and were getting ready to leave when she arrived.

"It's nice to see the night shift coming early so the day shift could leave home on time. Good work, Katarina," Matron Rosetta chirped on the way out the door.

"Thanks," Katarina replied in the low tone and rushed into the small room to change into her uniform. While changing, she wondered what kind of person would lie to her husband like this. There was no meeting; she made it up to get away from him, but then her inner voices reminded her. If she stayed, only one wrong word from her could have opened up millions of questions to which would never have been the end.

"Hello, Katarina." A voice from the door brought her back to reality. She turned toward it. "Maria, you're here," she replied.

"Yeah, where else would I be?" Maria said and went to put on her uniform. They both walked out of the room to take over the shift from the day nurses.

Later, as always, Maria made the coffee. "Would you like a cup, Katarina?"

"Yes, please," she replied as she picked up the patients' medical cards and placed them on their table. Maria poured a cup to both of them to drink while they were assorting their patients' medical cards. Through all the night, Katarina was quiet and barely spoke few words.

In the morning, just before their shift was over, Maria asked, "Katarina, you hadn't been yourself all night. Are you sick?"

"Well, I do feel very tired. I could be coming down with something. After all, I did get myself wet the night before when I went out," Katarina explained and rushed to change.

As days went by, the fury toward the animal who had mercilessly violated her body and soul consumed her. She was so preoccupied with herself that she paid no attention to her husband's demands. Each time Leo tried to make love to her, she would find some excuse to get herself out. He pleaded with her, day after day, "Darling, tell me what's wrong?"

"Nothing," she would reply and shrug it off.

One evening, after she rejected his advances, he became frustrated and lost patience with her. "Are you seeing another man?" he snapped angrily.

"Of course not! How dare you even suggest that?" Katarina snarled right back with indignation and stormed to work without explanation.

After that outburst, Leo distanced himself and was dispirited. He no longer tried to engage in intimacy with his wife, although he was civil to her. Her husband knew nothing about her problem except that there was something very wrong between them. The suspicion of Katarina's loyalty resurfaced in Leo's mind, driving them into daily arguments.

Suddenly, everything was coming back at her like a boomerang, and she had no clue what to do. So they both kept their distance for their own reasons.

Soon the narrow gulf between them widened and his suspicions of her faithfulness grew and their marriage began to suffer. The secrets and lies about the rape and the attack bottled up inside her kept eating away at Katarina.

Every time she checked on refugees in the barracks, day or night, she kept looking back. Her body trembled and was scared to death that the man who attacked her would come behind and kill her as he promised. Her insecurities increased and left her questioning her work performance and wondering how she could keep her job if she was afraid to leave the infirmary. All this just because she couldn't bring herself to tell him the truth. She was tired of everything and wanted to forget, but how? *Maybe I should tell him the truth?* she mused.

At the infirmary, refugees streamed in and out all morning, sick with influenza. By middle of the day, Katarina dragged herself like an old lady, frustrated and very tired.

Maria looked at her and wrapped her arm around Katarina's shoulders. "Let's have our lunch," Maria suggested and walked her to the coffeepot.

"I'm not really hungry, but I could use a little rest."

"I can see that. You look tired," Maria observed as she poured two cups of coffee.

"I didn't have enough sleep last night," Katarina quickly answered.

They took their portions and their coffees and walked into the small room to eat. Maria gobbled down her food. Katarina took a few sips of coffee and stared at her food.

"Eat, Katarina. It isn't going to bite you. The soup is good for you," Maria advised and added. "I noticed, ever since the night you were out, something has been bothering you. Is there something you forgot to tell me?"

"No. I haven't!"

"Then what it is? Why you are so scared? From whom you are running? Please talk to me. Talk to someone else. If you don't, it could destroy you," Maria was eminent.

Katarina looked at Maria, and her husband's question, 'Are you seeing another man?' flashed back at her. Leo no longer trusted her. He didn't want anything to do with her because he thinks she was having an affair. She was facing the moment of no return and she felt intolerably alone. *Maria is right,* Katarina thought. *I have to say something to someone, otherwise, my mind is going to explode from an overload.*

After a long pause, she finally decided to give Maria an answer. Almost in a whispering tone of voice, she replied, "Leo and I are drifting apart and I don't know what to do."

"Oh no. Is it that serious?"

"I don't know, I hope not because I do love my husband. My guess is we're both waiting who will make the next step."

Maria hesitated for second then asked, "I hope it isn't toward the separation because if it is, you are looking to remaining in the camp for years. If I were you, I would find the way to patch things up with your husband and quickly."

A touch of panic crossed Katarina's face. "No! I didn't know that! Are you serious?"

"Deadly serious!"

Maria gave Katarina a lot to think about. The lunch was over, and they both went back to work, but Katarina's mind was more on Leo's and her relationship than on sick refugees at the moment.

Finally, the day shift was over. On the way out, Katarina noticed few empty boxes lying beside the infirmary door and stopped. "These would be great in the room for my little things," she muttered and called. "Maria, may I have these boxes?"

"Go head, take it!"

She grabbed them, put one in each hand, and walked home, carrying the boxes into the room.

That afternoon, Katarina finally realized what she had to do to get Leo back. She reluctantly conceded that she would have to push her stupid pride aside and force herself to be a real wife to her husband because if she didn't, she'd lose him. She couldn't let that happen and certainly did not want to stay in the camp for years.

She opened the door, their room was empty. Katarina threw the boxes on her side of the bed, strolled around in the room, and noted the mess tins were missing. "He's probably gone to pick up the supper," she muffled and looked through the window, her plan for the evening kept turning in her head, continuously.

When Leo walked into the room carrying their supper, she rushed to give him a hand and said, "Oh, there you are, my love." She took the food and placed it on the cardboard-box table.

Leo threw her a suspicious look, but said nothing. They both took their food, sat on the floor, and began to eat in silence.

XXXX

Too much time had passed since they were last intimate. She had to find a way to turn things around and get their troubled marriage on the right track before it was too late.

After a long pause, Leo finally asked politely, "Did you have a good day?"

"Not really. There are so many people sick with influenza and pneumonia," she replied, casting glances from under her eyebrows in his direction. Occasionally, she smiled at him, studying his face, trying to read his mood.

Leo noticed her coy glances. "Don't even try it," he warned. "It won't work until you tell me what you are hiding from me or what's bothering you."

"Try what?" she asked.

"This little seduction you're planning." His voice was as distant as ever.

"Who? Me? I'm not planning anything," she smirked and stood up to clear the dishes away. But she also knew she had to do something more if she was going to save her marriage. So she rushed back before her husband had a chance to move and knelt down in front of him and kissed him without so much as a warning. "I love you!" she chirped and nibbled at his ear.

Her husband said nothing. She stood up then and began to unbutton her shirt. Leo remained seated and watched her from under his eyebrows suspiciously as she reached the last button at her neck and slowly slid her shirt off her shoulders and let it fall to the floor, smiling at him.

Leo leaned against the bed taking a leisurely pose, bound and determined to let her humiliate herself the same way he was when she pushed him away. He refused to make any effort toward her. For a while, he glared at her as if she was missing a few buttons out of her head. It was maddening to stand there, poised on the brink, waiting for him to react. But she withstood and continued her stripping, down to the underwear, but stopped there and sat on his lap, kissing him softly.

Finally, her husband couldn't resist. He groaned with the force of his passion and reached up abruptly to strip away her chemise, pulling it down and bringing the stockings with it so that she was naked. He stepped back and caressed her with his eyes as though memorizing every inch of her. Lifting his eyes to hers, he studied her face. His gaze flickered to her lips before returning to her eyes with an intimacy that was shattering.

"Oh, my darling. You made me wait too long," he whispered against the sweetness of her brown hair. "And now I want you so badly, I'm afraid I'll hurt you."

Katarina's heart leapt wildly about inside her as she listened to him, pouring out his love for her. "You won't hurt me," she said softly. "I love you, Leo."

He brought his mouth down to hers, moulding it with an exquisite mastery that took her breath away. "Ah!" she muttered, following the movements of his hand.

"Darling, I missed you so much!" he exclaimed, picked her up, and laid her gently on the bed, standing away so that he could strip himself of his clothing. Immediately, he lay beside her, gathering her close against him as he rained tender kisses on her face and neck. His hand moved to caress her breasts while his fingers brushed the sensitive peaks of her breasts, bringing the nipples to attention, then squeezing them gently between finger and thumb. Her breasts tingled, their nipples hardening at his touch. With questing hands, he explored farther down to her abdomen, sliding delicately over it to reach the point of coiled passion.

A rush of heat flooded Katarina's body, making her squirm with building desire. "Leo! Oh, Leo!" she breathed, overwhelmed by the force of her surrender to him.

When they had quieted, he lay next to her, brushing her hair back gently with his fingers and then tracing the lines of her face in silence. His eyes were clouded.

She stared into his eyes, and she was surprised to see the look of pain in them and knew what he was thinking. "There is no other man in my heart, but you. There never was. I want no one but you. I love you, Leo." Her body trembled in his embrace. "I'm sorry. I should have been more sensitive, but my stubbornness wouldn't let me."

"Hush, darling. It does no one any good to blame themselves. Destiny plays tricks with us sometimes and somehow love gets tangled in our lives."

She cuddled close to her husband, thankful she was able to push her ordeal to the back of her mind, at least for the moment.

The following morning, Leo and Katarina were both awakened by the blare of loudspeakers announcing the names of refugees scheduled for immediate transfer. At first, they ignored it, but the announcer kept repeating the message over and over with a kind of urgency in his voice.

Finally, Leo said, "Let's listen to it before it drives me crazy."

"Sure, why not." Cuddling in each other's arms, they stayed tuned as the message began: "Attention! Attention! The names I'll call are to present themselves at the gate with their belongings. They are to be transferred to another camp in Capua City. Please start packing now. The buses will be leaving in two hours."

They were both shocked to hear their name being called. Katarina jumped from the bed and angrily shouted, "I don't believe this! How dare the camp authorities do that to us again?" She was a little upset.

"I don't know, darling," he replied, not very happy himself and rose from the bed. "I only know we have to follow the rules. I hate to say I told you so."

"Well, I was convinced we'll find home here until we leave for Canada, but I guess I was wrong about that too."

They rushed to collect their belongings and pack them into boxes. Katarina flashed a disappointing look at him. "What rules? This will never end!" she thundered, punching their closed bags with her first. The fist and the punches brought back the memories of the rape but also the latest attack on her. She calmed down. Suddenly glad they were leaving, but how could she tell that to Leo now without telling him everything, she wondered.

Leo picked up the bags and said, "It's time to go, darling. We still have to pick up our breakfast."

"Just when everything is working out for us here," she shouted, "we have to leave." With a heavy heart, they walked out of the room that had given Katarina a few weeks of happiness. "I was happy here no matter what!" she exclaimed, dashing down the steps.

At the cafeteria, some noisy crowds were very unhappy because they had to move to another camp. "Only a few weeks after we arrived in here, we have to move again! Why?" they questioned and screamed.

"These are the same people we came from Trieste with," Katarina noted as they settled in the line for breakfast.

Leo glanced around, scanning their faces. "You are right," Leo whispered. "They are the same refugees."

After waiting a while, Leo and Katarina were given a few cookies and coffee and proceeded on the way to the bus. As they were striding toward the gate with their belongings, she bitterly complained, "I'm really getting tired of being bounced around from camp to camp. Why don't the camp authorities leave us in one place instead of herding us all around the country? It doesn't give us any time to live any kind of life. This time specifically, it didn't even give me enough time to say good-bye to my friends like Maria and Matron Rosetta. It's horrible if you ask me."

"That's it, darling. No one is asking you," Leo smirked and quickened his pace.

"Oh, so you don't care how I feel," she grumbled following him. But in fact, he began to worry too if they would ever leave Italy.

As they walked out from under the dorm, the two buses were in their sight lineup at the gate. The same procedures were used on the refugees as in previous transfers. So there were no confusions about that, everyone knew what to do.

Just before they were about to hand in their ID cards to the official, a voice from the crowd, yelled, "Katarina! Wait!"

She and Leo both turned toward the voice. "Hello, Maria! What are you doing here?" Katarina asked, excited she could say good-bye to her.

"I came to say good-bye to you," Maria chirped and hugged her. "We are going to miss you in the infirmary. By the way, Matron Rosetta said good-bye and good luck to you and your husband in Capua and gave me this to hand it to you," holding a white envelope in her hand.

"What's that?"

"Here, take a look," Maria said and handed her the envelope.

Katarina took it, glanced inside, and smiled. "Oh, I get it. Thank you, Maria, for all your help. You did a lot for me in only this short time. Say thanks to Matron Rosetta. I'm sorry I have to leave, but maybe it's for the best," Katarina replied, wiping her eyes.

"You could be right. Good-bye, Katarina, and you too, Leo," Maria said, shaking his hand and rushed away.

After they settled on the bus, Leo embraced his wife and finally said, "Everything will be fine," though not quite convinced himself.

She cast a sad look at him and in a barely audible tone replied, "Nothing will ever be fine. Sometime I think maybe if I never left home, it would be better."

"And let the Communists take advantage of you?" Leo suddenly blurted. "Use you against your own people like they do many others in the same situation like yours."

"What do you mean?" Katarina asked with wide eyes.

"Exactly what I told you!" he whispered, clamped up, and squeezed her against his body, reminding her, "We've passed through many hurdles, and we'll get through this too, just think positive." Leo didn't want to go any further with the Communist story for fear of someone listening, annoyed with himself for going even that far.

"Sure, think positive," Katarina echoed the words, slid her hand under his arm, and huddled next to him.

"By the way, what was in the envelope?"

"Here, look for yourself, it's not much." She handed it to him. Her head rested on his shoulder, and she stared into empty space as the buses sped south toward Capua.

After only weeks in Latina, Katarina and Leo were on the move again. At first, she was very upset they were going. Yet when she settled on the bus, for some reason she felt safe, and part of her was more than happy to be leaving. Despair and apathy flooded her face whenever she thought about the constant transferring they had been through, only in a few months. It diminished her some each time she said good-byes to friends.

After a long pause, she lifted her head from her husband's shoulder and asked, "How many more good-byes will I be forced to say before I could say that this is the last one?"

Leo placed his hand over hers and gently squeezed it. "I don't know. But I feel bad too you know. Things will work themselves out. Don't worry, darling."

"How can I not? Every few weeks, we move from camp to camp," she complained and turned to stare out the window.

Her husband rubbed his forehead with the flat of his hand and looked at her puzzled. "Are you sure there isn't something else bothering you?"

"No! I'm fine, just frustrated," she replied without turning her head.

"If there was, you wouldn't keep it from me, would you?" he asked, looking at her earnestly.

She glanced at him. "Of course not!" she replied untruthfully. However, hearing that question made Katarina feel uneasy as she realized once again that her husband still felt she was keeping something from him. It was a conversation she didn't want to have with her husband or anyone, so she turned her head back to stare out.

The sky was overcast with clusters of dark clouds floating through the sky, threatening with rain. The strong wind played with dry old leaves as it carried them through the air, leaving naked trees behind shivering in the forest. After watching for a while, she dozed off against the window. Leo and Katarina didn't speak again until the bus pulled up to the gate of the Capua camp.

# CHAPTER 13

Finally, the buses made it into Capua camp. The squeaking sound of the old gate as it was shut behind the buses startled Katarina out of her sleep. She opened her eyes and looked out. "We are here," she announced in a low dull voice and glanced at her watch. "That was quick. It took us only an hour and half to get here."

"Oh, you are awake," Leo replied and stood up to join her at the window. Together, they gazed out. The sky was overcast and a fog and drizzle blanketed the camp that prevented them to see much of it.

Katarina covered her mouth with her hands and through her fingers, whispered, "Oh no! It looks dismal in here!"

Instead of giving her an answer, Leo tapped his wife on her shoulder. "It's time to see what's waiting for us here, darling," he replied as the buses came to a halt in front of a church.

"Yeah, I guess," she replied unexcited. They both pulled away from the window and followed the others down the bus aisle and out.

The gray skies did little to raise their spirit. Katarina's eyes wandered, overwhelmed with the bleakness of the camp. Unlike Latina, there weren't many onlookers waiting to greet them. Although there were just as much trees as it was in Latina, the shacks were rundown, packed closely together with garbage scattered over the ground around them. The scene saddened her as she remembered the lovely setup they had to leave behind in Latina.

"Welcome to Camp Capua!" a loud voice blasted through the speakers getting everyone's attention. "ATTENTION! NEWCOMERS! After you picked up your things, please follow the guide directly to the supply room."

"Welcome to what?" Katarina said, gritting her teeth, still angry they had to move, even though she had the reason to be happy about it because the man that had attacked her in Latina was left behind. Leo just squeezed her hand as they walked to the other side of the bus where all the baggage was.

There was already a crowd of refugees scrambling to get their belongings when Katarina and Leo reached their destination. The drivers had, yet again, merely piled the luggage outside the bus in a big heap.

"Here we go again," Katarina grouched as they settled in yet another line to wait.

Leo was tired of his wife's complaints and tried to change the subject. He glared at the sky and said, "I wonder about this rain. Will it ever stop?"

"Obviously not!" Katarina answered, frowning. Finally, they picked up their bags and followed the others to the main building where the supply room was. But she didn't stop grouching. "My god, this looks worse than any other camp we've been through so far."

Leo was aware that the authorities were watching and anything could be used against them to keep them from emigrating. "Stop this!" he demanded, seizing her hand, and warned, "You're going to get us in trouble with your defiant behavior."

"Thanks. I feel that I've been scolded enough," she replied, surprisingly in a low tone. Katarina quickened her pace and didn't want to listen to anything he had to say at that moment. Oh, yes. He had to control her, he just had to! Her husband hadn't liked being ridiculed by the other men for not being able to.

When they reached the supply room, again they had to line up, but Katarina said not a word about it, realizing her husband was annoyed with her. After a while, the woman behind the wooden counter called out, "Mr. and Mrs. Lisic, here are your supplies." The woman threw two bundles on the counter in front of them as Katarina and Leo came forward.

"Thank you," Leo replied as he took hold of the bundles.

In her hand, the woman held two meal tickets. "With these, you'll pick up your food from the cafeteria," she instructed and then handed them to Leo. He put the tickets in his jacket pocket and they turned to leave.

"Wait!" the woman yelled.

They turned and walked back to the counter. "Is there something else?" Leo asked, staring at her.

"Don't you want to know where you and your lovely wife are going to sleep tonight?"

"Yes, of course," Leo replied, placing their bundles down on the floor beside his feet and waited for her to tell him. Katarina stood by his side but said nothing. After all, she didn't want to embarrass him.

The woman opened a big registry book that stood on the side of the counter and announced, "Mr. and Mrs. Lisic, you'll be staying in room number 1. There's a young mother with two small children in room 2." She handed a pen to Leo and ordered, "Sign here. The shack number is 5 and is located on the other side of the camp beside the small river that runs through the camp. Just follow the paved pathway."

"Thanks," Leo said and turned to his wife.

The number 5 brought back memories of the attack in barrack number 5 in Camp Latina. "Oh no, what's that mean? Shack number 5?" Katarina whispered, her mind spun into turmoil. Her heart sunk, her body trembled as it echoed in her head. She could barely keep composed and up on her feet.

"Is it something wrong, darling? You look like you've seen a ghost?" Leo asked, looking at her pale face.

"No! Nothing. My stomach just feels a little queasy," she answered with a deep sigh. *That was close,* she thought, tears welling up in her eyes. She had almost given away one of her secrets.

Leo wasn't quite convinced it was just her stomach and kept glancing at her, deep in his thoughts. *Oh no, not again,* Leo mused, still looking at her, tired of her mood swings.

Katarina noted her husband's stare and thought, *I better smart up, or else, one day I will give myself up.* She pushed the tears back, forced a smile, and hoped she looked physically unwound, although every muscle behind her trivially slack posture was tight with alarm. She picked up both their bags in her hands and ordered, "Pick up those bundles, my love, and let's get out of here." Her voice brought him back from his thoughts.

"Sure," he replied and lifted the bundles, one over each of his shoulder. Then they walked out.

The drizzle continued and the fog was so thick it was hard to see. Everywhere they looked, the pathways were strewn with craters made by human feet in the soft mud. "Which way should we go?" Leo questioned as his eyes wandered. "Where's the paved pathway?"

"What's the difference? There is mud everywhere."

"Let's take this path, it is least affected by the mud," Leo decided. But as they walked, their feet kept sinking one foot deep into the soft muddy earth.

"For God's sake! When will this rain stop?" Katarina shouted angrily while struggling to get her feet out of the mud.

Struggling beside her, Leo said, "We should have asked the name of the woman who will be our neighbor."

"What for! We'll find out when or if we ever get there," she replied, plucking her foot out the mud.

"Here, take my hand," Leo offered. She refused his help and kept on going. It took them quite a while to get there.

"Leo, look there is the river," Katarina shouted excitedly, pointing.

"Shack number 5 must be around here some place," Leo said, his eyes scanning.

"Yes, but where?"

"There it is!" Leo pointed and rushed toward it. He stopped right in front of shack number 5 and glanced at his wife. "This is our new home, darling," he announced. They paused and stared at it for a minute or so.

"Yes, here we are, but for how long this time, I wonder?" Katarina noted in a subdued voice.

"Don't be a pessimist, darling," Leo chuckled and continued toward the door.

"I don't want to be a party spoiler, but you have to agree. We are moving too much around," Katarina tried to justify her mood, following her husband closer to the shack.

"I'm sure this is the last move we will make," her husband said. "We would spend probably the rest of the time here while waiting for the transport to Canada."

XX

"I hope so."

Then suddenly a look of relief brightened her face as Katarina saw a little girl run out of the shack toward them and shouted, "Katarina! Katarina!"

"Look, Leo! It's Josipa, Manda's little girl," Katarina shouted, surprised but very happy to see a familiar face.

"I'm glad to see you, Katarina, and you too, Leo," Josipa said.

Katarina hugged the little girl and replied, "I missed you too. You'll never know how much."

The little girl turned and ran into the shack, calling, "Mama, Mama, Katarina and Leo are here."

Leo pulled a cigarette out of his pocket and said, "I'll be right behind you as soon as I finish my cigarette."

"Fine." Katarina followed the girl through a narrow hallway, hollering, "Manda! Manda! Is it really you?"

Manda came out of her room into the narrow hallway and said, "Yes, it's me. I'm happy to see you both."

"Leo is smoking outside, he'll be in soon," Katarina explained and rushed toward her friend. They embraced, happy to see each other. Excited, Katarina took a deep breath and chanted, "I can't believe my luck. I wouldn't have thought in a million years that our paths would ever cross again. Yet here we are!" She squeezed Manda tightly in her embrace before she let her go.

"Me either. I learned this morning we are getting a neighbor, but I would never have guessed it would be you two," Manda explained as they walked together into room 1.

Katarina dropped their bags into a corner, her eyes surveying the room. "Well, it doesn't look nice, but I know things will be fine now that you're here, Manda. Why wouldn't they be?" Katarina smiled and hugged her friend once again.

As they heard her husband walked in carrying the bundles, Manda turned toward him and said, "I'm happy to see you, Leo, and even more glad you are going to be my neighbor."

Leo threw the bundles down to the floor and greeted her. "Hello, Manda, we meet again."

"Yes, we do," she answered with a smile, walked over to him, and gave him a long passionate hug.

Katarina didn't notice the kiss as her eyes were inspecting their room. Unfortunately, there was not much to appraise except for two rusty iron beds with two old army mattresses that were coming apart at the seams. She was happy to see her friend here and that the room was theirs, only theirs alone. Also, the room had a beautiful large window. "There's a lot of fixing to be done, but I think it will be all right," she chirped, looking at Leo and Manda.

"We'll get it in shape, just like we did the one in Latina Camp," Leo promised and walked out after they chatted for a while in the middle of their empty room.

"I have to go too," Manda said. "See you later," and walked out after Leo.

Once again, Leo and Katarina were faced with the task of turning a barren room into their liveable home. She unpacked most of the things and began her construction. It wasn't hard; she knew what to do. After all, she had done that before a few times. She made their bed and was folding her clothes when there was a knock on her door. "Come in!" she called.

"It's only me," Manda said and walked in. "Let's go."

"Go where?" Katarina stared at her. "I have things to finish in here."

"We're going to the cafeteria to pick up our lunches. I'd be glad to return the favor and show you where it is, if you like," she smiled. "So get your mess tins and come."

"Sure. I'll be right with you. I forgot about food." Katarina put her raincoat on and grabbed the mess tins. "Oops, tickets? They are in my husband's pocket, I have to get them. I hope he's around," she said as they walked out the door.

"Where are you two going?" Leo asked, almost bumping into them with the cardboard boxes he was carrying into the room.

"We're going to get lunch," Katarina announced. "But I need those tickets you were given by the woman in the supply room, my love."

"Take it. They are in my pocket."

Katarina stuck her hand into Leo's pants pocket and pulled the tickets out. "Here they are," she said, and they were on their way to the cafeteria.

The rain had stopped, but the sky was dark and clouds threatened to unleash more rain. They had to hurry, but how? The mud was everywhere and their feet slithered on the soft marshy earth. "Which way should we go?" Katarina asked, her eyes wandering, but the thick fog prevented her to see much.

"Just follow me. There is a paved pathway somewhere here. I know that," Manda said and moved ahead.

Katarina followed behind cautiously. Sure enough, there was a footpath under the muss of mud that led between the shacks into the cafeteria. Her body shivered. "It's cold," she voiced and buttoned her raincoat, watching her each step.

"The wind in here can be ugly, I was told," Manda replied and continued her trek.

Then suddenly, she stopped in front of a building. "The cafeteria is in here, and all the other utilities are close to the main building. If you want me, I'll come with you another day to show you," Manda explained and pushed the cafeteria's door open.

Inside was a long line of noisy refugees waiting to get their lunch. As Manda and Katarina settled in the line and moved ahead, Katarina's eyes wandered around it. "This cafeteria is much bigger than the one in Latina. That means there must be more refugees here than in Latina," Katarina concluded.

"Really, I just know that there are a lot of refugees. How many I wouldn't know," Manda replied with a chuckle. Katarina knew by the whispered spurts of conversation behind her that the ears of those were tilted toward them, so she realized she better watch what she was saying.

It was more than an hour before they got served. When they returned with the food, they found Leo busy in the room. He had set up a cardboard table and a small tree stump to be used as a chair beside the window. "Here, put the food on the table," he said proudly, tapping it with his hand.

"Oh, wow! You're getting pretty good at this," Katarina chuckled, patting her husband on his shoulder. "In the future, I might not even mind moving from camp to camp since you are so good."

Manda glanced at her with worry in her eyes and asked, "You think there is a chance you'll be transferred to another camp again?"

Katarina sighed, "No. This one has to be the last move. After all, how many beginnings can there still be left for us."

"Are you telling me you used them all up?" Manda replied and felt relief flooding through her.

"I hope so," Katarina replied and placed the two mess tins on their new table.

Manda looked at her. "Why don't you bring the food into my room? I have a big table. We'll eat together and celebrate your arrival."

Katarina glanced at Leo. "Well, I guess it's all right," she said and picked up their lunch.

"Let me carry the food," Leo said and took the mess tins from his wife's hands.

Manda strolled next door to her room. Katarina and Leo followed her. Josipa and little Franko were playing in their beds when they entered. "Hello, children," they greeted the little ones. Leo placed their lunch on Manda's table.

"You room looks nice, did you have someone help you?" Katarina observed.

"Yes. A friend of mine, his name is Viktor," Manda explained. "He came at the same time as I did from Trieste and he is a good help to me, especially with the children."

"That's great," Katarina replied as they all gathered around the table and sat down to eat.

"I bet you I know what's in the mess tins," Katarina said, looking at them.

They lifted the covers and shouted in unison, "Spaghetti/macaroni."

Katarina frowned and stuck the fork into it. "I've eaten more pasta in the last six months than the rest of my life put together."

"Here, they occasionally cook other things like fava, fresh cabbage, and pasta fusili," Manda replied, spooning macaroni into two small handmade paper plates, which lasted long enough for children to gobble down their food.

"Well, we'll see," Katarina sighed, not quite convinced she'll be eating better food any time soon, and began to eat what was in front of her.

"Hurry, Mama. We are hungry," the children grumbled, licking their forks.

"Yes, I know," Manda said and handed them their plates with food. When Franko and Josipa finished their spaghetti, Manda settled them into their beds for the night.

"We should go too and let the children sleep," Katarina suggested.

"Don't worry. In two minutes, they'll be out like a light," Manda explained. She was right; it wasn't two minutes before the children were snoring.

Later, Manda handed a bottle of wine that she had bought in the canteen just a few days before. "Here, open this. Our chance meeting deserves a touch of wine," she chuckled as she fetched three crystal wine glasses she had brought with her from home. Before she handed them to Leo, she said, "These are my lucky glasses. I always carry them with me wherever I go. Fill them up, Leo."

"Thanks, Manda, that's very generous of you," Leo said and filled her glass first, then his wife's and his.

Manda lifted her glass and said, "This is to God who reunited us again."

"Here, here. Thank you, Manda." Leo and Katarina lifted their glasses to her toast and drank the wine, rejoicing in the moment with their friend and maid of honor.

Katarina's face beamed; she couldn't hide her happiness at seeing Manda and the children again. As she placed her glass down on the table, she commented, "Manda, I didn't know you are so sentimental."

"Oh, you didn't. I'm sure there's more that you don't know about me," she replied, chuckling.

"How long have you been in Capua, Manda?" Leo asked, looking at her.

"A few weeks," she replied and winked at him.

You must have left only a week after we did," Leo quizzed, still looking at her with a smile.

"Something like that," Manda answered, smiling at him.

*Hmm*! she wondered, glancing at them as they spoke. Was she wrong to think that her maid of honor has changed? Her friend was not as warm and friendly as she had been in Trieste. Katarina noticed the wink, but said nothing, but felt uncomfortable to stay there any longer. "It's getting late, we better go, my love," she said and was at the door almost instantly. Leo joined his wife.

"Bye, Manda, and thank you," they said.

"Bye, see you later," Manda replied and closed the door behind them as Katarina and Leo left.

They entered their new room and threw themselves on the bed, leaving the fixing of the room for after. Both were so exhausted that they quickly fell asleep and slept through the next morning.

The gleam of the sun breaking through the high mist shone on their window when they awoke.

"Good morning, darling. I'm starving!" Leo said and jumped off the bed to get dressed.

"Me too," Katarina agreed and got off the bed quickly. "I can't believe we had slept right through."

"I can believe it either, but I guess we're both exhausted," he replied and grabbed the mess tins. "I'm going to get breakfast for us."

"That's wonderful, thanks," Katarina said to her husband on his way out and got herself busy with the house chores. She made the bed, covered the table with that beautiful tablecloth they got at Red Cross at Latina, and finished folding her clothes on her side of the bed. But her husband wasn't back yet. She looked out the window and muttered, "Where is he? I'm hungry."

The gleam of the sun breaking through the high mist shone on the Capua camp. It had rained during the night, and in place, the small pools of water glimmered like crushed crystal. Wrapped in her coat, she went out in front of the shack, sat in the sun, and waited for Leo.

Time crawled and she started to worry. "What's keeping him?" she muttered and glanced up the pathway. To her surprise, she noted her husband, Manda, the children, and a young tall skinny man with short dark hair and nice looking face walking down toward her. She felt relief flooding through her; Leo was safe.

"Sorry, darling, I'm late. I was detained by these people here," he justified with a chuckle.

"Oh, by the way, this is Viktor, the man I told you about yesterday," Manda interrupted.

"Nice to meet you, Viktor." Katarina extended her hand to him.

"No, no, it's my pleasure to meet you," Viktor replied as he shook her hand. Katarina let go of his hand and took her mess tin out of her husband's hand. "Have you eaten, my love?"

"Yes, I did," Leo answered. "I couldn't wait. I was so hungry."

"I'm going to have my breakfast. You have to excuse me because I'm starving. See you later," Katarina said and rushed inside with her food.
xxxxxxxxxxxxxxxxxxxx

When the Communist people came for him, he was shocked as he had nothing to do with politics. He was going to tell them that they made a mistake, but as soon as he protested, one of the men struck him in the face, knocking his glasses to the floor and then stepping on it.

Xxxxxxxxxxxxxxxxxxxx

Later that day, Leo and Viktor went on a scavenger hunt and Katarina and Manda paid a visit to the Red Cross.

"I had brought a very little with me from home because I was afraid to be discovered by the police as a runner," Katarina said and emptied a box on the table, hoping to find things to make their room homey.

"I'm here to help you, I don't need anything," Manda said, turning over a box. "If I find something you need, I'll give to you." Yet at lunchtime, Katarina still had nothing to show for her effort. All they found were some clothes for Katarina and a few short-sleeved shirts for Leo.

"This is the last one," Katarina said and turned the box over and its contents spread over the table. Suddenly, Katarina shrieked, "Look at this, Manda!" holding in her hand an electrical coil cooker.

"Wow! That's good. You can cook on it," Manda replied as she rummaged through the things; she found a few cups for coffee. Katarina was ecstatic. They returned home very happy.

Leo and Viktor were also successful. They brought a bunch of old pieces of wood into the room, but before they were able to explain, Katarina interrupted.

"What are you going to do with these? There is no fireplace in our room," Katarina chuckled and kept her accomplishment a secret until later.

"I'll make a few stools out it," Leo replied. "And Viktor will help me." They began to work.

"How can you? You're not a carpenter," she commented, still giggling.

"Why don't you go to pick up your lunch instead of watching us work," her husband said and continued cutting and shaping the wood into a stool. Viktor was doing the same.

"How about your lunch?"

Don't worry about us. Viktor and I ate already," Leo replied as she was on her way out.

Her husband didn't want Katarina to see the stools until they were all done. So every day after they finished working, Leo would hide it.

The next week passed slowly, she was used to being active. Now both of them were out of work; there was nothing for them to do but to wait for an offer. Oh sure, they were busy making their room homey, but that didn't bring them any money.

There wasn't much left to the harvest season. Only few farmers who still were coming around to look for workers to harvest olive trees, but Leo was afraid to go out to the farms. So he tried very hard to make himself useful around the room and the camp.

Finally, on the end of the week, Leo and Viktor finished the stools and were about to reveal their work.

That afternoon, Katarina came home with lunch and was about to enter to her room when Viktor held the door and said, "You can't come in yet."

"What's going on?" she asked suspiciously, but there was no answer. They were rushing to set the stools around their cardboard table and clearing the mess.

Then suddenly, the door opened wide. "Darling, you can come in now," Leo called with a smile on his face.

"Wow! That's wonderful!" she shouted, staring at the stools around the table. "Thanks to both of you," she added and hugged her husband. "It almost looks like a kitchen set" and rushed to look at it. "Let me sit on it to eat my lunch."

"Of course, we can all sit down now," Leo said, looking at Viktor.

"No, thanks, I have to go," he said and turned to walk out.

"Thank you, Viktor, for helping my husband," Katarina yelled after him.

They sat on their stools and ate their lunch. That sparked some excitement inside her, lifting her spirit up a little. She pulled her surprise out of a bag and took a deep breath. "This room will soon look just as nice as the one in Latina did," his wife said and placed the cups on the table but hid the hot plate. "Now, if we only have some money to buy other things missing. I could make coffee for us."

Leo placed his arm around his wife's shoulder. "And it will be here as good as it was there. I'll find something to do," he promised, enjoying his achievement.

"Well," she smiled, "I must say that the camp isn't as bad as I first thought. It has many palm, spruce, and pine trees. Also the little river. And I do hope things will get better for us. Thanks," Katarina replied.

Their reveries suddenly were interrupted by a strange voice through a loudspeaker. "KATARINA LISIC, PLEASE REPORT TO THE CAMP INFIRMARY IMMEDIATELY."

They darted a look at each other, and she was certain in that moment that the same thought crossed both their minds, but neither wanted to express their feeling. "You better go quickly," Leo said and stood up to clear the dishes.

"You are right," she agreed and hurried to the infirmary to see why she had been paged.

She paused in front of the door. Her thoughts swung wildly, like a pendulum, and she realized suddenly that there was a possibility she might get the job, but she wouldn't dare think aloud.

As Katarina entered, she found two Italian nurses chatting at the main desk, both wearing white overcoats. "Hello, my name is Katarina Lisic. I was paged a short while ago to come here," she said.

"Yes, come with me," one of them replied and walked into an office with a file. The woman walked behind the desk and introduced herself, "I'm Matron Mateya. Sit down please."

"Thanks," Katarina said in a barely audible voice and sat down, shaking inside. While Matron was speaking to her, a sturdily built nurse with big black eyes and great cheekbones, twice the size of Katarina and dress in a white smock, strolled into the room. Her long brown hair was tied in a ponytail and bounced as she walked. She looked very much at home in the infirmary.

"Hello, I'm Lina!" she acquainted herself, towering over Katarina.

"That is Katarina. She'll be working with you, Lina," Matron pointed out.

"Hello," Katarina said, looking at her nervously, as she was still towering over her.

"Sit down, Lina," Matron ordered. Lina sat beside Katarina and listened to Matron instructing.

"Here, you're allowed to use all the nursing skills you have," Matron Mateya continued. "We don't get enough nurses, so we can use any help we can get. Lina is also our ambulance car driver. When she goes on her run with the ambulance, you'll be going with her to assist her whenever necessary. Also you'll be working night shifts with Lina. One important thing is that an Italian nurse is with you an every shift. The day shift it is me, and the night shift is Supervisor Emma. You'll do nothing without notifying the Italian nurse first. Now, do you want to work?"

"Yes. Of course, I do! I accept!" Katarina said with sigh of relief. She had been worried about what kind of job she would be doing here, but now that she knew, it made her happy.

"That's lovely," Matron replied. "When can you start?"

"How about now?" Lina intercepted. "I show you around and introduce you to the work, then you start in the morning 0700 hours." She rose to her feet and sauntered to the nearby cabinet and took a white overcoat from the shelf.

"Catch," Lina shouted and tossed it to Katarina.

Startled, she grabbed the overcoat. "What? Don't you wear a uniform, here?"

"No, not here," Lina replied. "So put the smock on."

Matron Mateya watched them for a while then interrupted, "Now, let's get back to work, ladies," and turned to the papers on her desk. Lina and Katarina walked out.

"I have been working here for quite a while," Lina said as they sauntered through the infirmary. "I'm waiting for my immigration papers to remain in Italy. Until then, I have to stay in the camp."

"Do you like it here?"

"What's not to like when you have to. It's not bad once you get used to it. The camp authority lets us use all our nursing skills and I'm learning a lot. Things like I would never learn in regular hospitals."

"I can believe that. What kind of patients do you get in here?" Katarina asked, wanting to know all the details.

Lina glanced at her. "Where do I start?" she asked. "The major problems here are tuberculosis, drug and alcohol abuses, dysentery, yellow fever, bronchitis, and secondary infections due to needle reuse."

"Same like in every other camp," Katarina agreed. "What's your routine?"

"Two weeks days and two weeks night shifts. The work is the same, day or night. Except during the night we prepare and sterilize the instruments, materials like needles, syringes, small and large gauzes, and other things needed for the day shift use. Sick refugees on medications have to come into infirmary for each of their doses in the time prescribed. For the ones who are too sick to come, the nurses take the medications to them in their homes. We take turns day or night. The most important part now: we get paid every week."

"It is the same as in the Latina camp infirmary. I like it. The practice could come in handy for me too," Katarina expressed. "I was afraid that things would be different here."

"That's all. I'm finished with the orientation," Lina said. "Unless you have any question."

"No, I don't, thank you," Katarina replied graciously.

"Well then, I'll see you bright and early tomorrow morning."

The orientation lasted for about an hour. Lina turned to her work and Katarina went home, delighted to be employed once again in the camp infirmary. Her face beamed when she entered their room. Leo took one look at her and guessed, "You got the job!" He hollered and rushed to hug her.

"Yes! Yes!" she chirped, happy things were turning out well for them.

Manda heard their laughter and came to join them in their celebrations. "I'm so happy for you," she said and wrapped her arms around Katarina.

The next morning, Katarina started her first day of work at the infirmary. She was buddied with Lina and said, at the end of the shift, "It's a lot to learn. I'm glad you were with me."

"I didn't mind, but tomorrow you're on your own, my friend," Lina replied, smirking.

"Yes, I know," Katarina acknowledged and walked home.

Outside, the wind blew chilly and the dark clouds floated through the sky, preparing to unleash a downpour of rain. She quickened her pace toward the shack.

The flu cases in Capua were rising daily as the bad weather persisted and forced the nurses to work long hours in the infirmary.

XXXXXX

The rain and chilly winds brought cold and flu to many refugees and forced Katarina and other nurses to work long hours. xxxxxxxxxx

Working together day in and day out, she and Lina soon became good friends.

On the last day after their two-week day shift was over, Lina suggested, "Let's go down by the river for a while so we can talk a little. Soon autumn will be over and then winter days will be right around the corner, and we won't be able to go there. It will be too cold and windy." Lina wanted to finish the conversation she started in the ambulance car on the way back from Naples.

"Yeah, let's," Katarina replied. "I like this time of the year." And they walked toward the banks on that late afternoon.

The sky was soft blue with maybe an hour more of sunlight. The chilly wind brushed against their faces as they strolled by the river, chatting and watching the murky water slowly move along the banks. Lina commented, "I feel peaceful here, listening to the water murmuring. I come here often, especially when I feel down."

"I can see why. It's so beautiful in here. Everything is golden, especially toward the evenings. The palm, spruce, and pine trees towering over the river makes it even more lovely. "Oh! It even has its fish," Katarina sighed deeply, taking the fresh air into her lungs.

"Yes, but it's only good for the gulls. What's your hubby doing while you're working?" Lina quizzed.

"He has been trying to get a job, but so far nothing. Since the harvest season is mostly over, the jobs are scarce. Also he is cautions about which jobs he takes after the scare he had in Latina with the secret police UDBA."

"What kind of scare did he get from the Yugoslav secret police?"

"They almost picked Leo up from the farm he and two of his friends were working at and take him back to Yugoslavia. He was able to escape, but the other two were not as lucky. We both got a big scare. Now, he would take an outside job only if the offer comes from one of his friends' employers, and even then, he feels it's risky."

"I understand Leo's and your feelings. I have heard about that too many times, I don't care to count. Besides, I witnessed one incident. I can tell you, you wouldn't want to do that."

"Tell me what happened," Katarina urged.

Lina hesitated for a short while; she turned and began walking to opposite side. "Well, all right, I'll tell you. One day, my friend, his girlfriend, and I were in the city. We walked back and were just about to enter through the gate. I was already at the gate, my friends were trekking behind. Suddenly out of nowhere, a black limousine came fast toward the gate. The driver accelerated and wrenched the wheel over to the couple, another car came in even faster from behind and braked violently. Two men jumped out of the first car, grabbed my friend and his girlfriend. 'Get in!' one of them yelled, pointing something at them, obviously a gun. But I couldn't see it, it was under his jacket. 'No!' the friend yelled, pulling his girl back. 'What's going on?' she asked. I could hear fear in her voice. They tried to run, but the men grabbed them and pushed them into the car then sped way just as fast as it could. There was no time for anything. I didn't even try to help them. I stood there as if I was frozen."

"Did you report to the Italian carabineers?"

"No. There wasn't any point. The carabineers wouldn't want to be involved," Lina said, still feeling sadness for her friend. "I wonder many times. What happened to them?" After all this, she decided not to persuade her to help as Katarina had enough on her plate to deal with, Lina thought. "Leo has to be very careful with whom he has business because there's a spy on each corner of the camp," Lina continued. "How many are in among us, I wouldn't even try to guess."

"You're right," Katarina said. "While I'm working, he spends his free time with Viktor and Manda, my maid of honor, and Viktor, a friend of hers. At least he's in a company of good people."

"That's very nice. Were you able to find something on your scavenger hunt for your room?" Lina changed the subject as it was depressing.

"Not yet. We did some hunting, but all we have to show is scraps of an old wood that Leo brought home, four coffee cups, and a hot plate for cooking that I found at the Red Cross office. It's hard to find much of anything as everyone else is also scavenging."

"What did Leo do with the scraps of wood?" Lina asked and gave a cynical laugh.

Katarina looked at her. "It's amazing, if you see it, you wouldn't laugh. He and Viktor made four such beautiful stools for around our cardboard table. It almost looks real. The only sad part is that we have to use someone's garbage to survive. And yet, we're lucky if we find any."

"We're also lucky this won't last forever," Lina said as they turned to walk back.

"We live in hope. That's the only thing we still have left. I'd invite you for coffee, but I'm still missing coffee and a coffeepot," Katarina said, arriving in front of her shack.

Lina looked at her and smiled. "You know what. I might be able to help you there. In the infirmary, it's an old pot in working condition. I'm going to give it to you next time we work together."

"Great! Are you sure no one would mind?"

"No. Don't worry, nobody is using it. See you in two days at the night shift," Lina said and walked away.

"I'll be there." Katarina walked into her room, but didn't find Leo there. She walked to Manda's door and knocked, "Is Leo here?" she asked.

"No," Manda replied. "He went with Viktor hunting for a job early this morning."

"And they didn't come home yet!" Katarina asked, alarmed.

"No. But don't be so concerned. Maybe they got the job and are working," Manda giggled. "Would you like to come in?"

"No. I'm going to get supper. See you later." She didn't feel at the time to explain herself why she felt alarmed.

Manda stood at her threshold when Katarina returned with her supper. "Have they returned?" she asked, pausing at her doorway.

"No. Would you like to come to my room?" Manda asked.

"No, thanks. I have some things to do before I go to work," she said and walked inside.

In the room, Katarina found herself wandering aimlessly around, fear was taking over her body. *I hope he's safe*, she thought. She opened the window and leaned out, shivering a little. Darkness was almost total, and her husband was still out there somewhere. The painful scent from an autumn bonfire drifted in and interrupted her train of thoughts, bringing with it a nostalgic memory of days when she was very young and helped her Papa burn the fallen leaves, twigs, and dry old grass on their farm at home. "Oh, Papa, would I ever see you again?" she muttered to herself, wiping the tears that were rolling down her cheeks.

"Hello, darling, I'm home," Leo said cheerfully as he entered.

His words jerked her out of her engrossment. She shot a swift look at him. "Where have you been?" she asked and rushed into his embrace. "I was worried sick."

"I worked!" he said happily.

"Worked? Where?"

"On one of the farms. I know, I know what you are going to say, but we need the money. I need extra money for cigarettes and maybe a beer or two, and you barely make to cover extra food that we buy occasionally. Besides, Viktor knows Marko very well, that's the man, and we're going to work around the house. It's less dangerous," Leo explained taking his dirty clothes off. Katarina was so relieved but also worried, but didn't want her husband to know. After supper, they lay on their bed and counted the money he brought home and made some plans.

Leo wrapped his arms around his wife and promised, "On your next days off, we'll take a run into the city of Capua. As the days are getting colder and the winter approaching, there aren't going to be many days nice to walk one kilometer to the city."

"Thank you, my love. I love to go, I heard it's an ancient city," she answered enthusiastically and lay her head against his shoulder, yawning. Exhausted, she fell asleep almost immediately.

During the two days off, Katarina washed their clothes and spent some time with Manda and children while Leo worked.

On her first night shift, Katarina came to work a little earlier. The evening shift left in the infirmary was only a guard. "Good evening," Katarina said as she entered.

"Hello, Katarina, you're working nights now," the guard asked.

"Yes, for the next two weeks," she replied and walked into a small room where the nurses kept their things. She put her smock over her clothes and walked out to the floor. The guard was gone, and she was now alone. Her eyes wandered, the infirmary was a mess. The sink was filled with dirty instruments, and there were many cases of needles to be sterilized. The garbage cans filled with dirty diapers full of baby feces. As she stood there with her mouth wide open, looking at it, she felt a hand on her shoulder.

"What happened in here?" Lina asked, buttoning her smock.

"I have no idea. When I got here, everyone was gone," Katarina replied and began to sort the instruments for the sterilization.

Xxxxxx

"I do. Today was the day of children's immunization, and it's obvious there were many babies here today with the dysentery." xxxxx

"Those poor babies with the dysentery were probably here again," Lina replied and began emptying the garbage cans into the special bags supplied by the camp.

"What babies?"

"A few days before you came, mothers brought their babies suffering of dysentery into the infirmary. The doctor examined them and gave their mothers medicine for their babies. I thought they were healed, but this tells me they were not." She opened the door and called, "Guard!"

"I'm here, Lina," he answered and walked over to her. "What can I do for you?"

"You can take this out please," she replied angrily, handing him the bag of stinky garbage. "The least the evening shift could have done, was to take it out."

"When I came, it was chaotic in here," the guard said as he took the bag.

"I realized that, but still they could have put the garbage out, so the infirmary doesn't smell so much." Lina closed the door, still somewhat upset, and returned to her work. They both worked hard, way into the early hours of the morning, thankful they didn't have any patients coming in.

"It's about time we have a break. Don't you think so, Katarina?" Lina said and sat down.

"Yes, you are right." She sat beside Lina and rested for a few minutes, then they both made over to the coffeepot.

Suddenly, Katarina remembered a promise Lina made to her the day they were by the river and turned at her. "About that coffeepot. Are you still thinking to give it to me?"

"Yes, I do," she said and strode into the small room and in minutes returned. "Here, it's all yours," Lina handed a small coffeepot to her. "With one request that I be invited for coffee."

"Wow! It's lovely. Thank you, and of course, you are invited. Just let me know when you can come," Katarina said as she took it.

"Great," Lina said, and they went back to work.

Katarina's first night was very busy, but she enjoyed it. She loved nursing, dreaming of one day being top nurse in her own right. She took her coffeepot and wrapped it into a brown paper.

"Time to go home," Lina said as she walked out the door.

"I know. I'm going in a minute." Katarina picked up her brown package and was about to walk out when Matron Mateya almost ran into her.

"Just the girl I want to see," she said and motioned to her to follow her into the office, and Katarina did. The matron didn't even sit; she pulled an envelope out of her bag and gave it to her. "This is for you, Katarina," the Matron said and handed the envelope to her.

"What's this?" Katarina asked with fear in her eyes and her face pale. Her hands were trembling when she took it, but she didn't open it.

"It's your pay, why are you afraid to open it, silly girl."

"Oh," Katarina said and looked at the envelope, blood flushed her face. "I'm not afraid. I was going to open it at home." She tried to hide her fear, but Matron Mateya didn't buy it.

"You thought you received a notice for another transfer, didn't you?" Matron quizzed.

Katarina glanced shyly at her. "Well, I'm afraid I did. Thank you for the money." And she walked home.

On the way, she counted the money and realized she was paid more than in Latina. "I'm rich! I'm rich!" she hollered, entering her door, not expecting to find her husband home.

"What are you yelling about?" Leo asked, rushing to get dressed.

"Nothing. Just that I got paid ten liras more than in Latina, that's all," she practically sang, taking her sweater off. "What are you still doing home?"

"As you can see, I'm running late, so please don't bother me." And he was out the door in minutes after she came home.

*What's bothering him*? she wondered; she only wanted to tell him she got paid more money. Exhausted, Katarina crawled to bed, but couldn't sleep, her thoughts swung wildly. She wondered if he had heard a word that she said.

Although happiness and love blossomed between them, there were times when she felt that something wasn't quite right in her marriage.

This was one of those times. Was it her fault, she wondered and blamed herself for the problem. After tossing and turning for a while, she fell asleep.

Through the dream, she heard a knock on the door and awoke. "Come in," she yelled.

"It's me," Manda said and entered with both of her children. "Would you like to come with us to pick up your supper?"

"Sure, thanks. It's nice of you to wake me up." Katarina climbed out of bed and got ready. Took her mess tins and they were on the way to the cafeteria.

After she returned, she did some cleaning around the room, added the coffeepot to the four cups in a small box, where she kept her dishes, the little she had. "Now I only need coffee, and I can make myself a cup of my own," she muttered and covered it with a tea towel.

By the time she finished her things and ate her supper, it was time for her to go to work. Before she left, she set her husband's mess tin with supper on the table for him when he returned.

XXX

The two weeks of Katarina's night shift went by uneventful and quick. Arriving home after her last night of work, she added another pay to the one she had, the little that was still left of it. The jingle of the change awoke her husband, and he asked, "Are we still going shopping tomorrow?"

"Yes, of course, my love. Not beer or cigarettes, I hope. You know, we can't spend too much," she replied, painfully aware that money was not coming from anywhere else except her work.

Leo gave her a sideway look and just smirked. "You get some sleep, darling," and walked out the room.

Katarina crawled in bed and tried to sleep, but whirling thoughts in her mind kept her awake. She hoped she would be able to buy something for herself when they go to the city, Capua, tomorrow. But now she wasn't sure because Leo hadn't being working in the last few days and the little money they had, it had to be for extra food. As she had no idea when or if he would find another job. In any case, she was delighted she would be going to see the city.

The following morning when they awoke, her husband asked, "Are we still going to the city?"

"Sure," Katarina replied and got herself ready.

"You know, the city is a kilometer away from the camp, I hope you can walk that far."

"No problem," Katarina chirped and was out the door first.

"Did you pack your raincoat?" Leo asked as he came out.

"Yes, you know I don't go anywhere without my raincoat." And they were on their way to visit the city of Capua. After the stuffiness of their tiny room, they enjoyed the air outside, which was sweet and fresh. It was chilly, even though the sun broke through clouds and shone on them as they walked.

On their way, Leo and Katarina encountered some refugees traveling to and from the city. They were amazed with those refugees returning back, how many things they had bought. After a couple had passed them, Katarina glanced and exclaimed, "How can they afford this?"

"I don't know, but we will," Leo said and walked in front of a few people going back. "Excuse me. Is someone in the city giving things free to the refugees?" he asked slyly.

A man chuckled. "No, I wish that were true. The farmer's piazzas are closing for the winter and they have a big sale."

"All right, thanks," Leo said and they continued their trek toward the city. As they were approaching, they noticed a vendor selling something beside the domelike gate that led into the city.

"Capua must be very old. The domelike shape entrances were built during the Old Roman Empire. If I'm not mistaken, the Colosseum in our city Pula back home was built during the same time."

"I suppose," Leo said and shrugged his shoulders, not very interested in the history of the city, his interest centered on the food it had to offer. As the fragrance of cooking wafted from the vendor's pot and reached their nostrils, Leo said, "Boy, am I hungry. Let's see what the man has for sale there."

"You know, my love, these kind of vendors are expensive," Katarina replied, not wanting to spend money, but her husband didn't care, especially when he was hungry. They made their way over; one customer was in front of them. While Katarina and Leo waited, they browsed around. On the vendor's counter stood an uncovered bowl filled with cooked beef cartilages sprinkled with only salt. No bread or anything else was visible.

"What can I get you? A kilo or a half?" the vendor asked, looking at Leo and Katarina after he had finished serving the costumer.

"How much is a kilo?" Leo asked, observing the food.

"Ten liras."

"Give us half of a kilo, we'll share it," Katarina jumped in before Leo had a chance to say anything. She wasn't sure if she would like it anyway. Her husband took the food and moved to the side, leaving his wife to pay the bill. When she finished, he was already eating.

"Oh, it's delicious. Would you like some?" Leo offered, extending his hand with a piece of beef cartilage to her.

Katarina looked at it and promptly refused. "I'm not hungry," she said and hurried toward the dome. Leo kept nibbling on the food as he followed her.

"This is the only way in, you know," she commented as they entered through the dome into the city.

"I don't know, history is your thing, not mine," Leo muttered, still munching on his food. As they climbed several crumbling stone steps and entered a narrow alley, they came upon a tiny restaurant crowded with Italians. She immediately noticed a sign written with big letters, PIZZA. Her taste buds began to grow, but it would turn out to be something totally different than what she thought.

They made their way over and Katarina saw her friend Lina through the window. Lina grinned at her from inside and came out. "What are you two doing here?" she asked and embraced them both."

"We thought we would see the city," Leo answered.

"Come inside and have coffee or something with me," Lina requested.

"Oh no, we shouldn't. There is still a lot of the city we hadn't seen yet," Katarina said, even though she did want to eat something too. Leo's nibbling on the beef cartilage made her hungry.

"Why not, let's have a coffee," Leo replied, glancing at his wife.

"All right," Katarina agreed and they went in.

Inside it was crowded, noisy, and scented with cigarette smoke. Young people rushed in and out. Lina pulled up two chairs and they sat down at her table. The waiters were quick on their feet when they saw new costumers come in. "What can I get you?" one of them asked.

"Three coffees and one pizza," Lina said.

Leo turned to Lina and said sheepishly, "We just want coffee. I'm off work now, and I don't like it when my wife has to pay for everything."

Katarina turned her head away and muttered, "Yeah, now that he's full."

"Don't worry, I'll pay for the pizza," Lina answered with a smile. Katarina wasn't about to stop her because she was getting pretty hungry and pizza was her favorite food.

The waiter returned quickly and placed three coffees and the plate with pizza wrapped in foil on their table. "Fifteen liras please," the waiter said, extending his hand toward Lina. She paid the waiter and he was on his way to the next table.

"I'm glad you two are here, otherwise, I would have to eat alone. I hate that," Lina said and pulled her cup of coffee in front of her.

"I'm sure it wouldn't be your first time," Leo replied and took his cup, but Katarina's eyes were fixed on the plate with the pizza. She was happy that she would finally get to eat pizza, a young chicken. She hadn't eaten chicken meat for a very long time.

"Katarina, aren't you having the coffee?" Lina asked and unwrapped the pizza.

"Yes, I'm," Katarina replied, her eyes drifting for a second from the pizza to her coffee. When she refocused back to the pizza, she was stunned. What's that dough doing here? Where is the chicken meat? Her inner voice screeched, but she remained silent and continued to stare.

Lina looked at both of them and said, "You two have never eaten pizza before, have you?"

"Better word is never seen one," Katarina replied sheepishly.

"Oh no. You thought?"

Don't say it," Katarina interrupted loudly. "It's embarrassing!"

"My wife thought this is a young chicken, *pica* and *pizza*, that's close if you want it to be bad enough," Leo explained.

"I know what Katarina thought," Lina replied. They all burst into laughter and ate their food.

"Lina, it was nice of you to treat us with the pizza and coffee, but we really have to go now. Thank you," Leo said and rose from the chair.

" Thanks, Lina, and I'll see you in a day or two at work."

They left their friend in the restaurant and went out to browse. Katarina stopped in front of the lady's boutique and peered through the window. "I wish I could buy one," she said, staring at the beautiful dress display.

Leo placed his arm around her shoulder. "Darling, if I had the money I would buy you as many as you want, but you know, as well as I do, we have to save money to buy extra food."

"I know. All right then, buy me that lovely dog figurine, it's a piggy bank," she smiled mischievously at her husband and rushed inside.

Leo followed her in. "Wait, the money can be used for something else."

"It doesn't cost much. Come on, Leo, please. I'll save some money for our journey to Canada in it. I promise."

He paused and stared at her with an upset expression on his face, then quickly shifted his eyes. He didn't know what to say. The truth was that Leo would rather have used the money to buy cigarettes and beer.

"Well, what?" Katarina asked, looking at him. The expression on his face gave her a sinking feeling. "Fine!" she thundered and turned to walk out.

"All right, all right. I'll buy you the dumb figurine." With a frown, he turned to the saleslady standing behind the counter. "Can I have that piggy bank, please?" and handed her the money.

The saleslady wrapped the gift into paper and passed it to Leo.

On the way out, he gave it to his wife and said, "Here, I know you like saving change."

"Thank you," Katarina replied, excitement filling her face. "You'll see I'll save money for our journey." She smiled and kissed the dog. "I have something I can call my own now," she muttered to herself as they walked toward the market.

When Leo saw how happy the figurine made her, he embraced her and kissed her. "I'm glad you want to save money for our journey to Canada, but I'm afraid you might not have any to save."

"I'm not sure if that day will ever come," Katarina glowered, realizing the day of their departure to Canada was still far, far away.

"Don't be sad, darling. The day will come and sooner than you think."

"Look, there is the farmer's market," Katarina pointed and quickened her pace.

The market was crowded. Many refugees and inhabitants were shopping. As Katarina and Leo were browsing and surveying the prices on the vendor's tables, they noticed many nice things, but the prices were still too high for their budget. Katarina and Leo couldn't afford to buy anything, even though some of the prices were slashed to a half.

After a long walk through the market, Leo said, "We can't go back without buy something."

"No, but we haven't checked that table on the end. Let's go there," Katarina replied and strode toward it.

"If you say so." Her husband followed her. They made their way over, and Katarina asked the vendor, "Can you give me a quarter of a hundred grams of Brazilian coffee, please?" pointing to it.

Leo stood aside and smirked. "Coffee?"

The vendor filled a bag and put it on the scale. "Here you go, twenty liras. Would you like anything else?"

"Yes, a few potatoes, tomatoes, and two sausages. How much would all this cost?"

The vendor weighted the veggies. "Ten liras. Did you want them?"

"Yes," Katarina answered.

The lady vendor placed everything into a brown paper bag and put it on the table within her arm's length as she extended her hand for the money. "All together thirty liras, please."

"Here are your thirty liras," Katarina said, placing the money in her hand.

Leo took the bag and said, "Now, we can go home, darling."

When they got out of the market, they went back by the same road they came. Katarina rushed ahead.

"Wait, my love," Leo called. "I almost forgot to tell you. We were invited to Marko's shack tomorrow night at seven o'clock for cake and coffee. It's his twin boys' sixth birthday. That's Viktor's friend who helped me get the job on the farm. You know Marko and his wife, don't you?"

She paused and looked at her husband. "Of course, I know Marko and his wife. How can I not? They live just across from us."

"Why are you angry?"

"I'm not angry. Just that they're both a little too stuck up for my taste, especially his wife. I said hello many times to her, she never responded. She thinks she's a goody-two-shoes." Katarina gazed at Leo puzzled. "Why is Marko inviting us into his home? He never invited us before."

"Who knows why he didn't invite us before?" Leo replied. "Maybe because we're much younger than they are. I don't know. I've worked with Marko, he seems to be a good man."

"I didn't say he wasn't," Katarina replied. "I bet you anything that Manda asked him to invite us, but why?" she quizzed.

Leo stopped abruptly and turned to her. "Why would you think that Manda had anything to do with him inviting us?"

"No reason. I just thought that since Manda is a good friend of ours and his, she might have said something to them. That's all I meant. What did you think I meant?"

"Nothing," he said and slid his hand into hers as they continued striding toward the dome.

They hadn't noticed the increasingly darkening sky until a sudden downpour of rain began. The strong wind tossed it in capricious spraying gusts, almost drenching them before they were able to pull their raincoats out.

Finally, they reached the dome and waited underneath until the big rain subsided. Then Katarina and Leo got out of the city and began to walk back.

On the way, the wind blew against them, slowing them to a crawl. "It's cold!" Katarina grouched, hiding her face in her raincoat. Her husband stopped and turned to her.

"I know. My clothing is wet too. I'll walk ahead of you and try to shield you from the wind's wrath, darling," Leo suggested and nuzzled his chin against his chest in an effort to escape the bitter wind, and he began to walk.

But her husband's back and somewhat wet clothes Katarina wore under her raincoat were little protection against the harsh wind that was piercing her chest as she walked. Her body shivered. "I'm freezing, if these winds continue, we'll never make it back!" she yelled and tried to quicken her pace, but got nowhere.

"Oh, yes, we will because we are here," Leo shouted happily and turned to walk into the camp. Katarina was bundled into her raincoat that she didn't noticed they were coming upon the camp.

Now she took the lead and ran home as fast as she could, but Leo wasn't far behind. They burst into their unheated room, both shivering. "It's just as cold in here as it was outside!" Katarina yelled.

They quickly changed into dry clothing. She wrapped herself in a blanket and sat on the bed. "Oh no. It feels like I'll never warm up," Katarina complained, still shivering.

Leo plugged in the hot plate and pulled the things out of the brown bags, grabbing the coffeepot they bought on the farmer's market. "You will, I'll make hot coffee," Leo said and rushed to the utility room to wash it and get some water for coffee. Leo made the coffee as he promised, and before he went to pick up their supper, they drank the coffee. "It's delicious!" Katarina chirped as she drained every drop out of the cup.

"Now that I have everything to make a coffee. I have to invite Lina one of this days for a cup."

"That's nice, but now, I'm going to get our supper, and after, I'll fry one of the sausages we bought, and the other one we'll leave it for tomorrow."

"Yes, that was my plan too," Katarina smirked, watching her husband walk out. After she drank the coffee, she felt warm and cozy under the blanket and dozed off until her husband returned.

He put the supper on the table, grabbed the sausage, and rummaged between the dishes. "You have to cook it because we don't have a frying pan. Use one of the mess tins," Katarina suggested.

"You're right," he acknowledged and placed the sausage into the mess tins and together on the hot plate. When the sausage was cooked, Leo and Katarina eat their supper.

"The sausage was very good," she said and returned to bed.

"See, I know how to cook too," Leo replied and soon joined her in bed.

# CHAPTER 14

The following morning, Leo awoke early and went out for a walk. The weather was nice, the sun shone, and the wind died down so he spent the morning visiting his friends. Katarina remained in bed a little longer, struggling within herself what to do, go to the party or not. After that wink she noticed from Manda directed to her husband, she had a hard time trusting her maid of honor.

"Get our clothes ready for tonight. We are going to the party," Leo ordered as soon as he returned.

"But, Leo," she replied, "I work in the morning. Besides, I have this feeling we shouldn't be going to Marko's tonight." That was a big mistake on Katarina's part, she thought, spreading the clothes they were going to wear to the party on the bed. She grabbed her own few pieces, her husband's shirt, and a pantaloon. "I'll be back soon," Katarina grumbled and was on her way to the laundry to iron them.

"I'll get the supper on the table," Leo said to his wife before leaving.

Just as they sat to have supper, Manda stopped by. "Hello, you two." She winked at Leo and smiled.

"We'll be there," Leo replied before Manda even opened her mouth for another word.

"Then see you there." Manda flashed a smile at Leo and rushed out of the room, all excited.

Katarina stared at her. Hmm, if she didn't know better, she'd think Manda was flirting with her husband. She quickly dismissed it as Leo hurried her to get ready for the party.

Marko's small room was already full of people when they arrived. "See, we're late," Leo frowned.

"No, we're not. It's not seven o'clock yet, my love." Katarina glanced at her husband. He didn't reply, but strolled up to his friend who was playing a harmonica, leaving his wife at the door. Her eyes scanned the room for Manda. She stood beside the table set with wine, coffee, and cake and was trying to feed a piece of cake to her little boy, Franko. Meandering through the crowd, she made over to them. "We meet again, Manda," Katarina said, staring at the half-eaten cake. "Oh no! It looks like I missed seeing the boys blow out the candles."

"I'm afraid you did," Manda replied. "Marko wanted the boys to blow out the candles early so he could serve the cake since that is all he has for the guests to eat. Besides, the children will have to go to bed early anyway.

"Where are the boys?" Katarina looked around. "They are not sleeping already, are they?

"No, they are over there," Manda pointed them out.

Katarina moseyed to them. "Happy birthday, boys!" she exclaimed and handed them a small package containing an old key holder to share, which she had found at the Red Cross office. Unfortunately, she had nothing else to give them.

One of the twins took the present and said, "Thank you."

She gave both of them a hug and reminded them, "You'll have to share the present, all right."

They nodded positively, and both scrambled to open the present. Katarina watched them for a little while then returned to the table with a heavy heart. She sat on the wooden bench with her back turned away from the table.

"Katarina, pour yourself a glass of wine," Manda suggested, showing her the one she was drinking.

"You what? That's exactly what I need right now," she agreed and turned to the table. Her eyes caught dozens of wine bottles there. "Wow! So much wine. Where did Marko get it?"

"The farmer that Marko works for donated the wine."

"Oh, that was nice of him," Katarina complimented and proceeded to pour herself a glass of white wine.

Suddenly, little Josipa came rushing to the table and sat on the bench beside Katarina. "Mama, can I have my cake now?" she asked, looking at Manda who was still busy with Franko.

Sipping on her wine, Katarina inquired, "Manda, is there something I can help you with?"

"Yes, thanks for asking," Manda replied and handed her a small plate with a piece of cake. "Feed this to Josipa. I don't want her to get all messy."

"Sure." Katarina took the plate, filled the spoon with cake, and said, "Here, open your mouth, babe."

"No! I'm not a baby! Give the spoon to me. I want to feed myself," she yelled. "I'm a big girl!"

"Yes, I know you are, but Mama wants me to feed you so you won't mess your beautiful dress. If you make a mess, next time you'll have to stay home."

"Oh, I guess it's all right then," Josipa acknowledged and opened her mouth.

Suddenly, a tall dark-haired woman came to the table. Katarina knew who she was but said nothing.

"Is everything all right in here?" the woman asked, looking at Manda.

"Yes, Rose," Manda replied. "Did you meet Katarina, Leo's wife?"

No, I didn't," Rose said and extended her hand to Katarina. "It's nice to meet you."

"It's my pleasure to meet you too, Rose. You have two handsome boys," Katarina complimented and shook her hand with a smile.

"Yes I do, don't I? They are my sweethearts," Rose replied. "I wish I have something more to offer you, but you know how it is. We are all on the same boat in here, no money and no food to speak of. Naked pasta, macaroni, spaghetti, almost every day."

"We have nothing," Manda sighed. "The living conditions are thrushes, especially for the children. They don't get, not even a bare minimum of food. My children are losing weight, and if we don't get out of here soon, I don't know what's going to happen."

"You are right, Manda," Katarina agreed. "Unfortunately, the children are not just losing their weight, but also their lives. Many died throughout the year from yellow fever, dysentery, and other diseases that are mostly caused by dirty water and bad nutrition combined with other things."

Their conversation was interrupted when Marko whirled around with a full bottle of wine to fill their glasses. "Ladies, pass your glasses."

"Not for me, thanks," Katarina replied and covered her glass with her hand. "I have to work in the morning."

"Where're you working, Katarina?" Rose asked.

"At the infirmary."

"Oh, you are a nurse."

"Yes, I finished nursing school at home."

"Well, girls, I have go to check on my birthday boys," Rose said and strolled away.

Most of the early evening, Katarina spent mingling with Manda, Rose, and other women and chatting and playing with the children while Leo spent his time with the men. Later, all the children were taken to Rosa's friend across the hall and put to bed.

After that, the party became wild and noisy. People were singing and dancing, and many were showing the effects of having consumed too much wine as Marko kept making continuous rounds with a full bottle, filling the empty glasses to compensate for lack of food. Leo and Manda extended their glasses each time and drank glass after glass as fast as it was filled.

Katarina was growing concerned, so after Marko passed almost a dozen times, she looked at Manda and reminded her, "You shouldn't be drinking that much. You have children to take care of."

"Mind your own business and don't worry about me. I can handle myself," she snapped with a slur.

Katarina realized she'd already had one too many and retorted, "Fine," as she walked away. She mingled and passed the next hour or so chatting with the other women.

Then her attention was drawn to Leo, having fun drinking with his buddies and dancing with Manda. He was so drunk that he began openly flirting with her as if his wife wasn't there. Barely able to stand, Manda hadn't resisted but slobbered over Leo, and her hands were all over his body as they danced. As Katarina watched them, her eyes rolled in disgust and she squeezed her fist tighter and tighter ready to lunge at them for making a mockery out of her, but she didn't want to make a scene. Instead, she tried to pretend she wasn't bothered by them, but her body told a different story.

About that time, Lina walked over and embraced her. "Wow! Your husband and Manda are having a lot of fun," Lina commented, looking at the flirtatious scene.

"Aren't they?" Katarina gnarled as heat flamed in her cheeks. "And things are getting worse by the minute. Just look at them: they're out of their minds, making a spectacle of themselves. I've never seen my husband drink that much before. I don't think he knows what he's doing."

"If I were you, I'd be more concerned about what's going on between Manda and Leo," Lina replied, still gazing at them flirting with each other.

"What do you mean? Nothing's going on!" Katarina stressed, realizing she told Lina too much.

"Well, look closely, my friend," Lina smirked. "I wouldn't call that nothing. Aren't you jealous?"

"Of course not," she answered and turned away to hide her anger.

Then, almost as if on a cue, her husband came over to his wife without a word, grabbed her hand, pulled her abruptly against his body, and began to dance.

Katarina felt her blood pressure rise and her heart pounded in response to Leo's aggressive and ridiculous manner. She gazed at him and wanted to shout, "What's wrong with you! Stop horsing around!" Instead, she gently suggested, "Let's go home, my love."

Leo shook her violently by the shoulders. "Who the hell do you think I am? Your puppet! If you want to go to sleep, go. I'm not leaving just yet!" he shouted, slurring his words. Then he pushed his wife aside and reeled toward the table with the wine.

A sudden hush fell over the room and the crowd stopped dancing, their eyes were pointed at her. Katarina stood there embarrassed, wishing she could disappear in a thin air. The awkward moment ended with snickers as the partygoers watched Manda stagger to the table and place her hand on Leo's shoulder.

"Don't worry. I'll take good care of you. Here, have one on me," she giggled, pouring him a glass of wine, even though she spilled half of it on the table.

Katarina felt somewhat relieved that the eyes of the crowd were no longer pointed at her and disappeared to the back of the room. The crowd resumed dancing; Leo and Manda drank their wine and joined the others on the dancing floor and continued flirting.

As Katarina watched from the back in dismay, her face flushed red and her heart was ready to burst. The sharp stabbing pain in her chest wouldn't let go. These were the first pangs of jealousy she ever experienced, and the only thing she could do was to stare in disbelief at Manda and Leo and wonder what was wrong with her. Why did Leo like Manda more than her? She stood still like she was glued to the floor, too ashamed to move.

Marko noticed tension in Katarina's face and approached her. "Don't worry," he said, placing his hand on her shoulder, wanting to calm her down. "They're both so drunk. They don't know what they're doing, but I'll talk to them."

She glanced at Marko but said nothing. It was all she could do to hold back the tears that welled in her eyes from bursting out. But her glare at Leo that said, 'I'll choke you, my love!' hadn't moved an inch.

Lina, who was dancing, returned to Katarina's side when the music stopped and, with a deep sigh, asked, "You're willing to let them do that to you, are you? What's with you, my friend?"

"You think I'm happy about it? Can you see they're both drunk? Neither one knows what they are doing. What can I do? Make a bigger scene than it already is," Katarina said, frowning.

"You're a fool, Katarina," Lina hissed through her clenched teeth. "If you believe this is only from the alcohol."

"But, of course, it is," she said stubbornly, Katarina wouldn't admit, not even to Lina, that her heart ached each time she cast her eyes upon them dancing and carrying on. She felt betrayed by her best friend and degraded by her own husband. Embarrassing as it was, Katarina was determined to keep her dignity and not let others see her pain.

Lina picked up on her emotion and saw through her facade. She understood how horrible Katarina felt and realized her provocative words hadn't done her much good either. She wanted to do something to uplift Katarina's spirit and take her mind off the situation, but what?

Suddenly she pulled her toward her and said, "Let's dance, my friend."

"Please, Lina," Katarina protested. "I'm not in the mood, all right," and tried to push her away.

Before she could free herself, Lina swirled her around and said, "It will do you some good," and swirled again and whispered to her ear. "You can't fool me, you know. Why don't you talk to me? Maybe I can help."

Katarina glanced at her. "I don't need help." Just when she started to calm down and her shakiness disappeared, the music stopped.

"I have to go, but if you feel like talking, you know where to find me," Lina said.

"All right, I'll see you tomorrow at work," Katarina replied and walked her to the door.

After Lina left, Katarina leaned against the wall and mumbled to herself, "Lina was right, I do feel more relaxed now." Her eyes instantly darted toward her husband and Manda's flirtation scene, which was still going on.

As the night wore on, however, Katarina's calmness disappeared. Her heart was ready to explode with jealousy and anger, and it became harder to keep her emotion under control. She felt alone and unwanted.

"Coffee anyone?" Rose offered, holding a pot in her hand by the table.

"Yes! Thanks!" Everyone yelled and rushed forward to get coffee, except Katarina. It was too much for her. She couldn't take it anymore and slipped out the door, leaving Manda and Leo behind and ran home.

Their room was a cold, silent dungeon in the predawn morning. She could hear her heart drumming and her bones rattle as her body shivered. Tears slid down her cheeks. "How could they do that to me?" she thundered, throwing her purse and shoes into the corner and herself across the bed on top of the covering. Her body wouldn't stop shivering so she crawled under the blanket and grumbled, "Am I overreacting or is there something going on between my husband and Manda?" She lay there for what it seemed an eternity mulling over the possibility before the wine and fatigue finally closed her eyes.

That night, what little was left of it, she slept fitfully, dreaming that Leo went alone to Canada, leaving her behind.

She awoke in a sweat, trembling in panic. Her teary eyes darted over to Leo's side of the bed. He was sound asleep beside her. Relieved, *Thank God, he's here,* she sighed deeply. She wanted to be furious with him, but she just couldn't. The love she felt for him was too great. Besides, she took the dream as a sign and decided there and then not to mention his behavior at the party since she wasn't sure what was going on.

She glanced at her watch. "Oh my goodness, look at the time. I'll be late if I don't hurry," Katarina whispered to herself, leapt out of the bed, and dressed quickly.

Before rushing out into the chilly morning, Katarina walked over to her husband's totally still body stretched on the bed. "Oh, my love. What's happening with us?" she whispered, bending down to kiss him, but the strong smell of wine, coming from his mouth, choked her. *Phew*, she thought. "Yes. He drank too much and he didn't know what he was doing. Of course, he didn't," she mumbled under her breath, hurrying to work.

"Good morning," Matron Mateya said and startled Katarina as she flew into the infirmary. She paused at the door.

"Good morning to you too," Katarina replied, wondering, *What's she doing here?*

"Lina is down with a bad influenza. That's why I'm here this morning on my day off," Matron quickly answered the unspoken question in Katarina's mind.

"Oh, I'm very sorry that she's sick. She has been looking very tired lately," Katarina agreed, taking her raincoat off.

"Katarina, you'll have to take Lina's load today," Matron Mateya announced. "I hope you don't mind."

"Of course not." Katarina began her shift with assortment of the instruments. But with Lina's workload, she felt overwhelmed, knowing she had a few hellish days ahead of her. "Are you really sick, Lina? Or you had one too many last night," Katarina muttered and took a deep breath, wishing Lina was there.

Even though she forgave her husband for his behavior the night before, she couldn't keep it off her mind and found it difficult to concentrate. Jealousy and anger raged inside her, and it interfered with her work so it took her longer to finish hers and Lina's load.

The long awaited day shift ended, Katarina was lucky that nothing out of ordinary hadn't happen. Leo was still in bed, nursing his hangover and feeling sorry for himself when she arrived home.

"I'm glad to see you, darling," Leo said as she entered. His wife glanced at him with wide eyes, but said nothing.

"I can see you're angry with me for getting drunk," he said as he pulled himself to a sitting position. She sat calmly on the small stump and turned her head toward the window and was silent.

But Leo saw through her mask and realized she wasn't buying it, and he had to do more to convince her. "You must think I'm stupid to drink myself into a stupor last night," he persisted, fingering his short blond hair nervously.

Heat flashed in Katarina's face and bitter bile rose up in her throat, choking her. She shot a fake smile at him, overriding the shrieking protest of her conscience and didn't reply. *Unbelievable!* she reflected. He was not apologizing for his contemptible behavior toward her, but acting like nothing had happened.

"What's wrong?" he asked.

Her suspicious brown eyes kept on casting glances at him as she wasn't sure whether he really didn't remember or was trying to hide behind the wine. More confused than ever, she huddled on her seat, her thoughts marching dizzily in a tight circle of shame, misery, anger, and betrayal as she pulled in a deep breath, feeling like a fool.

He noticed her glimpses from under his eyebrows and asked, "Why are you so upset? After all, it was only a party."

"I have a headache," she replied finally. Leo didn't say any more about it as though he were glad to be out of an unwanted discussion.

*Just as well,* she mused, unsure whether she would be able to handle herself if he continued the subject. She felt like a bubble, ready to burst and wanting to scream. "I'm going to pick up supper," Katarina stood up, patted her husband on the shoulder, and hurried out the door.

"Great! Now she talks," Leo groaned and lay down, pulling the blanket over his body.

At the cafeteria, Katarina saw Viktor at the door coming in. "Oops! Where you're rushing?" he asked as he almost ran into her.

"Home. Where else?"

"Where's Leo?"

"In bed, healing his hangover. We were at our next door neighbor, celebrating his two sons' birthdays. My husband had a few too many."

"What's for supper?"

"Spaghetti without meat."

"Will they ever give us anything else?"

"Yes, but not in here. See you later, Viktor," she said and left.

On the way, she passed by the canteen and grumbled, "Maybe I should stop and get some vegetables for soup." She knew soups were good for hangovers from her nursing training, but she wasn't sure her husband deserved her attention at the moment. Nonetheless, she bought two carrots and celery for the soup and two apples for a snack. She had tomatoes and potatoes that she bought at the market in the city at home.

"Here is the supper," she informed her husband in a soft voice and placed the mess tin of food on the table.

"My stomach is upset," Leo whined from the bed. "I don't know if I can eat."

She moved across the room, pulled out the other vegetables, and began to clean them and prepared to cook the soup. He watched her peel the carrots and potatoes and realized Katarina was making soup for him. *She forgave me,* he mused, smirking. The whole evening passed in eerie silence. She didn't speak nor did he.

For the next week, Leo made sure he behaved nicely toward his wife and spoke to her as if nothing had happened. But she wasn't eager to talk to her husband and spoke only if it was absolutely necessary. Her work kept Katarina busy now that she had to handle hers and Lina's load and allowed her to avoid Leo for hours.

When his wife was at home, Leo avoided talking about things he thought weren't worth discussing or that he didn't want to talk about, besides he wasn't prepared to accept responsibility for what he had done to her at the party. Moreover, for him, the party night became a distant memory, forgotten through the unspoken words that passed between them.

But for Katarina, it lingered silently in her heart and her thoughts, eating away at her. The extra work and her marital problems began to show: her dark eyes looked bleak and drawn inside their sockets. She was exhausted.

Finally, at the end of the week, Lina returned to work. She immediately noticed something was not quite right with Katarina. Lina wanted to ask her right there and then but realized it was too private so she left until lunchtime.

"You look terrible. Are you sick?" was the first thing Lina asked as Katarina entered into the small room for lunch.

"Hello, you too, Lina," Katarina replied shrilly. "Oh, I must have been sick, for I kept up with your work and mine for a week. You think that was easy?"

"You can't fool me, you know that. Come, come out with it," Lina demanded, realizing Katarina was probably still suffering from the embarrassment and betrayal of the friend and her husband at the party.

Katarina looked at her and hesitated for a second. "It's nothing," she replied and quickly turned, wanting to get away.

Lina gently grasped her hand, signaling she cared. "Wait," she said. "I can see you're worried."

Katarina felt trapped. She turned toward Lina, the lines of her face were taut with the shadow of anger. "You know, to tell the truth, I don't know what's real. Anymore. Yeah sure. I see little things transpiring between my husband and Manda whenever they are together, but they don't amount to much of anything. The only thing I know for sure is that Manda has changed. Any worries I have must be from my overactive imagination, that's all!" she shouted, angry at herself for even thinking there might be something happening.

"Oh, I don't know about that!" Lina responded with a dubious look. "She changed all right. I've heard that Manda has been flirting with other married men around the camp."

"No! I don't believe that," Katarina jumped to Manda's defense. "She has changed. I give you that. But to believe what you are saying is preposterous."

"Is it? How do you know what Manda's all about, hmm? How much do you really know about her?"

Katarina looked at her, puzzled. "Well, not much. Manda doesn't talk about herself, so I only know what she told me in Trieste. She said she came from Germany and she and the children are heading to Australia where her husband is waiting for them."

"That's what she told you, but is that the real truth?" Lina asked.

"I don't know. Do you know something that I don't? Do you?" Katarina yelled, defiant.

"No! But—"

"But nothing!" Katarina interrupted. "I don't want trouble in my marriage, and certainly, I don't want to be left behind because of it. As far as I'm concerned, they were both drunk and that's that, the end of the story. If you want to know, Leo doesn't even remember what happened that night."

"What a sneaky ploy. He's trying to make you feel guilty."

"You know what?" Katarina snapped. "I don't want to hear another word about it. I'm sick and tired of all this." She was furious with Lina for reminding her of the agony of that night; she stood up and wanted to leave.

"All right, all right. Sit down, I'll stop," Lina promised, at least for now, and glanced at her, adding. "This autumn is terrible! Too much rain." They both chuckled and finished their lunch and their shift on friendly terms again.

Lina could almost feel Katarina's pain as they worked side by side, day after day, but she knew she couldn't do much to help her friend except be there for her. She was determined to keep her promise and stay out of Katarina's business, especially that concerning Leo and Manda.

Linda would glance at her friend and say to herself. *She will just have to find out the hard way.*

One evening, after washing her clothes for work in the laundry room, Katarina returned to the room to find Manda and Leo sitting beside each other on their bed. Manda's hair was messy, and she quickly pulled her hand away from Leo's lower body and jumped to her feet. "I have to go," she muttered and headed toward the door in a frenzy.

"You don't have to leave on my account, a maid of honor. I'll be going to work soon," Katarina said sarcastically, pretending to have noticed nothing.

"Yeah, Manda, don't leave. You just got here," Leo agreed and sat on the stool at the table. But Manda rushed out anyway.

Katarina's heart hammered. She was terrified that Manda and Leo were really having an affair, but she didn't want to ask any questions for fear of being wrong. Barely able to control herself, she grabbed her purse and wanted to leave.

"It's still too early. Where are you going?" Leo asked then; realizing she was upset, he added, "There's nothing going on between Manda and me."

She had had enough of everything and threw him an angry, hurt look. "I have things to do," she said and ran out the door. So typical of him to deny and deny, but this time, Leo would have to do much better than that. "Lina was right. I don't know Manda at all. In that matter, I probably know just as much about my husband," Katarina muttered. "Either I'm losing my mind or the things I'm seeing is the truth."

The question still remained in Katarina's mind. "Are Leo and Manda having an affair?" No matter how much she tried to deny to herself, she seemed to come to a full circle, each time she thought about it.

Her head was in disarray. Only one thing she was sure of, her jealousy was growing inside her and she couldn't bear looking at her husband at this point. "I never thought I would be so happy that my night shift is here," she muttered, striding to the infirmary. There was little light, heavy clouds were rolling, obscuring the moon that was now up, and threatening with rain. "I better hurry otherwise I might get wet," she whispered and quickened her pace.

Things hadn't been right in Katarina's marriage since they arrived at the camp in Capua. *Is it Manda behind the trouble she was having with Leo*? she wondered, entering into the infirmary.

Except for the nurse, Emma, in her office, the infirmary was empty and quiet, and Katarina hoped it would remain that way because she didn't feel very energetic. She took her raincoat of and hung it on the hanger, put her smock on, strolled across the infirmary, and reflected. The shift she once hated, she now couldn't wait to start, and she hoped the night would bring some sense to the chaos in her mind. She glanced out through the window and noticed the downpour of rain. "Thank God, I made it before this," she whispered, watching the rain splashing at the window.

Suddenly, Lina burst through the door, "Oh, hell. We're going to be flooded. It's pouring out there!"

"You're here, thank God," startled, Katarina noted the gloom on her face.

"On a dreary, wet, cold night like this," Lina chuckled. "I wish I could be in my bed, not here, thank you very much." She shook her head as she closed her umbrella.

"Yes, I know," Katarina agreed. "I got here just before the downpour. I've never seen so much rain as I have here in Italy. It seems like it's raining all the time. But I'm glad to be here," she blurted, rushing to the sink to start the work.

Lina glanced at her puzzled and paused for a second or two. "Oh, why is that?"

"Nothing, nothing. Don't mind me."

Suspecting there was more to it, Lina walked to her and said, "I know I promised, but I have to ask, what's nothing?"

Katarina paused, fighting with her inner self to keep it hidden, yet dying to tell someone. "I grant you one thing, Lina. Manda had definitely changed, the kindness of her usual expression that I knew had been wiped out and replaced by bitterness."

"And so, tell me what I don't know?" Lina stared at her face, demanding more.

"Well, I found Leo and Manda together in our room," she said and went on to describe the scene she saw before leaving for work. "Leo said there is nothing going on, and I think he's telling the truth," she lied.

"Oh, that dog, he hurt you again!" Lina hissed through her teeth, not very pleased, and added, "You, my friend, couldn't see the truth if it hit you in the face."

Katarina glanced at her and was ashamed of what she had disclosed, so she turned to her work and said nothing more.

The peaceful infirmary turned chaotic, quickly when two women with babies in their arms burst through the door, shouting, "Help! Nurse, help!"

Katarina welcomed the interruption and rushed with Lina toward them and each grabbed a baby. "What's wrong with the baby?" Katarina asked its mother.

"He has been vomiting, has watery stools with blood, and has high fever, and wouldn't take anything by mouth."

As soon as both babies were examined and they took note of everything, Lina ran to the office to notify the Italian nurse Emma with the findings and explained to her what they are facing. After, it was up to Nurse Emma to call the doctor.

"These two babies had been in here before," Lina reminded her and stressed. "They are in a bad, bad condition."

Nurse Emma opened their files and quickly read through. "Dysentery, right?"

"I believe so."

"I'll call the doctor immediately," Supervisor Emma said and grabbed the phone. Lina returned to the examining room.

Katarina tried to keep both babies comfortable as much as she could while Lina was gone, but the baby kept on having small watery stools with blood and vomiting occasionally, it wasn't easy. When Lina tried to enter the examining room, the two mothers blocked her at the door. "What's wrong with our babies?" both mothers asked, trembling with fear.

"I'm afraid both of the babies are suffering from dysentery," Lina said, straight out.

"Oh my god, I thought this disease was healed," one mother screamed.

"I'm very sorry. But now you have to be patient and let us help your babies," Lina said and quickly entered.

"Lina, I'm glad you are here. These babies are getting worse by the minute. Here take this one, he is a little better. The other one, I don't know. I'm afraid to even say it, but I don't think he will make it through the night if we don't take him to the hospital soon," Katarina exclaimed with a deep sigh.

"Yeah, I can see. He's barely breathing. I wish I could take him into the hospital right now," Lina agreed. "But I can't do that. So let's do what we can." She filled two baby bottles with special water called electrolytes.

"Here," Lina handed one to her coworker. "I will offer fluids to one baby, and you do to the other as often as you can or as often it will take."

"Good thought," Katarina said and took the bottle and began her mission impossible. While the nurses inside were fighting to keep the babies alive, their mothers were in agony outside the door. They were crying and prying aloud when the doctor and Nurse Emma arrived.

"Doctor! Doctor, save our babies! Please!" both mothers screamed.

"He'll do his best, but you have to step aside," Nurse Emma said. "Come on, ladies," and pulled them a side to let the doctor enter the examining room.

As soon as the doctor examined the babies, he ordered immediate transfer to the hospital. "Lina, go get the ambulance car ready and hurry!"

"Yes, Doctor," Lina said and ran out for the ambulance car.

The doctor turned to Katarina and asked, "Did any one of the babies take any fluids?"

"This baby hasn't taken much, maybe a few drops, the other one took a little more," Katarina answered and continued to offer fluids to both of them while Lina was gone.

"What's happening?" both mothers shouted after Lina, tears running down their cheeks.

Upon Lina's return, she explained, "We are taking your babies to the city hospital where they are going to get better care than here. The infirmary isn't equipped to handle cases like these. You can come with us too," Lina suggested, hurrying into the examining room.

They bundled the babies and gave them to their mothers to carry them into the ambulance car. Katarina sat with the mothers and babies at the back of the ambulance car to keep eyes on them.

Lina drove off in a jiffy into the dark and wet night. It took them only fifteen minutes, and they were in the emergency room at the hospital. Lina and Katarina took the babies from the mother's arms and carried them into the emergency room.

"What do we have here?" the emergency people asked.

"Two very sick babies with dysentery," Lina said as they handed them the precious cargo.

"Take good care of them," Katarina said as they walked out.

The mothers outside the emergency room sobbed in silence, holding each other in an embrace. "Would you like a lift home?" Katarina asked, looking at the mothers' drained faces.

"Oh no. We'll stay here close to our babies," they said, wiping their eyes.

"We have to go back to work, take care of each other. And I hope your babies will be all right," Lina said as they were leaving.

They jumped to the car and rushed back. The infirmary was empty. The doctor was gone, and Nurse Emma was locked in her office. After two hours of frantic work with the babies, the infirmary was peaceful again.

"Let's have a short break and then we can clean up this mess," Lina said, placing a fresh pot coffee on the stove.

"Yeah, let's," Katarina agreed and sat down in a deep thought.

"Are you all right?" Lina asked, glancing at Katarina.

"Yes. But this is a first time I came across a person suffering with dysentery. Liquid bloody stool draining out of those babies' little rectums. It's horrible! It almost made me sick. Lina, do the babies with dysentery ever heal?"

Yes," she said and sat beside her. "They do, if you get help early, but here with all the pollutants, it's not easy. Dirty water, poor nutrition, poor hygiene, stress, drugs, alcohol, all these are the factors that play a big part in our lives and decide who will live and who will die. Many children and adults remain in here forever and some for a very long time because of the drug and alcohol abuses, and other diseases." She sighed and walked to the coffeepot.

"I don't mind telling you. When I saw those poor babies and the blood, I almost got sick," Katarina said, following Lina behind.

"My first encounter with dysentery was also a baby that later died. I was devastated." Lina remembered with tears in her eyes.

"I'm so sorry."

"Yeah, me too," Lina said as she handed Katarina a cup of coffee.

"Hmm! It's so good!" Katarina exclaimed, sipping at the hot cup.

Lina sipped on her cup and gazed out the window. Dawn was breaking over Capua, and the morning was quickly approaching. "We don't have much time. We have to hurry, there's still a lot of work to be done," she stressed.

"You're right, Lina," Katarina agreed, and they drank their coffee.

"I'll clean up the examining room, and, Katarina, you finish the instruments, which were left undone," Lina announced and rushed to her work.

"All right." Katarina walked to the sink to complete her task.

Just before their shift was over, the fathers of the babies walked to the infirmary. "Where are our wives and children?" one of the husbands asked, with panic in his voice.

"We took them to the city hospital during the night. The babies are very sick and they need to have special care," Katarina explained to the men.

"All right, thanks," the men said and rushed out. Lina and Katarina finally finished their first night shift of their set of five and were ready to go home.

Katarina paused at the door before going home. "What a night we had."

Yeah, I'm exhausted," Lina muttered, and they both walked out of the infirmary.

The weather hadn't changed: it was still drizzling with a continuous cold wind. On her way home, Katarina was so tired and couldn't wait to dive to her bed.

# A Hero

My hero is my grandma or what I like to call her Nona. My grandma is an amazing hero because of the things she accomplished in her lifetime. My grandma had 3 kids who she raised. My grandma`s husband died when he was 41 and it was a hard time for both my grandma, father and his siblings. My grandma never complained and always thought about the future. Even through the toughest times in her life she always stayed positive.

She always forgave people when they did the worst things. She consistently reminded me to be happy all the time. Sometimes it got annoying but it really paid off in the future. I tried to remind myself of her words over and over. Sometimes I put myself down over small things that I shouldn't even care about. Her words remind me to keep my head up. These words about being happy can really rub off on others.

My family is a very caring family and it`s because of her teachings to my dad and his 2 other siblings. My grandma never seeked attention in any sort of away. She lived her own life to her standards. No one told her how to live her life cause she already knew how to. She was a quiet person but I think I was the one who understood her. She told me ways to be happy and feel good about myself. She knew how to relate to my situations when others couldn`t.

She overcame many odds that stood in her way. She would smile and completely blow the negative distractions away. Sometimes it was impossible for me to believe she could do that without and complaining. With me I know that would be a challenge for me. Sometimes my confidence level can drop and it is difficult to face negativity. She made it look easy because she had an amazing amount of confidence inside of her.

She was a small lady with a massive heart and confidence. She would make you smile in rough times. It just came natural to her. She inspired me so much. When I think of her I just see a bright smile on her face. My grandma is a perfect example of a hero. Her self-esteem was full rates. She is a proactive person who could be herself everywhere. People judge all the time for actions or the way you speak or anything. But she never judged anyone ever. She saw everyone as a friend never an enemy. Some people see super heroes as the best example for a positive person. But, I see her as more than a super hero. I see her as an amazing women with the ability of herself to do anything she wanted. Life is difficult for everyone and she made it seem like she had no care in the entire world. That`s why I call my Nona a great hero that will always be remembered.

By: Jessica Djuranic: [redacted]

Jessica Djuranic

In Loving Memory of

KLAUDIA
DJURANIC

Born January 30, 1944
Crneloza, Croatia

Passed Away August 1, 2006
Calgary, Alberta, Canada

Age
62 years

PRAYER SERVICE
Pierson's Forest Lawn Chapel
4121 – 17 Avenue SE
Calgary, Alberta
Tuesday, August 8, 2006
at 8:00 p.m.

*Following the Interment, all are invited to a reception at the Church Hall*

FUNERAL MASS
will be celebrated at
Our Lady of M. Bistrica (Croatian)
Catholic Church
14680 Deer Ridge Drive SE
Calgary, Alberta
Wednesday, August 9, 2006
at 10:00 a.m.

CELEBRANT
Reverend Father Mladen Horvat

ORGANIST & SOLOIST
Colleen Reinhart

CASKET BEARERS
Robert Djuranic
Roger Djuranic
August Zec
Luciano Zec
Sean Barnes

INTERMENT
St. Mary's Cemetery
32 Avenue & Erlton Street SW
Calgary, Alberta

1972

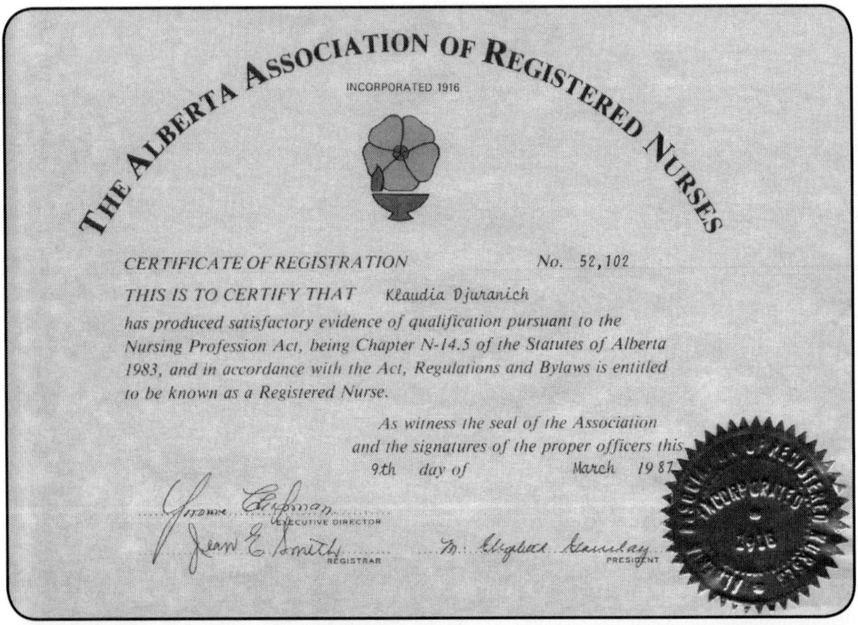

THE ALBERTA ASSOCIATION OF REGISTERED NURSES

INCORPORATED 1916

*CERTIFICATE OF REGISTRATION* *No.* 52,102

*THIS IS TO CERTIFY THAT* Klaudia Djuranich

*has produced satisfactory evidence of qualification pursuant to the Nursing Profession Act, being Chapter N-14.5 of the Statutes of Alberta 1983, and in accordance with the Act, Regulations and Bylaws is entitled to be known as a Registered Nurse.*

*As witness the seal of the Association and the signatures of the proper officers this* 9th *day of* March 1987

EXECUTIVE DIRECTOR

REGISTRAR

PRESIDENT

"You have to live through such things to believe them."

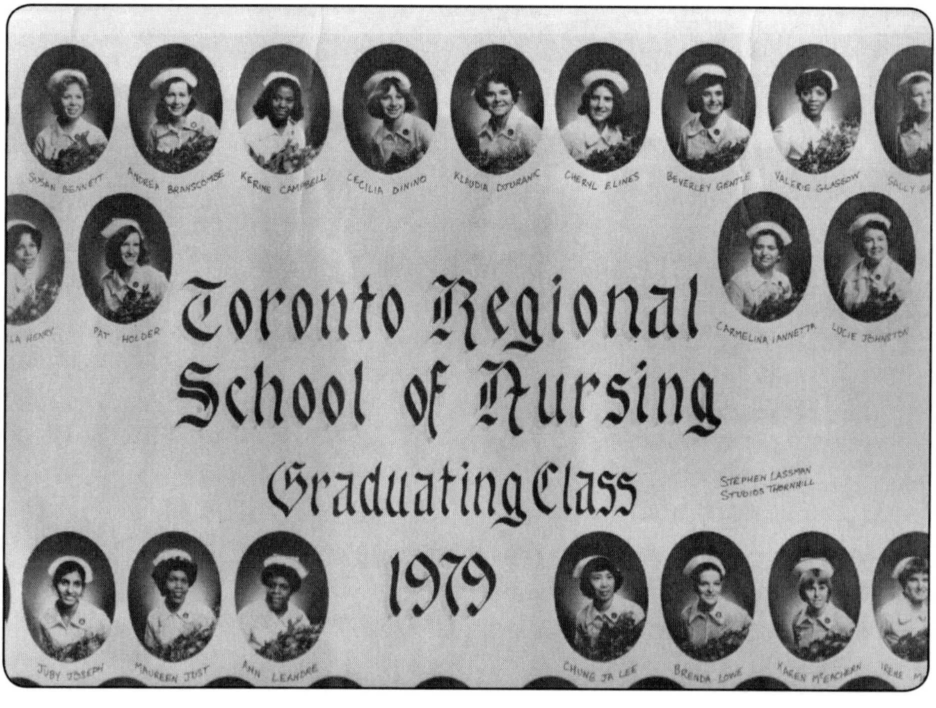

SUSAN BENNETT
ANDREA BRANSCOMBE
KERINE CAMPBELL
CECILIA DININO
KLAUDIA DZURANIC
CHERYL ELINES
BEVERLEY GENTLE
VALERIE GLASSOW
PAT HOLDER
CARMELINA IANNETTA
LUCIE JOHNSTON
Toronto Regional
School of Nursing
Graduating Class
1979
STEPHEN LASSMAN
STUDIOS THORNHILL
JUDY JOSEPH
MAUREEN JUST
ANN LEANDRE
CHUNG JA LEE
BRENDA LOWE
KAREN McEACHERN

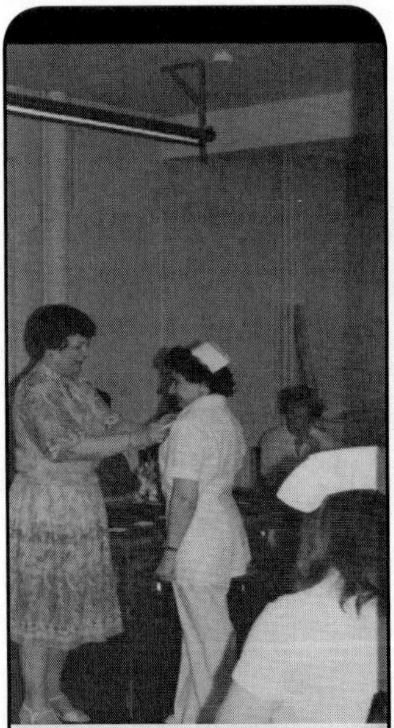

Graduating
Toronto School of Nursing

Practicum

Vera & Klaudia
relaxing after a long shift (6 West)
Holy Cross Hospital

Mother acting silly

School friend from Croatia.
"Toronto"

Graduating Picture

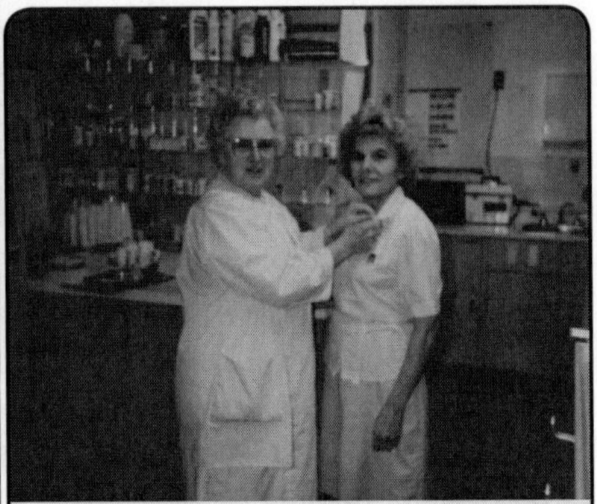

M$^{S}$G Head Nurse—Giving Klaudia a Nursing Pin

M$^{S}$G Retirement (Holy Cross Hospital)
Calgary, AB

Niagra Falls
Uncles & Mother
us children
Robert, Roger, Carolyn

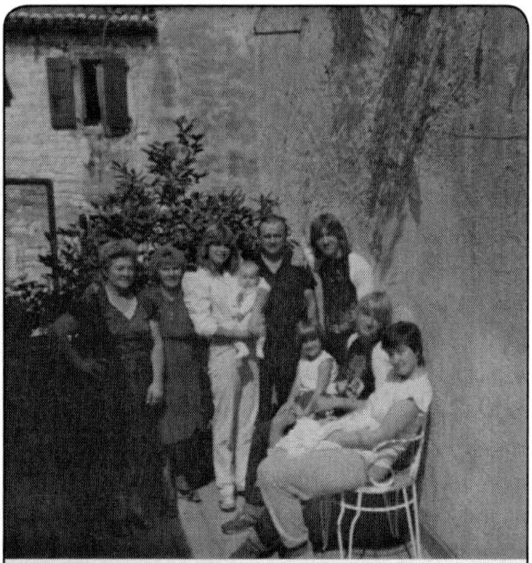

Umag, Croatia

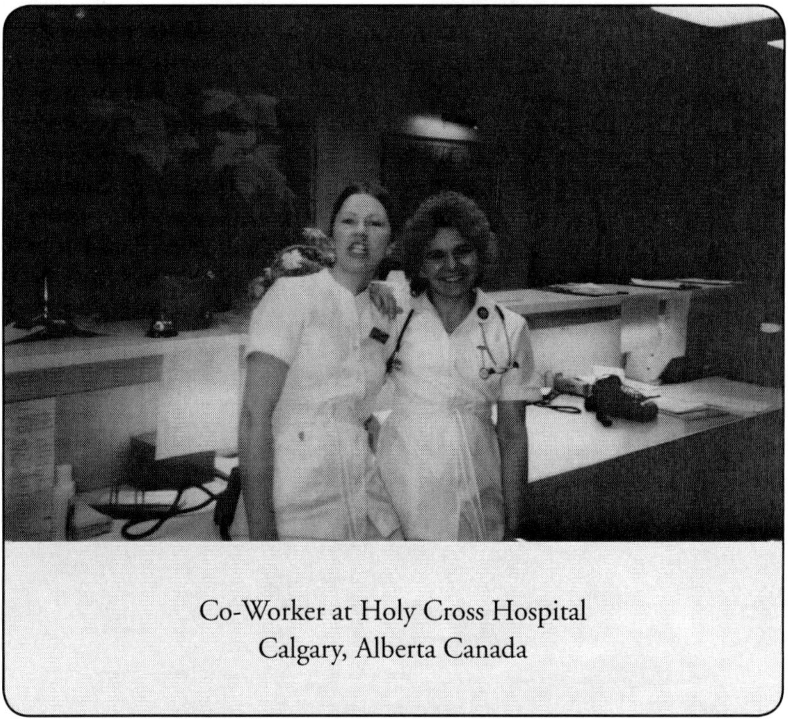

Co-Worker at Holy Cross Hospital
Calgary, Alberta Canada

Croatia, Umag
my mother and I

My Grade 9 Grad
and mother

Mother and I

Christmas
Calgary, AB

Mother, oldest brother
"Robert"
(Centre Island)
Toronto, Ontario

"Croatia"

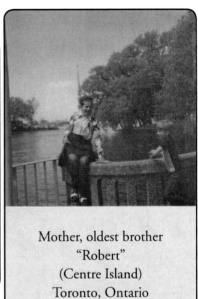

Banff, Calgary
AB.

Klaudia in middle.
She was in the hospital in Pula, Croatia

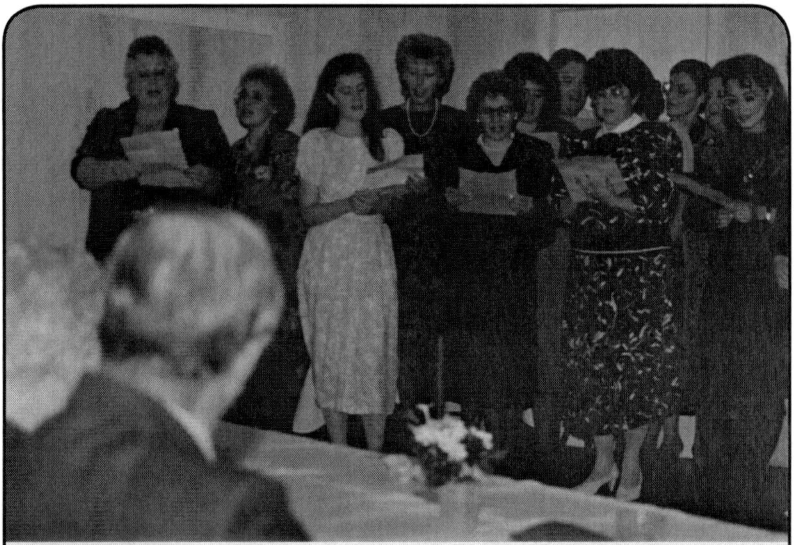

Mother with Nursing friends singing at the hospital.

Anniversary Mom & Dad

"Christmas"
"Toronto"

My Family (Toronto)

My Mom, Brothers and I

Klaudia
School
Friend

Klaudia
and
Father Ivan

Winnipeg, Manitoba

Josip & Klaudia
Winnipeg, Canada
Mom & Dad

Mother Writing Book
Journey to Freedom

Hospital Croatia, Pula

Going to Work

Robert's Mother in Law
and my Mother

Robert's Family

Roger's Family

Carolyn at Cochrane, Alberta CA 2012

# CHAPTER 15

The following few nights of their shift went by uneventfully. The weather hadn't changed; it was still raining off and on. The little river had risen within its banks and was ready to overflow and flood the camp.

As they began their fourth night shift, Lina glanced at Katarina. "We've been lucky the last few days. So far we didn't have any sick patients since the babies. We did have get Nurse Emma out of her cocoon," Lina chuckled.

"Who wants to go out on a mushy cold night like this?" Katarina smirked. "Even if I was sick, I wouldn't. Speaking of mushy. What do you think about the river? Will it explode and flood us all?"

"No! As far as can remember, it has never overflowed," Lina said.

Their reveries were interrupted just when they thought they would have another smooth night, a man in his thirties was brought into the infirmary by two friends. He was ragged, unshaven, confused, severely agitated, and had been vomiting occasionally. His body shivered, and his clothes were drenched as it was raining outside.

"What your name?" Katarina asked as she helped him change his wet clothes for dry ones she found in the infirmary closet, then she wrapped a blanket over his trembling body.

"Vojko," he replied through chattering teeth while chasing away imaginary creatures. He was barely able to say his name clearly, his words were so jumbled. Katarina realized she wouldn't be able to get the information she needed from him so she turned to his friends.

"Why did you bring Vojko to the infirmary?" she asked.

"He's been vomiting for a few days and doesn't eat. He trembles a lot. Then he scared us by shouting, 'Keep those snakes away from me.'

"'What snakes?' I asked. 'There are no snakes here.' I told him, but he kept shouting as if the snakes were attacking him," one of the men explained. "That's why we brought him here. We think there is something wrong with him."

"Has he been drinking?" Katarina asked. She could smell the distinct odor of alcohol on Vojko's breath and skin.

The friends looked at each other and chuckled. "Who? Vojko! He's always drinking, except for the last few days when he has been sick," one of them said.

"What does that have to do with anything?" the other man asked. "We'd just like to know what's wrong with Vojko. He's not going to die, is he?"

"No, he's not dying. Vojko is having a delirium tremens," Katarina said and glanced at Lina. That was the cue for Lina to go inform Nurse Emma.

"Delirium? What's that?" both Vojko's friends asked in unison, and chuckled.

Katarina looked at them. "Sorry, please forgive me. Your friend is in alcohol withdrawal. When he stopped drinking for a few days, the level of alcohol in his blood dropped and he became ill," she explained.

Then she proceeded to inject Vojko with a shot of vitamin B complex, which was used as a standard procedure for alcohol withdrawal. As she pulled the needle out of his buttock, she glanced at his friends. "This is the only thing I can do for Vojko until the doctor arrives and examines him. Although I'm not sure if this will help him much. He seems to be a very sick man," Katarina said and remained by Vojko's side.

The doctor arrived accompanied by Supervisor Emma. They both worked on the man, with assistance from Lina and Katarina, but they couldn't stabilize him. His condition hadn't improved, but got worse. He vomited more often, his body shook, and his mind was out of reach.

Finally, the doctor said, "The man needs intravenous therapy and psychiatric counseling, and for that, he must be transferred immediately to the hospital in Naples."

Katarina and Lina glanced at each other. Their eyes yelled, "Oh, no! Not that far! Not this week!" But they said nothing. The doctor wrote an order for a sedative to give Vojko and left; Supervisor Emma walked him to the door.

Katarina gave the injection to the patient and prepared him for the trip while Lina got the ambulance car for their journey to Naples.

As soon as Katarina came out of examining room, the two friends waiting asked, "What's happening, is Vojko all right?"

"No, he isn't. Lina and I are taking him to the hospital in Naples. The infirmary isn't equipped to handle cases like these," Katarina said.

"Can we go with him?"

"No, but you could help me get him into the ambulance," Katarina said as she placed a blanket over his shoulder to protect him from rain.

"Of course, we'll help," one of the friends said.

Lina drove the vehicle to the infirmary door and came in to help Katarina. The two friends took Vojko under his arms and led him out into the ambulance car.

"We'll come tomorrow to the infirmary to check on him, how he's doing," the friends said and walked away.

"Yes, you do that," Katarina said as she and Lina buckled him securely onto the stretcher and threw another blanket over him as he was still shivering and fighting imaginary snakes. They both hoped he would settle down once the sedative had time to work as they leapt out, closed, and secured the back door of the ambulance car.

"How far is the city Naples from here?" Katarina asked as they mounted the front seats of the ambulance.

"Oh, about an hour's drive, but because of the weather, it could take us up to two hours," Lina answered as she started the engine and took off.

Passing through the camp gate, she said, "Let's go this way. This is a shortcut. My favorite road. We'll get there much quicker." And she turned onto a dark muddy dirt road. Katarina looked at Lina with a question mark in her eyes.

"Don't worry, my friend. I know the road well. I've driven this way many times." She smirked and pressed on the gas.

"Don't get me wrong. I'm not questioning your driving ability, but I'm worried about the weather and the patient," Katarina replied and turned toward the window to look out.

"Are you saying that I don't care about the patient?"

"No. Of course not. I'm sorry," Katarina apologized. "It didn't even enter my mind."

"Then what did you mean?"

"I don't know what I meant. There hasn't been a single car along this road since we left the camp. It scared me a little."

"So what, it's been only twenty minutes since we left the camp. I know my way," Lina retorted, annoyed. As to prove her point, a string of car lights suddenly appeared in the distance. Keeping a strong grip on the steering wheel, she threw a pointed glance at Katarina with a huge grin on her face that said, "I told you so."

Katarina could almost hear her thinking it. Feeling foolish, she forced a smile and turned toward the window to stare out at the darkness and decided from then on to mind her own business.

After a short silence, a loud moan coming from the back of the ambulance broke the muteness between them. Katarina and Lina looked at each other as the patient began to thrash about on the stretcher, fighting the demons inside of him. Katarina stepped over her seat and walked to the back of the ambulance to check on him. "He's withdrawing further, his symptoms are getting worse."

"We can't stop now! There is nothing we can do for him except taking him to the hospital as fast as we can!" Lina yelled and stepped on the gas. Katarina returned to her seat and continued monitoring him from there.

After a short episode, the patient settled back to sleep. "Thank God!" Katarina sighed in relief.

The drive to Naples took more than two hours as the rain and mud slowed them down. When they finally approached the city, the morning showed as a pale wash of light. "Wow! Look at the fog, it blanketed the city," Katarina commented.

"Well, at least the rain stopped," Lina noticed.

"Yes, I can see, but look at the wind and its intensity," Katarina pointed; the wind whipped the boats that were tied to the dock, tossing them about on the tidal waves. "Goodness, this wind is treacherous," Katarina voiced, staring at them as they passed by the shore of the Tyrrhenian Sea.

"Yes, I know. I've seen it before," Lina replied holding on to the wheel tightly as the wild wind played with the ambulance car. It was so strong it shook the patient awake.

"Is the hospital far away from here?" Katarina asked, observing Vojko thrashing and groaning in the back of the ambulance.

"We'll be there soon," Lina replied without taking her eyes off the road.

"If the wind doesn't blow us and the city to kingdom come."

Lina chuckled. "This city has survived many disasters and it will this one too."

"What do you mean?" Katarina asked puzzled and wanting to know more.

"Well, on each side of Naples, the earth fumes and grumbles, reminding us that all this beauty was born of calamity. Toward Sorrento, Vesuvius smolders sleepily over the ruins of Herculaneum and Pompeii, while west of Naples, beyond Posillipo, the craters of Solfatara spew steaming gases. And near the city are the dark, deep waters of Lago d'Averno, legendary entrance to Hades. How you like that?" Lina said proudly.

"Oh, wow! You really learned Italian history," Katarina commented and added, "With these reminiscences of death and destructions so close at hand, it's no wonder that the southerner in general, and the Neopolitan in particular, take no chance plunging enthusiastically into the task of living each moment to its fullest."

"You are exactly right! People here always bustle. And you take time to visit this city and the surrounding area, you'll find it beautiful just as I have," Lina replied and halted the ambulance car in front of the hospital. "We are here." They both jumped out of the vehicle.

"I would like to see more of the Naples one day," Katarina said as they were taking out the patient. He was slightly calmer, although he still shivered, but that was probably part of his illness. They got Vojko out and into the hospital.

"You help him to the waiting room and I'll take the papers to the admitting nurse," Lina said and walked away. Katarina took the patient under his arm and walked slowly to the waiting room and helped him sit down on the chair.

Ten minutes later, Lina returned and they were about leave when the admitting nurse came running in panic. "I can't admit this patient!" she yelled, waving with the papers.

"Why not?" Lina asked, puzzled.

"The doctor from Capua has to make arrangements for this patient to be admitted, and he hasn't."

"I believe the doctor made arrangements," Katarina suggested.

"I'm sorry, but we don't have any papers and instructions signed by the doctor for this patient and no one called us. So, as I said, we can't admit him," the nurse advised and handed them the papers back before she walked away.

Katarina turned to her coworker. "Now what?"

"We'll have to take him back, what else?"

"You mean to tell me that we drove almost hundred kilometers in this weather for nothing?"

A sense of momentary helplessness settled over them. Then Lina ran after the admitting nurse and screamed, "There's no way in hell I'm driving the patient back to the camp."

The admitting nurse glared back. "You can't leave him here," she snorted and disappeared through a door marked No Admittance. Almost as if on a cue, the patient became violent and started to thrash about and foam at the mouth. His eyes turned upward showing only the whites of his eyes.

"Help! Help me! The patient is having a seizure!" Katarina yelled. After she helped him down to the floor, the only thing she could find around was his belt. She quickly pulled it out and stuck it between his teeth to prevent his tongue to be bitten.

Both the admitting nurse and Lina came running back. They helped hold him until he settled down again. "How long did the seizure last?" the admitting nurse asked.

"It lasted two minutes," Katarina replied, helping Vojko to the chair.

"The patient has to be seen by the doctor," Lina said, looking at the admitting nurse.

"Yes, of course. Let's take him to the emergency room," she ordered and walked ahead. Lina grabbed a wheelchair and they wheeled the patient to the room.

After waiting an hour, the doctor examined him and gave him an injection for the seizure and another sedative. "This will be enough to get him back to the camp," the doctor said as he pulled the needle out of his buttock.

"You can't send him back, Doctor. The man is very sick," Lina argued.

The doctor took another look at him before he sent him on his way. "He's fine to travel back to the camp," he reaffirmed his decision.

No amount of argument helped, Katarina and Lina had to take him back to the camp. As they walked Vojko out to the ambulance car, Katarina hissed furiously, "Holy God, I can't believe the hospital wouldn't admit him after all this."

Lina said nothing, just smirked, her teeth grinding.

It was almost midday and it began to rain again by the time they settled and secured Vojko in the ambulance. "I hope he sleeps through the trip," Katarina said, locking the back door of the ambulance car.

"We've lost all this time, for what?" Lina yelled as she climbed behind the wheel and slammed the door behind her, also angry at the hospital for not taking the patient in.

"Yeah, and no food, and I'm so hungry. We should have asked the admitting nurse to give us lunch or at least two coffees," Katarina growled as she settled into the passenger seat. Both were angry and famished and neither had any money to buy food.

Lina gripped the steering wheel as if to strangle it, pressed on the gas, and silently began driving back and let the anger filled the void.

Still upset, ten minutes later, she yelled, "How dare they play with people like this! They threw us out like a sack of potatoes with no regard for human life! I just about had it! I'll not stay on the side and just watch! I'll do something next time!"

Katarina stared at her friend, never seeing her so angry, and wondered where that anger came from. "I don't understand what you're talking about."

"The refugees are supposed to be fed, protected, medically insured so they can get help they need. What do they get? Nothing! Most of the refugees are ill-fed, their rooms are cold during the winter. There is no hot water and not enough soap to wash. Our babies are dying almost daily from dysentery. The camp is filthy with drugs and alcohol. And when something like this happens, it hits me hard." Lina didn't say much about what she knew, she wasn't sure if she can trust Katarina.

"Is there something anyone can do?" still staring at her friend, Katarina asked.

"Yes, there's plenty, but nobody wants to get involved," Lina quizzed as they drove along the muddy hilly road and watched the rain driven by the strong wind lashing against the windshield blurring their view.

Suddenly, Katarina noticed something in a beam of the ambulance light and shrilled, "Stop!" pointing ahead.

Lina took a deep breath and pressed on the brakes, full force, bringing the wheels to a screeching halt. "What's wrong with you? Do you have a death wish or something?" she shouted, gazing at her.

"Look, isn't he lovely?" Katarina commented, pointing at a beautiful wild gray-white rabbit that was spotlighted by the ambulance headlights.

The rabbit stood in the middle of the road on his hind legs and stared at the wheels.

They glanced at each other, and Lina burst into laughter. "Oh, that poor little bunny, it's all wet," she noticed. "It's probably scared, looking for food and a place to hide from cold and rain."

"There's certainly not much food left in the fields for them these days. He must be starving, just like we are," Katarina replied. They both watched and waited while the rabbit shook his hind legs and slowly hopped to safety.

"While I'm glad, you were able to stop in time, part of me wished I could eat it," Katarina blurted, almost able to smell Mama cooking it.

"Katarina!" Lina replied and stepped on the gas.

"What? I'm hungry. Besides, eating a rabbit is nothing new to me. My father is a hunter, so we did eat many rabbits, but I would never kill it," Katarina explained.

"Well, I'm so glad for that."

The back of the ambulance car was quiet; there was not even a peep out of their patient. He was sound asleep. "Thank God for that," Katarina sighed after checking on him.

The harsh rain and biting wind followed them all the way into the camp. When they reached it, the camp looked deserted. Everyone had taken cover inside to escape the brutal weather. As they drove through the gate, Katarina glanced back over her seat to see the patient still sleeping and smirked, "God granted my wish."

"What wish?" Lina asked as she brought the ambulance car to a stop in front of the infirmary.

"The one I made before we left the hospital in Naples. That I hoped Vojko sleeps throughout the trip."

"Oh. I never heard you say anything."

"I know," Katarina chuckled as they got out.

Lina helped her coworker get the patient out of the ambulance and into the infirmary. Vojko was still groggy from the injections and it took both of them to support him.

Matron Mateya looked at them with wide eyes as they brought the patient through the door and asked, "What's this? Why did you bring the patient back?"

"The hospital wouldn't admit him," Lina replied and they continued toward a chair with the patient.

"Why not?" Matron asked. "Don't they realize he needs medical attention? He's a very sick man." She was steaming.

"I told them the very same thing. The admitting nurse there just said that they hadn't received any phone calls from the doctor about Vojko's admission," Lina explained and placed the papers she had on Matron's desk after helping seat the patient.

"That's nonsense!" Matron Mateya yelled and picked the papers up. She waved them in her hand, her face was flushed red. "Mama mia! Weren't these papers good enough?" Furiously, she slammed them back on the desk.

Katarina finished settling Vojko as Lina parked the ambulance car. Exhausted, she and Lina went home then to get some rest before returning for the night shift.

When Katarina entered her room, Leo ran toward her. "I'm so glad that you're home, darling," he kissed her. "I went looking for you this morning when you hadn't come home. I was worried."

She didn't respond to anything he said. Her empty stomach preoccupied her mind. Leo poured her a cup of hot coffee. "Here, it will warm you up. I made it just for you," Leo said and handed her a cup of coffee.

"Thanks, but I'm starving. Where is lunch?"

"On the table, I just got it little while ago, so it's still warm. I waited for you to eat," he said and served it.

Katarina placed the cup down on the table, eagerly grabbed her portion and devoured her share of spaghetti as though she hadn't eaten in days. For the first time, she had no qualm with the food. "That was good," she finally said. She picked up her coffee and moved to her side of the bed. By the time she drank the last drop of coffee, she was getting drowsy. Her head became heavy and it pounded steadily. She threw a glance at her husband, who was lost in his thoughts, and lay down utterly exhausted. Within seconds, she felt her body drifting off to sleep.

A strong sneeze awakened Katarina from her deep sleep, and she glanced at her watch, it was 10:30 p.m. "Oh no, it's almost time to go back to work again," she said alarmed.

"You're finally awake," her husband commented as he sat at the table and read the newspaper. Well, mostly he looked at the pictures as he couldn't read Italian.

"Yes," Katarina answered coldly, dragged herself out of bed, and dressed slowly, still feeling tired from the trip to Naples. "Achoo!" she sneezed again. Her nose was stuffy and she began coughing.

"Are you all right, darling?" Leo asked, concerned. "You've slept nearly all day and part of the evening." He wasn't sure if Katarina was sleeping because she was sick or upset with him for what happened a few days before with Manda, but he was reluctant to bring the subject up. Instead, he tried hard to make up to her by being nice.

"Yes. Sure, I'm fine. I might have caught a cold," she admitted, sounding as miserable as she felt. "You know, the night shift is draining," she added, nibbling on the supper he had left her, but not feeling very hungry.

"Come on, eat some more," Leo urged, as he noticed she hadn't eaten much. "The night is long, you'll be hungry."

"I don't feel like eating," she said, staring at her food. The comfort of her mindless state was shattered when, out of nowhere, Katarina's mind wandered into the deep, forbidden space in her heart. The strain of her work and the shock of that evening's ugly experience at Marko's made her so tense and brought back the past. Suddenly, she was drowning in the flashbacks of the rape and all the other bad things that had happened to her. She glanced at her watch and said, "Look at the time. I have to go." And she rushed out the door.

As she exited, she sighed and looked up at the sky. There were still dark clouds covering the sky, but the rain stopped and the wind died down. "I hope the night will be quiet," Katarina muttered as she strode to the infirmary.

Arriving at work first, she began the night routine immediately determined to shake the bad thoughts from her head.

A little later, Lina made it through the door. "You're here already. You must really love this night work."

"Oh well, you know me, always punctual. I've set everything in the pot to be sterilized. It should start boiling soon," Katarina answered, interrupted by her own coughing, sneezing, and sniffling.

Lina said nothing and began to sort out her medicine cards, which was unusual for bubbly Lina. Katarina continued to chat so as to prevent the bad thoughts from coming forth in her mind. "What happened to Vojko?" Katarina asked, looking at her friend and coworker.

"Matron Mateya sent him by ambulance to the city hospital here in Capua. He was too sick to be held in the infirmary room," she answered distractedly and turned to her work with greater intensity.

Katarina was too sick to notice the sadness on her face so she persisted. "I'll get the medications ready for the outpatients. Do you know how many people I have to visit tonight?"

Lina didn't respond.

Katarina turned toward her and asked, "Have you heard anything I said?"

"I don't know! Check the books!" Lina shouted. "I have my own medicine to prepare." Her voice was laced with anger and torment.

"Fine, just don't bite my head off, for God's sake. What's wrong with you?" Katarina, put off by her friend's behavior, picked up the book. She wrote down the names of those needing medicine brought to them and said nothing more. She let a small silence pass between them and hoped that she would take it as asset. Then she asked, "Are you all right, Lina?"

"I'm sorry, my friend. I'm upset. Matron Mateya is very sick and she won't be back. Tomorrow, we're getting a new matron. Her name is Violeta. I heard she's very strict."

"Oh no! How awful. I'm sad to hear that she's sick. But how can that be?" Stunned, Katarina asked, "She seemed all right when we came from Naples, wasn't she?

Yes, she was acting a little unusual for her, but I hadn't noticed anything else."

"I don't know what had happened to her. They didn't say much. It isn't that I didn't want to share the news with you, it's because I couldn't bring myself to tell you. Please forgive me."

"Of course, I forgive you. I like her too. You must feel terrible. You worked with her for a very long time."

Because of the bad news about Matron Mateya, they ignored Katarina's harsh cough. At midnight, she had a list of people and medications and was ready to go.

"Hurry back," Lina said and went about her business.

"See you later," Katarina replied and strode out the door to dispense the midnight medications throughout the camp. It felt eerie walking around the camp alone, not a soul was out. The weather had settled, but the chilly wind blew fiercely. The camp grounds were soaked; her feet kept sinking into the mud so it took her more time to visit all the refugees on the list.

While Katarina was out, Lina dispensed the midnight medications to the refugees who came to the infirmary to get their last dose of the day that included: injectable and oral antibiotic, insulin, etc.

By the time Katarina returned, her cough and congestion had worsened. Her face was flushed red. Her body shivered.

"You, my friend, are sick. You're burning up with fever," Lina said, touching her forehead. She put a thermometer in her mouth. "Let's see how high it is."

"I'm just fine," Katarina frowned. "I don't have a fever," she said and pulled the thermometer out of her mouth.

"Then prove it. Keep it in your mouth for two minutes," Lina challenged her.

"Fine!" Katarina grabbed the thermometer and stuck it back to her mouth then turned back to work.

Two minutes later, Lina took it out of her mouth. "Oh no! You have a fever of thirty-nine degrees Celsius! You, my friend, are going straight home to bed."

"No. I'm not leaving until my shift is over," Katarina stubbornly refused. She looked at Lina with a grim face. "I'll make it to the end of the shift, if you leave me alone."

But after a while, Lina and the stubborn cold prevailed and Katarina went home.

It was about three o'clock when she arrived, hoping to find a warm bed by her husband's side, but he wasn't there. She knew he had been spending a lot of time with Viktor lately. "He must be there," she muttered, too sick and exhausted to give it a second thought. Her body shivered and her teeth chattered from fever and cold so she wrapped herself into a blanket and crawled into the cold bed and soon fell asleep.

Two hours later, a severe cough awoke Katarina. Leo still wasn't home. She glanced at her watch, "It's after four in the morning! What is he doing over there?" She groggily turned over. Suddenly the last two flirtation scenes of Leo and Manda on their bed and at Marko's flashed in front of her eyes. A tremor of anxiety fluttered within her. "Oh no!" she exclaimed, wondering what was going on and where was Leo really.

Despite her high fever, she crawled off the bed and walked around the room, wide awake. Then she opened the door and walked into the hallway. Before she knew it, she found herself outside Manda's door. The light was on and she could hear voices inside. While Katarina listened in front of the door, her knees weakened beneath her shivering body and she decided to turn back, but her suspicious mind wouldn't let her go, so without knocking, she opened the door.

"Oh my god!" Katarina shrieked, seeing Manda stretched across her bed while Leo massaged and caressed her body, which was covered only by a string bikini. Dazed, Katarina stood at the doorway motionless, glaring at them with both hands over her mouth. Her blood pressure rose with a rage that she couldn't hide. She wished she could sink through the floor or go up in smoke, but she couldn't even move for the next minute or more.

Leo stared at his wife, shocked to see her there, the look in her eyes told him more than she realized. "Darling, it's not what you think!" he shouted and rushed toward her. Without a word, she turned with one quick motion and rushed back to their room.

"But, but nothing happened, darling!" Leo repeated over and over as he followed her to the room. "Manda is suffering from low back pain and asked me if I wouldn't mind giving her a massage."

"Denial! Denial! That's all I've been hearing from you lately," Katarina replied, furious. Feeling dizzy, she threw herself on the bed, the tears running down her cheeks.

"Let me explain," he begged.

"No!" Tired and sick, she didn't want to listen to him or to his explanations. What could he possibly say to her that would make her refuse to believe the evidence she had seen with her own eyes.

"Come on, darling, I'm telling you, nothing happened. Why wouldn't you believe me?" he persisted without a guilty tone.

Suddenly, Katarina leapt from the bed and screamed, "Yeah sure, Leo, I believe you just like you would believe me in the same situation. Why don't we test that, huh?" Before he could answer, there was a knock on the door.

"Who the heck is now at our door!" she yelled, reaching for the doorknob. She jerked it open suddenly and saw Manda with her fist up ready to knock again. "What are you doing in here! Go away!" Katarina snapped and slammed the door to her face, but Manda pushed in.

"I didn't know you can be that mean," Manda said and stuck her foot to hold the door open.

"What's it with you? What side of 'Go home,' don't you understand?"

"Look! I'm not here to cause trouble. I just wanted to tell you that there's nothing going on between your husband and me. We were just killing time, and I asked Leo to give me a massage because I had pain in my back."

"You are killing time with my husband at four o'clock in the morning?" Katarina screamed. "What kind of fool do you think I am? Go home! Get yourself a man that's free to kill time! Any time!"

"I'm not going to leave until we settle this!" Manda was so stubborn and didn't budge.

"You're wasting your time. Go home!"

"All right, settle down," Manda suggested.

"When I need advice, I'll come call on you. Till then, stay away from my husband and me. Now get out!" Katarina tried to close the door, but Manda wouldn't move her foot.

"Both of you should cool down and stop yelling, everyone can hear you," Manda warned them.

All at once, Katarina went wild and had something like a rush to the head. "I don't give a damn!" she yelled brutally. "So get out!" She picked up a beer bottle from the corner of the hallway and threw it at the door. "Get out! And stay away from my husband!" The pieces of the bottle scattered all over the room. Manda exited quickly and pulled the door to a close.

Katarina realized what she had done. "Oh my god, I could have killed her," she said and slid down to the floor. Leo came to comfort her, but she pushed him away and got herself into the bed. Totally humiliated, she turned her back to him and sobbed in silence. In the flame of her fever, she drifted off to sleep almost as soon as her head touched the pillow.

The harsh cough and fever awakened Katarina three hours later and she felt very sick. She realized a visit to the doctor was unavoidable but said nothing to her husband. She got up and dressed, sneezing and coughing.

"Some cold you have there, darling," Leo noticed. "Where are you going?" he asked looking at her concerned.

"It isn't your business," Katarina replied angrily. Their wary relationship had just become even more distrustful.

"You're too sick to go anywhere alone. I'm going with you," Leo offered, hoping she planned to see a doctor for her cold.

"By all means, let's go!" Katarina said defiantly and strode out of the room, still furious with him. They walked in silence side by side. She could see Leo wanted to talk, but she was too exhausted to even think of anything. The decision has to be made: what was waiting for them two in the future, if there was any. But now her health was more important to her.

"I'll wait here for you, darling," her husband said as they arrived at the infirmary.

She said nothing but rushed in, choking on the harsh cough. Inside she met the matron. "Hello, my name is Katarina," and extended her hand to Matron.

"It's nice to meet you too. I'm Violetta. I heard you went home sick during the night. What are you doing in here?"

"I'm here to see the doctor. My cold has worsened and the fever is still high," Katarina explained, occasionally breaking into a harsh cough.

"Sit down then. The doctor will be here any minute," Matron Violetta said and returned to her office. While she waited, the day staff was running back and forth, doing their job.

"Come in, Katarina," the doctor called as he arrived. "What's wrong?"

"I have a high fever and terrible cough," she explained in between coughing spells.

After the doctor examined her, he pronounced, "Katarina, you have severe bronchitis. I'm going to order penicillin injection for five days with a lot of rest." He wrote a prescription, and she left the room. The doctor called for another patient.

Katarina handed the prescription to a day nurse and waited for her injection. After a little while, the nurse gave her first injection and said, "Now, go straight home to bed and come tomorrow for your next one."

"All right, will do," she replied and was on her way.

As he promised, Leo waited and accompanied his wife home. On the way, he asked, "What did the doctor say?"

But he didn't get an answer. She rushed ahead too sick to get into heavy conversation with her husband, not that she even wanted to speak to him. As she walked between the shacks, she noticed the swallows began their agitated low wheeling from the bushes to the eaves of the houses as the winter was nearing.

As they were approaching their shack, her stomach churned and she began retching.

Leo placed his arm around her shoulder. "Let me help you."

She cast an angry look at him, pushed his arm away, and shouted, "I don't need you to do anything for me!" In a flame of anger and fever, Katarina rushed ahead.

Suddenly a wave of nausea flooded over her. Knowing she wouldn't make it to the public washroom located in the laundry room, she ran toward the back of their shack and to herself muttered, "That's good enough," and threw up everything that was in her stomach and continued retching until there wasn't an ounce of reserved strength left in her. Nonetheless, without asking for her husband's help, she dragged herself to their room.

"Where have you been?" Leo asked, with alarm in his voice. She gave him a cold angry look and barely made it to the bed. Her face was pale tinged with a gray-greenish color, and she was sneezing and coughing.

The next several days, except the time she took to go to the infirmary for the injection, Katarina spent in bed sick, sleeping most of the time or pretending to sleep. This way she avoided talking to her husband as she had no energy left in her to argue.

Early one morning, Katarina awoke and realized she felt much better. The fever was gone and the cough was less intense. The autumn bitter weather persisted though. She could hear the cruel wind howling outside. Leo wasn't there, but she refused to speculate where her husband might be. She got up and walked to the window and peered out. There wasn't any rain, but the sky was cloudy and gray.

Her reverie was interrupted by a strong knock on the door. "Oh, please God, don't let it be Manda," she muttered, walking to the door. When she opened it, Katarina was surprised to see Lina standing on her doorway. "What are you doing in here?"

"What kind reception is this? Hello, my friend," Lina said, smiling, and entered. "How are you feeling?"

"I'm better, thank you."

"That's great, I'm glad," Lina said and sat on the stool at the table.

"Do you care for coffee?" Katarina asked and stood ready with the coffeepot in hand to make it.

"Sure, if you feel like making it, but today, I'm here to tell you to get well before coming back to work. Take another three to four days. Matron Violetta's order."

"I was planning to return tomorrow or the day after," Katarina sheepishly admitted, putting the water for coffee on the hot plate to boil.

"Somehow I knew. That's why I'm here. Let me help you with coffee. Sit down."

"Thanks."

"No trouble," Lina said, finished the coffee, and poured each a small cup. While they were drinking the coffee, Leo walked in.

"Oh, I see you're up, darling, and you have company. Hello, Lina," Leo said and put on the box-table the things he brought in. Lina smiled and nodded.

"Yes," Katarina answered without turning. Their relationship was a wary truce at this point. They spoke only when it was necessary.

"Good, maybe you can eat some breakfast," and he served the food and the strudel Leo bought in the canteen to his wife.

"I hope so," Katarina said and took the strudel.

"Would you like a piece of strudel, Lina?" Leo offered.

"No. Coffee is enough, thank you."

"It's so good, try some," Katarina suggested, stuffing her mouth with the strudel and looking at Lina.

"No, I have eaten already, thank you. Besides, I have to go to work." And she stood up.

Katarina chuckled. "Do you have to take my load too?"

"Of course. They will never get another nurse to fill times like these as long as we are here to do it. Thanks for coffee," Lina said and walked to the door. Before she opened it, she turned and teased, "Leo, take good care of my friend, or you'll have to answer to me," then walked out chuckling without waiting for an answer.

Leo turned to his wife and said, "That's great, you can take this time to recuperate now that your flu is clearing up."

"I know. Now if I only could clear up a few other things," she muttered, walking back to the bed.

"What was that you said?"

"Nothing, just that this is my first solid food that hasn't come right back up since I got sick," she replied, lay down, and turned her head away from him. Every time she looked at her husband's face, her imagination created visions of him and Manda naked in bed and her jealousy tormented her.

Katarina spent this few days getting stronger and trying to sort out the chaos in her head. She thought about the things that were happening in her life, even divorce crossed her mind, but she wasn't prepared to spend years in the camp because of it. Besides, in her mind, the possibility still existed that Leo was telling the truth and made her wonder what was real and what was not.

One thing was sure, severe reservations about Leo's love for her began to accumulate in her head. She struggled to make up her mind as to what to believe and what to do. She felt helpless and decided to do nothing.

What concerned her now was the fact that the autumn bad weather prevented her husband from finding any work; this meant he was off work and had a lot of time, time he might spend with Manda. It made her jealousy grow, and it severely tormented her. During her recuperation days, Leo spent most of his time with Viktor and Marko, hunting for jobs, that's what he told her, even though she hadn't asked. At home, they barely spoke.

After a few more days' rest, Katarina returned to work on the day shift. She was so anxious that she came a little early to the infirmary the first morning and had already began routine work when Lina walked in.

"Wonderful! You're back!" her coworker shouted and rushed to hug her, happy to see her well again.

"Thanks, I'm glad to be here too."

"How are things at home?" Lina asked immediately.

"Everything is just fine," Katarina smiled. "My husband was very attentive all those days I was sick. He even cooked soup for me one day, something he had never done before. Why are you asking?"

"No reason. I just wondered what you did about Leo and Manda," her coworker replied.

Katarina had forgotten that Lina knew about Leo and Manda's flirtation scene at Marko's and feared that Lina might somehow have learned about the latest interaction between her husband and maid of honor. She looked at her dazed, "What are you talking about?"

"Remember the story you told me during a previous night shift about your husband and Manda flirting on your bed," Lina reminded her.

"Oh, that. I forgave him, but he doesn't know that yet," Katarina chuckled. "I love him too much to let anything or anyone spoil my future with him. I had a long and hard look at things these days I was sick. I'm still not sure what happened between them, if anything. Besides, Our D-date, is bound to be near. If I make any waves now, it could delay our departure date for a long time as you know. God knows I don't want to spend another minute more in the camp than I have to. Manda will just have to find someone else. Leo is mine," she explained, but didn't want Lina to know about her latest discovery, at least not just then.

"Bravo!" Lina clapped. "Even though you've lost trust in Leo."

"Who said I did?"

"I can see in your eyes."

"Maybe just a little," Katarina admitted shyly.

"Well, you made up your mind. I'm not going to mention it again, at least not tonight," Lina promised and dropped the subject.

"Marvelous."

They both chuckled and went to their break. Katarina poured herself a cup of coffee and asked, "Lina, do you know what happened to those two babies we took to the hospital?"

"Yes, I just learned a few days ago, but you're not going to like it," Lina looked at her with a sad face.

"Oh no! What happened?"

"One baby died and the other one is still in the hospital fighting for his little life."

"That's horrible!" Katarina said and sat down.

"That wouldn't be as bad as it is, if there aren't many more little souls and big souls, too, suffering and dying from dysentery, yellow fever, and other diseases at this very moment," Lina said, wiping her tears.

"Why doesn't someone do something?"

"Who? We are just refugees," Lina glared at her.

"Are you telling me that no one cares?"

"Well, figure it out."

Katarina looked at Lina and said, "Let's go back to work." That was another subject she'd rather not discuss either; it made her sick to the stomach, remembering all that blood.

"You mentioned your departure before, are you getting ready for the journey?" Lina asked.

"What's there to get ready? The only thing I am doing is saving some money. When Leo and I went to the city, he bought me this beautiful figurine-bank, and whenever I have some extra money, I feed to the little doggy," Katarina explained with a smile.

"Did you save a lot? Maybe you can give me some," Lina teased.

"No. Just a little while Leo was working, now I can't even do that."

"Are you sure that's all it was?" Lina quizzed. Katarina glanced at her and turned to her work without further comment.

"Thank God, tomorrow is my day off. I'm so tired," Lina complained.

Katarina looked at her and agreed, "You must be, I remember how I was tired the time when I worked for you. Guess what, I'm off too for the next two days."

"Yes, you're a lucky dog," Lina commented and turned toward the voices coming from the door. "Here comes the evening shift, let's get ready to go home."

When the shift ended, Katarina rushed home. The fierce cold wind continued to tussle over the camp grounds and chilled her body to the bone. Her husband sat on the bed, reading a book when she arrived. "Brrr! We'll freeze in this godforsaken place!" Katarina screamed, wrapping a blanket around her shivering body, and laid down on the bed. In her mind, things were getting worse, there was no sign of the weather improving, their relationship remained wary, and there was no news about the anticipated trip to Canada. She began to lose hope.

"It isn't as bad, darling," Leo said and wanted to console her, but she pushed him away.

"It is almost as cold inside as it is outside, and you're telling me it's not bad," she replied angrily and began pacing the floor. She stopped at the window, putting her hands on the windowsill to look out and feel. The wind forced its chill through the holes in the window and into their unheated room making it colder. "Here it is! Where the cold is coming from!" She pointed and grabbed a few old pieces of their clothing and stuffed it against the window.

"Let me do it," Leo said and began pressing the clothing against the window.

"Sure, by all means," she said and returned to her seat, watching his strong hands working. He worked with his sleeves rolled up. The cold didn't bother him as he was used to even worse, she thought. Where he comes from, the snow falls up to five feet high every winter. On the other hand, it never snowed on the coast of Adriatic where Katarina comes from. Even though, Capua lay south, close to the Adriatic Sea, but the weather here was much more harsh and cold.

"There, that will help a little," Leo said as he finished and picked up the hot plate. "Let me make you a hot cup of tea to warm you up."

"Where did you get the tea?"

"At the cafeteria. They gave us extra because of the flu and cold."

"That's nice, make it," she urged him. After Katarina had her tea, she wrapped herself in the blanket and lay down. The cold harsh weather was depressing, she just wanted to sleep.

During the night, it was so cold, she could barely sleep. After tossing and turning most of the night, she couldn't take any longer and got up wondering what to do to warm up the room a little while making a cup of tea. Cooking steam would do it, she thought, but she needed something to put into the pot and she didn't have any money. The only choice she had was to take money out of her doggy bank.

Katarina glanced toward the bed, Leo was still sound asleep. Quietly, she walked to her side of the bed, picked up the figurine to get some money out, so she could buy some vegetables. The change inside rattled and awoke her husband.

"What are you doing?" he asked groggily.

"I'm getting some money out of my bank to buy fruits and vegetables. I hate to do that, but there isn't any other money. I can barely remember the day when fruit or veggies were served in the cafeteria. Besides, it's my day off and I would like to cook a veggie soup for us. It would give me something to do," she replied and carried the bank to the table.

"Don't!" Leo shrieked and jumped from the bed in his underwear. "We'll manage without it. This money is for our trip, isn't that what you said?"

"Yes, but," Katarina looked at him and noticed the doggy bank felt lighter than she remembered. "You didn't take any money out, did you?" she asked, with wide eyes.

"Well, just a little," he admitted sheepishly.

"Just a little! It looks like there is half missing!" she thundered angrily as the money spilled on the table. "Oh my god, what else is going to happen to me!"

"I needed it for cigarettes," he calmly answered and rushed back to bed.

"And for beer, no doubt. How dare you?" she shouted, took a few hundreds of liras, and returned the doggy bank back to its place. "Don't you touch it again," she said with a stern voice and was about to walk to the canteen when the loudspeakers blared.

"THE LIST WITH THE NAMES OF REFUGEES LEAVING ON THE NEXT TRANSPORT TO CANADA IS POSTED ON THE BOARD OUTSIDE THE MAIN ADMINISTRATIVE BUILDING."

"Wow! Did you hear that, my love?" she shouted and jumped to her husband in bed, showering him with kisses. "I can't believe it, it's here! Our D-day, it's here!"

The announcement came like a miracle to Katarina and gave her new hope. Everything else was forgotten or pushed at the back of her mind. Her head filled with cheerful thoughts. Instantly, she leapt out of bed and began to dance around the room and sung, "We're going to our promised land! We are leaving! We are leaving this cold place!"

Still stretched on the bed, Leo asked, "Are you all right, darling?" staring at her as though she had lost her senses. "I know there's a possibility that we're on the list, but don't get yourself all worked up. I want that just as much as you do, but what if we aren't on the list? You know just as I do, we haven't been here that long." Leo was very careful not to get his hopes up. He had been there before.

Katarina took his face between her hands, staring straight into his eyes. "Well, I'm not wrong. You'll see. There's no doubt in my mind. We're on the list," she said, planting a kiss on his lips. "Hurry!"

"How can you be so sure?" Leo chuckled as he got dressed.

"Come on, hurry," Katarina pleaded. "I want to go and check the list." She was so eager that she rushed out into the cold windy morning, forgetting all about cooking and vegetables. Leo grabbed his jacket and followed her.

The announcement sent the whole camp scrambling in anticipation and euphoria. Everyone who signed to go to Canada was up on their feet rushing toward the list, anxiously wanting to know if their names were on it. Emotions were high. People cried, laughed, shouted, and sang as they scurried toward the stated building.

"Oh, look at the people," Katarina commented as they arrived to the main building. The area was buzzing and swarming with refugees.

"I can see," Leo replied, staring anxiously at the noisy crowd. Everywhere, people were pushing and shoving as they tried to get close enough to the board to read the list.

"We better line up, otherwise, we'll never get there," Katarina said and took her place behind the mass.

"You're right, darling, otherwise we'll be here all day in this biting wind," Leo replied and followed her, but soon the mob pushed forward and separated them, almost crushing Katarina's ribs. Nevertheless, she managed to squeeze inside the crowd, ignoring the shoulder-to-shoulder throng. Her small size let her wiggle between people and she began to move ahead, but Leo was left behind.

"Come on!" she yelled back to Leo, but her voice was drowned by the horde so he didn't hear her. Katarina, however, continued to struggle through the mob and eagerly inched forward, her heart filled with happy and hopeful thoughts.

Way in the back of the line, Leo realized he'd never make it to the board and decided to wait on the side of the crowd. "She'll make it. Her body is small, she'll get through the crowd easier than I can," he tried to convince himself under his breath. Sporadically, he would jump up in the air, extending his neck, but he couldn't see Katarina. She was lost in the crowd. He could do nothing but watch and wait in anticipation.

Two hours had passed and the day was getting colder. A fierce wind penetrated everyone's clothing causing the throng to grow riotous as no one wanted to stay outside longer than necessary.

"Go on, darling," Leo shouted, cheering her on, though he doubted she could hear him. He followed his wife's progress whenever he could see her; most of the time, however, she was shrouded by the mob.

Just before Katarina reached the list, she noticed the departing refugees' faces. Some were laughing, others were crying, and wondered which she would be after seeing the list.

There were four long pages with the names of four hundred refugees who would be leaving together. She carefully scrutinized every page, her hand trembling as she turned each page, scared to death that her husband might be right and they hadn't made the list.

"Hurry up, lady! What's taking you that long?" Someone from the crowd shouted toward her. She ignored them and continued slowly and carefully checking each name.

Finally in the middle of the third page, she found their names. Her trembling hands covered her mouth instantly, and she could do nothing but stare at the list for a few seconds, shocked in disbelief. "Oh my god! Oh my god! I was right! It's true!" she began screaming, joyful tears pouring down her cheeks as she joined those in jubilation. With arms above her head, she turned, began to wave, and shout, "We're leaving! We're out of here!"

Her words never reached Leo's ears. They drowned in refugees' voices as they shouted, "GOOD-BYE, CAPUA. HERE WE COME, CANADA!" The chant, laughter, and songs echoed throughout the camp for the rest of the day and weeks before their departure.

Even though Leo couldn't hear his wife, seeing her hands up in the air, he knew meant their names were on the list. Excitement flooded his face. He waved back to her over the crowd, jumping up and down jubilantly.

Katarina extracted herself from the mass and ran into her husband's embrace, yelling, "See, I told you so," she bubbled with happiness. "The ship leaves from Naples on December 31! And we'll be on it!" she chanted.

"Wow! Imagine, we'll be standing on Canadian soil in about six weeks!" Leo shouted, kissing his wife as he swirled her around.

"Yes! I can't believe it! Finally, it's going to happen! It's going to happen!" Katarina enthused, happy tears wetting her cheeks. Her delight boiled in her, she couldn't stop talking. Leo didn't have a chance to utter a word, so he just listened and absorbed it all quietly.

They wrapped their arms around each other and savored the victory for a moment in silence. "This is the happiest day of my life!" Leo shouted and squeezed his wife closer.

"I thought marrying me was your happiest day!" Katarina teased.

"Hello, Katarina," a voice startled her out of Leo's embrace. It was Lina. "Congratulations! I'm so happy for you two and somewhat sad because I'm losing a good coworker and great friend," she said and hugged them both.

"Thank you, Lina. We're grateful to have a friend like you," Katarina replied with a big smile on her face.

"By the way, what're you doing here?" Katarina asked, puzzled.

"I just arrived from the city, and I knew you are going to be here so I came to see you. Just in case you need my shoulder to cry on," Lina chuckled.

"Thank God, I don't!" she said joyfully.

"In that case, I'll be going." She hugged Katarina. Over Lina's shoulder in the distance, she noticed Manda and the children in the distance coming toward them, but said nothing.

"Thanks for coming, Lina. See you at work," Katarina quickly grabbed Leo under his arms, "Let's go to the canteen to buy the veggies," and rushed him away from Manda.

"Take it easy! I'm coming. Why are you pulling me so hard?"

"Oh, no reason. Sorry! I guess I'm too excited," Katarina chirped and let him go as they entered into the canteen.

She chose two small carrots, two potatoes, a tomato, an onion, and small stick of celery. "How much are these?" she asked, handing them to the shopkeeper.

He took the veggies and put them on the scale. "Fifty liras. Do you want them?" he asked, staring at Katarina while she decided.

"Yes, I do," she answered, pulled fifty liras out of her pocket and placed it into his extended hand. While she was shopping for veggies Leo observed other things. As soon as she got her veggies, they walked out together.

They had barely reached their room when a new announcement came through the loudspeakers. "All those refugees who are leaving December 31 need to report to the immigration office for further travel information and instructions. We'll start tomorrow morning calling alphabetically."

"Our name will probably not be called until the day after," Katarina commented and began to cook the soup.

"That depends how fast the official works," Leo replied. "I wonder if Viktor got in?"

"Is he going to Canada too?" She was surprised as she didn't know.

"I believe so if I'm not mistaken. I'm going to find out," Leo said.

"Great! Leave me here alone!" she yelled, but she was too excited to be angry, not today.

"I'll be right back," her husband said and left. Katarina finished her soup and ate some, leaving the rest to him as Leo still wasn't back.

She stood up and walked outside the door; to her surprise, the wind subsided, and the sun peered from under the clouds. "It's not as bad," she muttered and took a walk as she didn't want to be in front of the shack, just in case Manda came out. Katarina wasn't ready to face her yet. Before she realized, she found herself on the banks of the small river.

She stood by the river, watching a gull, its great wingspan stretched, plunging through the sky, diving into the water for the fish hiding between the rocks. The swift faultless action gave her a sense of the power of even a bird to be utterly itself. It was her lesson, and she needed one. She had to hold on being herself again too.

Suddenly she shivered. "I'm getting cold. You better go back, before you freeze," she ordered herself and turned to walk home.

By then, Leo was home and worried about her. When she entered, anxiously he asked, "Where have you been?"

"Down by the river," she chirped calmly and happily.

"Where have you been?"

"At Viktor's place and guess what?"

"He's going too," Katarina finished his sentence. "I'm happy for him."

After their supper, they both laid down under the blankets because that was the most comfortable place as the room was cold. Leo turned to her and began to stroke her arms, but Katarina didn't want to rush. "I'm too tired," she said and turned her back to him.

"Oh, come on, darling. I missed you so much," he said, but she didn't hear him. All the excitement and cold air made her tired and she was fast asleep. So their relationship still remained wary.

The next morning, they both were up early afraid to miss the call from the immigration office. There was a long silence between them, each of them doing their own thing. Leo smoked like a chimney and Katarina tidied up their room. "You think we'll be called today?" she asked.

"Maybe. Let's go for breakfast," he suggested, not wanting to say much.

As they walked to the cafeteria, the cold wind brushed against their cheeks, making them red. In the cafeteria, they met Viktor and they sat down with him after they picked up their breakfast. "Have you been called yet?" Leo asked as he sat beside Viktor.

"No, not yet."

"I guess we don't have to worry about this. We are on the list, that's what counts, right?" Katarina said.

"Well, you are probably right," Viktor agreed and stood up to leave.

"Where are you rushing? Wait, we are almost finished, then we can walk out together," Leo said.

"All right, I can stay for a while," Viktor replied and sat down again. It didn't take long, and Leo and Katarina were ready to leave. As they stood up to go, an announcement came through the loudspeakers. "THE NAMES WE ARE GOING TO CALL NOW ARE TO COME TO THE OFFICE AS SOON AS POSSIBLE."

Dead silence covered the cafeteria as it began to read the names. Each time a name was called, a jubilant voice was heard of the person as it exited the cafeteria and ran to the office.

Halfway down, it called, "LEO AND KATARINA LISIC." And right after Viktor's name.

"Yeah!" Katarina exclaimed.

The three walked together to the office. The refugees were crowded at the door and noisy when they arrived. "I guess we have to wait," Katarina said.

They took their places behind in the line. "Let's hope this wait won't be as long as the other was," Leo replied, moving slowly toward the door.

An hour later, they were still waiting, and they were not even near the door. "I have to go to work tonight, you know. I almost forgot all about it," Katarina said.

Viktor chuckled. "What are you talking about? It isn't even lunchtime."

"I know, but I need to get a little sleep before I go to work."

Before Viktor or Leo had a chance to say anything, the office door opened and an older dark gray-haired lady official appeared. "Mr. and Mrs. Lisic, come in," she called and returned inside.

"We are coming," Leo said and they entered to the office.

"Sit down. Please."

"Thank you," they said in unison and sat on the chair beside the desk.

The lady official handed them some documents and a pen, among them a packet of papers about the voyage. "Here, these papers need both of your signatures. It's about your travel expense. In the packet are instructions on how to pack and secure your belongings for the transport to and off the ship. Also, inside you will find when they'll be picked up. Read it carefully," she explained.

Katarina didn't hear a word the official said. She was transfixed by the picture of the ship on the cover of the packet. "Are we going to sail to Canada on this huge luxurious liner named *Cristoforo Colombo*? Who is going to pay that?" she asked puzzled.

"Yes. You two and 398 more refugees are sailing to Canada on that ship, and the Canadian government is paying for everything," the lady official said and smiled.

"Wow! That's very nice of the Canadian government to pay for our ticket and everything," she gushed, still staring at the picture.

The official stood up and said, "Well, I'm finished unless you have any questions."

"No. Thank you." And they exited.

On the way home, Leo informed her. "Yeah it's nice that the Canadian government is paying, but they are not giving us the tickets free. We'll have to repay the money back to them once we begin to work and make money."

"So what? We have the rest of our lives to do that," Katarina replied, so jubilant her body quivered. It didn't matter to her who paid for the ship, so long as Leo and she were on it, and they were on their way to Canada and far, far away from Manda.

"I know, but it would be nice if we don't have to pay the money back. Wouldn't it?" Leo smiled and opened the door of their room for his wife.

Grabbing her head with both hands, she exclaimed, "Oh no! We have lots of things to do!"

"Yes, but." Leo picked up the packet and sat on the stool. "Let's see what it says in here," he said and began flipping through until he reached the part they needed. "It says, you're not to pack perishable food and that everything has to be safely packed and locked by December 17. Pack clean clothes only. See, there's a lot of time. You're going to sleep now as you have to work tonight, remember," her husband reminded and kissed her.

"All right, all right." As soon as she lay down, the thoughts of their voyage began whirling madly in her head. Katarina wondered, would they succeed in getting to Canada? What kind of life would they have in there? What kind of a husband will Leo be there? There were so many questions. Her mind was so consumed by thoughts of leaving that she couldn't fall asleep, so she just lay there, frustrated. After tossing and turning for a while, finally she dozed off.

Quietly, Leo continued flipping through the packet, taking a close look at the picture of the ship Katarina liked so much while he waited for his wife to fall asleep, so he could go out and let her sleep.

At work that night, Katarina couldn't concentrate. Her mind played tricks on her, making her believe she was not on the ship already sailing for Canada. Instead of working, she just stared at the empty space.

"Katarina, what are you doing? You haven't even started your work," Lina said.

Lina's voice hit her like a ton of bricks. "What?" she responded, annoyed, when she realized she was standing in the infirmary.

"Finish your things. Don't just stare at them. You're lucky we're not busy," Lina laughed, realizing Katarina was daydreaming about her ship.

"All right. All right," she sighed. Still she was anxious to get home and begin her washing and packing. Consequently, the night seemed to last forever.

The next morning, as soon as Katarina got home from her night shift work, she collected some of the clothes and headed for the laundry room.

At the door, she ran into her husband. "Where are you going?" he asked.

"To the laundry to wash," she said and wanted to exit.

Her husband took hold of her arm. "Wait! Where you're going to put your clothes once you washed it? Have you thought about that?"

She looked at him and put the bundle down. "No, I have not. Let's hear what's your plan then."

Leo closed the door, and they sat at the table. "First we have to go to the city and buy a chest so everything we have fits in," he said.

"I know we need a chest, but we can't buy one now. We don't have the money," Katarina acknowledged. "Until then I can wash, iron, and fold the clothes, but you're probably right, it would be better to have the chest ready."

"How about the money in your doggy bank?" he asked.

"I don't know how much is still left. You spent most of it, remember," Katarina reminded.

"How about your pay?"

"Next week. I can check how much is still left in my doggy bank," Katarina said and hurried to get it. It was in her interest, too, to get things going, even though it upset her to think what he had done. She opened it and they counted the money. Inside, they found a little less than a thousand lira and her husband took it all of it.

"You go and buy the chest and wake me when you get back so I can at least start washing. No beer or cigarettes until you buy the chest, all right," she warned and crawled to bed. "You're right, I do need some sleep. I'm exhausted."

Leo took the money and stuffed it into his pocket. "I'll be back soon, darling," he said and walked out. He didn't feel like going to the city alone so he stopped at his friend's place to see what was he up to and maybe he could convince Viktor to go with him. When Leo arrived at his shack, Viktor was on the way out. "Where are you going?" Leo asked.

"To the city to buy myself a chest to pack in my things," Viktor answered.

Leo laughed. "What a coincidence. I'm on my way to Capua too to buy a chest, and I was going to ask if you want to come with me."

"Great! Now we can go together," Viktor replied, and they were on their way.

The beautiful sunny November day kept them in the city almost all day. They spent it walking through the markets looking for the cheapest chest they could find, at least Leo was. He forgot the promise he made to his wife.

Katarina awoke on her own; it was late in the evening. She was furious with her husband and was ready to scream when she realized how long she had slept, but he wasn't back yet. "Where the heck is he?" she called out. "I wanted to see the chest before I go to work."

The whole time she'd been rambling he had just stood by the door, his stare fixed on her. A blind man couldn't miss the tension in her demeanor. Leo walked in with the chest in his arms. "Here it is!"

She looked at the chest that her husband held in his arms and ignored the question she wanted to ask. "Wow, it's lovely! Do you think it is big enough for all our belongings?" she asked.

"Oh, I'm sure it is. We don't have much stuff."

"Wonderful!" she exclaimed. "In the corner, there's a small bundle of summer clothes clean and ironed, ready to be packed. You could start with that, and I'll start washing in the morning," she hinted and walked to work.

The next morning, she marched home from work determined to begin to wash their clothing. Leo wasn't there and she asked under her breath, "Where is that husband of mine?" Then she noticed a piece of the cardboard box lay on the table. *What's this?* Katarina wondered, looked closer, when she noted there was something written on it. "Oh! It's a note from Leo," she muttered and read it. "I went to pick up breakfast, love, Leo."

"Perfect! He won't be able to stop me," Katarina chirped, gathering a load of clothes and rushed to the laundry. If he was here, he would insist she get some sleep first.

The area in front of the utility room was already crowded when she arrived and the line extended way out, inching forward. Katarina decided to wait no matter how long it took. "What time did these people come here to wait?" she asked the lady standing next to her.

"Who knows, probably five, six o'clock," she answered and moved a step or two ahead.

When Katarina finally got a free sink, she began to wash. With little soap and no hot water, she had to scrub the clothes hard to make them clean. "I wish the camp authorities give us more soap at least since there isn't any hot water," she complained, looking at the lady washing in the next sink.

"It would cost them too much money," the lady chuckled and continued to scrub her clothes.

After a few hours of plunging her hands into cold water, her fingers started to go numb. Cold and exhaustion took over her body, forcing her to stop and return to their room. By then, it was drizzling outside, and there wasn't any room on the clothing line inside the laundry room to hang the clothes she washed to dry. So she brought them wet with her into their room.

Her husband stared at the wet clothes and asked, "What're you doing? These clothes aren't dry."

"I know, Leo. I have to spread them out in here because there isn't any space in the utility room. Hammer some nails into the walls," she ordered while spreading some of the clothes over the boxes and stools.

He grabbed some nails and said, "All right, but there's only a few more left." She followed behind him with the wet clothes and hung them on the nails until they were all gone.

Exhausted and sleepy, Katarina crashed on the wooden stump and said, "I washed as much as I could today, but there are still a few loads left."

"Is there anything else I can help you with?" Leo asked, placing lunch and hot cup of coffee in front of her.

She took hold of the coffee and replied, "Of course, there is. Find out everything that we need for the voyage. Did you get the lock with the chest?" she asked, sipping on the coffee.

"Yes. The lock comes with the chest," Leo replied.

"That's good. We'll need an extra for the bag." Katarina ate her food, drank the coffee, and crawled into bed to get a few hours' sleep.

Before she left for work, she glared at the wet clothes spread around the room, suddenly impatient. She realized with so many refugees leaving and the bad weather, it would be harder than she thought to get her washing and drying done. Then idea popped in her head. She kissed her husband and rushed to the infirmary.

"Hello, Lina," she greeted her friend, bubbling. "I'm so glad you are here."

"Where would I be?" Lina asked with wide eyes. "What are you up to?"

"Oh, nothing, but I was just wondering. You are off tomorrow, aren't you?"

"Yesss," Lina responded slowly. "Why?"

"Well, could you work for me? Please say yes. I have to wash everything, including a blanket and tablecloths that I found at the Red Cross. It will take time to wash and even more to dry if the rain persisted. Besides, the wait in the line for the sink at the laundry is so long. Please don't say no," Katarina begged.

Lina paused and looked at her. "All right. I'll do it, but only this one time."

Katarina gave her a hug and said, "Thank you, my friend. This will give me two days off, yours and mine the following day, and then we are both off for two."

"And then it gives you four days off on the row. You figured that just right, smart lady," Lina said before they both turned to their nightly routine. Katarina could hardly wait for the morning to arrive.

As soon as her shift ended, Katarina rushed home, thankful Lina let her have her day off. On the way, gusty wind blew her clothes around her like a tourniquet, slowing her down. She looked up, threatening dark clouds were moving through the sky rapidly. "I hope it doesn't rain," she muttered as she reached their shack. Leo was bundled in the blankets and was sound asleep.

She picked up the unwashed load and quietly hurried to the laundry. It was still early in the morning; the waiting line was much shorter when she arrived, and it didn't take long for her to get a sink and began to wash.

After immersing her hands into cold water for hours, her fingers became numb, frozen, and totally blue. She shook and rubbed them against each other, trying to warm them up.

The lady at the sink next to her said, "Put your hands under your pit, you'll see how fast they'll warm up."

She smiled and put her hands under her pit. She was ready to do anything to get them going so she could continue her washing. "I hope you're right."

Sure enough, it worked. "Thanks," she said to the lady and continued her washing.

Suddenly, she felt a hand on her shoulder: it was her husband. "Come for lunch, Katarina," he said.

"I have to finish this load," she replied and continued scrubbing the clothes.

"Look at you. You're shivering and your hands are freezing. You need something hot to drink and some food," Leo said, trying to convince her to come inside to warm up. Stubbornly, Katarina refused to listen; she didn't even allow herself time to eat because she wanted to be finished.

"For God's sake, you are going to get sick. Come inside," her husband demanded.

"All right. Bring me a coffee," she requested.

"I'll do that, no problem," Leo replied and returned to their room to get the coffee.

After Leo left, the lady next to her looked at Katarina and said, "You know, you should listen to your husband. Go have something to eat and rest a little, then return. You don't want to get sick, do you?"

She stopped and replied, "No, I don't. Maybe I should stop. I'm getting a little tired." She thanked the lady, picked up her clothes, and walked home.

They met at the door. "I'm hungry and cold," she announced as she entered and placed the wet clothes on one stool and sat on the other one.

"Here, drink the hot coffee," Leo offered and placed it on the table in front of her. "I'll get your lunch."

Katarina sipped on the coffee while Leo warmed up her food, and suddenly, she began to cough and sniffle. Her husband glanced at her with alarm. "I was afraid of that. You caught a cold, haven't you?"

"No, no. I'm just tired. After a little rest, I'll be fine, and I'll be going back to finish the load," she explained, ate her lunch, and went to sleep. Before she fell asleep, she ordered, "Leo, wake me up in two hours please."

Her husband sat at the table and watched as she drifted to sleep. His eyes darted to the wet clothes on the stool. "Maybe I should hang that clothes for her," he muttered and walked out to check the weather and the laundry.

The wind blew wildly and the dark clouds threatened to unleash rain so he chose to hang up their clothes to dry in the laundry and let his wife sleep until she awoke on her own.

It was late in the evening when the wind whistling through the hole in the window awoke Katarina. “Why didn’t you wake me?” she asked her husband, sitting at the table and reading a book.

“You looked so tired, I felt sorry for you.”

“You know, washing and drying is moving slowly. If I continue procrastinating like this, I won’t be finished in time, then what?” Katarina sniffling.

“All right, all right. Let’s not argue,” Leo said. “Come, I’ll make hot tea, supper is on the table, eat something.” He poured some water into a coffeemaker to boil for tea and placed it on the hot plate.

She tried to get up to eat, but when Katarina stood up, she started to cough and sneeze. The excitement made her head spin; she became dizzy and almost fainted.

Her husband grabbed her to help her back to bed. “You are not going out of this bed tonight.”

But she wouldn’t have it; she walked to the stool and sat down at the table. “As soon as I eat and have a cup of hot tea, I’ll be fine,” she said. “Don’t worry. I only have a few sniffs. I’ll get some rest and I’ll be all right in the morning.”

He smirked and said, “I’ll get your tea.”

She drank her tea, then changed into pajamas and dragged herself back under the blankets and fell asleep.

# CHAPTER 16

The next morning, Katarina awoke to a severe harsh cough and her body was shivering and burning with fever. She felt horrible. Nevertheless, she got dressed to go to the laundry. Besides, Leo wasn't there to stop her.

As she opened the door with the load of a wash in her hands, Leo ran into her. "Where do you think you're going? You have to see a doctor, darling. I don't want you to be sick now," he stressed.

She glanced at him and realized he wouldn't let her be. "Fine, I'm going," she replied, throwing the clothes on the floor and storming out.

He came after her and suggested, "Let me come with you."

"No. I can do this by myself," she snapped harshly and strode to the infirmary.

The sky was still cloudy and cold wind blew, but at least it wasn't raining. Walking caused her to gasp for air, making her throat dry and her cough more severe. By the time she reached the infirmary, she could barely speak.

"Oh, my dear girl, you sound horrible," Matron Violetta exclaimed and wrapped a blanket around her shoulder while leading her to the examining room.

"Hello, Katarina, you're sick again?" the doctor asked as he entered. She coughed so hard she couldn't answer him, but nodded, with her head.

"I guess I don't have to ask you what's wrong. That's a terrible cough you have there," the doctor said and proceeded to examine her. "Well, Katarina, it looks like you have severe bronchitis again. You need to take better care of yourself. I'll prescribe like before five injections of penicillin for you to have the next five days and lots of rest, so you are off work. Since you'll be leaving us soon, there's no need for you to come back to work at all. Matron Violetta will see to it that you get paid. Good luck to you and your husband in Canada."

"Thank you, Doctor, for everything, and good-bye," she said in a muffled voice accompanied by the harsh cough.

After only a few days rest and penicillin injection, Katarina began to be anxious and didn't feel she had time to rest anymore. December 10 was quickly approaching and she barely began. Following her second injection, she went to the laundry room to finish her wash. The cough and sneezing slowed her pace, but she finished the half load that she left the day she got sick in the early afternoon. She glanced at the clothesline inside and muttered, "Goodness, there is room on the clothesline in here today for my things too," and spread her clothes on it. She returned to their room, coughing and sneezing to find Leo busy packing other things into their chest.

"Where are the rest of our clothes?" her husband asked, looking at Katarina.

"At the moment, everywhere. In the laundry drying on the line. Some still dirty. Others, we are wearing," she said and walked to make herself a cup of tea. "Tomorrow, I'll finish the last load and then the clothes we are wearing will be going into our carry-on bags," she said and went to sleep.

She awoke to a beautiful cold December morning, the soft billows of cloud that clung to the horizon tinted lavender and pink. The air was wet and sea-fresh, but Katarina couldn't enjoy it as she spent the whole day in the laundry; the evening and late into the night she worked hectically. She dried those clothes that hadn't finished drying with the iron and folded everything.

With a little help from Leo, she filled and locked the chest with their belongings that evening. "I don't know if I'd have done this in time, if Lina and the doctor hadn't give me the time off," she sighed as they parked the chest beside the door ready to be picked up by the truck in the morning.

"Don't forget my help," Leo chuckled.

"Some help you turned out to be," she said as she put up water for a cup of hot tea before turning in for the night.

Early the next day, the truck picked up the chest with their clothes, but they couldn't relax. There were many other things left for them to do before their D-day. As they stood at the door of their shack and watched the truck pulled away with their chest, she realized this was real; she turned to her husband and said, "We are finally leaving, aren't we?"

"Yes, we are, darling!" They hugged each other and returned inside.

They were both so busy preparing for the trip that Katarina barely found the time to run for her injections. She still coughed occasionally, but for the most part, her bronchitis was healed. That day, Katarina felt so well that she forgot to go for her last shot, but Matron Violetta didn't.

She ordered her paged over the loudspeakers. "Mrs. Katarina Lisic, please report immediately to the infirmary."

Katarina ignored it; even though she knew how important it was to take all of the antibiotics, she decided against going. She had more important things to do on the sunny day like this than get poked, she thought.

"They are paging you," Leo reminded his wife. "You didn't go for your injection today, did you?"

She cast a shy look at him. "No. I feel like myself again. Besides, I don't need it." She hated the needles and didn't want to be poked anymore.

After lunch, the second page came while Leo and she were getting ready to visit some of their friends and say their good-byes. "Why don't they let me be?" she said glowering.

His gaze met hers levelly. "I know you're better, but you have to go. We don't need any trouble now, do we?"

Knowing she was going to have to go. "I am, I am." She gave in.

They exited their room together, Katarina walked to the infirmary for her last injection and Leo went to their friends. Alone. Not even in his wildest dream, did he think he might never see his wife again.

As Katrina walked through the door, she was faced with an angry Matron Violetta. "I've been waiting for you all morning. What took you so long?" she yelled in her face.

"I am fine. I don't need the penicillin anymore," Katarina returned.

Matron Violetta gazed at her from under her wire glasses. "The doctor is the one to decide if you need it or not. He ordered five, and you will have five." There was no arguing with Matron Violetta. "Yes," was the only answer she'd accept.

Lina came to take over as Matron usually didn't give out medication and specially not injection. "Don't worry, I'll take care of Katarina," she said and rushed to fill a syringe with penicillin. Lina was shocked to hear her say that; she knew Matron Violetta well and she couldn't remember when she last gave an injection. Lina looked at Katarina and returned to her previous work.

Matron soon returned and stood facing Katarina. "Presto! Presto!" She rushed, tapping her foot on the floor. "I don't have all day."

Katarina glared at the needle, a shiver ran up her spine. "Fine!" She stormed into a small room, pulled her dress up, and stuck her hip toward Matron. "Go ahead! It's the last of the five injections anyway."

Matron Violetta jabbed the needle into her flesh. "Here, that wasn't so bad." She pushed the penicillin into her muscle without aspirating to see if she was in the right place. Consequently, she wasn't aware that the needle had pierced Katarina's blood vessel. Penicillin found its way into the bloodstream and reached her heart.

Almost immediately, Katarina's heart began pounding and racing so fast she became lightheaded. On her way out, she stopped in the middle of the infirmary stunned and looked panic-stricken at Matron Violetta. "What's happening to me? What did you gave me?" she yelled, clutching her chest with both of her hands as she walked to the closest chair and sat down.

Matron Violetta said nothing but hurried toward the medical cabinet. Lina screamed from behind the counter. "Oh my god, what did you do to her? She looks like she's dying!"

At that moment, Katarina felt herself drifting away, so she gripped the chair. Lina's words echoed in Katarina's head, but she couldn't comprehend what was happening to her and why. Through the fog, she saw Matron Violetta rushing toward her with another syringe filled with some kind of medication. Lina stopped her halfway, and they started to argue. Katarina heard their voices and their words as if through a dream.

"Don't give her anything!" Lina begged.

"This will help," Matron was eminent and continued toward Katarina with the injection in her hand. She wanted to escape but couldn't move.

"Lina, help!" she heard herself saying.

Lina came after her. "Noo!" she yelled and knocked it from Matron Violetta's hand. The syringe tumbled under the desk. Obviously, Lina thought differently as she grabbed Katarina and rushed her to the hospital in Capua. "I can't believe the anger drove her to do a stupid thing like this!" Lina yelled, pressing on the gas.

By the time they reached the emergency room, Katarina began to feel better, although very shaken and scared.

The doctor examined her and said "You have experienced an allergic reaction to penicillin. You'll be fine, but I still want you to stay in the hospital for a few days so you can recuperate."

Lina stood on the side watching while Katarina stared at the doctor mesmerized. "Hospital? I have to stay in here?" She could barely get the words out. She just couldn't believe her luck.

He looked at her gloomy face. "Don't worry. It's just precautionary. You'll be fine," He tried to reassure her before he left.

"Great. If I'm fine, why doesn't he let me go back to the camp?" Katarina said, turning to her friend Lina with suspicion and fright in her eyes. "I don't understand, the doctor had said I had an allergic reaction to the penicillin, but I had penicillin many times before and nothing happened. Besides, I don't have the usual allergic symptoms. Why do I have to stay in the hospital if I'm healthy? What's going on here?"

Lina gave a sigh of relief and explained, "It appears that you suffered penicillin shock, not an allergy to the penicillin as the doctor said. A small amount must have gone into your heart. Thank God, it was only a little, otherwise you would have died. You're very lucky, my friend. It's known, only a small percentage of people survive penicillin shock."

"I remember now," Katarina said. "Matron Violetta didn't aspirate before injecting the penicillin into my flesh. She was so angry with me for being late, she probably forgot. Oh no, I could have died." Her face paled and she shivered.

"Yes and just before you are to leave the camp forever. What an irony that would have been," Lina frowned.

Katarina gazed at her face alarmed. "What're you suggesting, that she wanted to hold me back?"

"No, no. That wasn't her intention. She was negligent, pure and simple," Lina said.

"Then tell me why the doctor kept the truth from me?"

"Are you kidding?" Lina said. "They're not going to tell you or me that you had penicillin shock. That would spell trouble for Matron Violetta who happens to be the one who injected you, who happens to be an Italian nurse. We're the only ones who know that she was at least negligent, that when she injected you, she didn't follow proper procedure. That's criminal," Lina whispered angrily.

"Why the admission to the hospital then? The doctor could have sent me right back to the camp," Katarina asked searching for answers, despite of her inner warning against it.

"Why do you think the camp authorities phoned ahead and requested that you be admitted?"

Katarina's face paled and she grabbed Lina's hand. "The admission was requested by the camp authorities? Oh no, but why?"

"They want to make sure you are all right. It wouldn't look good on their record if a healthy young refugee died just days before transport. Canadian government has a list of refugees coming already and there would be a lot of questions asked if you didn't show up," Lina explained.

Katarina gazed at her. "You're kidding, right? As if anyone would really care for a little refugee like me and ask questions?"

"Yes, the human rights organization would," Lina assured her.

"How do you know all this as a refugee?"

Lina squeezed her hand. "I've been in the camp for a very long time. And I have good pair of ears."

Katarina wouldn't let go of her hand until she asked, "What if they keep me in here for a long time? What will happen then? Could Leo and I be taken of the transport list or just me? Is it possible the camp authorities won't want me to go because of what happened?" she rumbled chaotically. "I don't want to stay in the hospital."

"Slow down. I know you're scared at the moment, but everything will be all right," Lina assured. "I'm going back and I'll tell Leo what happened if he doesn't already know."

Katarina's fearful eyes watched her. "What are you going to tell him?" She was worried that if Lina told Leo the truth, he might do something stupid, like beat Matron Violetta, and that would make things even more complicated for them.

"I'll tell him you had a reaction to the penicillin, just like the doctor said. We won't tell anyone what we suspect or know. I mean anyone," Lina emphasized.

Katarina sighed. "Good. It's a deal. I don't want you to get into trouble and I don't want my husband either, otherwise, we'll never get out of here."

"See you later," Lina chirped and strolled out of the emergency room, just as the male aide came in with a stretcher to roll Katarina to the medical floor.

Lina returned to the camp to see a crowd of refugees in front of the infirmary entrance. "Oh, I hope it isn't what I think," she grumbled to herself, quickly parking the vehicle and rushing to the scene. Matron Violetta and Leo were standing at the infirmary door arguing and being cheered by the mob.

Katarina's husband was livid. The fire in his blue eyes pierced Matron Violetta as he threatened her with his fist. "If my wife dies, you will too," Leo screamed.

The little hair on Lina's neck bristled with alarm when she heard Leo's threat. She broke through the mass and came behind him. "Stop that!" she shouted. "Katarina will be all right!" Even though it was loud enough for him to hear her warning, he didn't acknowledge it. She grabbed his hand and again said, "Katarina will be fine!"

"Let go of my hand!" Leo tried to shake her hand, struggling with her, as if he hadn't heard a word she said.

Lina kept pulling at his hand and shouted, "No! I won't let you go! You have to come with me!" She knew the carabineers would be called in as they always were when an Italian was involved.

"She hurt my wife!" Leo yelled as he fought to free himself from Lina's grip.

"Matron Violetta didn't hurt your wife. Katarina had a reaction to the penicillin. She'll be fine." Lina yelled into his ear, making sure he heard her this time and held tight to him. She had to get Leo away from Matron Violetta before the carabineers came.

Matron Violetta turned to Lina and said, "I'm glad that Katarina will be all right. Thank you for your help."

"No problem," Lina acknowledged her thanks as she struggled with Leo, but he resisted. "Come on, friend!" she screamed, pulling on him. She was strong though and wouldn't go. "I wish you hadn't done this. Your ship leaves soon for Canada. Do you want to be left behind, do you? Because if you touch her, that's exactly what's going to happen. The carabineers will take you away. They are on their way here as we speak, I can assure you. You and Katarina will never see Canada. Never! Now come on! I'll take you to your wife!"

He saw the carabineers marching toward Matron Violetta and finally he calmed down. "Oh no, let's get out of here!" he said in a panic.

"Sorry, friend. It's too late. Now you are under Matron Violetta's mercy. Whatever she chooses to do," Lina said sharply, staring at the carabineers approaching Matron Violetta and praying she would be merciful.

"What's going on, here?" one of the carabineer asked, looking over the crowd. "Violetta, do you need our help?"

"No, officer," Matron replied.

"Are you sure?"

"Yes. One of the refugee girls that work in the infirmary got suddenly sick and was taken to the hospital. Her husband was a little upset, but now everything is under control," Matron Violetta said, staring at Lina and Leo who stood still, fearing for the worse.

"You're lucky, my friend, that Matron Violetta didn't tell them the truth," Lina said, still holding Leo's hand. They turned and walked to the ambulance where Lina ordered him in. She climbed into the driver seat, took a deep breath, and stepped on the gas. All the way to the hospital, she didn't speak. Nor did he.

Lina parked the vehicle and said huskily, "Go see your wife." Leo glanced at her and was about to say something, but she turned her head away. Leo jumped out and rushed toward the hospital entrance. She was so angry with him that she remained behind; she didn't want Katarina to get upset too.

The hospital was affiliated with the Catholic Church and many of the duties were performed by nuns. The male aide rolled Katarina's stretcher from the emergency to a room with thirty other patients. One nun waited at the bedside as the male aide came with the stretcher down the room aisle. Another signaled to him and said, "In here," pointing to the bed beside the window.

"Gracia," the aide said and wheeled the stretcher close to it. "Now hop over," the man told Katarina.

She laughed ironically as she moved into the bed. "I see my luck hasn't run out on me yet."

"What's so funny?" the male aide asked as he turned to roll away the stretcher.

"Oh, nothing," she answered and turned her head to stare out the window. A few tears slid down her cheeks as she worried how long her luck might hold.

As soon as the aide left with the stretcher, the nuns began to straighten the sheets on Katarina's bed. "Are you feeling all right, my child?" one of them asked.

"Yes, thank you," Katarina replied, without turning her head and wishing they would leave her alone, but they kept fussing around.

"Hello, darling," she heard a familiar voice say and quickly turned. Her husband was standing beside her bed. The nuns were shocked to see him there as visiting hours were over but kept quiet.

She leapt into his arms and said, "I want to go home with you."

"You can't. Not yet. The doctor said he wants to keep you in just a few days for observation and recuperation," Leo replied, by then calm.

"How did you get here?"

"Lina drove me here."

"Where's Lina?" Katarina asked, surprised she hadn't come up with him to see her.

"The visiting hours are over, and the doctor let only me in for a few minutes. She'll come and see you tomorrow," Leo lied without mentioning anything about what had happened in the camp.

Before Katarina could say much of anything, another nun came by. "Visiting hours are over, sir, and we would like you to leave," she announced. "Our patients need rest." The nun left, but the other two continued straightening the sheets on Katarina's bed and wouldn't move.

Leo glanced at the nuns. "I'll see you tomorrow. I have to go anyway. Lina is waiting downstairs to take me back." He kissed her good-bye. She stared after him with tears in her eyes as he walked down the room aisle to the door.

"I'd like to go back to the camp with my husband," she said out loud.

"No," a nun panicked. "You can't go back just yet. Your body experienced a shock and it needs time to heal."

"What shock?" Katarina pretended she had no idea what the nun was talking about.

"Penicillin shock. You could have died, my child," The nun confirmed Lina's suspicions. It wasn't that she didn't believe Lina. Being a nurse, Katarina had suspected it herself, but hearing it from the nun was the proof she needed. Even though she wasn't planning to do anything with it, especially with their D-day so close, she was happy to know the truth.

The supper wagon rolled down the aisle and interrupted her reverie. "Here is your tray, Mrs. Lisic," a man said and placed it on the bed table for her. She didn't feel like eating and ignored it.

A nun came and lifted the cover of the plate. "Eat some spaghetti, they look delicious, my child," she said.

When Katarina heard the word *spaghetti*, her stomach churned. "Oh no! If anyone offers me spaghetti one more time, I'll scream," she muttered. But when her stomach began to growl and demand food, she peeked at the plate and realized this spaghetti was different. There were pieces of meat and the spaghetti was covered with plenty of delicious Italian sauce. "Oh, wow! A banana and orange too. I haven't seen these since who knows when," she voiced as she picked up a piece of the fruit.

"Eat, my child, eat," the nun urged and finally walked away.

"Thank God!" Katarina whispered to herself, watching her go. The swarming nuns around her bed made her even more nervous and worried.

The next morning after breakfast, the doctors were making rounds; as soon as they reached her bed, she asked, "Can I go home today?"

Her doctor glanced at her and then at her chart. "Not today, Mrs. Lisic," he said and continued on.

Lina was authorized to use the ambulance car to transport Leo to visit Katarina in the hospital, as for any other refugee who was sick, but not every day of course.

Four days later, Katarina was still in the hospital, not very amused with the situation she was in. At first, she enjoyed being pampered. Her only problem was choosing which fruit to eat or so she thought. But as the days wore on and she still was in there, she began to wonder, *Why doesn't the doctor release me? There has to be a reason. I must be very sick. Maybe I'm going to die? They are keeping it from me.*

*No! No!* her inner voice raged. Your suspicious, always-doubting nature was getting the better of you. But she couldn't stop the doubts from playing her, and every day she stayed, she worried Leo and she were going to miss their ship to Canada.

She just couldn't let that happen, but what could she do? Just the thought of being left behind sent a shiver up her spine and brought tears to her eyes. "Oh, why did this have to happen now?" she agonized.

"Hello, darling. How are you today?" Leo's voice brought her down to earth. He sat beside her on the bed, subdued, and didn't even kiss her.

"Just as good as I was yesterday. I'm ready to go back to the camp. I still have a lot of things to do before our departure. Besides, in a few days is Christmas, and I want to spend it with you, home, in our room. Why won't the doctor let me go?"

She stared at him waiting for his reply and realized he was looking at her as though he had something to tell her, but the words wouldn't come. Fear welled up inside her. *Oh my god, it's true. There's something wrong with me, I must be very sick.* Her eyes filled with terror and fixed on his. "Tell me the truth!" she blurted. "I deserve that much from you, don't I?"

"Tell you what, Katarina?" Leo asked, surprised.

"You know that I won't be going anywhere because I'm dying," she choked out between tears.

Shocked, Leo took a deep breath. "No! No, darling. Where did you get that idea? You're not dying." He hugged her. "I would take you home now if the doctor would let you leave."

"Then why do you look so worried and crushed, did something else happen?" she asked in a hushed tone.

"Yes, there is," he whispered. "I don't know how to tell you this, but the camp authority told me that if you're not out of the hospital and back in the camp by Christmas day, we'll be taken off the transport list. And so far, the doctor is refusing to discharge you. He keeps saying you need to recuperate."

"Nothing of this makes any sense to me. Can we do something?" Katarina asked, very anxious.

"What can we do? I have to go and meet Lina, she wanted to speak to me about something. See you tomorrow," Leo said and left in a hurry.

Leo was concentrating on something else instead of her. *What about me?* she wondered, watching him walk away. It wasn't that she was envious of Lina, but she wanted to get out of the hospital.

He met Lina in the hospital parking and they talked about how to get Katarina out of the hospital before December 25. She arrived a little early and picked up a few papers from the hospital administration and waited in the vehicle for Leo.

They wanted to tell Katarina, but her hospital room with thirty other patients wasn't a good place to do that, especially when Lina wanted that to be a secret. As soon as he arrived, she handed to him the papers.

"What are these papers for?" he asked, with interest as he settled on the passenger seat.

"They are called release of responsibility. You have to sign them agreeing to take full responsibility for your wife upon yourself, which then releases the doctor of his responsibility for her. This way he can't stop Katarina from leaving the hospital. However, the doctor has to witness your signature," she explained on the way back to the camp.

"I'll do anything to get my wife out so we don't lose this transport. Thank you, Lina," Leo said as they arrived to the camp.

"The only thanks I need from you is to get your wife home, and please not a word of this to anyone. We'll go tomorrow and bring Katarina back to the camp," Lina said and stopped the ambulance for him to get out.

The following day, Lina picked up Leo at his shack and drove him to the hospital to visit Katarina. She was all wrapped in her thoughts, worrying and wondering what was going on and why the doctor was keeping her in that she hadn't seen her husband coming down the room aisle.

"Penny for your thoughts?" she heard a familiar voice say. She jumped and hugged him, glad to see him.

"What are those?" she asked pointing to the papers in his hands.

"Never mind this. Did the doctor say anything new this morning?" he asked.

"If you're asking if he said I can go home. No." Katarina turned her head away. "There has to be a reason. Otherwise, why all this hovering over me and double portions of everything?"

Leo rushed out of the room without responding. Her mind whirled. She didn't know whether to be more afraid of dying or what Leo might be doing.

Ten minutes later, he returned with a smile on his face. "You're going home, darling, as soon as the doctor arrives."

"Are you sure?"

"Yes, I am. So get dressed."

"But what does that mean, am I sick?"

Leo took her face into his hands and stared into her eyes reassuringly, "Be patient a little, the doctor will be here soon."

Katarina crawled off the bed and got dressed. By the time, the doctor arrived she was ready to leave.

He glanced at Leo and then at Katarina and smiled, "You know, Mr. Lisic, I couldn't release your wife because of the hospital police. Hand me those papers. Sign here, here, and here." He pointed to the marks on the papers. Then he witnessed it with his signature. "Katarina, you're free to leave."

"Thank you, Doctor," Leo said and shook his hand, then took his wife's hand. "Let's get out of here, darling."

Lina was waiting with the ambulance car in the parking lot to take them back to the camp. She sat inside the vehicle while Leo and his wife approached. "Thanks, my friend," Katarina said and climbed into the passenger seat with Leo.

"It's my pleasure," Lina smiled and drove back to the camp, dropping them off in front of their shack.

Happy, full of joy, and grateful to be home, Katarina hugged her friend. "Come for coffee, we need to talk before Leo and I leave for Canada."

"Yes, soon, but now I have to go to work," Lina chuckled and drove away.

They walked to their room, still cold as ever. Katarina felt shaken from the ordeal she went through, and spending days in the hospital worrying didn't help. "It's cold in here."

"Let me help you in bed," Leo offered.

"I'm not going to bed, I had enough of that in the hospital." She took a blanket and wrapped it around her shoulder and sat at the table.

"I'm glad you're home and well again." Her husband reached down to kiss her forehead and said. "I have to go to see Marko for a few minutes. I'll be back shortly."

"I'm glad I'm home too. I wouldn't want any other way," she smiled and snuggled into the blanket. He spun on his heels and was gone.

After he left, Katarina wandered around in their small room and checked their supplies and the things she still has to do for their trip. She invited Lina for coffee so she better have some when she comes, she thought, looking into the brown bag. "Good, there's enough for a few more coffees," she muttered to herself.

An hour went by, Leo hadn't returned and she was getting tired. Still wrapped in the blanket, she lay down on the bed and listened to the sound of music coming from outside through the window holes. "People are starting to celebrate the holidays already," she said under her breath, drifting off to sleep.

xxxxxxxxxxxxxxxxxxxxxxxxxxxxxxxxxxxxxxxxxxxxxxxxxxxxx

She awoke to a smell of food the next morning. Her husband was up and tiptoed around not to wake her. Refreshed and much more energetic, Katarina chirped, "Good morning, Leo."

"You're finally awake. It's lunchtime, not morning. You've slept through it," he said and went to embrace her. He kept his arms wrapped around for a long while.

"Let me go, I'm hungry."

He laughed as she dug her elbows into him. "You forget, I've climbed mountains. I'm hard and tough. Your elbows are like thistledown."

"You never told me that you were a mountain climber," she said surprised and moved to the table where lunch was waiting for her. Just as they were finishing their food, Lina walked in.

"What are you doing, friends?" her husky voice was so loud that the neighbor could have heard it.

Katarina stood up and hurried toward her. "We are just fine. Come in, come in. And how is my best friend?"

"Yeah, you know me. Nothing new, working hard. At least, we have nice December weather. The wind is blowing a little, but it's not bad."

"That's good. Sit down," Katarina offered. "You didn't get any help in the infirmary yet?"

Lina sat down on the stool beside Leo. "No, not yet. Matron Violetta is working on it, that's what she said." Leo and Lina nodded hello to each other with their heads in acknowledgement.

Katarina let them alone and rushed to make a coffee, hoping Leo would leave so Lina and she could talk. Her suspicious mind just couldn't leave things alone. She needed to know why they kept her in the hospital if she was healthy and Lina must know something. When the coffee was done, she poured two cups and turned to the table. "Leo, would you like a cup too?"

"No, darling. I'm going to see what Viktor is up to." He stood up and left.

She brought the coffee to the table and placed one in front of Lina. "The coffee I promised you when you brought me from the hospital. Sorry, I packed my cups so you have to drink the coffee out of these paper cups," and sat on the opposite side to her.

Katarina's thoughts were running wild as they sipped on the coffees. She hesitated for a moment, but she felt that Lina was expecting her to say something about the hospital. "Tell me that this nightmare was a dream. It didn't happen, right?"

"Wrong. It did happen and it happened before and is happening now, so don't you forget it," Lina stressed.

"But this is absurd. The camp authorities were going to use my illness to keep us back. Why, Lina?"

Lina hesitated. "I wasn't going to tell you, but I learned you could be trusted so here it goes. In one word, money. The camp authorities stand to lose a lot of money in donations if it comes out that an Italian nurse was negligent. They get a lot of money to take care of us, but the sad part is that they barely spent 0.5 percent for the refugees. Here, we are eating dry spaghetti almost every day. No meat, no fruit, no veggies. There's so much corruption no one knows who is doing what. Everyone is misusing the money the camp gets for the refugees.

And quite frankly, filling their pockets."

"I knew it! It has to be a reason." Katarina sighed, relieved it's finally over. Please watch yourself, and don't worry. I'll never tell a soul about this. I hope Matron Violetta won't cast suspicion on you."

She stood up to leave. "Matron Violetta won't suspect me, thanks to your husband."

"My husband? What do you mean?"

"Oh, he didn't mention anything to you about what he had done the day you were admitted," Lina smiled. "He attacked Matron Violetta and threatened to kill her, if you die." As she headed to the door, she turned to Katarina. "But don't tell him that I told you."

"I was afraid he might do something stupid like that. I don't understand how could he do this? Doesn't he realize he didn't do himself a favor?"

"He wasn't thinking. Leave it at that now. Mention this to him after ten or fifteen years in Canada, if you still remember. And now I really have to go," Lina chuckled.

"Wait! Here, take this hot plate back. Give it to someone who might need it," Katarina handed it to her and escorted her friend out.

Strong cold winds blew and the sun disappeared behind the horizon. Lina glanced up. "I hope we won't have a storm," she said, looking at the dark clouds hurrying through the sky as she walked away.

"I hope so too." Katarina remained a few minutes on the threshold of the shack, watching sparrows get shaken off the palm and pine trees by the wind and cuddled under the roof of the shack, trying to escape from the biting wind.

Later, she walked slowly back to the room, collected the dishes, and went to the laundry to wash them and brought a few bottles of water inside.

Leo still wasn't there. The room was cold; she lay down on the bed and bundled into a blanket to keep warm. Cozy under the blankets, she drifted off to sleep.

# CHAPTER 17

Several hours later, she awoke to the sound of the wind whistling through the window holes. Leo wasn't there. She got up and walked to the window. Darkness had swept through the camp so she couldn't see a thing, but there was lots of commotion as people were singing and shouting. The whole camp buzzed with the double festivities of Christmas and the upcoming departure of a group of refugees. Katarina listened to the music and smiled to herself, happy that Lina had helped Leo find a way to get her released from the hospital. Otherwise, their names would have been taken off the list, and she wouldn't be home to see or hear this celebration.

Her daydream was interrupted by Leo rushing in and slamming the door. Excitedly, he announced, "We're going to the church tonight to midnight Mass. Can you make it, darling?"

"But, of course, I can make it!" she confirmed, annoyed with her husband for even suggesting that she couldn't.

"Sorry, I don't mean to sound careless. I just thought because of the weather you might want to stay home. The wind is strong and cold." Leo smoothly got himself out of trouble and began to dress up.

Katarina was just as determined to accompany her husband to the midnight Mass and wasn't about to let him out of her sight, if she can help it. "The wind won't bother me," she smiled, half-dressed.

When they arrived, the small church was crowded with worshippers who had come to say a prayer and give thanks to the baby Jesus for helping them get out of this place, at least some of them. "There's no more empty seat," Katarina whispered to her husband as the Mass had began.

"Come here. We're going to lean against the wall," he said in a low tone, and they moved to the wall and began singing with others.

Her body broke into a cold sweat before the Mass was half over. Her knees began to buckle and her stomach churned, but she said nothing to Leo. No matter how well she pretended to be, she couldn't bear the hot stifling atmosphere inside the church. Grabbing her husband's hand, she whispered, "I don't feel well," fearful that she might faint.

Leo took a hold of her and glanced around for open spaces, but the only window in the church was too far away for them to reach. So he wrapped his arms around her waist and whispered, "Come with me, darling." He led her out of the church before anyone could see she wasn't well because he was afraid the camp authorities might send her back to the hospital and that would spell disaster for them and their trip.

She didn't answer but did what he asked of her. He helped Katarina to lean against the church wall outside and asked, "Are you better?"

After a few deep breaths, she replied, "I'm fine. I just needed some fresh air."

Soon, the blowing wind chilled them and they shivered. "There's certainly a lot of fresh air out here," Leo said and glanced at her. "Let's go back inside."

Katarina felt much better, but she wasn't about to go back into the crowded church, even though she would miss seeing baby Jesus. "I'm going home," she said and turned to walk away.

"Wait! I'm going with you," Leo called and rushed toward her.

"No! No, you go back into the church, kiss baby Jesus, and say a prayer for me," his wife replied and continued down the pathway.

"Well, if you insist. I'll come home as soon as the Mass is over, I promise," Leo yelled after his wife and hurried into church. Katarina tried to quicken her pace, but the gusty wind slowed her down, stinging her face and blowing her clothes around like a tourniquet.

When she finally reached their room, she shivered, "I'm so glad to be out of that biting wind." Immediately, she grabbed a blanket and bundled herself in it, then laid down on the bed. Warm and snugged under the blanket, she fretted in and out of sleep, restless and tormented by concerns for their upcoming voyage. The things Lina told her, she couldn't get them off her mind, and she was afraid there was still time for things to go wrong.

Suddenly, she was wide awake. Her husband wasn't home yet. She glanced at her watch. "Three o'clock in the morning?" she said out loud and jumped from her bed in alarm. "Where's my husband? The Mass must be over by now." She walked to the window and gazed out through the glass.

The night was so dark that she couldn't see a thing. But she could hear music and people celebrating Christmas and the imminent departure day. Everyone was having fun, and here she was, alone. Sadness wrapped around her heart. "Leo and I should have been celebrating with them together," she muttered under her breath.

The coldness in her room chilled her body and forced her to return to bed, but she couldn't relax and was out of bed again and begun anxiously to pace back and forth. "Where could he be?" Bad thoughts raced through her mind and made her worried even more. When she couldn't stand it any longer, Katarina rushed to the door and opened it to peer out. By then, the wind had risen dramatically and it almost pushed her back inside, but she stood her ground and stared into the pitch-dark of the night. Though she could see nothing, snatches of music and voices came in waves carried on the wind, like a sound of a wolf moaning from deep in the mountains.

It didn't take long for the cold wind to force her to retreat to the warmth and safety of her room. "I better get in," she grumbled. While she wrestled with the wind to close the door, she heard a familiar voice. "Oh! It's my husband's voice!" she spoke softly to herself and ran inside, leaving the door open. She grabbed her coat and rushed toward the sound of the voice singing. The wind carried it on a twisted path, making it difficult for her to find him, but finally Katarina stood in front of the shack.

Suddenly, she felt foolish. "Come on, turn back! You're acting like a crazy woman." Before she could decide what to do, she heard voices coming toward her. Embarrassed, she ran to the side of the shack to hide so no one could see her. Standing behind a pile of bricks stacked under the window of the shack, she could clearly hear her husband's singing. Then a female voice joined Leo in singing. Katarina's stomach fluttered. "Who is she?" she asked herself in a whispering tone. Wanting to know, she climbed up on the pile of bricks and peered through a tear in the window covering to see him embracing another woman. "Oh no, that bastard! How can he kiss and dance with another woman when he's married to me?" she hissed through her teeth, still not knowing who she is. The woman's back was toward the window preventing Katarina from seeing the face of the other woman in her husband's life. She freaked out.

Questions nudged forth in her head as she stood frozen under the window, still peeking in, even though the cold wind kept biting her. *How can he forget about me? Why didn't he come home? Would they laugh at her if she went inside?* she wondered. "Of course, they would," she answered her own question and began her descent from the pile. "Go back to your room!" she commanded herself, but the panic boiled inside her, muddling rational thought. She was so upset she slipped and fell in the mud. "Oh no! Look at you!" she grumbled as she shook the mud off her hands. This mishap enraged her even more. Katarina just couldn't leave without knowing what was going on and who that woman with her husband was. The rage blinded her, she didn't care who laughed at her.

She stormed through the door, mud dripping from her hair and clothes, and headed straight for her husband and the woman he was dancing with. When Leo turned his dancing partner to face her, Katarina's heart sunk to her feet and filled with anguish. "Oh no! It's you! You bitch!" she shrilled and instantly slapped Manda across the face, then pushed her away from Leo. "Stay away from my husband!"

Everyone laughed.

She walked to Leo and screamed into his face, "How could you do this to me? You son of a bitch!"

"Did what to you?" he asked nonchalantly, pretending he didn't know what she was talking about.

"We were just dancing," Manda interrupted.

"A likely story," Katarina shouted in rage. "You . . . you . . . BITCH! You husband snatcher, stay out of this! You stole the best night from me!" She pushed Manda with both hands so hard that she flew into the corner. Katarina spun around and ran out into the night, leaving everyone staring with their mouth wide open.

"Wait!" Leo called, running after her. When he caught up to her, he asked, "What in God's name do you think you're doing? Do you know they can use this to take us off the list, do you?" Struggling not to raise his voice.

"That's good. That's really good. What a hypocrite. You asking me what I'm doing! How about what you're doing?" She pushed past him and strode home. Leo followed her into their room, both angry at each other.

Choking on her tears, Katarina screamed, "Look what you made me do. You promised you'd come back right after the Mass was over! Instead, you went to celebrate our departure with Manda, my so-called maid of honor. I see now why you sprang me from the hospital. It wasn't because you wanted to be with me, but because you were afraid you'd be left behind with me!"

"I got sidetracked!" Leo yelled back, getting his clothes off. "At the church, Marko asked me to have a drink with him and I accepted. We walked to that place where they sell wine under the table, and we had a drink."

Katarina anxiously listened to him and spat, "But I didn't find you drinking with Marko, did I? I found you in Manda's arms!"

Settling in bed, he replied, "Marko left just a few minutes before you burst in. You can ask him if you don't believe me. Manda asked me to dance with her—"

"Let me guess. You couldn't refuse," Katarina angrily finished his sentence.

"Exactly. I had one dance with her. Is there something wrong with that? You went home from the church sick so I thought you were too tired to go out," Leo replied and pulled an extra blanket over himself.

A hot anger coursed through her body, stopping her shivering. She swallowed hard and turned to stare. "You asked me if there is something wrong. Let's see. I fell in the mud and got all wet and dirty. I embarrassed myself in front of a bunch of people. You and Manda made me the biggest fool who ever existed for the second time. You figure it out!"

"Nothing happened! There's nothing going on between us," Leo tried to convince her. "I danced with a friend once, that's all!"

"Some friend!" Katarina screamed. "Silly me, here I thought you loved me and that you would return to me as you promised. Instead, you left me all alone on Christmas Eve and went to celebrate our departure with someone else! Is that what you call nothing? I can't believe that I thought you loved me."

Instead of responding, Leo stared up at the ceiling with his hands behind his head and a smirk on his face ignoring every word she said.

"You, bigot!" she yelled and took the wedding ring from her finger. "Here! You can have this back," and threw it at Leo's face. "I have no use for it anymore. We're finished! You're no longer my husband." She turned away from him, spewing fire.

Anger replaced the smirk on Leo's face, and fury ignited in his eyes. He abruptly stood up, accidentally knocking over Katarina's doggy bank. He violently kicked the figurine across the room and grabbed her shoulders, spinning her toward him. "How dare you come after me like that, insulting and angry?" he yelled in her face and pushed her away from him. Katarina's body struck hard against the hard brick wall and slid down to the floor. Her hands shook as they covered her mouth and silenced her sobs. She stared at him with fear and disbelief, trembling.

Leo lifted his hair off his forehead as if to try to comprehend what had just happened and rushed to her. "Now look what you made me do! Come on, darling, let's not fight. We are leaving in a few days. You wouldn't want to spoil that, would you?" he asked in a softened tone, the fury in his eyes gone.

Reluctantly, she grabbed his hand and let him help pull her up, but only because she wanted to be on that ship sailing for Canada on December 31. "There you go," he said as he wrapped her shivering body in a blanket and guided her into bed. He tried to gaze into her eyes to weigh her mood, but she refused to meet his.

"Leave me alone," she said. "I don't need your help." She turned away from him and wept in silence, but could feel Leo's blue eyes entreating her to forget everything. Katarina hated being this conscious of him, especially when she was furious with him. But somehow he was always in command of her thoughts, feelings, and actions as if he knew every thought that spun through her mind.

The light of dawn came upon them quickly. Katarina barely slept a wink as she sobbed most of the night while her husband snored beside her and was still sleeping. She got up, wrapped herself in one of Leo's cotton shirts, and sat on the stool beside the window, heavyhearted.

The sun rose bright and clear. "Christmas Day," she whispered, trying to absorb some cheer from the sun's rays. However, even the sun couldn't brighten her spirits and she moaned to herself, "This should have been one the happiest days in my life, instead, it is one of the saddest." It just didn't feel like a holiday without her family, she still missed them so much. Her eyes filled with lonely tears. She thought Leo would be her family forever, but now she wasn't so sure about that either. She glanced at her husband stretched on the bed, still sound asleep. She drew a deep long breath, "Oh, God, how I feel alone."

Katarina wanted to punish him because he had hurt her so deeply, yet her dark eyes burned with desire and her heart ached for his touch. *How can she punish him?* she wondered and turned back to stare out the window with a promise to never speak to Manda again.

They had been the best of friends, but now, just the thought of her name gave Katarina heartache. Even more painful were her feelings for Leo. "How could he do that to me?" she asked herself under her breath, again and again, wiping the tears running down her cheeks.

She could still remember, as vividly as if had happened yesterday, the lovely summer night they spent together under the open sky. It was full of mystical moonlight and magic stars, the scent of lilacs and lilies of the valley filled the air. After making love for the first time on their wedding night, she had expected the best to follow. Now it seemed like such a long, long time ago. Everything was falling apart just as they were about to depart for their promised new home. She was clueless to what was the best to do.

Her thoughts were interrupted by Leo's touch as he wrapped his arms around her shoulders from behind. "Merry Christmas, darling. I'm sorry for last night," he whispered in her ear. "I drank a little more than I should have." He kissed her softly on her neck and silently slipped the wedding ring back on her finger. Then he turned her toward him and looked at her face. "I love you very much. You're wrong to think otherwise."

Katarina stared into his blue eyes with an unsettled feeling in her heart. Leo seemed to always know which of her strings to pull. Even so, it felt good to have his arms around her body, she admitted. So, as before, she ignored the voice of caution that intruded on her senses and forgave him yet again. "I'm sorry too. I acted like a crazy woman. Merry Christmas," she said after a long pause. "I'd never forgive myself if I were the cause of us being left behind."

"I know you wouldn't," Leo agreed.

She pulled herself out his embrace. "I know you do, but I will not let that happen," she said and went to get dress to go to the Christmas Mass.

"Are you ready to go, darling?" Leo asked and headed to the door.

"I'm coming," she said and grabbed Leo's hand. They exited and strode to the church with hands entwined. Dignity and privacy was important to Katarina. It wasn't easy for her to face the people at the church and especially those in front of whom she made a fool of herself. In the camp, there were no secrets. She was sure that by then almost everyone knew what she had done, but she wanted to show everyone that what had happened the night before hadn't affected their relationship. More than anything, she wanted to send a message to Manda.

The church was jam-packed when Leo and Katarina entered. "We better stay close to the exit," Leo warned, glancing at his wife.

"I'll be fine. Don't worry about me," she replied with a smile and leaned against the wall beside the door. Just then, Manda entered with her children. Katarina's blood drained from her face. She quickly turned her head and avoided the contact with Manda the whole time they were in church.

It was midday and lunch was about to be served when the Mass was over. Leo and Katarina rushed home to get their mess tins to pick up their food. "Let's eat our Christmas lunch in the cafeteria," Leo suggested on their way over.

"All right, but we better hurry if we are going to find empty seats," Katarina agreed and quickened her pace.

As they came to the cafeteria, the entrance was jammed with refugees waiting to get in. "Merry Christmas," they chanted in unison.

The crowd responded the same way. "Merry Christmas to you too."

As they reached inside of the cafeteria, Leo turned to his wife and ordered, "You go look for seats and I'm going to get the food."

"All right," she replied and went to look and watch when someone gets up and leave.

On the far side, she noticed an arm up and gesturing her to come over. When she got close, she noticed their friend Viktor. "Do you have two seats free?" she asked looking at the full table.

"If you wait a little while. This two are leaving in a few minutes," Viktor explained.

"I'll wait, thank you," Katarina replied. "Are you ready for the long trip, Viktor?"

"Oh yeah, long time ago. I don't have much. What I have is on the ship already."

In the meantime, the two people left the table, and Katarina sat down. Leo picked up the food and was looking for his wife. She saw him by the counter and waved. He walked over. "Hello, friend," Leo said to Viktor, placed the food on the table, and sat beside Katarina.

She peered into her mess tin. "Dry spaghetti on Christmas Day! God, couldn't they cook something else, at least for today?" She barely touched her food.

Viktor looked at her and chuckled. "You still didn't get used to it!"

"I did, but I'm not hungry," Katarina sighed. "I'm going to visit Lina, wish her merry Christmas, say good-bye to the matron and some other girls." She smiled and walked away.

On the way to the infirmary, she enjoyed the walk on the beautiful, sunny Christmas Day; the wind blew lightly, but it didn't bother Katarina until Manda crossed her path and stopped her. "I would like to speak to you," she said, standing in front of her.

"Leave me alone! Haven't you done enough? I never want to speak to you again!" Katarina retorted and stormed away.

Anger boiled inside her, so she changed her mind and decided to take a walk down by the river. The murmuring water of the river calmed her and washed away her bad thoughts, even if for a short time. Her eyes were fixed on the debris and trash the river carried ahead. Piece after piece tumbled along its way. "The water has to carry many loads and make its way past numerous obstacles before it reaches its destination," she muttered under her breath. It captivated her so much, she hadn't felt the temperature drop. Her body shivered. She took a few deep breaths of fresh air into her lungs and hurried back.

On the way, she stopped at the infirmary. As she entered the door, Lina was on the door out. "Merry Christmas, my friend. I was hoping you'd stop by. Let's go to the cafeteria and grab a cup of coffee."

"Merry Christmas to you too. It sounds so great to say it freely out loud, Merry Christmas!" Katarina replied and smiled as she turned and walked out with Lina.

"You mean, without looking over your shoulder if someone is listening?" Lina replied. "I remember those days and my parents whispering while talking. Also, I have vivid picture of Christmas holidays, when two weeks before, the Communists cleared everything from the shells of the stores: sugar, flour, banana, oranges, eggs, and anything else that would prevent the Catholics to celebrate Christmas.

"As soon as December 25 passed, they returned them to the stores for the New Year's celebration. I remember that. I also remember the jails were full of Croats, Catholic, who went to the church and sung their songs.

"My most memorable part was when I went with my parents to church in the middle of the night to the christening of my baby brother. I didn't know then that the children were forbidden by the Communists to be christened," Lina said, entering into the cafeteria. Inside, there were only a few people left by the time they arrived. Leo and Viktor were gone.

In the cafeteria, sipping on her coffee, Katarina looked at her friend askance and wondered what Lina was up to now. "I've been feeling you want to ask me something. What is it?"

Lina glanced at her with uneasiness in her eyes. "I heard a rumor," she began tactfully, "that's being whispered throughout the camp." Then she came right out and asked, "What happened last night? That Leo! He's been giving you a lot of undeserved grief lately, hasn't he?"

Katarina nodded positively.

"Why don't you leave him?" Lina asked, anger flashing in her eyes.

"I could never do that now," Katarina frowned. "Besides, if I were to take such a step now, we might, no, we would be both left behind in this camp forever at least until the things cleared. I couldn't stand being here for one minute more than I have to."

"I don't understand after what he had done to you. Why would you want to live with him?" Lina asked once more.

She paused and threw Lina an empty stare, surprised, not about the way Lina felt about Leo, but that she would encourage her to leave him now, five days before their departure. Katarina was worried her friend knew more than she was saying. "I told you why," she finally answered.

"You could find someone else," Lina persisted. "Whom you might love as much, but in a different way and who would give you the respect you deserve. Leo doesn't deserve you."

"For God's sake, Lina, let it be, this isn't the time to talk about things like that," Katarina said, annoyed at her friend. "In a few days, we'll be gone from here on our way to the promised land. I'm sure things will work themselves out once we get to Canada. If not, I can always leave him then and there."

"Hmm, there's still a glimmer of hope for you two, I suppose, since Manda isn't traveling your way," Lina smirked.

"Amen to that!" Katarina agreed and added. "I have to go, Leo will be furious. I've been gone for a long time."

"We'll see each other before you two leave, right?" Lina quizzed.

"Of course, we'll be leaving December 30 in the morning from the camp. We still have a lot of time to see each other," Katarina affirmed and rushed home.

The sky was clear blue and the sun shone bright, but the nasty wind blew strong, swaying the branches of the palm and pine trees, making Katarina rush home. As soon as she walked through the door, "Where have you been for so long?" Leo demanded. "I've been worried sick."

"I strolled down by the river. I had a lot of things to sort out." She took her coat off and hung it behind the door.

Leo rushed to her and wrapped his arms around her. "How could you go down there? Do you know how dangerous that place is? Many refugees have been found dead there, killed by someone." He held her tightly against his body. It seemed hours before he let her go. She felt suffocated. "You scared me," he voiced his concern as he let her go. "Don't ever go there again."

"Oh, come on," she said and gazed into his face suspiciously, wondering how important she really was to him. Her judgment was clouded by all the recent unhappy moments, but not that bad not to recognize Leo's big crocodile tears. However, how Leo felt about her she wasn't sure anymore. Should she believe him or not after all the mixed signals he'd been giving her? She didn't know. Only one thing was clear in her mind, departure day. "I won't let anything spoil that," she promised herself and sat on the stool.

The Christmas Day passed in a peaceful atmosphere between Katarina and Leo. The following morning, Katarina leapt out of bed as soon as she awoke. "Only a few more days left. Have we forgotten to do something?" she asked excited, glancing at Leo.

"I don't think so. Our chest of belongings is already on the ship. We'll sign our last papers and the documents on December 30. Relax!" he chuckled.

Katarina ran back and forth, around the room, checking every corner to make sure nothing worth was left behind. "You are right. We'll get the passports and some other papers just before we board the ship. I just wanted to make sure everything is in order."

Their banter was interrupted by a knock on the door. Leo sprang to open it. A man stood on the threshold holding a big carton box. "Mr. Lisic?" he asked.

"Yes, that's me," Leo answered, staring at the man, wondering what he was doing on their doorstep.

"I have a delivery for you."

"Delivery? From whom?" Leo asked, puzzled.

"The box is from the camp authorities. Sign here," the man ordered, handing Leo a pen. He signed and took the box inside. "Let's open it, and see what's in it," a curious Leo said as he tore the box open and emptied the contents on the floor.

There was a letter included that read:

"This is a gift from us, the camp authorities. The clothing is warm and it will come handy in a cold, freezing Canada."

While Leo read the letter, Katarina rummaged through the clothing and pulled out a huge skirt that was obviously intended for her, three sizes too big. She held it in front of her body. "Some gift! Whom is this for? It's most certainly not for me, and army clothes at that? I thought we were sailing to a democratic and peaceful country, not a war zone."

Leo turned toward her holding a pair of large-sized army pants in front of him. "Look, mine are the same ugly things. I bet they kept the money that was intended for our clothes and gave us these used army things for our journey."

"That is disgusting! How they can do that is beyond me," she replied and eagerly continued digging through the clothing, but everything she found was at least two or three sizes large for her. "I wouldn't be caught dead in this!" she yelled. "There's nothing here I can use. They must have thought I was as big as an elephant." Angrily, she threw them back into the box, but before she did, she noticed a plastic bag stuck at the bottom of the box. In the bag was a beautiful pastel two-piece lady's top made of cotton with short and long sleeves. "Oh my god, look at this," she chirped. "This is a miracle." Katarina quickly tried it on, and it fit her, almost. "It's a little too big, but I'll keep it. It will go well with the burgundy suit I plan to wear on the ship. It's perfect! And, of course, the raincoat." She decided.

"But, darling, you need to take at least the army coat. Your raincoat won't do, if you remember, that Canada is a cold country, as we were told by the camp authorities," Leo warned, looking worried.

"Yeah, I remember. But how much colder could it be than it is here?" Katarina smirked, ignored his warning, and threw everything back into the box, except the pastel set she found. "There's no way! I'm not going to wear this . . . this junk!"

Leo shrugged his shoulders. "Who knows how cold Canada is? But we need to be prepared for whatever the weather is."

"Don't worry about me. You wear whatever you want, and I'll wear what I want." She took the lovely sweater set and added it to her belongings.

# CHAPTER 18

Leo and Katarina were busy signing papers and collating their documents at the administrative building.

The day before departure, when they finished and emerged from the building, their emotions were high. Katarina screamed, "Wow! We did it, my love! We're on our way to Canada!" Filled with energy, she leapt into Leo's embrace.

"Don't get too excited. We're not even out of the camp yet," Leo replied. "We still have one more night."

Katarina glanced at him. "What's wrong with you? You sound as though you don't believe we'll be leaving tomorrow. What can possibly go wrong now?"

Leo gazed into the sparkling happiness of her eyes, smiled, and slipped his fingers through hers. They continued on their way without further comment on the subject.

On the way home, Katarina said, "Let's go say good-bye to our friend Lina, she is working day shift today."

"All right, I'll be glad to," Leo agreed and they walked into the infirmary.

Hello, you two," Lina said, approaching them. Matron Violetta rushed to her office as soon as they entered. She didn't want to face Leo and Katarina.

"Hello, yourself! You are not working too hard, are you?" Leo teased with a smile.

Katarina silently hugged her friend, tears flooding down her cheeks as she faced leaving yet another good friend behind forever. After a short pause, she squeezed her close. "I hope your papers are ready soon so you can start your life too. You've been waiting long enough."

"I hope so," Lina replied grimly, adding, "But I'm so happy for you and Leo that you are on your way. I'll certainly miss you both. Good-bye."

"By the way, Matron Violetta didn't have to run. I wanted to say good-bye to her too. I don't hold her responsible for my allergy reaction. Tell her that for me, will you, Lina? Could you also give me your address, so I can send you a letter when we arrive to Canada?"

"Oh, that would be lovely," Lina said and quickly wrote on a piece of paper her address and handed to Katarina. "Here, and don't you forget me."

"I'll never forget you. Thanks for everything," Katarina said, pointing out, "If it wasn't for you, we might not be saying good-bye to each other today. And I'll miss you too so much. Good-bye." Katarina squeezed Lina little tighter before letting go.

Still holding on to her hand and with a sad face, Lina said, "Never give up, my friend."

Choking on her tears, Katarina said, "I'd better go before I explode," and quickly pulled her hand back and rushed away. Leo said his good-byes to Lina and followed his wife home.

Katarina and Leo were apprehensive and restless just as were the other refugees leaving in the morning. Their last hours in the camp were ticking away too slow, it seemed as if they would never pass. There was no place they could settle and find peace; they were continuously on a go. "Let's get over that list one more time," Leo suggested.

Katarina pulled the list out and began to read it to Leo. "Everything seems to be in order," she said and folded the list and put it in her purse. She took another look around and threw herself on the bed. "Now what?"

"Now we're going to the cafeteria, supper will be served soon and we're going to have our food there," Leo said, and they strolled out and to the cafeteria. As they walked, the sound of music and singing could be heard from the inside of the camp.

"Some refugees are still celebrating," Katarina said as they entered.

At the door, they ran into Viktor, rushing out. "Where are you running to?" Leo asked.

"To the party. A bunch of us are celebrating our last night in here," Viktor said and rushed out. Leo and Katarina sat down for their supper. Halfway into it, Manda came to pick up her food and looked around.

Katarina noticed Manda and turned her back to her. "I hope she doesn't come over here," she said, looking at her husband.

Leo shrugged his shoulders and continued to eat his supper without glancing toward her. When Manda saw they're not reacting, she got her food and left. "Thank God, she's gone," Katarina sighed in relief and enjoyed the rest of her meal.

During the hour or so Leo and Katarina spent in the cafeteria, their friends came over and offered their wishes and said their good-byes to them. They also said good-byes to many friends and acquaintances. "Now, we're going to our room and get a good night's sleep," Leo said and stood up to leave.

"Do we have to go already? The night is still young," Katarina pointed out, she wasn't sleepy at all.

"Yes, we have to. You'll thank me in the morning," her husband replied and strolled toward the door. She followed.

Their last night at the camp, Leo and Katarina went to bed early. "The morning will come quicker," her husband said as he snuggled under the blankets.

She went over the list again before she cuddled beside her husband, but they were too excited to sleep. Instead, they tossed and turned as their minds were overloaded with emotions: happiness, sadness, and worry.

Eventually, Leo fell asleep, but Katarina couldn't stop her rolling thoughts long enough to fall asleep. The night seemed endless. Finally around dawn, her eyes closed only to be ripped open a few hours later by the loudspeakers blaring an announcement: "All the refugees leaving for Canada today are to report to the front of the church by eleven o'clock."

Stretching her body over the bed, Katarina shouted almost in a singing tune, "Good morning, world, and good-bye, Capua camp! Today is our departure day! What a wonderful time to be alive!"

Her husband awoke from the racket. "What's all this commotion?" he replied, half-asleep, and turned on the other side. He would have preferred to snooze for a few more minutes.

Katarina, however, was charged with energy. She rolled over on him and said, "Oh no, you don't. We still have many things to do before we leave. You know, my love, this journey could be the honeymoon we never had." She smiled devilishly and gave him a long passionate kiss, then jumped out of bed to get ready.

Leo seemed to be having a hard time waking and still lazed around in bed by the time Katarina finished dressing. "Get up, lazy bones, unless you want me to leave you here," she chuckled and started to tickle him.

He turned onto his other side and said, "Just let me snooze a few more minutes."

"No. It's getting late. We have to get ready and go for breakfast." She rolled him down from the bed and yelled, "Now, get dressed!" She grabbed a towel and rushed out to the public showers, giggling.

"Oh, I'll get you for this," he raged in a playful manner, running after her.

After their quick cold showers and their breakfast, they returned to their room for the last time. Katarina picked up a few remaining clothes and stuffed them into her carry-on bag. Leo did the same and was already standing at the door. "Are you ready, darling?"

Katarina took another look around. "Yes! Yes!" she shouted excitedly, so happy they were finally leaving.

"Then let's go," Leo commanded and walked out the door with their both carry-on bags in his hands. From the doorway, Katarina turned, glanced around, and whispered, "Good-bye," to the room that had been their home for close to three months. She had no plans to say good-bye to Manda. Katarina wanted to slip away without seeing her, but that wasn't to be.

As they came out, Viktor was saying good-bye to Manda and the children in front of the shack. "Oh, great!" Katarina whispered under her breath. Before she could think of anything else, little Josipa came running into her embrace.

"Listen, people are singing," Josipa said and pointed toward the church. " Good-bye, Katarina, I'll miss you."

She wrapped her arms around both of the children, kissed them on top of their heads, and said, "Yes, Josipa, people are singing because they're happy to be leaving this place. I hope you and your mama leave soon." She squeezed them close to her body and whispered, "Good-bye, my little ones."

"Good-bye, Katarina," they said in unison. She let go of the children and, without saying a word to Manda, marched ahead. She didn't hate her, but she resented her betrayal and for encroaching upon her life.

Leo kissed the children and said, "Good-bye, Manda," but didn't hug her. She replied the same way. Viktor and Leo hurried to catch up to Katarina. Leo got hold of his wife's hand, and they walked away with hands entwined.

It was a cloudy and cold December morning, but the sun shone in Katarina's heart as brightly as ever as she strode hand-in-hand with her husband out of the compound. Just before they turned the corner, she glanced back at Manda and smiled, "Poor Manda. I wonder how long she'll have to wait to get her travel papers to Australia."

Viktor glanced at Katarina, puzzled. "I thought she said her husband was in the USA."

"Well, I don't know anything about USA. She told me in Trieste that her husband was in Australia," Katarina replied, just as shocked. Anyhow, she was glad that Manda was staying behind and would never get a chance to take Leo away from her.

As they approached the church, the singing voices of the refugees grew louder; they smiled at each other and quickened their pace.

The front of the church was filled with the commotion of exhilarated refugees singing, shouting, and crying. "Wow! The buses that will take us to Naples are here already. And they are buried in the noisy crowd," Katarina shouted by Leo's ear, making sure he heard her.

"Yeah, and they're only three, which means it would be a fight for the seats again," Leo noted.

"I guess we just have to be prepared to fight," Viktor said and settled behind a long line of refugees. "Come on, you two. Get in here."

"We'll never break through this wall. We'll probably be here tomorrow morning, still waiting in the line," Katarina replied with a touch of sarcasm as she lined up behind her husband and Viktor.

Leo immediately pulled out his ID cards. "The officials will be asking for them," he reminded her, dangling it in his hand.

"They always do before boarding, I know that," Katarina replied and pulled hers out too. She surveyed the buses and each official standing on the steps of the bus, holding a long list in his or her hand. "Tell me. Which bus you think will take us to Naples?"

Leo paused, staring into Katarina's eyes, with a wide grin on his face and teased, "Guess what, you tell me on which list our names are?"

They were grounded by Viktor. "Oh, you two. Stop bickering. You'll know when the officials call you," he said and move forward a little.

Katarina's impatience began to gnaw at her gut. "If there is one thing in my life I hate, it's waiting in line," she said, restless.

One hour and half passed by the time an official called, "Mr. and Mrs. Lisic."

"Finally," Katarina whispered as they walked toward the official standing on the steps of the bus.

As they approached the lady official, she asked, "Your name?"

"Leo Lisic and my wife. Here," he said, extending his hand with ID to her. Katarina did the same thing. The ID cards trembled in their hands as they showed them. Realizing every step they made brought their dreams closer to reality.

"Thank you. You can board now," the lady official gave them permission. They proceeded to climb onto the bus as the priest continuously prayed in the background and giving blessing to the refugees leaving the camp.

"God bless you and is with you. Go in peace, my children. Never forget where you come from wherever you go." Those were the only words Katarina and Leo heard from their priest and took them into their hearts.

From the bus door, they glanced back and waved good-bye to the refugees remaining behind. They moved forward only a few steps when Leo spotted two empty seats right behind the driver. "Here," he called, pointing at them. "After you, darling." He stood aside and waited while his wife took the seat beside the window.

Katarina settled on her seat and her husband sat beside her. "Thanks," she said and glanced around. "Where's Viktor?"

"I don't know," he said, stretching his neck over the seat to see if he was down the aisle.

"You looking for?" Viktor asked, just coming into the bus.

"Oh, there you are," Leo said. "Here, sit down here beside me. We're all skinny, we can fit."

"Thanks, it's a long way to Naples for me to be standing." Viktor sat beside Leo and they started to talk.

As always, Katarina turned to stare out the window and plunged deep in her own thoughts. Her eyes scanning the camp and storing its picture deep in her memory so she would never forget the pain and sorrow it had caused her. She also noted the camp looked as desolate as when they first arrived. "At least, there isn't any rain and fog this morning," she muttered aloud without turning her head.

"You are talking about the day we arrived, aren't you?" Leo quizzed.

"Well, yes," she answered and glanced at her husband. "You didn't forget, did you?"

"No. How could I?"
"And we never should," she replied and turned back to stare out.

"I, too, remember that day I was here," Viktor said. "The weather was horrible for a few days."

When the drivers started their engines and began to move the buses toward the big gate, a huge roar was heard as the refugees left behind yelled, "Good-bye until we meet again!"

"Yeah, until we meet again!" shouted the departing refugees through the windows of the buses, including Katarina and Leo.

The buses rolled down by Capua City, on to the highway, and began their trip toward Naples. Katarina said a silent good-bye to the city, which lay shrouded in a haze, and said a prayer for God to keep her husband and her safe. She hoped they would never have to go through things like this again. But again, they are going far, far away to the country they knew nothing about, and no one knew what was waiting for them there.

Leo looked cheerfully at her stressed face. "Relax, darling, we're on our way. Nothing can stop us now."

"I hope you're right," she replied, with a hint of doubt and turned to cuddle into his shoulder.

"Listen, Katarina, don't give us more worries. We'll find out and we'll worry when we get there. It's too late now anyway. No more talk of nonsense. Let's sing with the crowd," Viktor smiled.

Katarina smirked and turned to stare out the window. "Never give up." The message echoed in her head as it had for the first time after Katrina was raped in Trieste camp. She was grateful for having listened to the voice then and several times thereafter as it had helped her pull herself from a brink of destruction. She hoped now it would give her strength on their voyage to Canada.

As the buses rolled down toward Naples, Katarina drifted off to sleep against the window. She hadn't slept much during the night.

The refugee buses arrived in Naples, around four o'clock, and were plunged into a traffic jam. Naples was a tumultuous, animated city that was frantically alive, and everyone in it seemed to be on the move. The city was throbbing with buses, Vespa scooters, and small fiat cars crowding the downtown streets and slowing the traffic down to a snail's pace. Every driver of the vehicle on the street was on their horn. It felt like a million fire engines with their sirens on rushing to the nearby fire.

Katarina awoke to the loud street noises and asked, "What's all this racket?" and looked out the window. "This must be Naples, right?"

"Yes. People are yelling and buzzing their horns because we are stuck. The buses are barely moving," Leo explained and joined her admiring the city. Her eyes drifted to the beautiful Christmas and New Year's decorations dangling from the light poles, buildings, stores, and houses, ignoring his complaint.

Their buses continued to crawl through downtown until they turned onto Via Colombo, which took them along the waterfront.

Fifteen minutes later, they stopped at the maritime terminal in front of the hotel where the refugees were to spend the night before boarding the ship the next morning.

A crowd of refugees from the back of the bus stood up and screamed, "Stanzione Maritime!"

"Hurrah! We arrived finally!" others yelled while laughing and singing as they began disembarking.

Katarina's eyes widened as she stared through the bus window at the majestic luxurious liner docked at the pier. Shocked, she shouted, "Wow! This must be it! Look, Leo, look. *Cristoforo Colombo*!" She read aloud the name of the ship.

"They all can see that, darling," Leo retorted as he stood up to disembark.

Following her husband off the bus, she snapped, "All right. All right. I got carried away. Other people are staring at the ship too."

On the way to the hotel, everyone chatted and chuckled, occasionally casting their wide eyes at the ship and making funny comments. The one that stuck in Katarina's memory the most was when someone from the mass shouted, "I will buy myself a ship just like this when I get to Canada!"

"Yeah, sure, you will! Call us when you do! We'll all take a trip back on your ship!" another voice retorted from the crowd. Everyone burst into laughter and roared so hard that no one made any more comments.

As the refugees entered, the hotel employees met them in the lobby. "This way please," the hostess said and began leading them down the hallway. They followed him noisily into the dining area where the tables were reserved for them.

Overwhelmed, Katarina grabbed Leo's hand and held on to him, following the crowd. Their eyes floated around the hotel captivated by the luxury as they admired beautiful Christmas and New Year decorations. "It's gorgeous!" she voiced, twirling her head as they walked through the aisle to the table beside the window overlooking the Tyrrhenian Sea where the big liner was docked.

"Yes, they are, but keep your voice down," Leo urged and sat down opposite to her. Viktor, who silently trekked behind them, sat beside his friend.

Katarina ignored his warning. Her eyes darted to a corner of the room. "Look there, my love," she chirped, pointing at a little barn. "Mary and baby Jesus are inside, surrounded by animals, donkeys, cows and sheep." Not waiting for her husband's response, she rushed to see it up close.

Not very pleased with his wife at that moment. He didn't like to be ignored, especially not by his wife. Viktor noted Leo's frowning face as he was looking after his wife and said, "Let her be, she hasn't seen anything like this before."

With all the excitement and festivity going on, his mood didn't last long. When she returned to the table, he asked, "Would you like some water, darling?"

"Yes, please." And her eyes wandered over the room again. All the refugees were settled around their tables but continued to chat and giggle loudly. They were very noisy.

One of the camp officials stood up to speak. "Hello, everyone!" but no one paid attention to her. After repeating herself a few times, finally, she banged the spoon over the plate to quiet down the crowd. As soon as quiet occurred, the official began her speech. "Hello, everyone! I know you are excited, but please be patient just a little longer. Tomorrow, at eleven o'clock, you will begin your journey to your new beginning in a new country, Canada."

"All right! That's wonderful! It's about time!" the refugees interrupted, shouting and clapping.

The official looked around, smiled, and repeated, "First, I have to tell you a few things. We'll meet again in here at six o'clock in the morning, and the boarding commences at eleven. Thank you."

At the end of the speech, all the refugees rose from their chair and in unison shouted, "Happy New Year!" And with their glasses of water in their hands, cheered.

The officials distributed room keys to the refugees, then a delightful Italian supper ensued. The waiters in black-and-white outfits rolled in food. "Something smells so good," Katarina commented.

"Yeah, I can smell it too," Viktor said, rubbing his hands in anticipation. Leo just waited without comment, sipping on water.

The chicken soup was served first. Katarina tested it. "It's good. It tasted like my mama's chicken soup," she said and continued to spoon it, her sadness showing on her face. Leo and Viktor glanced at her, but said nothing.

Followed by spaghetti alla pescatore with seafood sauce and side orders of mashed potato and spinach, radichio salad dressed with olive oil and vinegar, served on exquisite porcelain dishes and silver platters, and for decor, a bottle of red Italian wine for each table. To top off the meal, a few men walked in with the mandolins. They began to play and sing.

Leo poured a glass of wine to Katarina, Viktor, and himself. "Cheers!" they yelled together with the other refugees, to the musicians, this time with glass of wine in their hands.

After they applauded the singing men, Katarina dug her fork into the food and exclaimed, "Wow! It seems that spaghetti can't escape us, but this kind of spaghetti I can eat anytime. They are delicious!" she chuckled, her cheeks were blooming. It felt like a dream, one from which she never wanted to be awakened.

Her husband looked at her with a smile. "I hope you'll always be as happy as you are this minute."

She cast a naughty look at him and replied, "The combination of spaghetti and mandolins. It is an irresistible!" and continued to enjoy the food and music. Viktor enjoyed the food and the music in silence and left the niggle to Leo and Katarina.

Later, some of the refugees celebrated with a small going-away party. That was, of course, for those who still had money left. Others, who didn't, walked out of the dining room and watched from the threshold.

Leo glanced at his wife with a smile and gave her his hand. "Let's go up to our room. We'll have our own celebration."

She rose from her chair without letting go of his hand and teased, "You mean the one I missed in the camp." They both glanced at Viktor.

"I'm staying," he answered their unspoken question.

They walked out of the dining room area and began to climb the polished stone steps to the second floor. Leo unlocked room number 12 showed on the key and opened the door for her.

"Here you go, ladies first," he said, showing her in with his hand.

Katarina entered slowly, her gaze seemed to float about the room like an aimless balloon. Finally, she said, "Wow, it's lovely. Leo, how much do you think the Canadian government paid for all this luxury? Do you think this is included in our tickets?"

Her husband chuckled and closed the door. “Well, I hope so. Otherwise, we might have to wash some dishes before we leave. I heard it’s cheaper sailing than flying though, I can’t even begin to guess how much this all costs. But I do know why we were sailing at this time of the year.”

“I’m sure you’re going to tell me. So why?”

“In the winter season, there aren’t many tourists moving up or down the Atlantic Ocean, so the ship would be sailing half-full to Canada or USA if there were no refugees on board. Also the ship carries more people than the plane does, so it costs less,” Leo concluded, proud of his knowledge.

“Where did you find this information?” Katarina asked wide-eyed.

“Oh, from sources around the camp,” he said, undressing himself.

“I have heard that one before. That doesn’t tell me much,” Katarina replied, coming out of her clothes. “In any case, I don’t care who paid what, I’m just happy to be leaving Italy.” She threw her clothes over the back of the chair, and both of them settled into a soft cozy bed under white sheets and downy cover.

“Where is the celebration?” Katarina teased, giggling.

Leo squeezed his wife close to his body and peered into her eyes. “Here it is!” He plunged a big kiss on her mouth and began to make love to her.

Holding his wife in his embrace after they made love, he asked, “Would you like to live in Naples? It seems like a lovely city.”

“No, Naples is a rowdy and a dangerous city,” Katarina replied. “Lina told me that from all four sides of Naples the earth fumes and grumbles, ready to explode at anytime. I wouldn’t want to live under that kind of pressure.”

"Oh, what else did Lina tell you?" Leo chuckled because he didn't believe her.

"Many other things about Naples, but to tell the truth, I don't remember. And anyway, I want to go to Canada."

"Yes. I'd rather go to Canada too," Leo said and began talking about the plans he had for the two of them. Katarina's face glowed like a shining star in the sky when he said, "I'll buy you the most beautiful house you can imagine."

"Yeah, and the wedding you promised," she reminded her husband of his pledge he made to her on the wedding day.

Leo squeezed her against his body and confirmed, "No doubt, that too."

Katarina nestled against her husband's rib cage and asked, "Can you tell me something about Canada, my love?"

Leo paused, staring at his wife, but didn't answer. Neither one had any clue about Canada, except it was a very cold country. Instead of answering, he began to tickle her so she couldn't ask any more questions. Of course, that didn't stop overzealous Katarina from doing just that. "Come on, say something," she insisted and pulled away from him.

"Brrrr! It's freezing!" Leo laughed and resumed tickling his wife.

"Haha, tell me something I don't know," Katarina pleaded, through the chuckle and their conversation turned to their new life together. It was the longest chat they ever had on the subject that lasted late into the night and she was pleased.

After a while, Leo turned away from her and fell asleep. Katarina continued to toss and turn in bed as thoughts about Canada and the journey whirled in her head. Especially a few questions rolled over and over in her mind. How would their journey over the Atlantic be, and would they survive the voyage? The huge liner floating in the cold ocean upside down kept flashing in front of her eyes, causing the knot in her stomach to tighten instead of loosen. "Oh, go to sleep, Katarina," she ordered herself. "You're scaring yourself." She was scared. She had never traveled a long distance on a ship before. Just as she finally managed to drift off to sleep, Leo suddenly jerked awake and sat in bed in a sweat, muttering something incoherent.

"What's wrong with you now?" Katarina asked, annoyed that he had awakened her just as she dozed off.

He turned toward her struggling with words. "Oh no! I dreamed that the ship sank in the middle of the ocean and we all drowned." His body trembled.

"Oh, go to sleep," Katarina said groggily; she turned on the other side and fell back asleep, not realizing how much her husband was shaken by the dream.

The morning drew too quickly for both of them as they just began to sleep. Leo awoke and immediately consulted his watch. "Oh no! It's six already! Get up, darling!" he yelled, jumped off the bed, and frantically began dressing. Without a word, his wife followed. Neither one of them mentioned the dream Leo had had that night. Their minds were too preoccupied with other things to remember.

"Make sure you pack all of the clothes," Katarina said, combing her hair.

"Hmm, right," he replied and took another look around the bed and between sheets, then walked to the door. She still wasn't ready. "Hurry! Otherwise, we'll be in big trouble."

"I'm coming!" she hollered and was at the door.

They rushed down the steps. The hotel lobby was seething with refugees as they gathered to wait for the officials to arrive. Leo and Katarina made it down the steps just seconds before them. He wiped sweat off his forehead and sighed, "Good. They are not here yet."

Before Katarina had a chance to say anything, they heard a voice behind them. "Good morning. I hope everyone is here," one of the officials said as they descended the steps and went into the dining room.

The refugees stopped talking and turned to follow them. Everyone settled at the same table as yesterday, but unlike yesterday, the refugees sat quietly. Their eyes were on the officials. An eerie lull swept across the room as they anxiously waited for their last instructions. "After this, we're on our own," Viktor whispered to Leo and Katarina.

Just the same spokesperson as yesterday stood up and looked around and said, "I trust you slept well. Breakfast will be served as soon as I finish." Holding up a paper in her hands for everyone to see, she continued, "This is called a landed immigrant card. You'll find it in your passport which my coworker is distributing around to everyone as I speak. Please take good care of it, it's very important. Without it, you won't be able to enter Canada." She paused and waited for everyone to get their passport and travel documents.

When Katarina received her passport, she stared at it for a while and then turned to her husband. "I thought I would never see one of these," she whispered and carefully placed it in her handbag, smiling.

Before her husband could respond, the official began to speak again. "Now, you're on your own and officially no longer a refugee. The only thing left for us to say is good-bye and good luck!"

"Hurray! We made it!" the former refugees shouted and clapped their hands while the officials waved and smiled. Then the boys in black-and-white rolled in carts filled with platters of sliced mortadella, cheese, and other kinds of salami, glasses of juice, and Turkish coffee. By then, everyone had worked up an appetite.

As the waiters began serving a scrumptious European breakfast, the refugees relaxed. They chatted and enjoyed their last meal in Italy, excitement filling the room. Katarina took a sip of her coffee and called out, "Now, this is real coffee, not the chicory we drank in the camp." For her, even a little improvement from the way things were in the camp was grandiose.

"Yeah, yeah, I know. Drink your coffee, it's getting cold," Leo retorted; he and Viktor were trying to eat as much as they could.

The officials finished their breakfast, rose from their chair, and tried to sneak out quietly. Just as they were about to exit the dining area, the refugees shouted, "Happy New Year. Thank you and good-bye!"

"I hope we'll never see you again," Leo in a barely audible voice.

"Here. Here. My thoughts exactly. I never want to be back in a camp anywhere," Viktor replied, and they all chuckled.

Katarina became a little nervous as she realized they were completely on their own after the officials were gone. "What now?" she asked. "There is still almost two hours until we board the ship. I wish some of my friends from camp were here, going to Canada."

"Which one, Manda?" Leo teased with a smirk on his face.

She cast a sharp look at him and thought, *How dare he remind me of her?* And turned to stare out the window, wrapped in her own thoughts, slowly sipping on her coffee and observing the brilliance of the sunrise colors gleaming on the sea.

Leo and Viktor studied the ship that towered in front of the hotel and fiddled with their coffee cups as if they didn't know what to do next without someone telling them. Suddenly, Leo said, "Isn't she a beauty?" pointing to the ship.

Viktor smiled toward it and replied, "You're absolutely correct, she is a beauty. Nothing can touch her."

Still feeling a pang, Katarina was somewhat apprehensive, but she too put her two cents in. "Yes, but the sea is much bigger and stronger," she replied, finally with a deep sigh. Her eyes floated to the horizon and she asked, "Viktor, do you know what's on the other side?"

"No, I don't, I have never been there."

Leo covered his wife's hand with his and said, "I didn't mean to hurt you. That was a stupid remark. I'm sorry, darling."

"Forget it. I'm fine."

Viktor stood rose from the chair. "See you later," he said and walked out of the dining room.

They both turned to stare at the sea and the liner and pretended to enjoy the moment in silence. However, they were both running scared, secretly worried they might never make it, but neither one wanted to admit it to the other.

Their daydream was interrupted by the noise some of the refugees made as they left the dining room for a walk.

Looking at them as they exited, she leaned toward Leo and whispered, "We shared part of our lives with these people, but when we reach Canada, we might never see any of them again."

"That shows you we can only depend on each other. The friends are coming and going, in and out of our lives. It's just you and me. We're the two that are solid," Leo said bravely.

Katarina glanced at him under her eyebrows and said, "Are we really that solid?"

Instead of responding, he glanced on his wristwatch, rose, and gave his hand to his wife. "Let's go out for a walk too."

Still holding his hand, she pulled herself up. "Sure. I'd love to," she replied, looking at his face. To her astonishment, she saw fear in his eyes and, at that moment, realized she was not alone with her fear. She also remembered Leo's dream during the night and wanted to know more.

As they strolled across the room to the exit, she said, "Tell me about the dream you had last night, Leo."

"Oh, it's nothing. Besides, I don't remember much," he replied, not wanting to scare his wife more than she already was.

They walked out to the pier under an overcast sky and a strong wind blew. "We should have come out earlier while sun was shining," Leo commented as they began to stroll toward the ship.

"Why didn't you say so?"

"Oh, I don't know."

Leo and Katarina walked in silence side by side for a short while, occasionally ducking the wind-driven water that sprayed the pier, each of them occupied by their own thoughts, questions, and doubts. At the same time, they surveyed and admired the huge giant floating on the water beside them. "Look at those men working hard," Katarina noticed, observing columns of men going in and out the ship continuously, like ants, carrying boxes, barrels, chests, suitcases, and other things, preparing the ship for its long voyage over the Atlantic.

"Yes, that is heavy work," Leo agreed, but wasn't really paying too much attention; he was concentrating more on the ship than what his wife was saying.

Katarina stopped in the shadow of the ship and stared at it. "I wonder if this beauty can handle all the cargo it's about to take on and arrive in Canada in one piece."

"Of course, it can," Leo said and continued to observe the ship. "There is nothing to worry about. This ship is strong and one of the safest that ever floated. Its length is about seven hundred feet and width around ninety feet. Engine, steam turbine double reduction, and it carries around six hundred passengers plus crew. Its speed is twenty-three knots. Just look at it, it's huge. It can't be capsized," he smiled, but there was a hint of worry in his eyes as if he was also trying to convince himself.

"Yeah, are you sure about that?" she quizzed, her eyes shifting to the huge murky sea that lay endlessly ahead. "Maybe you are right, but it looks so scary over there. Oh god, if we get lost in the middle of the Atlantic Ocean, no one would ever find us."

"Look out!" Leo yelled as a wave of water spray was coming straight for Katarina. Leo grabbed his young wife's hand and they rushed away. "You almost got drenched, darling."

She shivered, blood drained from her face. "Thank God, you were able to get me away from that splash of cold water," Katarina said, and they continued their trek down the pier.

Suddenly, an image of her family nudged her head. "Do you think we'll ever see any of our family again?" she asked, glancing at her husband, her voice filled with sadness.

He lay an arm around her shoulder and said, "One day, I'm sure we will. Goodness, you are shivering. Let's go back inside."

As they walked back toward the entrance of the hotel, a dark shadow blanketed them. She looked up to see an ominous cloud floating rapidly across the sky as though it was hiding the answer to her question in its darkness. "It looks like we might have some rain soon," Katarina said, entering the hotel lobby.

"It better wait until we are safely on board the ship," her husband smirked and went on to the dining room.

Katarina didn't answer. She was happy they were leaving, yet there was sorrow in her heart mixed with fear of unknown. It was one thing escaping to Italy, but quite another going overseas to an unknown place alone.

In the dining area, they ran into a waiter. "Two cappuccinos please," Leo ordered; they were allowed two extra coffees each with their ticket.

When they arrived to the table, Viktor was already there. "You are back?" Viktor said, sipping on his coffee. "I wish the time goes by quicker."

"Patience, my friend, patience," Leo teased as they sat down. Katarina's eyes flew around the room.

The waiter brought the coffee promptly and placed it in front of them. "Here, two cappuccinos," he said and rushed away.

"Thank you, Leo. A hot cup of coffee was exactly what I needed," Katarina leaned her head toward her husband and gave him a kiss.

They sipped on their coffee and listened to the nonstop Italian music while anxiously waiting for the boarding to begin. "It won't be long now," Viktor broke the silence between them.

They both consulted their watches, and sure enough, it was ten to eleven. "Maybe we should stroll out," Katarina said, dying to climb the ship.

"We should get prepared and slowly saunter to the pier to see what's going on there," Leo agreed, and all three together walked out the hotel.

At eleven o'clock on the dot, the refugees streamed out of the hotel toward the ship in respond to the urgency of its whistles, announcing the boarding to the ship. The threesome just made it to the pier when they were taken over by the crowd. Before they made any headway, there was a jam of bodies in front of the ship crowding the gangway.

They lined themselves behind it. "This is going to be a long wait," Leo announced and slowly began to move forward.

"I hope not, it's cold," Katarina replied, bundling herself into her raincoat to protect herself from the biting wind.

The refugees continued to push, each of them trying to board sooner. Soon a dispute broke out between two men in view of Katarina, Leo, and Viktor.

"Look, Leo," Katarina called in alarm. "Those two men there are going to fight each other. The man in a hat touched another man's arm, turned and spoke to him angrily. Then he raised his hand and appeared about to strike the other."

But before her husband could answer, the crowd shouted, "Shake him up! Shake him up! It's cold in here!" Everyone laughed.

"That will warm them up," Leo replied and followed the others in cheering the two men to fight. His wife gave him a puzzling glance and frowned.

As they watched for what was going to happen next, two stewards came rushing to the scene and stepped between the two men. "Stop this now!" But the men didn't listen; they kept trying to reach each other. "That's it, we are taking you in," the other steward yelled and grabbed one of the men.

"I don't think the man in the hat is one of the refugees," Katarina noticed as they watched them being dragged away by the stewards.

Leo chuckled and quizzed, "How could you tell by just looking at them?"

"Easy. He's dressed too nicely to be a refugee," she giggled, despite the cold wind brushing against her cheeks. Soon, the cold wind and dark clouds overhead, threatening to burst into rain any minute, took their toll and more refugees started to push and scuffle.

The stewards had to come back to make peace and order, but this time they insisted, "Form a double line, and don't step over this," pointing to the yellow line in front of them and then with an authoritative voice announced, "All the tourist passengers, please step in front. You'll begin boarding first, then the refugees."

The threesome were halfway down to the gangway by then and found themselves way back in the line because of the change. "That's just great! We're back at the same place we began," Katarina grumbled, watching the tourist passengers taking place in front of them.

"Well. It's obvious we're still refugees," Leo replied as they slowly moved ahead in the line that was now farther away from the entrance to the ship. Viktor sighed, but said nothing.

"I'm not sure if we will ever lose refugee status," Katarina said and prayed it wouldn't rain until they boarded the ship. Shuffling forward, they finally reach the gangway again, but it took them an hour and it was cold. "It's about time," half-frozen Katarina sighed and began to climb; her husband and Viktor followed.

When they reached the top of the gangway and were about to enter the ship, suddenly, an indescribable feeling of peace and fear came over Katarina simultaneously. She felt as if she were arriving at heaven's gate. The entrance of the ship was decorated with colorful lights and New Year's decorations wrapped around the door. Above their heads, a huge green, white, and red flag waved at the side of the door as if it was saluting them as they stepped inside.

An officer sat behind a long desk not far from the door demanding, in a gentle but firm voice, "Passport please."

"Here," Leo pulled his traveling papers and handed it to him first. Katarina surveyed him from head to toe. His medals on his white jacket hanging down from his pocket shone each time he moved. The green strips on the sides of his black trousers glittered as he stretched his long legs under the desk. With high-ranking officials like this, they can't go wrong, she mused.

"Next!" the official called after he finished with Leo.

Katarina stepped forward and smiled, "Here you go," as she handed over her passport and other papers. But as he flipped through the pages of the passport, her heart sank. She remembered another time an officer had flipped through her papers and shivered. Then she realized she had nothing to worry about. "I'm free and on my way to the country I want to live in," she whispered to herself.

The officer placed the seal of approval on her passport and papers then handed them to her. "Have a nice trip," he said before taking the next papers.

"Thanks, I will!" Trying to shake her fear, she quickly walked to the waiting area, where the names had been called as they coming in, and glanced around. "It's beautiful in here."

Leo threw a hard look at her with a fake smile that meant for her to be quiet. "For God's sake! We're not in church," she whispered in his ear, annoyed and turned to watch the other refugees entering the ship.

"Mr. and Mrs. Lisic," a young tall, blue-eyed, and blond-haired steward called as he stepped forward and called a few more refugees' names waiting to be settled in their cabins.

"Here we are," Leo said, raising his hand.

"Those whose names I called follow me," the steward requested and turned to walk down the steps. With all the noise and bustling, Katarina hadn't heard their name being called as she was too busy staring at the other passages crowding the entrance.

"Let's go, Katarina," Leo called, grasping her shoulder.

"Where?"

He grabbed her hand and pulled her after the steward and the other refugees before they lose them. They followed him in silence along the narrow dim corridors that twisted and zigzagged deep down into the ship.

The steward paused on the threshold of a narrow passageway labeled "Third Class" and pointed his finger at Leo and two other men. "You and your wives follow me. The rest of you wait here," he said and began to stride toward the other end of the corridor.

The steward stopped in front of a small cabin door inside the nose of the ship and unlocked it. "This is your cabin, Mr. and Mrs. Lisic," he announced, handing Leo the key and added, "The third class and most of second has been reserved for the refugees. All the passengers will dine together in the second-class dining room and will use the second-class decks. Bon voyage." The steward smiled as he turned and walked away.

"Bon voyage to you too," Katarina replied, staring after him as he rushed to the others.

Without warning, Leo grabbed his wife and lifted her into his arms.

"Wow!" Katarina exclaimed, giggling. "What are you doing?"

"I'm carrying you over the threshold," he asserted. "Isn't that what you're supposed to do when two people get married?"

Katarina smiled and wrapped her arms around his neck. "Yeah, but isn't this a little too late?"

"No. If you remember correctly, when we were married, there was no a real door to our room."

Holding on to him tightly, as he stepped inside with her in his arms, she laughed, "Hahaha, I remember. How could I forget? But you did have a few other chances, for example, at the hotel."

"I did, but I thought this would be the most appropriate time. You did say this could be the honeymoon we never had, didn't you?" Leo exhaled as he put her down inside the cabin.

Katarina grabbed his face between her hands and kissed him. "Oh, you did hear that! Thank you for remembering. It's very thoughtful of you." She quickly sat on the lower bunk bed. "I'll take this one," she asserted. For a moment, her face became serious and she stared at her husband. "There was a time I thought we'd never make it," she sighed in relief and stretched her body across her bed.

"Well, you see, darling, I knew we would," Leo boasted, taking off his coat and placing it over the chair beside the small built-in table, then he sat on the chair, placing his carry-on bag on his knees, and pulled clean underwear out. "I'd like to take a quick shower now," he said.

"You can't do that. Read this." Katarina pointed to the note taped to the cabin wall, which read: "Do not use showers or bathroom until the ship reaches the open sea."

"Oh gee, thanks," Leo replied unhappily.

"You'll shower later. Let's go up to the deck. The ship is about to sail, and I'd like to wave good-bye to Naples and its people. Besides, we don't have a window, and I don't want to miss anything. Hurry, Leo," Katarina said and dashed out of the cabin.

"Wait for me," Leo yelled and came running after her. "I wonder where Viktor got his cabin?"

"I don't know, we might see him up on the deck, you can ask him," Katarina suggested and strode up the steps to the second class and on to the deck.

# CHAPTER 19

The deck was crowded and noisy, excitement and joy overflowed. Laughter and song greeted Katarina and Leo as they emerged in time to watch the luxurious ship set sail. They paused on the deck threshold, their eyes wandering. The strong wind blew cold and dark clouds scuffled across the sky, still threatening to unleash their rain. She cuddled close to her husband and exclaimed, "Wow! The ship is even bigger than I thought."

"I told you, darling. You have nothing to worry about," Leo bragged as they began to wrestle through the mass to find a place at the deck railing.

The refugees walked around; they were not held up in one place for long. Just as Katarina and Leo reached the railing, a couple moved away. "Thank God," she said as they filled the space.

"You can say that again," Leo voiced, squeezing beside her. They leaned over the deck and joined the others in jubilation. The fierce wind whipped Katarina's long brown hair, stinging her face and turning her nose red, but that didn't force her to retreat inside. She just brushed the hair from her face, tightened her raincoat against her body, and continued singing, cheering, and waving. "Are you cold, darling?" Leo asked, looking at her red, mostly blue, nose and face.

"I'll be fine," Katarina answered between the singing.

Suddenly, one long blast of the ship's whistles signaled the departure of the *Cristoforo Colombo*, elating the crowd even more. "Good-bye!"

they shouted almost in unison and continued to sing and wave to the onlookers below.

"Bon voyage!" the onlookers' voices echoed over the deck.

Amid the cheers from onlookers and the passengers crowded against the deck railing of their respective decks, the captain gave the orders for the mooring lines to be slipped. From the deck, the passengers watched wide-eyed as the tugs began to take up the job of manipulating the ship from the Naples dock. "We're moving!" Katarina shouted, glancing at her husband with exuberance.

"Hurrah to that!" a familiar voiced yelled; they turned. It was Viktor.

"Oh, there you are. We wondered what happened to you." Leo asked and consulted his watch. It was exactly four o'clock, New Year's Eve, when the luxurious liner began to inch its way out of Naples' dock. But by then, Viktor moved on.

"Good-bye and good luck to all of you!" the onlookers yelled and waved as the ship was moving away toward the open sea.

Everyone from the deck shouted, "Good-bye, all of you down there!" They sang and waved again and again.

When the tugs had maneuvered the majestic liner to his turning arc, the engines were started and they slowly began to turn. The tugs' shrill whistles saluted the big *Cristoforo Colombo* as it cleared the dock. A huge single plum of white steam shot into the overcast sky and vanished in the wind as the liner left Naples' harbor.

Leo, Katarina, and the other refugees were finally beginning their voyage through the Tyrrhenian Sea, into the Mediterranean, and across the Atlantic Ocean to Halifax. The ship sirens screeched one more time as they began steaming west, nothing ahead of them but an ocean. "Now! We are on our way!" Katarina sighed in relief and embraced her husband, her eyes alive with happiness.

Everyone again sang, cried, and jubilantly yelled, "Canada! Here we come!" while watching the city of Naples shrinks away. They stayed to enjoy the colorful New Year's decorations, shining brightly on the city skyline, and bright decorations turned into small dots of lights in the distance.

Katarina's body tingled as she watched the city disappear into the sea. "Good-bye! Naples!" she yelled.

"Hello! Canada!" someone shouted from the deck, which was followed by a jubilant cheer.

After the flaming sunset across the horizon, the rushing darkness surrounded them quickly and cleared the deck. Most of the passengers retreated into the ship except Leo, Katarina, and a few other couples. Despite the cold biting wind, they remained on the deck after the city of Naples was no longer visible and continued to sing.

Approaching darkness and cold forced the other couples to retreat inside and Katarina would have to, but Leo resisted. He leaned over the rail and stared at the dark ocean water, ignoring the others and his wife. "Is there something wrong?" she asked, but he didn't respond. She grasped his hand and leaned over the rail beside him.

They both listened as the ship cut through the deep dark sea. The only sounds they could hear were the hum of the engines and the steady splash of *Cristoforo Colombo*'s wake. Holding each other's hand, Katarina felt like honeymoon had only just began.

But Leo didn't move, his eyes were fixed on the sea, his thoughts apparently somewhere else. He looked lost in time. Katarina studied his face, wishing she could see the thoughts behind his inscrutable stare, but she couldn't. Perplexed, she asked, "Are you all right, my love?"

Leo's head jarred to attention as he was abruptly brought back to the present. "Yes, Katarina. I was just wondering if things will turn out the way I pictured them in my mind."

Katarina had no clue what came over her husband or what he was saying and asked, "What do you mean, Leo?" Again he didn't answer. He just frowned and turned his attention back to the wake in the sea. "I'm scared too," she softly admitted, shivering as the cold permeated her body. "But it couldn't have been any other way for us, for me. I thought you understood that, my love. Besides, there's nothing we can do about it now. We're on our way to Canada. Are you sorry?"

Leo's eyebrows lifted as he turned toward her, but without a word again. His eyes were crystal hard, flaring with anxiety. She stared at him, still holding his hand and worrying what was bothering him. His reaction puzzled her. *Had she done something to offend him*? she questioned.

Suddenly, a frightening thought occurred to her. *Was it possible that Leo was in love with Manda*? she wondered, with a crushing feeling in her heart and now he's having a sudden attack of conscience. Finally, she said, "Let's go inside. It's getting cold." The chattering of her teeth was masked by the constant sound of waves breaking against the ship. Leo glared at her, frowned, and turned his attention back to the wake in the sea as if to say, "You're on your own, Katarina." He got what he wanted, a voyage to Canada.

Her blood boiled inside her. Glaring back at him, she wished she could yell and scream, but she couldn't. "Fine," she hissed and retreated into the warmth of the ship, leaving him standing on the deck. Thoughts of their honeymoon vanished from Katarina's mind into the dark sea.

She only made it past the entrance door before her shivering body forced her to stop and lean against the wall beside it. While waiting for her body to stop shivering, Katarina's mind whirled frantically. Why didn't he say something to her before? Why now? Had her husband fallen out of love with her? Had he ever been in love with her? Was it possible that he was one of the spies for the Communists after all? She didn't know what to think or do anymore. She was tired of him giving her mixed signals and worried what would happen when they reached Canada. "Hell! He'll probably drop me like a hot potato by the looks of it," she whispered to herself. In attempt to settle these thoughts, Katarina promised herself she would not force him to do anything he didn't want to do. "If he loves me, he'll come to me," she decided. Her husband's mood swings took up too much of her time to notice what was happening around. Each day her life was more miserable than the last, and she didn't like that very much. In the camp, she took his nonsense because she wanted to keep peace, but no more.

Her pondering was interrupted by a strong voice that came through the loudspeakers: "SUPPER IS BEING SERVED."

Immediately, Leo walked in from the deck. It was obvious to Katarina he had heard the announcement. One thing her husband would never miss was a meal. He sneaked behind his wife and wrapped his arms around her shoulders. "I'm sorry, darling," he said and kissed her on her neck and gave no other explanation.

*Are you really?* Katarina mused, fuming. If he thought he would get off that easy this time too, he had another thing coming. She gently shrugged off the arms he laid on her shoulders. "Sorry for what?" She threw him a fake smile, no longer wanting to argue.

"I heard supper has been served. I'm hungry," Leo said and stepped back.

"Yes, let's go to eat then." She took him under an arm as they strolled into the dining room.

The smell of strong coffee wafted through the doorway and filled their nostrils. "There's the hot cup of coffee I been craving for," Katarina announced as she took in the colorful decor of the dining area and the huge silver platters filled with delicious hors d'oeuvres, assorted antipasto, cheese prosciutto, and mortadella. Two bottles of wine, one red and one white, graced each table and loud Italian music played through loudspeakers. She was overwhelmed. "I can't believe that I forgot today is New Year's Eve!" she exclaimed as they began maneuvering through the aisles of the dining room and crowd.

"How could you have missed that?" Leo teased, his hungry eyes staring at the food.

Determined to enjoy herself no matter what happened, "That's a good question!" she replied with an upbeat voice, ignoring her husband's attempt to make her feel bad. She smiled and turned to admire the goods on the tables.

Leo skimmed over her and chuckled, "I'm so glad to see the table set with delicious food and wine. I can barely wait to get some of it in my stomach."

"I can see that," Katarina's face crinkled into a mischievous smile. She just couldn't pass that one by. "All you ever think about is your stomach. Where we are going to sit?"

Without lifting his gaze off the tables, he replied, "Table 21 is assigned to us for the journey."

"Great. We won't have to struggle to get the table when we come up to eat," Katarina was relieved and continued to scour for number 21.

"There it is, table 21," Leo pointed.

"Good for you. I didn't think you could get your eyes off the food long enough to look for our table," she titillated as he led her toward it. Leo sat right away and dug into those delicious hors d'oeuvres, but Katarina remained standing for a little while and let her eyes wander around the dining room. Finally, she took a deep breath and remarked, "This is beyond my wildest dream."

Meanwhile, Leo was going red in his face as he was worried she'd embarrass him and began to tug at her sweater. "Sit down!" he demanded through clenched teeth.

Katarina gave him a hard look and sat opposite him, frowning. He was always worried about being embarrassed and she respected that, now was his turn to respect hers. Here she was on this beautiful liner and on New Year's Eve at that. She wanted to see, feel, and express herself without being worried about embarrassing her husband or anyone else.

"Wine, darling?" Leo asked, lifting the red bottle of wine.

"Not now," she replied with a sharp tongue, annoyed with her husband because he wanted everything to be his way. Besides, Katarina didn't care much for red wine. Unfortunately, Leo believed red was the real wine and white was just lowly water.

"I think I'll partake," Leo said and poured himself a glass. Katarina had forgotten her hunger for a while, but she noticed it again when she smelled the fragrance of salami. Her eyes darted toward the delicious hors d'oeuvres on the table, her mouth watering as she stared at them. "I wonder where Viktor got lost?" she said.

Oh, he's someplace over there, I'm sure. We'll look for him after we eat the supper," Leo answered and continued to fill his stomach.

"Shouldn't we wait for everyone to arrive before we start to eat or can I help myself?" Katarina asked finally, in a low tone, and cynically added, "I don't want to embarrass you."

"I can't hear you. It's too noisy. What did you say?" Leo asked.

"Never mind." She decided to wait until the other refugees arrive and let her eyes wander around the dining room.

Meanwhile, the dining room was becoming packed with happy faces of refugees and regular passengers. Excited to be here, they laughed and chatted away and began to enjoy New Year's Eve as they waited for their main course to be served. The noise level crescendoed.

A young couple strolled over to table where Leo and Katarina sat. "Is this table 21?" the man with dark short hair asked, fixing his glasses.

"Yes, it is," Leo said and rose from the chair.

The man extended his hand to Leo and said, "My name is Istvan and this is my wife Greta. We're the couple you'll spend the trip dining with." He held the chair for his lovely, five-foot-one-inch tall, long brown-haired, blue-eyed, a little on the plump-size wife to sit on, then took his jacket off and hung it on the back of his chair.

Leo and Katarina silently stared at them. Then Leo suddenly realized he was still holding the bottle in his hand. "Wine, anyone?"

"Of course," Istvan accepted flamboyantly. "Hungarians never refuse wine, but my preference is white."

"Of course," Leo picked up the bottle of white wine. Istvan sat down and extended his glass to Leo.

"Hungarian, hmm? But you're speaking Croatian. Where are you from?" Leo asked, filling his glass with white wine.

Istvan took a sip of wine and explained, "We came from the Republic of Croatia on Yugoslavia, Hungary border. Both of our parents live at the Village Sopije along the banks of River Drava. Our grandparents were born during the Austro-Hungarian Empire. They were Hungarian. After the borders were changed, our small village became part of Croatia."

Katarina turned to chat with his wife. "I don't recall seeing you in Capua camp. Which camp did you two come from?"

"We came from Latina camp," Greta replied. Her long hair dangled over the table as she selected hors d'oeuvre.

"Oh, I thought, there were much more passengers here than our four hundred refugees, but I didn't realize refugees from other camps were sailing with us."

"What did you think?" Greta asked, looking at her.

"They were tourists. What else?" Katarina answered and extended her hand to pick an hors d'oeuvre.

"Haaaahaaaah," Greta chuckled. "If the Italian shipping company could get that many tourists in the winter season, we would be still waiting in the camp for someone to transport us to Canada."

"You are probably right," Katarina replied and they both giggled. Suddenly, she took another look at Greta's face and said, "Oh my god, I know you. You are the woman," she got closer to Greta's ear and whispered, "with the severe sores on the buttock. I worked briefly at Latina in the infirmary during the September month. How are you doing?"

"I remember you now. I'm doing fine. Things completely healed," Greta said, not willing to talk about it. So Katarina didn't ask any more questions.

Leo and Istvan were too busy chatting and stuffing their faces with prosciutto and wine to hear a word the girls were saying.

"Supper is coming!" someone shouted from the dining area. They looked up to see a parade of ship's stewards swarming in all directions, carrying silver platters and bowls full of hot food. Delicious odors of roasted meat wafted through the dining room.

"More food?" Katarina exclaimed as the stewards placed platters of food with a big bowl of chicken soup on their table.

"Bona petito," they said and carried on.

Katarina scooped up chicken soup into a small soup bowl and tasted it. "It's very good. Have some, Greta," she suggested and continued to spoon it.

"I'd rather have some roasted piglet," she replied and dug some out into her plate.

Halfway through supper, a voice broke through the loudspeakers. "Welcome to my ship. This is your captain speaking."

Complete silence fell upon the dining room and the passengers' heads lifted from their tables. Their eyes darted toward the voice as everyone wanted to hear the man guiding then into a free and better life. He finished his speech with, "Happy New Year! And bon voyage to everyone."

The dining room exploded in hand clapping. "HAPPY NEW YEAR!" the passengers shouted, lifting their wine glasses in cheers.

Then another voice spoke, "The New Year's Eve celebration dance will be held in the ballroom, beginning at nine o'clock tonight. Entrance is free and everyone is invited. Happy New Year!"

"Hurrah! Hurrah! Happy New Year!" they yelled and continued with their supper. It couldn't be a happier time than that one for them. Everything was going as it should have.

Katarina turned back to her plate and made a point. "Wonderful! I love dancing." Her eyes were shining with happiness.

"We all do!" Greta yelled jubilantly.

They sat at the supper table almost two hours and were overindulging in the good food and wine. Leo managed to drink the whole bottle of red except one glass that Katarina had. After the wine took over his body and mind, Leo became restless and stood up. "We'll see you two later in a gala," he informed Istvan and Greta and helped his wife up from the chair.

"See you later," Katarina said and they strode away.

"Yes, later," Istvan echoed and turned to his wife.

On the way to their cabin, Katarina glanced out through the window of the second class. Outside was dark, not even a star of lightness could be seen. The sky was overcast. "It looks scary out there."

"It's night, silly!" Leo noticed and staggered down the steps. Upon returning to the cabin, he chuckled and threw himself on Katarina's bunk bed.

"That's my bed," she protested, but didn't get an answer. Her husband was a little tipsy, and as soon as his head touched the pillow, he fell asleep.

She sat at the room table in disbelief. "This is our honeymoon?" she mused, staring at his sleeping face. She was hoping to spend some quality time with her husband; instead, she had to listen to him snoring.

The longer she watched him, the angrier she became. *Oh, damn! How dare he fall asleep on her?* she fumed inwardly. This was supposed be their honeymoon. She missed his arms around her body and longed for his deep, full, passionate kisses. There was something so magnetic about his blue eyes, so mystical and compelling. Katarina just couldn't stay away from him, but she did promise herself that she would no longer force the issue. She lay hushed at the foot of the bed and settled into one of her miracle dreams in which she so faithfully believed. Eventually, she too drifted off to sleep.

They were asleep just a short time when Katarina jarred awake. "Oh no! How awful!" she shouted, jumping to her feet and waking her husband.

He lifted his head still groggy and asked, "What happened?"

"Nothing happened yet! Thank God, but if we don't hurry, we'll be late for the dance," his wife said and eagerly began getting ready.

A few minutes later, Leo dragged his body out of bed, still half-asleep, heading toward the shower. "I'll be only a minute," he announced. By then, his wife was already dressed.

"Hurry, my love," she said. "I don't want to miss even a minute of it." They have been deprived for so long of things like these, and she hated to be late. An overzealous Katarina bubbled and began practicing her dance around the room as she waited for her husband to get ready.

He stepped out of the shower, leaned against the bathroom door, and watched her as he dressed. She spun around and around and practically sung, "We're going to the ball, the ball, the ball! It's unreal! Just yesterday, we were in camp, barely surviving each day and scrambling for crumbs of food. Now we're here on this beautiful luxurious liner with more food and drinks than we could ever finish."

"Look at you," Leo commented finally. "You're positively flying with excitement. Calm down." Katarina was too excited to see him come out.

Her husband's words startled her, but she continued, "It feels like a story from a book of fairy tales," she whirled around and chuckled, drunk with happiness. Her eyes twinkled like diamonds. "And in Canada, it will be like this all the time."

"These are big dreams. Are you sure about that?" Leo asked and smirked.

"Of course! Aren't you?"

"Yes, but let's hurry. Otherwise, we'll be late," Leo said, almost grouchy, and exited.

She took a deep breath and forced herself to calm down, determined not to be bothered by his moody remarks. "Look who's rushing now?" Katarina titillated, climbing the steps.

At the crowded entrance to the ballroom, loud music met their ears. They paused and stared in. "There are so many people here!" Katarina remarked.

"Where else are they going to go?" Leo chuckled. Katarina didn't respond.

Their eyes drifted around the hall. At the far end, up on a podium stood a huge orchestra, and its members, dressed in green-and-red dinner jackets, played. Katarina's eyes caught the stewards meandering through the crowded ballroom and around the dancing partners, carrying a full tray of drinks on their hands and tensely observed. "How do they do that?" she muttered to herself, and her eyes continued to wander.

Her reverie was interrupted by a new song the band began playing. She recognized the lyrics. "Oh, wow! They're playing "Tequila," that's our song!" she announced, excited, and slipped her hand into her husband's.

Leo looked at his wife. "You still remember the song?"

"Of course! It played in the Uljanik garden the night when we first met. Don't you remember?"

"How can I forget? It played almost all evening," Leo answered and let his eyes wander around the hall, occasionally pausing on a beautiful young woman. Katarina glanced at her husband, not sure what to make of his pauses.

Her heart wilted though as it reminded her how much things had changed between them and how far they really were from home. "Let's go to find our companions," she suddenly suggested and pushed forward.

Leo grabbed his wife's hand. "Yes, of course," he obliged and began guiding her through the crowd as they scoured for their friends.

"Look over there, Istvan and Greta," Katarina said, pointing to the bar. As they maneuvered their way toward them, the loud music made it difficult for them to hear anything but the gibberish of the crowded ballroom, so they decided not to talk until they got to the bar.

Finally, they broke through the mass and found themselves standing in front of their newfound friends. "Hello, you two," Leo said with a smile. "Are you enjoying yourselves?"

"Immensely!" Greta giggled and glanced at her husband.

"You made it," Istvan said and picked up a red bottle of wine.
"Drink, Katarina?"

"Yes, please," she said and turned her head toward the dance floor, admiring the couples dancing and longing to have a dance with her husband. Katarina hadn't danced with him since he had met her at the camp and that one didn't really count.

"How about you, Leo? What would you like to drink?" Istvan asked as he handed a glass to his wife.

"The same as Katarina, red," Leo replied and let his eyes wander again. "It's very lovely. Beautiful decorations."

"Yes, it is. I've never seen anything quite like it," Greta noticed, glancing around the room and sipping on her wine.

Katarina was enchanted and conceded, "I've never been to a party like this!" She chuckled and wiggled with her body. "I love it!"

Leo extended his hand to his wife. "May I have this dance, darling?"

Heat flamed in her cheeks as she bowed, "But of course, you can, my love." He swooped her into his arms, and they waltzed and glided across the shining wooden floor, like a white swan on the lake, as did Istvan and Greta, including many other passengers.

The crowd was wild. It screamed, chatted, and laughed. After a few dances, the music stopped, and the dancers traveled to the bar, had a drink, and returned to the floor to dance again. The evening was superb and the Italian music intoxicating. "I'm having a marvelous time, are you?" Katarina smiled, looking up at her husband's face, adding, "I almost forgot what a good dancer you are."

Leo stared down at her dark-brown eyes. "You are not bad yourself, darling," he noticed, whirled her around and around, holding his arms out to protect his wife from being elbowed.

XXXXXXXXXXXXXXXX

Suddenly, she was blinded by a camera flash. "Look, that steward is taking our picture," Katarina voiced.

"It's not us. Why would he take our picture?" Leo asked and continued to whirl his wife around, refusing even to acknowledge the possibility. She wasn't sure if the picture was of them or someone else, but she ignored it and turned her attention to her husband and the dance.

Finally, an hour and half before midnight, Katarina became exhausted. "Let's rest for a while," she suggested and walked on the side.

"Sure. Let's have a drink," Leo agreed, wiping sweat from his forehead as they began to stroll to the bar. Istvan, Greta, and a few other refugees gathered around the bar, drinking and chatting as Katarina and Leo arrived.

Leo poured two glasses of red wine and handed one to his wife. "Here you go, darling," and took a sip out of his, moving close to the men. "What are you up to?" he asked, puzzled.

Istvan turned to him and said, "We are planning to visit the captain on the bridge."

"Why?"

"To wish him a Happy New Year, and perhaps see outside a little, and get some fresh air," Istvan explained.

"That's great! Can we girls come too?" Katarina asked giddily.

"Absolutely!" Greta chirped. "We can't let the men go alone."

"Can I come too?" there was a familiar voice coming from the crowd. It was Viktor. He was a young nice-looking bachelor and was all over the ship. "I would like to see some of the African continent," he said.

"Sure you can, my friend," Leo said, shaking his hand in wishing him a New Year.

"Then it's settled. Let's go," Istvan gave the command and added. "However, we cannot see the African continent tonight. It will have to be tomorrow night because that's when the ship sails through the Straits of Gibraltar, not tonight," Istvan explained.

Together, they ventured toward the captain's bridge, armed with bottles of wine. As they were climbing the steps to the bridge, they met a young officer coming down. "What are you people doing in here?" he asked.

Istvan paused, put his hands behind his back, and said, "We would like to see the captain please?"

"Well, the captain won't be here for a while. Is there anything I can do for you?" the young officer answered.

Leo and Istvan looked at each other. "We wondered if we could go up to the bridge to wait for the New Year. Maybe we'll see some ships on the high sea," he said sheepishly.

"Go ahead, but it's very dark, you might see nothing," the officer warned and let them to go up and was on his way.

"Hurray! We did it!" the group shouted and proceeded to climb the steps to the captain's bridge.

They reached the bridge in just a few minutes. The night was dark, foggy, and cold, the wind blew fiercely from the sea, but nothing could be seen, just something ahead in the sea. They couldn't figure out what was. "It's probably a mirage?" Viktor chuckled and took a drink of wine from his bottle.

"Oh no!" the men all sighed in disappointment. They had all been so excited about seeing something more besides their ship sailing in the same direction, they had forgotten to take account that it was winter night. When they realized, nothing could be seen. "Now what?" they asked in unison, and everyone turned to leave.

"Where are you going?" Istvan protested, somewhat tipsy. "We came here to wait for the New Year, so let's wait."

"Yeah! Yeah," they said. Despite not being able to see much, everyone decided to wait on the captain's bridge for countdown to New Year and they pulled out their supplies.

"I brought my drink," Leo chuckled as he pulled out a bottle of red wine.

"You are not the only one," Istvan said and several other men as they sipped from their bottles of wine. They hollered in laughter as the strong Mediterranean Sea wind ruffled their hair.

Everyone held something in their hand, a bottle of wine or a drink in a glass to toast in the New Year. At the stroke of midnight, the ship sirens started to screech wildly announcing the New Year.

XXXXXXXXXXXXXXXXXXXXXXXX

They all shouted, "Happy New Year!" The tinkle of glasses and bottles was louder in their ears than the sirens. They toasted the New Year as the ship sailed quietly across the Mediterranean Sea. The strong wind that blew hadn't touched it.

"Bad weather is approaching," Istvan announced in his high-pitched voice.

"How would you know that?" Leo asked. "It's dark out there."

"I can smell it in the air," Istvan chuckled, staggering toward Leo. Istvan laid his hand on Leo's shoulder and said, "I was a marine in Yugoslav army. I passed through here many times on an army destroyer, accompanying Tito's ship *Bijeli Galeb*, on trips to visit Africa and other third-world countries. I don't have to see it to know." He chuckled as he lifted his bottle and took a sip of white wine.

"Yeah, I'm sure you can," Leo said cynically.

"Yes! Yes! Yes!" Istvan said.

The steady cold wind blew mercilessly against their faces as they listened to Istvan yak on and on. Katarina and Greta's bodies were shivering and their teeth began to chatter as they waited for the men to say was time to go back inside. They were dancing on the spot to keep warm. Finally, Katarina suggested, "Let's go inside."

"Yes, that a wonderful idea!" Greta agreed, her teeth chattering. They rushed off the captain's cold and windy bridge without telling their husbands and descended to the warmth of the ship.

"That's better," Katarina sighed as they sat at the bar in the ballroom.

The bartender glanced at their frozen faces and asked, "Can I get you something to drink, ladies?"

Trying hard to prevent her body from trembling, Katarina replied, "Cappuccino please."

"Make that two," Greta quickly added, rubbing the palms of her hands against each other.

A short while later, their husbands returned from the captain's bridge, their bodies shivering. "Brrr! Is it ever cold up there!" both of them exclaimed, and they took a few sips of hot cappuccino from their wives' cups. "Let's dance, girls," Istvan suggested.

Without waiting for an answer, they grabbed their wives and rushed to spin them around on the floor to warm up. Katarina enjoyed Leo's spin dancing so much, he couldn't have made her happier even if he tried. After they warmed up, Leo squeezed his wife close to his body. "From now on, it's smooth sailing," he commented as he slowed down his spins.

"Yes, smooth sailing!" she agreed, looking at her husband joyfully, hoping that was a new beginning for them. They kept dancing, oblivious to everyone else in the room.

When the music stopped, after the last dance of the evening, Katarina noticed the passengers gathering at the podium. "What's going on over there?"

"I don't know, let's see," Leo replied and they made their way over.

"What's those stewards doing on the podium?" Istvan asked, coming with his wife behind Katarina and Leo, and at the same time Viktor arrived and settled at the back, she noticed.

"We just got here," Leo explained. They were curious and kept pushing closer, but the passengers in front of them gathered together so tightly not even a fly could have made it through.

The stewards gathered around the microphone with their smiles on their faces and some papers in their hands. "Happy New Year!" one of them said and explained. "Every New Year's Eve, we have a dance surprise contest. We surveyed and watched the dancers throughout the evening, then we take pictures of everyone dancing tonight. Then we chose the best dancing couple."

"Wow!" the refugees screamed, interrupting him with their surprise at being photographed while dancing.

Katarina turned to Leo and said, "I told you so!" He just smirked and turned his head toward the podium.

When the crowd settled, the steward continued, "And now, we're proud to announce the winners, and they are Mr. and Mrs. Lisic! Come down here!"

For a second or two, Katarina and Leo looked around; they were shocked beyond belief that their names were announced. Then the steward repeated, "Mr. and Mrs. Lisic! Come down!"

"Oh my god! It's us!" she shouted as they threaded through the crowd.

A huge applause accompanied them as they climbed to the podium. "Congratulations!" the crowd shouted again and again and Viktor, Istvan, and Greta cheered them on.

The steward shook their hands as they posed for another picture and said, "Congratulations to you both." Then he presented them with a small certificate to acknowledge the achievements.

Katarina accepted the certificate and said, "Thank you very much. My husband and I are proud to have been chosen the best dancers of the New Year, on your ship tonight. We'll treasure it forever." When she unwrapped it, she asked, "Where's the picture?" shocked that it wasn't there. She wanted the picture.

"Oh, but the picture costs two dollars, young lady," another steward replied.

"Two dollars!" Katarina frowned. "I don't have two dollars. Better yet, I've never seen two dollars. The picture means so much to me. Please may I have it?" she begged. "I really don't have any money."

But he wouldn't hear it. "No money, no picture," the steward insisted that those were the rules of the ship. He wouldn't dare break them and walked away. Later, their picture was posted under a glass frame with the other winners, which hung on the wall outside the ballroom.

As Katarina and Leo descended from the podium, Greta hugged Katarina and shook Leo's hand. "That's very nice for you to win the contest," she said.

"That goes for me too," Istvan agreed.

Also Viktor came through the crowd to hug them and congratulate them. "Let's all have a drink," he invited and sauntered toward the bar. Leo and Katarina followed him but was late and many passengers were preparing to leave for their cabins, including Istvan and Greta.

Leo and Katarina paused. "Are you two leaving already?" he asked and tried to convince him. "Stay just for one drink."

"It's getting late and my wife is tired and sleepy," Istvan said and they turned to walk away.

"See you in the morning then," Leo replied, refusing to accept the night was over. He watched Istvan and Greta as they walked out, and he and his wife continued toward the bar where Viktor was waiting for them at a small table.

They sat down and were about to decide who was going to drink what when they heard the bartender from the bar yelled, "This is the last call for drinks!"

Viktor went to the bar, grabbed a bottle of red wine, and brought it on the table. "We should enjoy it while it lasts," he commented as he was filling their glasses. "Cheers to you two for winning the dancing contest," he said and took a sip from his glass. Leo and Viktor started chatting and chuckling, by then very tipsy.

Katarina would rather have coffee or something else instead, but she said nothing and took a sip anyway. "Thank you, Viktor," she said and her thoughts whirled around the picture. A little disappointed at not being able to obtain it for future remembrance, she said, "Let's go to sleep."

Leo looked around. There were only a few passengers still mingling. "They are passengers still celebrating," he replied and turned to Viktor and their chatting.

It wasn't until the stewards announced the ballroom closed and the wine was gone that Leo and Viktor were ready to go sleep.

At the door, Katarina noticed the big frame filled with pictures and stopped, "Wow! Here's our picture!" she said in a high-pitched voice, pointing at it. Her heart sunk as she could only look at it, but couldn't touch it.

Leo and Viktor just glanced and staggered on their way. "Oh, you two don't care about anything except wine," she muttered, following them down to the third class.

It was three in the morning when they strolled into their cabin and both were exhausted. However, Leo staggered most of the way as he had had a little too much to drink so when he tried to take his pants off, he fell down. Rolling over on the floor still struggling with his pants, he chuckled and teased, "Don't worry, darling. When we get to Halifax, the Canadian government will give us money. Then you'll see how the dollar looks."

"Too bad they didn't give us money before we left for Canada. I could have had the picture now. Anyway, this was a night I will always remember." She smiled, throwing her clothes over the chair, getting herself ready for bed. Katarina had drunk only a few glasses of red wine, but that was enough to put her to sleep as soon as she lay down.

Two hours later, she awoke, almost screaming from a nightmare. Her nightgown was soaked with sweat. The red wine gave her a headache and made her so hot and thirsty she threw back the covers and got off the bed. "I should have never touched that wine just to make my husband feel better," she muttered, walking toward the water fountain, holding on to her pounding head. She drank a whole glass of water, took off her dampish long-sleeved nightgown, and tossed it on the foot of the bed. Then rummaging through their carry-on bags to find something cooler, she plucked out one of Leo's old short-sleeved shirt, wrapped herself in it, and went back to sleep.

In the morning, the loud breakfast announcement awoke them both. "Oh no!" Leo moaned. "My head is pounding like a drum. It's going to explode. I need a hot cup of coffee fast." He rolled off the bed and walked to the bathroom holding his head.

Slowly getting off the bed, Katarina teased, "Hangover? You should have drunk less," even though she didn't feel much better with only the few glasses she had had. Imagine how she would have felt if she had had as many as her husband did.

Without a comment, he dressed and was out the door.

"Wait. I'm coming too!" Katarina rushed after him. He didn't stop but walked swiftly as if he hadn't heard her. Before he reached the dining room, his wife caught up with him and grasped his hand. "Hold on," she said and they strode inside for New Year's breakfast together.

The tables were laden with cold cuts, fruits, sweets, and fresh brewed coffee. As they walked down the dining room aisle to their table, Leo's eyes widened. "Look at that food!"

His wife glanced at his hungry eyes askance. "There seems to be no end to the food and apparently to your hunger. I thought you only wanted coffee," Katarina noted and put out her cup toward him.

"I do, but also other things," he replied, pouring coffee into his cup and filled her cup too. Then he began attacking the cold cuts, his favorite was prosciutto.

A few minutes later, Istvan and Greta arrived at the table. He was subdued, with black circles around his eyes, and his face was pale, as if he hadn't slept a wink.

"Istvan, you're pale as a sheep. What's wrong?" Leo asked, staring at him. He probably would have chuckled if his own head wasn't giving him severe pain.

"Haha," Istvan replied, barely able to turn his head without experiencing vicious throbbing.

"He drank too much wine and grappa last night. Just like you did, Leo," Greta intercepted and finished her husband's sentence.

Leo chuckled. "Oh, but the trick is not to mix. Besides, I didn't have any grappa last night."

"But you had headache when you woke up this morning anyway," Katarina butted in. Leo just cast a glare at his wife and said nothing.

Istvan poured himself a cup of coffee and conceded, "I don't usually mix drinks, but last night, I was overjoyed and I overdid it, I know. I'll be fine."

As soon as everyone was seated, the stewards came with French toast and three-minute boiled eggs. They placed them on the table and Leo and Istvan were all over them. Even with hangovers, they had no trouble eating breakfast. Both girls stared in disbelief. "The way you two sounded earlier I thought you would never be able to look at food again," Katarina said, ready to burst into laughter.

"You would think so, wouldn't you?" Greta agreed with her mouth full of food. Their husbands didn't even glance at the girls; they just continued filling their stomach.

Suddenly a loud voice boomed through the speakers and momentarily hushed the din in the room. Everyone stopped eating and lifted their head to listen to the announcer.

"WE ARE NEARING THE PORT OF MALAGA, SPAIN. IF ANYONE IS INTERESTED IN LEAVING THE SHIP TO GO TO VIEW THE CITY, THEY CAN DO SO, BUT THE SHIP WILL NOT WAIT FOR ANYONE IF THEY ARE LATE. ONE MORE THING, PLEASE DO NOT TOUCH ANYTHING, ESPECIALLY THE ORANGES LYING ON THE GROUND, IF YOU WANT TO CONTINUE YOUR JOURNEY," the speaker warned.

"Hurray! Hurray!" the passengers yelled, clapped, and cheered, pleased to be able to visit the city in Spain.

Katarina looked at everyone at the table and said, "Hmm, that sounds good. A short view of the city would be nice, but what was that about oranges?" she asked and stuffed a last morsel into her mouth.

Istvan took a sip of his coffee and chuckled, "I can see you would be confused about the oranges in the middle of winter. But the climate, with more than three hundred days of sun and year-round average temperature of twenty-three degrees Celsius makes Malaga perfect location to grow lemons and oranges and olives. The oranges are on the ground, that was what the warning was about."

Xx

They glanced at each other and at Istvan. "Are you telling us that in Malaga at this moment, it's summer like weather?"

"Yes, that's exactly what I'm saying." He took his last bite of his breakfast and washed it down with a gulp of coffee.

"How long do you think the ship will take to get to the port?" Leo asked.

He shrugged his shoulders. "Oh, I really don't know. Depending on the ship's speed," and turned to his coffee.

Leo covered her hand with his and asked, "Did you say you would like to leave the ship for a while, darling?"

"Yes, I'd like that," his wife replied. "The question is, will you be able to go?"

Leo cast a sharp look at her, annoyed, but didn't answer. He stood up and asked, "Is everyone ready to go up the deck?"

They rose from their chairs and sauntered to the deck together.

# CHAPTER 20

The sun played a game of peekaboo, with the clouds making the morning cloudy and chilly. Katarina, Leo, and their newfound friends strolled and mingled with the other passengers on the deck, viewing the sky and the sea for about an hour, when Viktor joined them. "It's a wonderful day, isn't it?" he commented, looking around.

"Yes, it is, if it wasn't for this chilly wind. It would feel like spring," Greta said and snuggled closer to her husband as they continued to saunter.

Leo leaned over the side and pulled a cigarette out of his pocket. "A cigarette anyone?"

"Don't worry, we got our own," Viktor announced and gave a light to both of them. All three smoked like a chimney, continued watching and anxiously waiting for the liner to arrive at the port.

Katarina's eyes were fixed on the ship's wake as it nudged its way toward the Spanish port of Malaga. The acrobatic performance of the seagulls over the surface of the water got most of her attention. Suddenly, strains of music began to drift toward them. "Listen! Everyone! Spanish music!" she shouted and turned toward the direction of the music.

The passengers moved closer to Katarina and turned to listen. "Where is the music?" some asked and listened again.

"Where is it?" Leo turned to his wife, staring at her in disbelief.

"Look over there," she pointed excitedly toward the direction of the sound. Everyone's eyes followed her finger. Then, right in front of their own eyes, a city began to rise from the Mediterranean Sea. "See I told you," Katarina chirped and widened her eyes at the city as it rose completely. "It must be the city of Malaga!" she yelled, staring.

"Wow!" they shouted and began jumping up and down. It was still too far to see how the city looks, but they were elated to know they were close to Malaga.

As soon as they entered the Spanish horizon, they began to feel the weather change. The wind blew warmer and the sky was clear blue, and there were barely waves in the sea. The closer the ship nudged to the city port, the warmer the air was getting.

The passengers with the warm coats began to take them off and enjoyed the sun as they waited for the liner to dock at the port. "Can you feel the warmer air?" Greta giggled, taking her coat off.

"Yes," they answered. Everyone revelled in the warm air that blew lightly from the coast of Spain.

"It's a huge and beautiful city!" Katarina exclaimed, still staring in the direction of it. "Look! There is a band on the pier accompanied by majorette dancers in black-and-yellow costumes the color of the Spanish flag."

"And the small crowd of spectators," someone yelled from the back. Suddenly, the ship sirens began to wail announcing its arrival. The single plume of white steam shot into the sky and vanished in the wind, then the engine stopped working.

Leo, Viktor, and Istvan leaned against the deck, looking at the tugboats coming toward them to meet the great *Cristoforo Colombo.* "Here we go again," Istvan said.

Leo and the male company had their eyes on the tugboats while their wives strained to watch the girls dancing on the pier and listened to the beautiful Spanish music. "I love this kind of national dancing," Katarina noted and added. "At home, we were forbidden to dance national dances and sing national songs."

"I know. The police used to come around when there was some kind of national holiday for Croatians or Hungarians. They used to run after us and beat us with those straps called *pendreks*," Greta remembered.

"Yeah, those pendreks left severe pain but no marks on the body," Katarina noted. "Thank God, that period of our time is over." She noticed a long line of horses and buggies waiting patiently on the far side of the pier until the great ship docked. "What are those horses and buggies doing down there?" she asked, looking at them.

Istvan chuckled, "They're waiting for passengers who want to ride around the city. But for a price, of course."

"Of course."

Ship docked right in the commercial harbor adjacent to downtown Malaga, only a five-minute walk to the center. The city center was beautifully decorated for the New Year holidays, it could be seen even from the ship. As soon as the *Cristoforo Colombo* docked, the passengers crowded the exit for the tour around the Malaga. Everyone wanted to see the city where the grass was green, the flowers bloomed, and the oranges were still on their trees even during the Christmas and New Year season. The foursome followed the crowd out of the ship and got separated. On the pier, Leo glanced back. "Greta and Istvan, where are they?"

"It looks like we've lost them in the crowd," Katarina replied, scrutinizing the area. 'Oh, there they are, just ahead of us." She pointed to the buggy they were walking toward.

Leo and Katarina both ran. When they caught up to them, their friends were standing beside the buggy. "Are you going to take the buggy?" Leo asked, scanning a small price list attached to the buggy.

Istvan chuckled, looking at them. "I don't think so. Are you?"

"No," Leo replied quickly. "The day is nice and warm, in spite of a little wind. We're going to walk. Exercise and fresh air will do us good."

"All right then. Let's go. We're walking too," Istvan said. They gave their hands to their wives and went on foot to view the city, leaving the buggy and horses to someone else.

Leo turned to his wife and said, "I don't have ten dollars to pay for a ride for us."

"Five dollars for a ride, wow!" Katarina exclaimed. "That's very expensive!"

"Yeah, that's a lot. We don't have that kind of money to give for a ride neither," Istvan said and continued to walk.

They moved out of the harbor and turned to walk up a small hill that would take them to the center of the city. They came upon the orange trees heavy with ripe fruit, growing alongside the Mediterranean seashore.

"Oh, wow! Look at this!" Katarina sputtered, surprised to see so many ripe and bruised oranges lying on the ground around the trees. She was even more perplexed that nobody had touched them. "This must be what we were warned not to touch."

"It looks that way," Leo answered, wondering the same thing, why nobody had touched them.

Istvan chuckled as he watched them wondering. "Yeah, this is exactly why the steward warned us. If you get caught taking even one orange, you could go to jail for stealing."

Leo turned to Istvan and asked, "Why they don't harvest them?"

"Yeah, why they don't do that and give them to the poor children?" Greta questioned.

"Why? I have to admit I don't know. Probably national pride and their culture," Istvan answered sheepishly.

They all laughed.

"What a shame to let such lovely oranges waste away," Katarina giggled and made a motion as though she were going to take one.

Leo grabbed her by the hand. "Are you crazy? You can't do that," he yelled, almost piercing her with his sharp look. "Did you forget what the ship steward told us?" he asked with a stern voice. "'Don't touch the oranges, if you want to continue your journey.' Remember those words."

Katarina laughed. "You didn't think I was that stupid, did you?" She teased and pulled her hand back. She just wanted to play a little, to make the trip more enjoyable. Greta joined Katarina in laughter and they rushed ahead.

Her husband looked at her slightly cross but said nothing. It bothered him that she was having fun at his expense, but he didn't want to make a big deal out of it. After all, it was a New Year's Day.

They all laughed and continued their trek toward the center.

It took them fifteen minutes to get to downtown Malaga. The center was almost empty; there were only a few people here and there. Everything was closed. The streets were strewn with New Year's garbage: old flowers, shriveled wrapping papers, and decorations that were falling apart from the buildings. The wind kept blowing them down and shuffling them from street to street. As the foursome strolled around downtown, the shriveled trash kept tangling around their feet. "Look at all this junk. I can barely walk," Leo said as he untangled himself from it, and the wind blew them away.

As soon as Katarina pulled a few colorful ties off her feet, she turned to Istvan. "Where are the people?"

"It's a New Year's Day! People are sleeping," Istvan answered, and his eyes scanned around.

"Istvan, you seem to know a lot about the city, tell us a little about it," Leo said as they continued to walk around.

"I'll be glad too." Istvan accepted the challenge and began. "The town of Malaga is a very fascinating town with a rich and unique history, which gives visitors a great variety of interesting things to do and see, museums, cathedrals, Gibrseforo theaters, which we can't do or see anything today."

"What's that huge building in the middle of the city?" Katarina intercepted, pointing at it.

"That is a beautiful high-rise hotel Larios next to the Plaza del Obispo and the Plaza de la Marina. The hotel enjoys a great location between the cathedral of Malaga and Paseo del Parque with a picturesque view out over the port," Istvan explained and continued. "A few years back, I had visited Alcazaba Palace, you can see it on the far end, this ancient over a thousand-year-old palace, you have to see it to believe how beautiful it is. Down farther are the Moorish fortresses and Museo de Bellas Artes, home to some of Picasso's paintings are among the most prominent attractions here as Picasso was born in this city."

"I wish we could go and visit some of these places," Katarina said after they had listened tentatively every word he was saying about Malaga as they walked along the streets viewing the city buildings at the same time.

"Me too, but we don't have much time, in fact, it's time for us to turn back," Istvan said, and they turned to walk to the harbor.

Suddenly, Leo stopped and said, "This feels creepy. It's like we're walking through a ghost town. There's barely a few people around."

"Of course, it is. What about those drunks over there, still wandering through the streets, and that one there, taking a nap under a bench, don't they count?" Katarina pointed at a few bodies down the road with a chuckle.

"Yeah! They are the citizens too," Greta giggled. Everyone laughed.

"Oh no! The time is running out," Leo shrieked after consulting his watch. "We better rush."

"You're right," Istvan replied. They grabbed their wives' hands and quickened their pace, pulling them along with them.

"Hey, slow down!" Katarina yelled, unable to keep up with her husband.

"The ship won't wait for us. We have to hurry," he replied and continued his pace dragging his wife with him.

When they reached the pier, they were all almost out of breath, especially Katarina. Istvan and Greta noticed horse and buggy stationed beside the ship where the passengers were having their picture taken. "Would you two like take pictures with us?" Istvan asked, walking over to the buggy and horse.

"We'd love to, but we don't have the money for it," Leo answered for both of them.

"Don't worry. I'll pay for them. Come in," Istvan said, and all four climbed up to the buggy. The driver was selling a small stuffed Spanish toro to take pictures with it. Istvan bought one and handed to his wife as they yelled "Cheese!" to the camera.

When the cameraperson handed them the pictures, Istvan paid for them and said, "Here, Leo, these two pictures are a gift to you and Katarina so you could remember us by."

Leo took the pictures and smiled at Istvan. "Thanks, it's a lovely thought."

While they were taking pictures and chitchatting, the other passengers crowded entrance to board the ship. They had to stay in line, but they didn't care because the day was beautiful, like summer. The air was warm, a little windy, but nothing they couldn't handle. Katarina turned to Greta and said, "I wish this weather would accompany us to Canada."

"Yeah, me and you both, but I'm afraid that's not going to happen," Greta disagreed with a frown.

As soon as the passengers boarded the ship, everyone walked out to the deck. Leo and the company strolled up and down the deck, chatting and surveying the city, sea, and the sky, waiting for the *Cristoforo Colombo* to sail. "It feels like summer here," Katarina complimented enjoying the nice warm weather.

"Isn't it," Greta agreed and sighed deeply.

Katarina glanced up: there were no clouds, the sky was clear blue. But she did notice a man on the first-class deck leaning against the railing sunbathing. She looked closer and said, "See, Leo, I was right."

"Right about what?" he asked, glancing at her.

"Look at the man up on the first-class deck. That's the same man the stewards dragged away from the ship in Naples. Remember?"

"Oh, so he is," her husband replied, looking up inconspicuously.

"I told you he wasn't a refugee," she had to rub it in.

"All right! All right! Enough already!" he asserted testily.

"You two are bickering again," Viktor said, suddenly coming to the deck, out of nowhere. "You're going to miss this beautiful Spanish music and girls." He leaned against the deck and began waving to the dancing girls below; they were getting ready to dance.

As the tugboats began their job, the girls began to dance accompanied by the beautiful Spanish music. Excited, the passengers lined themselves against the deck rail, leaning over, waving to dancers, musicians, and the small group of onlookers that arrived at the last minute to the pier, shouting "Good-bye, everyone!"

"Adios! Adios!" they yelled from below and waved.

It was one o'clock in the afternoon when the tugboats dragged *Cristoforo Colombo* out of the Malaga dock and the engines of the ship took over. The single plume of dark steam shot into the sky and disappeared in the wind. The ship bid farewell to Spain, their music and dancers, with its sirens and began its voyage toward the port of Lisbon in Portugal.

"I wonder if we're going to stop in Gibraltar," Leo asked, still leaning against the deck railing.

Istvan looked at Leo and said, "I know the ship has to stop, but we might not be aware because it will be after midnight when the ship passes through. We all will be asleep. I would like to see Africa as we sail through the Straits of Gibraltar."

"Why don't we ask the captain as we did the night before? He might let us to the bridge to see it," Leo suggested with a smile.

Their wives put their two cents in. "We would like to see the African continent too, so count us in," Katarina said.

"Yeah, count us in," Greta confirmed. The husbands said nothing, just smiled.

A group of passengers stayed on the deck, waving and watching the girls dancing until they were no more visible. Then most of them retreated inside, including Istvan and Greta.

Leo grasped his wife's hand and they strolled around the deck a little longer to listen to the beautiful Spanish music, which could be still heard in a distance. They reveled in the warm air that blew from the coast of Spain. Leo was interested in the sea and the wake of the ship.

Katarina was intrigued by the lovely white seagulls flying merrily above their heads, scanning for food, and by the sea. "Will these birds accompany us all the way to Canada?" she asked.

"I don't know," her husband said. The ship picked up speed, intensifying the wind, and it turned blowy. They turned to walk inside.

Lunch was announced just as they entered, so instead of going to their cabin, they strolled into the dining saloon. It wasn't any lunch. It was New Year's lunch, with added trims and decorations. "Wow! It's so beautiful!" Katarina exclaimed with a dazzling smile of joyous amazement.

"Yes, they're lovely," Leo said, less interested. His head was turned to the tables, soaking in the lovely aroma of the food as they walked to their table.

*Hmm,* Katarina thought. *He hadn't heard what I said as his mind is on the food.*

By the time they arrived, Istvan and Greta were already sitting down. "You beat us to it," Leo commented.

"I guess we did," Istvan replied. Greta smiled and said nothing.

Katarina immediately picked at the hors d'oeuvres. "I'm starving. This outing gave me a huge appetite."

"Hold on a minute," Istvan called and placed both bottles of wine in front of himself.

"All right, all right," Katarina grouched and glanced at him. "What is it?"

"I said to wait one minute," Istvan said, took four glasses, and placed one in front of each of them and poured the wine: red for Leo and his wife, white for Greta and him.

"I knew there had to be a reason that you two came earlier than usual," Leo chuckled, watching him and wondering what he was up to.

Istvan smiled as he lifted his glass in a cheer to them and said, "Here now, a toast to all of us and our new beginning. We're sailing to our new promised land. I wish all of us a long happy life, full of love, laughter, and prosperity."

"Here! Here! I'll drink to that," Leo replied joyfully as the tinkle of glasses rang through their table. The dining room was noisy and no one paid any mind to them. After taking a few sips, Leo put his glass down and continued, "My wish is that we meet again in twenty years on this very ship, sailing the other way, for holidays, of course." He laughed and winked at his wife.

"And I toast to you, Istvan and Greta," Katarina cheered and took a sip of her wine. "But, Leo, I can't lift a glass to your toast. Don't you remember that the ship will be retired as soon it returns to Italy, weren't we told in Naples when we embarked that this is *Cristoforo Colombo*'s last voyage?"

"I'm sorry I forgot," Leo mumbled, exasperated and a little embarrassed. He hated to be corrected, especially by his wife, but he didn't let it show. Katarina knew he was furious with her for modifying his statement, but she didn't let that bother her, she was determined to keep her spirits up and enjoy the voyage.

After they finished eating, Leo sprang from the chair and extended his hand to his wife. "Let's go out on the deck for some air."

She smiled and took his hand. "I accept your invitation with delight, my love," she said cheesily.

Together, all four of them sauntered out to the sunny deck. By then, the ship was well underway toward the port of Lisbon, still sailing in the Spanish water, but no longer could the music from the coast be heard. They walked around on the deck and reveled in the warmth of the sun.

Throngs of seagulls circling the big liner provided relief from the desolation. Katarina's eyes fixed on them as they were flying noisily over the surface of the sea. "Aren't they beautiful?"

"Who?" Leo asked.

"Those white seagulls. I can't believe they are still with us." She pointed at the birds.

"But not for long," Istvan interjected and added his own observation as he viewed the sky. 'When they sense danger, they began to fly away, just as they're doing now." He shifted his glasses anxiously as he watched them fly way, flock by flock. "A big storm is coming our way!" he announced, shifting his eyeglasses.

"You're kidding, right?" Leo, quizzed. "You're not suggesting what I think you are, are you?"

Still inspecting the sky. "Yes! I am! And I'm not kidding!" Istvan stressed. "That's how sailors know when a storm is closing in, and I'm a sailor!"

Leo gazed at the perfectly clear and blue sky and chuckled, "Who knows? You could be right. We might have a storm."

Oh, you men," Greta lashed out at them. "You merely want to scare us girls."

"It's a lovely sunny day," Katarina said. "Let's not spoil it with a talk of a storm."

"Yes, it was, but now the sun is bidding farewell. Look how lovely it is," Greta replied, watching the sun slowly sink, bathing the sea in gold and hundreds of other beautiful colors on its path below the horizon.

Katarina stopped and stared at it. "Wow! You are right. The sunset is so beautiful. It's one of the most colorful sunsets I've ever seen." Fascinated, they all leaned against the railing and watched it.

"I've heard you can see the most beautiful sunsets from the ship," Leo said. "But I never dreamed it's that lovely."

"Yes, but this one isn't the kind of sunset that gives the sailors delight," Istvan noticed, looking worried.

"Oh, Istvan! You always have something different to say. What do you mean by that anyway?" Katarina quizzed.

"It's the kind of sunset that warns the sailors of a coming storm," he replied stubbornly.

"Oh, sure. I meant to ask you, where is the storm?" Katarina smirked and looked up. "There's not even a cloud, the sky is clear blue. Greta is right. You just want to scare us, don't you?" They all chuckled, except Istvan.

He frowned. "I'm not kidding!" and continued to observe the sky. "I'm a sailor, I can smell it!" That brought even more laughter.

After the sunset, the darkness of the night was quickly approaching and the gentle wind turning cool. The girls cuddled against their husbands' bodies to keep warm and listened to their husbands' discussion, trying to figure out if the clear sky was about to unleash a storm upon them.

The debate ended abruptly when Viktor arrived. He was constantly on the move, here and there, you never knew when he was going to pop up. "Are we going to try to see the African continent tonight as we pass through the Straits of Gibraltar?" he asked.

"That's a good idea!" they said, and everyone was so excited.

"Now, we go inside and get something warmer to wear. Later, we'll climb the captain's bridge," Greta said, and the girls quickly retreated inside the ship.

"All right. We are going to get ourselves a drink," Leo said as they followed the girls in. They found each other at the dining saloon and had their supper.

Later, they strolled toward the captain's bridge. At the bottom of the stairs, they encountered the same officer from the night before. "You again," the steward said with a smile. "I know, you would like to see the captain. Am I right?"

"Yes, you're," Leo smiled shyly.

"You can't see the captain, but you can go up and see Africa. Though I'm not sure if you're going to see much," he told them and walked away.

"Thank you," they all said and began to climb the steps up. On the bridge, it was dark. A fresh cool breeze blew and brushed against their faces.

Katarina glanced up. The sky was clear, dark, and full of twinkling stars. "Oh no! There's no moon tonight."

"It's quiet and the sailing is smooth," Greta commented, looking ahead into the sea.

For a few minutes, they listened as the ship moved forward. The only thing they could hear was the splashing of the ship's wake as it cut through the deep Mediterranean Sea. "We should be entering soon into the Strait of Gibraltar," Istvan said suddenly, looking ahead, but it was dark and could see nothing. "I think we just began to sail through the strait, I can feel the colder breeze coming toward us from the open Atlantic Ocean."

"Yes, I can feel it too," Leo agreed. "Istvan, you seem to know a lot about Spanish history, tell us something about Gibraltar."

"Well, Gibraltar was Spanish once, but now it belongs to England, their army won it in a war in 1700s," Istvan said.

"What about the Rock of Gibraltar? I heard the people saying like you're my Rock of Gibraltar. I know it must mean something special, right? But I don't know much about it," Katarina questioned.

"Look on your right. There's standing a huge Rock of Gibraltar," Istvan said. "You can't see much now because is night and is dark. But I know it's there because I saw it when I passed through here during the daytime. The Rock rests at the crossroads of the Atlantic Ocean and the Mediterranean Sea."

"What's the name of the part of the water that our ship is sailing through into Atlantic Ocean?" Greta asked. "I know it has a name, but I don't remember."

"The stretch of water that separates Gibraltar from North Africa is called the Strait of Gibraltar. That's our ship is sailing now. On your left side is Africa," Istvan pointed out.

Everyone strained their eyes to look for anything they could see. Unfortunately, only a few faded lights could be seen in the distance, some on the right side of the small city harbor call Gibraltar and some on the left. The men sighed in disappointment, still staring ahead into a dark night. "We've entered the cold, unpredictable Atlantic Ocean," Istvan announced finally in his high-pitched voice.

"How do you know?" Leo chuckled. "It's dark out there." Looking around, but could see nothing that would tell him they entered the big ocean. The only thing was the weather; it began to change as soon as the ship plunged into the Atlantic Ocean. The wind blew a little colder, ruffling their hair and caressing their cheeks.

"I know. I don't have to see it to know," Istvan grumbled annoyed, staggering toward Leo and laid his hand on Leo's shoulder, "I don't have to see it to know. I'm a marine." He lifted his bottle and took a sip of wine.

"It is the weather?" Leo asked. "As we are now behind the boundary of Spain."

"No, it's not!" Istvan said. "In Portugal, the weather is similar to the one in Spain, but winters are cooler because of the cold Atlantic wind."

"I'm amazed how the weather can change so much in such a short distance," Katarina commented, tightening her sweater around her body. "We better go inside, I'm a little chilly." They had all been so excited about seeing Africa from the ship, they had forgotten to take into account that it was winter everywhere except in Spain; of course, neither one brought their coats to the bridge.

As they were leaving the bridge, Greta turned to her husband. "Too bad that this tropical warm weather won't stick with us all the way to Canada."

"That would be nice, but that is wishful thinking on your part, Greta," Katarina chuckled, descending the steps slowly. As they walked to their cabins, the only people they encountered still awake were stewards running around, preparing for the next stop.

"Good night," Istvan said as they parted. One couple went left, the other right. The girls didn't even notice when Viktor left them, they were so busy discussing the weather. Viktor was like magic: he seemed to appear and disappear just like that; he made Katarina wonder if he could be a spy.

While almost everyone slept and dreamt about Africa, the *Cristoforo Colombo* slipped quietly through the Straits of Gibraltar into the Atlantic Ocean without stopping and sailed toward the port of Lisbon, Portugal.

"The ship will be anchored here for two hours. If anyone likes to explore the City of Lisbon they can do so now. The same conditions apply as in Spain." A voice through the speakers awakened Katarina and Leo.

She jumped from the bed and asked, "What's that?"

"I don't know, but I think we arrived at Lisbon," Leo answered, still sleepy. He consulted his watch: it was seven o'clock in the morning. They both got ready and walked up to second class. The smell of fresh aroma of coffee wafted all over the dining saloon. They grabbed each a cup and walked to the deck.

Istvan and Greta were leaning against the railing and watching the tugboats doing their job. Leo and Katarina joined them. "What's going on?" Leo asked and leaned against the railing to watch the tugboats once again, maneuvering the great *Cristoforo Colombo* to the Lisbon pier.

"Nothing much except you two missed to see the great Tower of Belem from the sixteenth century," Istvan informed them.

"Where? How?" Leo was little annoyed for missing to see such an old monument.

"It stands guard at the entrance to Lisbon harbor, look over there. Portugal, just like Spain, is full of history. And of course, like our Croatia," Istvan explained, pointing at it. "Ooops. I meant Yugoslavia." They both laughed.

"It looks lovely," Leo replied, straining his eyes looking into its direction. "Unfortunately, we can't see it."

When the tugboats lined the ship against the pier, then they started pulling out. "Hurry!" someone hollered and rushed toward the side of the deck that faced Lisbon's pier. Katarina, Leo, Greta, and Istvan were standing at the same side. Everyone expected to see a crowd on the pier welcoming them, but nobody was there, except a few working men and women.

"Where are the band and the dancing girls?" Katarina asked, looking around.

Watching the tugboats sail away from the liner, Leo chortled, "I guess there's no welcome wagon here."

Everything was funny to him but she wanted to know, so she asked again, "Why is it that nobody welcomed us here as in Spain?"

Leo hesitated. He had no answer for her, and Istvan made up one. "According to my information, Portugal is a very poor country. They are probably too busy trying to earn money to greet us," Istvan butted in. Of course, he was kidding.

They looked at each other, just then the loudspeakers announced, "Breakfast has been served."

Casting a glance at the passengers who began walking off the ship to view the city of Lisbon, Leo asked, "Are you and Greta coming off the ship sightseeing?"

"No. We'll stay on board. Greta doesn't feel like going," he answered.

"See you later then," Leo rushed with his wife after the others off the ship.

It was still early in the morning when sun just rose. Gazing at the dark clouds scuffling through the sky, Katarina suggested, "We can see the city from up there," pointing at a small hill close by the harbor.

"Yeah, maybe you're right," Leo answered, a little concerned. They decided it was better not to go far from the harbor, so they began to climb the hill.

But as they continued their trek up, his eyes wandered, and he became a little concerned where the road was leading them. The houses looked like old dilapidated shacks. Garbage was scattered along the backyards and back roads. Children ran around dressed in tatters.

Suddenly, Katarina shivered. "This reminds me of the camp in Capua."

"Yes. It looks like we ended up in a poorer part of the city. It's nothing like Spain. Here everything is subdued and quiet, like the calm before a storm," Leo replied.

"I have a feeling we should have stayed on the ship," Katarina said, barely finishing her sentence when a bunch of hungry children, dressed in torn rags, surrounded them. They grabbed them by their clothes and began to push and pull, from all directions, begging for food, money, other handouts. At least that is what Katarina and Leo surmised since the children spoke Portuguese.

"I'm sorry! I've nothing to give you. I'm just as poor as you," Katarina said in Italian, hoping the children would understand. Instead, they continued to push and shove and shout in Portuguese. Her body trembled. "What're we going to do, Leo?" she cried, glancing at her husband.

But before her husband could answer, a familiar voice behind said, "Don't do anything, just stay calm," Viktor instructed them.

Viktor said a few words in Portuguese and the children ran away. "I don't know what you said to them, but I'm so glad to see you. Thanks," Katarina said and gave him a big hug and kiss.

"That goes for me too, without the kisses, of course," Leo said and shook Viktor's hand. They returned all together to the ship.

On the way, Katarina asked, "Viktor, where did you learn Portuguese?"

"At Zagreb, and it isn't Portuguese. The language is called Esperanto. Everyone can understand it," Viktor said.

"Well, I'm glad that the children understood you," Katarina was thankful.

As they reached the ship, they paused under the gangway. "We should have never gone out. However, I'll never forget this experience. Thanks to Viktor, we can board the ship," Katarina said and began to climb the gangway.

"Hell!" Leo thundered. "We could have missed our ship, my wife is right, if it wasn't for you my friend, we might not be boarding now. Thanks," he said once again. "By the way, what were you doing up there alone?"

"Istvan told me you two were gone off the ship sightseeing. I came looking for you, and by the looks of it, I'm glad I did," Viktor explained.

"Well, you found us," Leo said sheepishly. He was slightly embarrassed for being in the position, but they all chuckled anyway as they entered into the ship.

On the deck, they found Istvan and Greta. They were sitting on a bench, chatting and watching other passengers stroll past. "Hello, you two lovebirds," Leo called as they approached.

"Back so soon?" Istvan asked, glancing at Leo with a smirk. "What happened?"

"You didn't happen to know anything about this, did you?" Leo asked, looking at Istvan suspiciously.

"About what?"

"We got ourselves in trouble, a bunch of poor children attacked us," Leo said.

XXXXXXXXXXXXXXXXXXXXXXXXXXXXXXXXXXXXXX XXXXXXXXXXXXXXXXXXXXXXXXXXXXXXXXXXXXXXXXX XXXXXXXXX

Istvan stood up and asked, "Why would you think that I would know something about that?"

"I smell a rat in here," Leo smirked. "Besides, you did say that you had passed through here many times. I thought you knew more than you let on."

"Bickering, bickering, that's all I hear when I'm with you fellows. I'm leaving. Bye," Viktor said and strode away.

"Tell me, Katarina, what really did happen out there?" Greta asked curiously.

"Don't even ask. It's a long story," she answered and wouldn't talk about it.

Disappointed, Greta rose to her feet.

"You are not leaving, are you?" Katarina's eyes fixed on her.

"Well, I'm getting tired sitting here," Greta complained, trying to keep the hair off her face. "Let's go for a walk."

They began to saunter along the deck. "Too bad it isn't really summer so we can get a dip," Katarina said, eyeing the huge swimming pool that stared empty and taking most of the room on the front deck.

"Yeah, that's a real shame. I would enjoy that very much."

They were so preoccupied with each other that they didn't notice the ship was ready to pull out of the dock, and the tugboats were in place to do their job until the siren began whistling.

"We are ready to depart! Let's go say good-bye to the people of Lisbon!" Katarina shouted. They rushed to the railing and leaned over, but the pier was empty, just as empty as they came in.

"There's no one there!" Everyone sighed; disappointed, they turned to watch the tugboats. As soon as they did their job and pulled the big liner out of the Lisbon harbor, its engines took over, and the ship's sirens screeched a farewell to Lisbon and its people.

The *Cristoforo Colombo* began steaming west, carrying them closer to their destination. Nothing was ahead of them, but the dark, cold, threatening Atlantic Ocean.

"This is it! No more stops. The next one, Canada!" Katarina exclaimed joyfully, bidding farewell to the tugboats returning to the pier.

"God willing," Greta replied, glancing ahead into the murky ocean.

The men wrapped their arms around their wives' shoulders, and Leo said, "Now it's smooth sailing all the way to Canada."

Istvan glared at him, but said nothing, squeezed his wife, and turned to stare at the ocean and at the sky. He just couldn't shake the feeling of an upcoming storm. They all reflected in silence, listening to the splashes of ship's wake as it began to increase cutting through the deep water.

Slowly, the passengers began to return inside; the foursome remained a little longer. The day was mostly sunny, and a light wind blew; the ocean was calm, and there were no waves to speak of. They enjoyed strolling on the deck, and the seagulls were always there. "It's a lovely day," Katarina mused, looking at the birds flying around the ship and diving into the ocean.

"Amazingly, it is," Greta looked at Katarina and they continued to stroll and giggle.

An hour into the voyage, lunch was served and they returned inside. They walked to their table and sat down. The dining saloon was packed; everyone was there, chatting, laughing, and singing. The smell of food was inviting and the coffee was so delicious.

"The food smells good," Katarina said and packed her plate.

"I'm hungry too. All this clear air gave me an appetite," Greta replied and dug into the food. In fifteen minutes, their plates were empty. No word was needed for their husbands: they were always hungry and their plates always full.

Later, the men stood up from their chairs. "We're going for a smoke," Leo said, and Istvan nodded to Greta before they walked down the aisle.

The girls moved to two seats at the window and passed their time observing the ocean and sipping on the cappuccino. Greta looked at Katarina and asked, "Where're you and your husband settling in Canada? What city?"

"I believe it's called Winnipeg. And you?"

"Hamilton. That's close to Toronto," Greta explained. "My husband has some family there."

Disappointed, Katarina looked at her. "Oh, that's nice. I was hoping you're going to Winnipeg too."

"No. Sorry."

The afternoon passed in a calm, relaxing manner. After finishing the cappuccino, Katarina said, "I feel a little tired. I'm going to our cabin to get some rest." She stood up and left.

"Wait! I'm going too," Greta said and rushed after her. They walked down to the third level together. "See you later," she said, turning to her cabin.

Yeah, later," Katarina agreed.

She lay down on her bed and fell asleep. She didn't remember when her husband returned as she slept until the next morning.

It was almost eight the following morning when she awoke. Leo was still asleep. The waves were rolling against the ship; as their cabin was located inside the nose of the ship, every little wave could be heard like a thunderbolt.

She got up to shower and dress; the lurching of the ship began to be more noticeable, she couldn't finish her shower. When she came out, her husband was awake and waiting at the bathroom door.

"Good morning, darling," he said and covered her mouth with his as he planted a big kiss upon her lips, then went into the bathroom.

"What was that for?" Katarina said, but he hadn't heard her as he was under the shower already. She didn't think it was a very good morning anyway.

As they walked up to the second-class foyer, Leo glanced through the window. The murky and wavy Atlantic water stretched to meet the gray overcast sky at the horizon. He recalled the seriousness of Istvan's face when he told them, "The storm is coming," but he shook it off. Katarina stood beside him and stared out with wide eyes. Leo looked at her and teased, "There's one thing for certain, ahead of us lies an open and treacherous cold Atlantic Ocean." He chuckled, still not convinced that a huge storm was on its way.

Katarina clung to her husband as the ship wobbled. "Thanks! If you wanted to scare me, you just did. I don't know how to swim and I'm petrified of sharks."

Leo said nothing but stared at the dark and wavy ocean. Suddenly, he remembered the dream he had in the hotel in Naples, of the ship sinking and everyone drowning. "Could that happen?" he muttered, but quickly dismissed it. He didn't want to believe in that hocus-pocus that his wife does.

"Did you say something?" Katarina asked. Her mind was so preoccupied with her queasy stomach, she hadn't heard him.

"No," Leo replied, without turning his head.

Just then Greta and her husband arrived. "Are you two coming for breakfast?" Istvan asked, glancing in their direction as he and his wife continued ahead.

"Yes," Leo answered and guided his wife into the dining saloon.

As soon as they sat at the table, Leo's attention was distracted by the food, as always. His wife sipped a hot cup of coffee, which she hoped would have settled her stomach. Her eyes wandered over the tables. Everyone seemed relaxed, there wasn't undue worry seen on their faces, she told herself and relaxed. "This will pass, and my stomach will settle," Katarina said.

"But of course, it will," Greta agreed. She seemed confident that the weather will settle soon.

"No, it won't!" her husband countered. "I told you, a storm is coming."

No one said anything, but turned to their food. On the sight of what was happening outside, no one wanted to comment. Katarina took only a bite of her boiled egg and waited for others to finish theirs, finishing her coffee.

Later, they walked into the foyer outside the dining area. The girls glanced out. "Storm or not, I know the waves are rising and my stomach is queasy," Katarina complained, feeling sick. "I'm going to the cabin." And she stormed on her way.

"Mine too," Greta echoed. They retreated to their cabins together, leaving their husbands behind, settling the storm score.

Istvan placed his arm on Leo's shoulder. "Let's go to have a smoke. I get a little nervous when I see the storm coming."

They strolled to the smoking room. Many refugees were there already, smoking like chimneys, some worried, some just for fun of it. The smoking room was paneled in mahogany. Chairs were set around iron-legged tables. The large room dimmed with cigarette smoke and loud with the laughter of men drinking brandy. Leo and Istvan took corner seats and lit their cigarettes. "Two hard drinks please," Istvan ordered as the steward came around their table. When the drinks arrived, Istvan paid for them and handed one to Leo.

"No. I don't have the money to pay you back," Leo protested.

"It's all right, I'm not asking you to." Istvan took a sip of his brandy and motioned to Leo to do the same. They sipped in silence for a few minutes and then Istvan spoke first. "What brought you here?" he asked.

Leo was shocked at his question and looked at him suspiciously. "Why don't you tell me your story first?" Their eyes met and stared at each other for a few seconds. Surveying each other's thoughts, they realized they don't trust each other and they knew why.

Istvan turned his head away. Since he started all this, he thought it's just fair that he goes first. "Look, during this few days I came to know you and Katarina well enough to be able to trust you. I believe you're not any kind of spy. So yeah, I'll answer your question. I am here because I hate the Communists. My father was in the partisan army fighting for the country, but most of all for justice. My father was a general. I was only twelve years old then and so proud of my father. We were so happy, Mama and I, to have him home safe and sound after the long years of brutal Second World War. My father was an older man, he wore glasses and his hair was gray, but he was sharp. He remained in the army and worked hard in the office. He should have been working until his pension."

"I gather he didn't retire. What happened?"

Istvan sighed deeply. "After a few years, on October 15, 1949, to be exact, my father went to work as he did every morning since the war was over, but that day he didn't return home. He disappeared from his office without a trace. The next day, Mama went looking for him, but no one was able to tell her anything. OZNA then, now UDBA, the secret police of the Communist Party, they also had nothing to say. The last thing they told her, that he probably ran off with another woman, and they laughed in Mama's face."

Leo placed his arm on Istvan's shoulder. "Did you ever learn the truth about your father?"

"No," Istvan said. "Later, when I got older, I started to ask questions about my father. I found out many other people disappeared the same way. According to some men that were with my father in the war. Before the fight for the country began, they agreed among themselves, when the war ends, Croatia and Serbia would get their independence. But after the war was over, everything changed, the top Croatian partisans who were pushing for Croatian independence disappeared, some without trace, including my father. But we all know what happened to him. The OZNA killed him, just like many thousands of others who didn't agree with Communist ideologies, and buried them in unmarked graves where we'll probably never know. All the Intelligencia knows what happened and still is happening, but they are silent and by turning away accepted it. Oh, there was concern in someone's eyes, even some sympathy, but what the mothers, wives, and children are going through would not interrupt their dinners later on or affect their work or keep them from the soccer at the hippodrome or the music opera. So long as it was not personal, it had no effect." Overflowing with sadness, he turned his head and wiped his forehead of sweat.

After Istvan finished, Leo moved closer to him. "I'm so sorry for what you are going through. I'm just lucky my story isn't that horrifying. I'm a son of a Communist father too, and until not too long ago, I adored the Communists and was a member of their party. But since Katarina ran away and all my Croatian friends either disappeared, were jailed, or ran out of the country, I decided to look closer at the party I belong to. And I can tell you the discovery was shocking. My research shows Croatian people are disappearing even today as we speak, in big numbers, and not just in the country, but outside in the other countries like Germany, Argentina, USA, Canada, Croatian people have been killed. So we have to be very careful who our friends are and what we say no matter where we're living because you never know who is listening. So if I don't tell you the details, you'll understand, but when the time comes, I will. They already tried to kill me once in Latina, I don't want to give them another reason to try again. " Leo finished his drink and glanced over the table to see other smokers.

"Two more," Istvan said, and they lit another cigarette. "You see, Leo, you are a son of a communist, but I'm a son of a partisan. It's not the same."

"Yes, I understand. Most of the real Communists were for Yugoslavia and against the Croatian independence. I know that now," Leo explained.

"Yes, they are and that's why my father is dead," Istvan said.

The drinks came, and they took sips on their drinks and smoked their cigarettes in silence, listening to the waves coming apart as they splashed against the ship.

Istvan took one more puff from his cigarette, drowned the rest of it in the ashtray, and drained his drink. "I have to go," he said and walked away.

Leo nodded, finished his drink, and followed him. It was time for lunch; he wondered if Katarina would come up to eat. He strolled to the cabin carefully as there was noticeable wobbling of the ship. His wife was sound asleep, and he didn't want to wake her. So he had lunch alone with Istvan. Greta also didn't come up for lunch.

By the end of the day, the weather remained the same. Everyone thought it would settle soon. Encouraged by it, Katarina decided to accompany her husband to the dining saloon for supper, despite of her queasy stomach. "I'm so hungry," she said as they exited from their cabin.

But as they were climbing the steps, the ship careened and they leaned severely to one side and bumped against the step railing. "Oh no," she grouched alarmed and grasped Leo's hand to help herself off the last step.

"Are you hurt?" he asked as he helped her up.

"No."

Leo took his wife's hand and led her to the dining saloon for supper. Their partners sat quietly at the table subdued and a worried look was on their faces: Istvan picking on his food, Greta just staring at it. The ship continued to wobble at the low intensity.

Leo poured his wife and himself a cup of coffee and glanced at Istvan. "Are you two all right?"

"I am, but Greta has an upset stomach. But I told you people that a storm is coming," Istvan blurted out. His wife glanced at him with a frown, but said not a word.

"Oh, come on, Istvan. Stop it! You're scaring the girls," Leo finally said. "Are you all right, darling?"

Holding her stomach, Katarina answered, "No! But I will be, if the ship stops reeling." However, the lurching didn't stop instead. The presence and the smell of food suddenly made Katarina's stomach churn. She picked at the food on her plate, but ate very little; it just wouldn't go down her throat.

The ship's rolling worsened every minute. After a while, Katarina couldn't stay at the table any longer. "Let's go!" she said alarmed and grasped Leo's hand to help herself up.

"Just hold on, darling, until I finish my supper," he responded and continued to pig out without any regard for her.

"I'm sorry, but I can't wait," Katarina said and walked away, slowly and carefully.

Leo rushed his supper and caught up with her on the middle of the steps going down. "Why didn't you wait?"

"You didn't want me to throw up all over the table, did you?" Katarina answered and continued on her way to the cabin.

"Of course not," Leo dashed ahead to open the cabin door for her. They retreated early to the cabin as did most of the passengers that night.

The next morning, the waves rose even higher, thundering against the ship as it cut through them. The storm wasn't subsiding. "I hope this doesn't get any worse," Katarina said and crawled off her bed.

"I hope it doesn't too," Leo responded as they were dressing for breakfast. They wobbled into the second-level foyer like drunks. Katarina felt even sicker when she saw many passengers squatting against the wall, feeling nauseous and using their sick bags, which the stewards were passing them out along with seasickness remedies. The doctor simply sent the pills around with the instructions to be passed to the passengers. As soon as Katarina received them, she popped one in her mouth.

Greta hadn't shown up. Istvan took the pills from the stewards for his wife and went to the cabin to give them to her.

"Let's go to have breakfast," Leo said to his wife and began to walk toward the dining saloon door. As soon as he mentioned food, her stomach churned.

"I think I'll wait her until the pills settle my stomach," she replied and turned to peer out the window.

Leo went for breakfast alone. At half-past eight, there were only a few passengers scattered about the huge dining saloon. Leo sat at their table and soon Istvan joined him. "How is Greta?" Leo asked.

"She'll be fine as soon as the pills start to work," Istvan replied and sipped on the coffee. The storm hadn't affected them; they had their full breakfast and returned to the foyer. Katarina was still leaning against the window looking out; she didn't like what she saw. The storm worsened; the waves were bigger each time they came rolling against the ship.

"Are you feeling any better, darling?" Leo asked as they approached.

"No! But I will be if the ship stops reeling," she replied, holding her stomach. However, the lurching didn't stop.

Most of the morning they spent in the foyer, Leo keeping eyes on the boiling ocean and Istvan ran between checking on his wife and the foyer. Katarina, trying to settle her stomach, gripped the rail in silence, hoping the weather would subside soon.

Finally, close to lunch, it seemed that the storm had subsided slightly. Katarina felt some relief, her stomach was much better, and she felt she could eat something. Just as Leo and Katarina settled at their table, Istvan and Greta wended their way in and sat down. The stewards carrying hot food were right behind them. "Oh no!" Katarina grumbled; the smell of food made her and Greta retch violently. Both of them rushed into the powder room.

Just as they returned to the table and sat down, the old liner began to shake, shudder, and wobble. Suddenly the floor tilted, sending the passengers scrambling in panic for some kind of handhold. Everything: tables, chairs, and other loose things were on the move.

"Oh my god! What's going on?" Katarina shouted as their table began to slide forward and they, on their chairs, with it. She grabbed the table with one of her hands and Leo's hand with the other, clinging desperately. With the free hand, Leo grabbed a bottle of red wine off the sliding table. Istvan saved the white wine. "Just what we need," he commented.

A pale-faced Greta rose from her chair. "We're all going to die!" she yelled and braced her feet tightly against the tilt. Her plump white hands gripped the table so hard that her rings cut into the flesh of her fingers and drew blood as she attempted to hold the table back. But it kept sliding and threatened to crush her if she didn't get out of the way. Fortunately, there was a pillar behind her and Greta was able to hide behind it, just before the table smashed into it and stopped.

Katarina and Leo, still in their chairs, also came to an abrupt stop as they crashed into the table.

"Are you hurt, Greta?" Istvan called and hurried to comfort her.

"No, no. I'm fine," she replied, holding her arms tightly around the pillar. Her husband wrapped his handkerchief around her bleeding hand.

Leo rose from his chair. "I'll be right there!" he said and went to help Istvan and his wife after his wife let go of his hand. Katarina wasn't hurt, but her body shivered, like a leaf on a tree branch; she couldn't move. She still sat on the chair when Leo returned. "Come on, darling!" he stressed and pulled her toward his body just before another tilt came, this time going the other way.

Frantically, they hurled themselves toward the pillar and all four held on for dear life. "On no! We are goners!" Greta said, wide-eyed and pale-faced.

"Oh my god! This can't be happening!" Katarina gasped, listening to the people screeching, children crying, and dishes crashing to the floor. With the bedlam came fear, which spread swiftly even to those who normally were fearless.

"Settle down, girls. Everything will be all right," Leo and Istvan said in unison calmly, pretending to be immune, but Katarina and Greta could see the fear they hid in their eyes.

Even though the passengers were convinced that they were capsizing, the ship's crew wasn't. They merrily staggered around, reassuring their passengers and picking up rolling bottles that might cause someone to stumble.

Greta looked up at the steward in alarm. "Listen, that was dangerous, wasn't it?"

The steward replied, "Not really, madam. I've seen him do worse than this. CC can't go over, ma'am, not the way he's built." And he continued on his way. Everyone was rattled.

"He'll be all right! He always levels off!" shouted Silvestero, one of the stewards serving at the time. Their words were calming but not totally convincing to Katarina and Greta and many other passengers whose screams, long-drawn-out and high-pitched, were compounded with the agony of human fear. They were too frightened.

"It'll settle, darling, just hold on," Leo again stressed, squeezing the bottle of red wine in his hand as he waited for the ship to stop shuddering and listing so much.

There were two large sways, each lasted only a few minutes, then the ship straightened, but the pitching and wobbling continued along with minor rolls. It wasn't until then that they realized that they were wearing the food that had been served for lunch. "Yeah! Look at this!" Katarina cried, pointing to her messy clothes splattered with spaghetti and other food.

They all glanced at their clothes and everyone's lunch was on it. "Don't worry, they can be washed," Leo replied and embraced his wife. She said nothing as her stomach kept sinking with a dipping of the bow of the ship.

"Please calm down and slowly walk out to the foyer until we clean this mess then a second lunch will be served, but it will be dry," Silvestro and the stewards pleaded to the yelling, crying, and vomiting passengers.

One by one the passengers wobbled out of the dining saloon, their eyes filled with fear. Their clothes and the floor were strewn with food that had fallen off the rolling tables. It looked like they had been in a food fight. Katarina was in shock; she let go of the pillar but still clasped Leo's hand as they walked outside into the foyer.

It became obvious to the ship's crew that the storm would not subside quickly. They placed guide ropes along the stairways and hallways for the passengers to grab when they walked. The stewards, keeping order in the foyer, instructed, "All passengers, please hold on to the ropes. Keep children close, so they can be safe. Move around slowly."

Panic-stricken, Greta and Katarina finally released their husbands' hands and grabbed for the rope, with one hand and brown bag in the other. Istvan and Leo reeled to the window and stared at the angry Atlantic Ocean as the strong wind carried the water wide and high, spraying it on the second-class windows and clouding their vision.

The captain concluded the storm ahead was more severe than they had seen a long while and ordered the crew to nail all the tables and chairs to the floor. He also called for the ladies to use flat shoes if they have any, if not to walk barefooted.

It took a while for everyone to get their bearings when Katarina got hers and calmed some. She staggered closer to Greta. "Come, let's look outside," she suggested; trying to conquer her fear, she turned toward the window.

"No. I wish I had never boarded this ship," Greta blustered fearfully between retches.

"You don't mean that," Katarina replied, trying to calm her down. "The storm will pass and we will be all right."

Panic gleaming in Greta's eyes. "You don't know that."

"No, but I do have hope," Katarina said and hugged her. "At this moment, that is all what's left."

They slowly tottered to the window. Katarina peered out to the horrifying scene that made her hair on her head stood up. "Greta, you were right. It wasn't a good idea after all," she muttered and turned toward her. "Let's go see if lunch is ready." Holding on to the rope, she began to walk toward the dining saloon.

"How about the window?" Greta asked, gazing at her.

"Never mind, we'll do it later," Katarina answered and opened the dining saloon door. The stewards were still working, cleaning up the mess, preparing another lunch and nailing the tables and chairs to the floor. She closed the door just as Greta arrived. "Is it ready?"

"They are not finished yet," Katarina said and leaned against the wall in the hallway as her stomach churned.

Greta got closer to the door and heard the pounding inside the dining saloon. "What's that banging?" Greta asked, looking at her, puzzled.

"The crew is nailing all the tables and chairs to the floor."

"Oh my god! You know what that means, don't you?" Greta exclaimed.

Before Katarina could answer, the captain began speaking to the passengers through the loudspeakers. "My crew is well equipped to handle any kind of situation that might occur. I promise you that no harm will come to any of you. Please obey the rules my staff put in front of you. This is only a safety precaution," he finished.

Leo and Istvan made their way over to their wives. "What's up?" Leo asked, leaning against the door of the dining saloon.

"See! We'll all be fine, the captain said so," Katarina affirmed and took her high heels off. She clung to the captain's promise and wasn't about to let go.

"Darling, of course, we'll be all right," Leo agreed and peered into the saloon. "I'm hungry. What's taking them so long?"

"But the storm that I warned you about is here!" Istvan chanted. He wasn't about to let them forget how right he had been.

"Yeah. Yeah, enough already," Leo snapped and turned to his wife.

Katarina tried to smile, but instead, she began to retch. "Anyway, when will this lunch be ready," she said, tired of waiting. It wasn't for her because she was sure she wouldn't be able to eat a bite, but her husband was starving.

Suddenly, Steward Antonio opened the door and announced, "You can all come in. The second lunch will be served now."

Leo and Istvan's eyes lit like a Christmas tree. "Finally," Leo exclaimed and they both rushed in, leaving their wives behind. Since many passengers had retreated to their cabins, there wasn't a crowd and Katarina and Greta had no trouble entering.

"You two rushed in as if someone would take your place," Katarina chided as they arrived at the table.

"How could you be so selfish?" Greta scolded, looking at both of them.

Almost immediately, the stewards, carefully bracing themselves against the tilts of the ship, brought dry food and coffee to the table. They didn't have too many to serve because the dining saloon was almost empty.

"I'm sorry, Istvan, for being short with you," Leo apologized as they began to dig into the food.

No, no. It was my fault, I didn't realize until the last minute how upset everyone was. I only wanted to tease the girls a little. You know how they get squeamish."

"I realized that, but still I should have been more patient," Leo admitted and poured himself a glass of red wine. "I don't know, something snapped inside me."

While most of the passengers who came to lunch were shaken and too nauseous to eat, Leo and Istvan were not. They enjoyed every bit of their food, especially the wine. Both girls felt even sicker to their stomach as they watched their husbands eat. "I can't believe my eyes. Those two are totally unaffected by the storm," Katarina said, glancing at Greta who was busy trying to keep from retching.

Greta gave her a green-tinged glance, but didn't respond. Both of them kept popping the seasick pills provided by the ship doctor, but nothing seemed to help.

"Maybe some fresh air will help," Katarina voiced. Immediately, she rose from her chair and, holding on to her stomach, staggered onto the second-class deck with the help of the guide ropes. "Oh, stomach, please settle down," she begged under her breath and grabbed for the exit door. As soon as she opened the door, the ferocious wind-driven water sprayed all over her and pushed her back, but she never let go of her hold on the door. Katarina stood at the doorway of the deck transfixed with fear as she watched the treacherous waves march forward regally. She could taste the salt in the air, on her skin, and her lips. The chill in the wind stippled the flesh on her arms with goose bumps and she shivered. "Oh my god! This will never end," she muttered, not sure if she still trusted the captain's promise.

Indeed, the storm showed no signs of passing quickly. The ship was caught in a huge boiling pot with everything around it bubbling and splashing, and the wind-driven water sprayed, continuously flooding the deck.

A sudden violent crush of waves against the ship caught Katarina's attention. She tightened her grip on the door to steady herself and stared at the scene of endless rows of angry gray waves rolling over on themselves in repeated crushes of foam. The ocean formed one dish of darkness and the sky, another dish inverted over it. They were trapped right in the middle.

"Oh god! We're doomed! I don't want to watch this," she mumbled and turned to leave when a sudden severe list sent her flying.

Istvan had already taken his wife to the cabin as she was severely nauseous so Leo came looking for Katarina just in time to grab her before she fell. "Are you all right, darling?" he asked, staring at her greenish-gray face.

"Thank God, you're here, my love," she groaned and blacked out in his arms. When she came to, she began retching violently and felt severely ill.

Leo propped her up against his body. "You'll be fine," he assured her and practically carried her down the steps. Katarina kept her hand over her mouth as her stomach was still retching and said nothing. When they got to the cabin, her husband helped her settle into bed. You'll be safe here," he promised. "Get some rest. I'll bring you food from the dining room later."

"No! No food!" she shouted. Her stomach churned at the mere mention of it. However, just before Leo left for supper, Katarina asked, "Bring a lemon please."

"Sure, lemon it is." Leo kissed her and sauntered alone to the dining saloon. Katarina's stomach settled somewhat as she lay there. Spent, she shut her eyes and drifted off to sleep, but the ship continued pitching and thunder kept awaking her.

Leo and Istvan both were present at the supper table. On their way, they noticed many passengers sitting and squatting along the steps and the corners of the foyer with their brown bags in their hands, not quite making it to the dining room. The stewards with their food trays made their way through the aisles of deserted tables of the nearly empty dining room. "Those poor people, they didn't make it," Leo acknowledged, glancing around the room before he dug into the sandwiches.

"Yeah, not too many are here. Including our wives," Istvan noticed and quietly began to polish sandwich after sandwich. They had their supper without any problem; between the shakings of the ship, they could hear the occasional clink of a fork and plates. It was rather a silent meal; the passengers' voices were kept down.

When Leo returned to the cabin, she was awake. "Are you any better?" He asked. "Here, I brought you a sandwich and a few oranges and lemons."

"Thanks, put them on the table," she replied and crawled out of her bed. She took a few bites of the mortadella and cheese sandwich and immediately ran to the bathroom. Her stomach couldn't take it and throw up everything. She grabbed the lemon and sucked on it before settling in bed.

The ship continued pitching throughout the night. To add to the unhappiness of the retching Katarina and everyone else, things in the cabins came alive. Throughout the night, everything unattached: chairs, handbags, bottles slid from side to side. Clothing hung upon pegs took on animation, swaying outward and back again. Nerves were further jangled by the protesting creaks and groans of the old ship's joints and the crashes of breaking waves against it. Even the oranges and lemons joined in, making loud continuous thumping noises, which prevented Katarina from sleeping, not to mention her nauseous stomach. "God, please let it stop!" she shouted in the middle of the night and sat on the side of the bed. Her husband didn't hear her, he was sound asleep. After munching on the lemon, she lay back to sleep, but there was not much sleeping. By morning, she was exhausted and even sicker.

At seven o'clock, a voice called through the speakers with a loud urgency awaking all the passengers. "EVERYONE, PLEASE REPORT TO THE BOAT DECK." Leo slept through the noise.

Katarina staggered off her bed and shook her husband awake. "Why are they calling everyone to the boat deck? What's happening?" she asked in a breathless grave voice.

"I don't know, darling," Leo replied and got up. "But let's get dressed and go and find out." He was quickly dressed and ready to go, but it took his wife much longer. Katarina was so ill that her body shook and she could barely dress herself. However, she managed to hide it from him.

"Are you ready?" he asked, leaning against the door, waiting. "I just need to put my shoes on to go out on the deck," she whispered, staggering toward him. "I'm not going out in my bare feet."

He extended his hand to her and said, "Just hold on to me."
She grasped her husband's hand and they walked out of their cabin.

They made their way to the stairways leading to the boat deck where they met other passengers coming from their various quarters. Everyone was slipping, sliding, clinging to each other, and shouting warnings such as "Watch out! Hold on tight to the ropes!" as they negotiated the last set of stairs, one step at the time.

In front of Katarina, Mario and little Nada refused any assistance from their parents. They, like the other children passengers, tried to assert their independence, but the pitching of the ship was too strong for them. As soon as they climbed a few steps, the ship would tumble them to the bottom again. "Here, Nada, Mario, take my hand!" their mother yelled, extending her hand to them while holding on to the rope with the other.

Everyone's eyes turned to watch them, anxiously waiting for them to climb the first step and angrily wondering why their parents were not more forceful. And Katarina's patience was running thin as she became more nauseous and dizzy. "What a time to show off their ability," she complained, turning to her husband. "But then, they are only children and they don't know better. I guess it is better this way than they are too scared to climb," she justified.

"Exactly my point, they are children, wouldn't you think their parents should have more control over them?" Leo grouched.

Upon on their sixth attempt, finally, their parents said, "That's enough." They grasped their hands, pulling them up the steps.

"It's about time," Leo whispered to his wife's ear. She felt too nauseous to answer but continued to climb.

The ruthless wind whisked the waves so high that they drenched the deck.

Everyone was given a yellow raincoat so they don't get too wet, as the ocean water, driven by the strong wind, rained everywhere. All of the passengers shivered, some from cold and some from fear as they wondered how much danger they were in.

"Go over there," the stewards handing out the yellow coats would direct each of the passengers, pointing to where a dozen stewards were preparing for the drill on safety gear, how to use the lifeboats, and life jackets.

Katarina listened to the stewards for a little while, then for a moment she experienced that sickening feeling at the pit of her stomach and asked, "What's this? What's happening?"

"It's just a drill test, don't worry," someone said from behind. Leo and Katarina both turned and saw Istvan and Greta standing there. Istvan knew it wasn't just a drill, it was preparation in case something went wrong, but he wasn't about to frighten the girls any more than they already were.

The other passengers weren't fooled and their heads quickly filled with fear and terror. Everyone silently began to ask themselves, *Are we going to make it through this storm? Will we ever reach our destination?*

Suddenly, one of them could no longer keep silent. "Why do we need this? What's going on?" he asked anxiously.

"It's just a drill," one of the stewards responded calmly and continued his presentation.

Meanwhile, news that the ship had been sailing off course for two days to bypass floating icebergs circulated amid of them, adding to the fear and panic spreading through the ship like wildfire. "We'll never make it to Canada!" one of the refugees shouted.

Then another yelled, "We're all going down with the ship!"

Those words destroyed the little faith Katarina had; she closed her eyes and shook her fists like a child in temper and let out a squeal, "I don't want to die! We're all going to die and all you do is yackety, yackety, yackety! Oh Mary, Mother of God, save us!"

Leo wrapped his arms around his wife and squeezed her close. "No one is going to die," he said, trying to calm her.

Istvan, holding his wife tightly against his body, said, "The storm will pass soon. I have been through these types of storms many times, and I'm still here."

But that was a little consolation to the girls when the ship was rocking with no signs of stopping. "Well, I hope you make it through this one too because I don't think I will," Greta answered, holding on to her husband tightly, her body shaking in fear. But neither the storm nor the passengers were calming down.

The stewards, realizing the passengers were panic-stricken, stopped the drills. "Calm down! Nothing will happen to anyone!" one of the stewards shouted.

Still they couldn't get the crowd to settle, so one of the stewards pulled a gun out and shot into the air a few times. "Please! Quieeeeet! Listen here! We had to sail around the iceberg to avoid crushing into it," he shouted, his face as red as a lobster tail from excitement. "Now! All you return to your cabins. Hold on to the ropes and walk carefully. Nothing will happen to any of you, Captain said so," he added. This quieted the passengers somewhat and they began to walk back inside.

Propped by their husbands, Katarina and Greta were led back inside. On the way to their cabins, the girls were lurching, retching, vomiting, and crying, just as the other passengers, except Leo and Istvan and a few others.

As they entered the cabin, Leo guided his wife toward the bed. Her face was pale and drawn and he wanted her to get some rest. "Darling, lie down and don't give up, be strong. The storm will pass, even Istvan said that. We'll be fine," Leo assured her.

Even though she felt exhausted, she wouldn't have it. "No!" she yelled and began pacing the floor back and forth. Her husband's attempts to calm her down went unheeded as a nightmarish scenario kept surfacing in her mind. All of them were drowning as the ship capsized and she saw herself being eaten by a shark. Fear began to envelop her, a dark sense of dread descended upon her. "Oh my god! We're not going to make it to Canada," she screamed, suddenly totally out of control.

"Keep those sharks away from me!" she shouted and hysterically pushed her husband away. Then she began throwing insults and lemons at him as though what was happening was his fault.

Leo stared at her in disbelief. "What sharks? There are no sharks in our cabin!"

He quickly tired of what he thought was a childlike outburst and his eyes flared with anger, shining like a spark waiting to ignite. He threw his arms up in the air and shouted, "I give up!" still glaring at her.

Katarina saw hatred in his unrelenting eyes. "You don't love me anymore," she spat and wobbled on her heels, then staggered angrily out of the cabin. "How dare he treat me this way," she said under her breath. She began to climb the stairs, eyeing the passengers squatting alongside the stairways and hallways, vomiting into their little brown bags. Their pale, bewildered, and panic-stricken faces telling their agonizing story.

"I need some air," she muttered; weak, pale, and as sick as the passengers she passed on her way up, she headed for the deck but never reached it. Katarina collapsed a few meters from the deck door and was taken to the ship's infirmary, unconscious.

Her husband was paged over the loudspeakers to come to the ship infirmary. "Oh no! Katarina! What happened now?" he muttered and rushed up to the infirmary.

When he arrived, he ran to the first steward that he met on the scene and said, "I want to see my wife."

The steward looked at him and said, "I'll tell you, but first calm down and tell me her name."

"Katarina Lisic," he answered, very upset. "Can I see her now?"

"Yes, I'll take you to her, but first I need to know a few things. I'm her doctor and that would help me to treat Katarina better."

"All right, go ahead, ask," Leo gave permission to the doctor.
"Has she been taking any solid food or drinking many fluids since the storm began?" the doctor asked.

"No, mostly she sucked on the lemons, she couldn't eat, because she was retching too much. After we got off the boat deck, she had an outburst and started seeing sharks that weren't there and stormed out the cabin. That was the last time I saw my wife. I don't know what else to tell you, except that my wife is petrified of being eaten by a shark. Now can I see her?"

"Sure," the doctor said and opened the curtain. "Here she is, but she's still not responding."

Leo rushed to her side, kissed her forehead, and sat beside her. "Darling, wake up," he exclaimed. "I thought she was just scared because some of the passengers on the boat deck yelled. 'We are going to drown,'" Leo said, his eyes were moist with tears.

The doctor looked at him and said, "The sharks are not your wife's problem. She is dehydrated from having lost much of her body fluids through vomiting and not taking enough fluids. That's what caused her hysterical outburst and hallucinations. We need your permission to treat your wife."

"Of course, you can have it. Do whatever you think needs to be done for my wife. I want her back," Leo said and turned to her.

"Great!" the doctor said and raced away. He quickly returned with a bag of fluids and the IV pole and tubing. Soon, she had fluid running through her veins into her body.

Leo stared at her motionless body, waiting for any movement. "Why did I argue with her? Why didn't I see that she was sick?" He blamed himself, wiping tears from his cheeks.

"It's not easy to recognize the symptoms if you don't have a medical background. She'll be fine once she gets enough fluids," the doctor replied as he finished establishing Katarina's IV and ran off to see the other patients.

Katarina emerged from her unconscious state and grabbed Leo's hand. "Take that shark away from me!" she shouted, still incoherent and hysterical.

"Doctor!" Leo called, "Come quickly."

The doctor rushed over to Katarina's bedside and took a one look. "I'm going to give her a sedative to relax and get some rest," he said and proceeded to fill a syringe.

"Oh no! You're not!" she screamed, still holding tightly on to her husband's hand. Staring at the doctor, she cried, "I'm going to die, and you'll throw me to the sharks! Get them away from me!" She sat up in bed and began pushing the imaginary sharks away.

"See what I mean, Doctor?" Leo said. "My wife's seeing the sharks again."

"I know," the doctor said. "She will get better, but she needs this medicine and the fluids. Mr. Lisic, you'll have to hold her so I can give her the injection."

Leo hugged his wife and exposed her upper arm. "Here, Doctor," he said, holding her tight against his own body.

Katarina, petrified of dying and even more afraid of being eaten by sharks, fought hard. "No! No! Leo, don't let him eat me if you love me. Keep that shark away from me!" she implored, striking her husband's shoulder with her free hand. But her weak body soon buckled under Leo's strong arms and he didn't have any trouble holding her still.

The doctor was quick and injected the sedative into her shoulder muscle. "There. It's all over."

"I know," Katarina replied, glancing at her husband with a sad drawn face. "This is my last crossing, isn't it? I'll die."

"No, darling, no. You'll get better. Now just close your eyes and get some rest. You're so exhausted," he suggested.

But she refused to shut her eyes. She clung to his hand, fighting the sedative. Her deep dark eyes were filled with fear. "When I'm dead," she persisted, "they'll throw me to the ocean. You know, just like they did in that movie we watched. You remember, Leo, don't you?" She kept babbling as her eyelids grew heavier and heavier.

Trying to convince her otherwise, her husband hugged her trembling body and said, "Don't talk that way." But the sedative was strong and beat him to it. The drug soon took over her body and mind, and she fell asleep.

Later, the doctor came to check on her and found her husband settled to stay beside her and glanced at him. "You wife will get more rest if you are not here, Mr. Lisic," he suggested.

"If that's the case, I'm going," Leo said and returned to their cabin.

For supper, Leo met with Istvan and Viktor at the foyer in front of the dining saloon and told them about Katarina. "I wanted to stay the night with her, but the doctor said no, so I came here."

"My wife is sick too, she can't handle any food," Istvan complained. "At least, she isn't in the ship infirmary."

"You have to encourage her to take fluids, if not, she could end up like Katarina," Leo suggested as they wobbled to their table.

"Viktor," Leo called, "If you like, you can come and sit with us."

"Sure," he said and followed them to the table 21.

They sat at their table with their heads bowed, eating their supper and quietly worrying about their wives while the ship careened without a stop. There were only a few male guests in the dining saloon, and not everyone enjoyed their food, their faces were tinged greenish pale. Viktor, Istvan, and Leo had no problem; they were gobbling down their food and drinking the last drop of wine.

"How is Katarina?" Viktor asked, breaking the silence.

"She'll be all right, but if this storm doesn't subside soon, I don't know what's going to happen to her," Leo replied and took sips of coffee.

"I know what you mean," Istvan said. "I worry about my wife too, she still isn't better. You are right. While this storm persists, I'm afraid, no one will feel good." He finished his last morsel of supper and poured white wine into his glass.

The three of them continued to be among the hardy few who continued to stuff their mouths with cold cuts and wine, despite the rolling and pitching of the ship.

When Leo settled for the night, he hoped that in the morning the storm would be subsiding. But that wasn't so, it continued with the same force as it did day before.

On the way to visit Katarina, he ran into Istvan, who was on his way to the dining saloon. "I can see that Greta isn't better," Leo commented.

"No, she isn't, but she's not worse. That's good sign," Istvan responded. "You're going to check up on your wife?"

"Yes, then I'll see you for coffee," Leo answered and moved unsteadily toward the ship's infirmary.

When Katarina opened her eyes, the first words she heard were Leo's, "Good morning, darling. You feeling better?"

"Hello, my love." She smiled and looked around. "Where am I?"

*Thank God. She's herself again.* Leo sighed as he gave a kiss on her cheek and replied, "You're in the ship's infirmary."

"What am I doing here? What happened?" She sat up in bed, puzzled, staring at her husband. She hardly remembered anything.

"Yesterday, you collapsed in front of the door to the second-class deck according to the doctor. You'll be fine," Leo explained.

"I see the ship is still seesawing," Katarina commented.

"Yes, the weather is still bad," Leo agreed. He visited for a while longer and then said, "I have to go for breakfast, but I'll be back later for you. The doctor said you're well enough to leave the infirmary after you eat your breakfast. So be ready when I come." He smiled and walked away.

After Leo left, a steward brought her a tray of dry food with cup of coffee. "The doctor said you must eat all of it if you want to go back to your cabin," he warned as he laid the tray in front of her.

"All right," Katarina promised, but ate only a little. Then she listened to the storm roaring above and under her, rocking the ship as badly as ever. She tried to remember what happened to her the day before, but instead remembered the moment when the ocean had turned wild and the waves attacked the ship as if they were alive. *Is the ocean really a living thing?* she wondered. Then suddenly a quote from her old geography teacher popped in her head. She recalled it well as he made her learn it by heart as punishment for talking in class.

"'All our pathetic adjectives about the ocean are insufficient,' he said. 'The ocean is not cruel or angry. How could it be? The terrible thing about it is that the ocean is not alive. The ocean and the sea are inanimate, an eyeless particle of the universe. And it kills us not in rage, but with apathy as casual by-products of its own incomprehensible harmony,'" she recited to herself and wondered if they were the chosen ones?

"What are you muttering?" Leo asked as he walked in. "You are not ready yet? Don't you want to come out with me?"

His voice startled her back to reality. "Oh, yeah, yeah, I'll be ready in one minute," she said and begun to crawl off the bed.

He walked to her, took her hand, and asked, "Do you want me to help you, darling?"

"No, I'll be fine," Katarina replied, pulled her hand back, and managed to get down on her own and grabbed her clothes. "I'm sorry if I said something to hurt you. I remember bits and pieces and I feel embarrassed."

"No, darling, I'm sorry. I should have seen that you were sick."

"Katarina," the doctor called from behind the curtain and stepped in. He handed her a small bottle of pills. "Take these, one per day for seasickness. They are a little stronger than the ones you received from the stewards. You should be fine. One more thing. You must force yourself to drink fluids, no matter what, coffee, tea, juice, water. Anything. Just drink!" he said.

"Thank you, Doctor," Katarina managed to say before he disappeared. She popped a pill from the small bottle the doctor gave her in her mouth and washed it down with juice that was left from her breakfast. "Now we can go," she said and walked out with her husband by her side.

When they returned to the cabin Katarina lay down on her bed and, almost immediately, fell asleep. Leo decided to venture up to the second class to see how things were going with the storm while she was sleeping.

In the foyer, he met Istvan and Viktor watching the waves rolling against the ship. "Is there any change?" Leo asked as he approached them.

"See for yourself," Viktor said and moved aside to give Leo room at the window.

"Oh god. It looks direful," Leo commented, staring at the murky, dark water, dancing wildly over the ocean.

Istvan slowly turned toward the men and took a deep sigh. "I'm concerned about my wife. I don't know how much longer she can withstand this."

"I know what you mean," Leo acknowledged. "I brought mine home today, but I'm not sure if she's any better. They have to start eating. Otherwise, they're not going to get better."

"I know, but you can't force them," Istvan said as they slowly moved toward the dining saloon.

xxx

Instead of setting the tables, the stewards assembled the sandwiches, fruit, wine, and coffee beside the entrance door and served as the passengers entered as they didn't want the food find itself on the floor again because of the unsteadiness of the ship.

Xxx

"Supper for three," Istvan called out as they stepped inside.

"Are you all from the same table?" one of the stewards questioned as he handed him a bottle of white wine.

"No," Leo answered and added, "I don't drink white wine."

The steward turned to Viktor and said, "How about if I give a bottle of red wine to him with his supper and you all sit together?"

"Great," Leo agreed and added. "Can you please put in a brown bag a small sandwich, a few lemons, and a fruit juice for my wife, she just got out of the ship infirmary, and she couldn't come."

The steward nodded with his head, gathered all the items, placed them into the bag, and handed them to Leo and they were on their way to the table. Istvan, Viktor, and Leo still continued to be among the hardy few who continued to stuff their mouths with cold cuts and wine, despite the rolling and pitching of the ship.

After Leo finished eating, he brought his wife fruit, juice, and a small sandwich. "Here, I hope you can eat," he said and handed everything to her.

"I took another of those pills the doctor gave me. I hope it works," she replied, taking the food off his hands, and forced herself to eat. Her stomach wasn't settled at all, but she wasn't about to tell that to her husband. After all, he did take time to think about her as he was stuffing his face.

Leo sat on the chair and watched Katarina devour all of the food he brought without any trouble. "Excellent! You're much better, darling," he observed, gave his wife a kiss on the cheek, and crawled up to his bed.

"Now, if only the ship would stop pitching, we might have a good night's sleep," Katarina managed to mutter before she was back in the bathroom vomiting.

Two more days went by with no change in the storm. On the third morning, they were awakened by the ship public address system as it blared out the weather report. "The worse is over, the storm is subsiding," it said.

Katarina jumped from her bed and shook her husband. "We're going to see Canada, after all," she shouted jubilantly, ignoring her weak and retching stomach.

"Of course, we are. I told you so," Leo replied nonchalantly, though relief was etched on his face. He slid down from his bed and began to dress.

Katarina smirked and began to dress up too. However, the lurching of the ship persisted as did the fierce wind and waves, despite the weather report. Even so, the report brightened her spirit and gave her hope, at least for the moment.

"I'm going up to see what's happening. I'll be back soon," he said anxiously and rushed out the door. Before Katarina could respond, he was gone.

When Leo arrived up to the foyer, Istvan was already there, observing and studying the ocean and the sky. "You think the storm is subsiding?" Leo asked as he approached him.

"I hope so, but I don't think it would subside just yet," he answered without taking his eyes off and continued searching the sky. Leo also glared through the window, but the only thing he could see was the steaming Atlantic with its huge waves rolling over each other and spewing ice-cold water all over the ship's windows, clouding their view. Leo had no words to add, but stared at it. Just as the passengers had waited in anticipation of the storm subsiding as the report had announced in the morning. xxxxxxxx

But by late evening, the ship was still rocking hard, so was Katarina's stomach and most of everyone else's on the ship. xxxxxxxxxxxxxxxx

For the first time since the storm began, they had enough of it and walked to check on their wives. Doubts began creeping in Leo's and Istvan's minds, even though they tried hard to hide from them.

Silently, Leo reeled into the cabin. Katarina glanced at him curiously and quickly asked, "So what do you think, my love? Is the storm subsiding any?"

"Well, you can see for yourself that the ship is still lurching," he answered and crawled up to his bed to lie down without offering any further explanation.

"I guess it isn't," she said disappointed and rushed to the bathroom retching. When she returned, Leo was snoring like a tractor.

Xxxxxxxxxxxxxxxxxxxx

The next morning, Katarina was jolted awake by a thunder of waves pounding against the ship. Her stomach turned, and she had to run to the bathroom, retching. Inside, she debated with herself whether to join her husband in the dining saloon or not, even though she didn't feel strong enough to go. Realizing her nausea would not disappear until the pitching of the ship stopped and the storm subsided, she decided to take a chance. Besides, she had been cooped up in the windowless cabin for days and needed a change.

While Katarina was in the bathroom, Leo awoke, slid off his bed, and got dressed. He was already so accustomed to going alone that he no longer asked if she would like to come along. When she came out, he was ready to leave. She didn't like that very much. She glared at him from under her brows. "Wait! I'm going with you," she advised him immediately and rushed to get dressed.

"Oh, I thought you were not coming. Hurry then," Leo replied and leaned against the door as he waited.

"I need some fresh air," she answered and threw one pill into her mouth and the package in her handbag and added, "I'm ready."

Outside their door, they grabbed the rope that was secured along the sides of the hallway. Holding on to it tightly, they wobbled toward the steps and climbed up to the second class. Alongside them, passengers squatted, their faces tinged gray-greenish, with their brown bags in hand ready to vomit. "Oh god, nothing has changed, it's just as same as the first day. When will this end?" Katarina voiced and continued to climb on.

Xxxxxxxxxxxxxxxxxxxxxxxxxxxxxxxxxxxxxxxxxxxxxxxxxxxxxxxxxxxxxxxxx
xxx

# CHAPTER 21

Katarina and Leo made their way to the second-class foyer. She staggered to the window and grabbed for the nearest pillar, held on to it, and glanced through the window. Her eyes searched a large area ahead, but saw nothing to mark the passing of the storm. High waves continued their unrelenting march over the Atlantic Ocean to smash against them, spraying foam and knocking the ship around. "Please, stomach, stop already!" a passenger shouted, interrupting Katarina's trance.

She shivered, shook her head, and turned to Leo. "The seasickness remedies that had been dispensed by the stewards unfortunately aren't helping any longer. Thank God, that mine are a little stronger," Katarina said, leaning against her husband.

"You worry too, don't you?" she asked and continued to rumble. "Will the storm ever subside? Will the great liner be able to withstand this monstrous storm? Or will the newspapers around the world, in a day or two, be plastered with the news: GREAT *Cristoforo Colombo* LOST IN THE MIDDLE OF ATLANTIC OCEAN, FULL OF REFUGEES? As if anyone would care, except maybe our parents and families if they know we are on the ship. Mine don't, how about yours?" she asked, looking at her husband.

"Stop that," Leo said and hugged his wife. "The storm will stop and we'll all be fine, you'll see."

When they let go of each other, suddenly, they realized there was something different about the ship. Katarina yelled, "The ship is no longer rocking and creaking as it had when fighting its way through the huge waves."

"You are right!" Leo agreed and embraced her again.

The passengers squatting around the foyer and the steps froze; their eyes stared at them for a while in silence, then they stood up and cheered. "We'll not be needing these anymore," one of the passengers said and threw the brown bag in the garbage.

They crammed at the windows with their cheery faces to see and listen to what was happening outside. "It is clearing up!" someone shouted from the bunch.

"Yes, it is clearing up," Istvan agreed as he and Greta approached them. "I think the storm is finally over."

Leo looked at his friend. "There you are. I wondered where were you two this morning?" he said and they shook hands in the triumph of their survival.

"I'm sure the captain has thanked his lucky star that he has gotten off so lightly because this was a horrible storm," Istvan commented.

Leo turned to the window and peered out into the ocean. "I know he has, but so have we," he replied, without turning his head, still wondering if the storm was behind them.

Istvan joined him to the window, stared out for a few seconds, and then again said, "Yes, the storm is definitely subsiding, and it will be over soon."

Istvan's words made Leo very happy, he chuckled. "If you say so, I believe you." Both of them exhaled a breath of relief. Nevertheless, they were still apprehensive and continued to carefully scan the dark, murky ocean and the sky for any further trouble ahead. The wind still blew strong and cold, but the waves lessened, and the dark clouds were clearing off the sky.

"The sky has begun brightening," Katarina announced, excited to see the sun peeking beneath the still dark clouds.

Everyone laughed as they were witnessing through the window the demise of the ugly storm and the calm that had finally began to silence the madness. They were all happy to be alive. "By afternoon, it will all be clear," Greta forced a smile. Her stomach wasn't quite settled yet.

Leo and Istvan slid their hands under their wives' arms and in unison said, "Let's go have our breakfast."

At the door, Leo paused and sucked in his breath. After so many days of the dining saloon being mostly empty, the crowd took his breath away momentarily. "Wow, they are all back," he said, chuckling as they made it to their table.

Istvan looked at him. "What do you think, they are not hungry? Or you are the only one who's the right to be here?" he asked with a huge smile on his face.

Leo threw a glance at him. "I don't understand what you want me to answer to these," he asked and turned quickly toward the entrance where the smell of bacon and fresh percolated coffee drew his attention. "Here they come," he announced.

Reinvigorated, the stewards entered carrying a hot breakfast for the first time since the beginning of the storm. They rushed in and out of the dining saloon with smiles on their faces, serving the hungry passengers as they gathered around their tables. Most of the passengers had not fully recovered, but that didn't matter. They came anyway to join in the celebration with a hot breakfast and coffee, excited the storm was finally behind them.

Istvan wanted an answer. "Well, what is it?" he asked, staring at Leo as they waited in anticipation to be served. Leo, no longer used to waiting, was impatient and walked over to one of the stewards.

"Can I have a pot of coffee please," he asked cheerfully before his table was served.

"Yes, of course," the steward said and handed him a pot.

"The steward will bring the food soon," Leo announced and poured everyone a cup of steaming hot coffee.

Katarina looked at them and smirked. "As far as I know, you two are the only passengers who held firm against this monstrous storm," she said, knowing her husband wasn't about to answer that question to Istvan. She had to intervene. She picked up her coffee and sipped it. "Coffee never tasted better," she declared and continued sipping.

By then the steward brought a plate of food and placed it in the middle of the table. "Enjoy," he urged and strode away.

The smell of food overpowered Katarina's urge and she immediately cut a piece of bacon and devoured it. "It's delicious," she said and continued.

Watching his wife stuff her mouth with food, Leo smiled but advised, "Take it easy, darling. Your stomach is still weak."

She rose from her chair and kissed him impulsively. "Thank you for caring, my love. Without you, I would have never made it through this horrid ordeal. You're my rock, solid and eternal as Gibraltar."

Leo blushed, a little embarrassed. He didn't know what to say. His crooked smile showed for the first time in a very long time. Then, and only then, did Katarina feel there was still a glimmer of hope for them and their marriage. She looked at him full of admiration and also realized that the food she had eaten was staying down in her stomach. "I feel so good, I don't have to rush to the cabin. I can spend time with you here," she exclaimed happily.

Istvan turned to his wife and asked, "How about you, Greta?"

"I, too, feel stronger, but my stomach is still somewhat weak," she replied.

"Good," they both replied and rose from the table. "We'll be on the deck."

The girls said nothing but watched their husbands walk out through the deck door, stunned they didn't even ask them to come along. "How quickly they forget us," Greta muttered as they moved to a two-seater table beside the window.

After viewing the ocean through the window for a while, slowly sipping the delicious-smelling cappuccino, Katarina commented, "It looks lovely outside."

"Why don't you go out on the deck for a while?" Greta urged.

"It's freezing out there, I don't want to catch cold," Katarina replied, glancing at Greta's pale face and asked, "Greta, are you all right?"

"No, I'm not. My stomach isn't settled yet, and the coffee made it worse. I'm sorry, I can't drink this," she replied, pushing the cup away.

"You don't have to, just leave it," Katarina suggested and turned to stare out. Greta also turned to stare out the window across to the horizon. Each wrapped in their own thoughts silently enjoyed the calm of the ocean and watched the lingering dark clouds slowly clearing from the sky. There were no signs of a storm ahead, but the ocean remained murky.

Without turning her head, Katarina commented, "God, am I glad to be alive, but is the bad weather really behind us? Or will the frigid Atlantic boil below the ship again before we reach the Canadian coast and bury us, without mercy, deep in its dark bottom?"

"I think the storm is over, let go of your fear, Katarina," Greta tried to reassure her. Her voice was barely audible.

"I want so desperately to believe you and the captain's words when he said, 'No harm will come to any of you.' But we are still days away in the middle of Atlantic Ocean with no end in sight. Considering what we just went through, I'm not sure if I believe anything anymore," Katarina argued.

"We are all scared, but the captain is right. If you don't want to believe him, it's your prerogative. Maybe you should tell your husband," Greta advised.

"No way!" Katarina exclaimed with a high-pitched voice. "He should never know that I'm scared. You can't tell him that. Promise."

"All right. All right, I promise. Don't go crazy on me," Greta said.

"Thanks," Katarina said and turned back to stare at the ocean, her dark eyes fixed on the distant horizon, unable to determine the ocean's next move. The feeling of uneasiness in her heart persisted. She glanced at Greta and finally said, "I won't feel totally at ease until we step on terra firma." She was so wrapped in her thoughts that she didn't see Leo come inside.

"The sky is clearing and the ocean is much calmer. But it's getting colder out there. The smell of ice is in the air," Leo announced as he bent to his wife. "That must be a sign we're moving closer to Canada," he added, standing beside the table, smiling as he rubbed his palms together.

His wife looked at him and replied, "I don't know if we have something to smile about, if ice is synonymous with Canada personally, I don't think it's as cold as people want us to believe."

"For now, that's the only thing we have to go on. However, if other people survive and live there, why can't we?" Leo answered, still standing and rubbing his palms together.

"Yeah, yeah. Sit down," Katarina said. "You're blocking my view."

"I'm going to get myself a cup of coffee first. Would you two like coffee too?" he asked, looking at the girls.

"Nothing for me," Greta said quickly.

"Bring me a cappuccino please," Katarina requested.

"All right, one cup coming up," he briskly walked away bouncing on his feet.

Leo quickly returned and placed the cup in front of his wife. "Here. Be careful, it's hot," he warned and sat at the next two-seater table behind the girls. His gaze darted at the window. "It's much better out there today than it was a few days ago. The sky is almost clear and the wind has died down considerably. However, it's getting colder."

Katarina peered through the window glass out at the sky and the ocean. Even though she liked what she saw, shivers went up her spine as she remembered the stormy days that had passed. "You are not kidding about the sky," she chuckled. "I just hope the weather holds like this at least until we get to Canada."

"The storm is over. There's not going to be another one, darling," Leo tried to assure her with intense sincerity.

But his wife had a hard time trusting or believing anything after what they went through. "Wow! When did you become a weatherman?" she giggled, looking at her friend Greta, trying to hide her real feelings about it. His gaze followed hers as he hadn't bought her bravado look.

Xxxxxxxx
Leo glared at Greta. "The storm is over. Isn't that right?"

"Yes, Leo, you are right. I told her the same thing myself," Greta said and turned her head to stare out, not wanting to get involved in a squabble between them.

Leo didn't want to bicker with his wife either so he grasped her hand. "Would you like to come out on the deck for a short walk with me? It's cold, but it isn't that bad."

Katarina paused and glanced out the window, still holding his hand. The bright sun shining upon her face was so inviting. "All right," she chuckled. "I'll go, but only for a while."

"I'll stay here," Greta quickly answered as she didn't have the energy to fight queasiness and the cold at the same time.

Katarina stood up and sauntered out to the deck with her husband. The ship sliced through the wavy, dark, ice-cold Atlantic Ocean with ease. The air was cold and the wind was sharp and strong. It quickly wrapped Katarina's body like a sheet in a freezing chill. "You are right, Leo. There is the smell of ice in the air. This wind has teeth, it bites at my cheeks.

I told you. We are not far from Canada," he chided as they strolled along the deck.

"I don't know where we are, but it certainly is freezing up here," Katarina complained, snuggling her face against her husband to protect her nose and cheeks from the ice-cold wind. They were both shivering, but refused to go inside. "Where's Istvan? And we haven't seen Viktor for a while, what happened to him?" she asked, lifting her nose from Leo's chest.

"Istvan must have gone inside to check on his wife. Viktor? I don't know, he seems to appear and disappear like a Christmas elf." They both chuckled and walked a few more feet before Leo stopped and leaned against the deck rail to stare into the gloomy ocean. Katarina cuddled beside him to keep warm.

"Look! Darling," he shouted suddenly.

Katarina's eyes darted into the ocean. "Look where?" she asked, puzzled as she saw nothing.

"There. It's speeding toward us," he said and pointed his finger at something in the ocean.

She took a closer look and saw the fin of a huge shark swimming speedily toward the ship. "Oh no! It's a shark!" she screamed and leapt away from the railing.

Leo laughed. "Don't be stupid. It won't get you up here."

"What's so exciting over there?" Istvan asked as he and Greta appeared in front of them without being noticed.

"Nothing," Leo smirked tauntingly. "Just a little harmless shark," he teased.

"Harmless? You call a big shark like that harmless?" Katarina protested.

"Yes," Leo answered, chuckling. "Especially when he is down there and I am up here."

They peeked at the animal that was very close to the ship now and laughed. "We're quite safe here, you know, Katarina," Istvan said.

Leo glanced at Istvan and Greta. "My wife is petrified of sharks," he chuckled.

"At least I'm big enough to admit it, something you probably couldn't do," Katarina spat with fire in her eyes. She had had enough of his sarcasm and strode away fuming.

"I'm sorry, darling. I didn't mean to upset you," Leo yelled after her.

Katarina didn't turn her head, but kept on going straight to the cabin, furious with her husband for mocking her. Yes, it was good to have some breathing space, away from the overwhelming maleness of him. He insulted her and judged her constantly, and she always comes up short. She slammed the door after entering the cabin and threw herself down on her bed still huffing with anger.

Question after question lined up inside her head. What was going on with him? One moment he was loving and the next he was as distant as ever. "What is going to happen when we arrive in Canada, if we ever get there?" she muttered to herself and jumped off the bed and into the shower, trying to wash away any warm feeling of love she still had for her husband. Still, no matter how long she used the water, she couldn't.

Leo returned to the cabin and, when he didn't see her, called, "Darling, are you here?" There was no answer. Then he heard the water running and he knew she was in the bathroom taking a shower. He undressed and threw himself on the lower bunk and dozed off.

She finished showering, wrapped herself in a towel, and peeked out the bathroom door to see if Leo had come in. He was stretched on her bed with his arms under his head and stared straight up, snoring. As she watched him from the door, a cold suspicion lurked at the back of her mind. *Will things ever be the same between us again, my love?* she wondered, then giggled inwardly and muttered, "Not unless I do something about it. Instead of fighting him and acting like a spoiled brat, green with jealousy. Face it, Katarina, you'll always love him, no matter what. You should join him."

She emerged from the bathroom, wrapped only in a towel, and leaned against the door. Her dark-brown eyes watched his sleepy face with a mixture of wonder and weariness.

When Leo awoke, he appeared preoccupied with his own thoughts and didn't notice his wife at first. Suddenly, realizing she was standing there, Leo asked, "You're not still angry with me, are you, darling?" And he stared at her with his big blue enchanting eyes.

When her eyes met his, her anger dissipated and she was filled with love for him. "No, I'm not angry with you," she said. Then with shy eagerness, she held out her hands and let the towel slide from her body. "Come to me, my love," she called in a soft voice.

Without a word, Leo stood up and caught her in his arms. Gently slipping her arm behind her back, her hand still locked in his, he pulled her against him and looked down into her eyes, slowly maneuvering her toward the bed, showering her with kisses.

Katarina closed her eyes, dizzy from the rush of blood into her head. They kissed slowly, tasting the texture and scent of each other as if they were kissing for the first time.

Leo groaned with the force of the passion. "Oh, how I love you, my darling," he whispered and picked her up then laid her gently on the bed.

"I love you too," she finally said and pulled him down to kiss him.

He lay beside her, gathering her close against him as he rained tender kisses over her naked body. As they were making love, Katarina reeled in his arms and burned with desire for more. Tears of happiness were in her eyes as she knew then that she finally had her husband back again completely. Afterward, they lay awake in each other's arms without a word for what seemed to be on eternity.

The loudspeakers announcing supper forced them back to reality. "Oops, we'd better get dressed and go," Leo said and jumped off the bed.

"Yes, I'm starving," she replied and followed him. They both got ready and walked into the dining saloon with bright faces and huge grins.

Istvan and Greta were already sitting at the table when they arrived. "Hello, you two. You looked like cats that ate the canary. Where have you been?" Istvan asked with a chuckle as he studied them, then turned his smile toward his wife. He had a good idea what they had been doing.

"Why? We didn't miss the supper, did we?" Leo glanced at him and pulled out a chair for Katarina.

She sat down, threw a surprised look at her husband, and said, "Thank you, my love." Leo didn't usually do those kinds of things for her; it threw her off for a few seconds. But the smell of the steaming chicken soup in the serving bowl got her back on track. She pulled it closer, filled her soup plate, and began to eat.

Everyone was enjoying their food except Greta. She just stared at it. Katarina lifted her head from her plate long enough to ask, "Aren't you eating?"

"My stomach isn't quite well yet," Greta replied with a frown.

"Why don't you try some chicken soup? It's delicious. And your stomach will feel better that much quicker if you eat," Katarina advised and continued spooning her soup.

"All right, Nurse Katarina, you win," Greta sneered and slowly began grabbing soup out of her plate. Their husbands were too busy filling their mouths with food to comment.

Katarina wanted to ask Greta several questions so she was hoping they would be able to talk for a while after dinner but wondered if she should since Greta was still sick. Even so, she decided to ask, "What city are you and your husband settling in?"

"I think the name of the city is Kitchener," she whispered and added. "If you don't mind, I really don't feel like talking. My stomach is still so upset, I have to leave. I'm sorry," Greta said before she and her husband left for their cabin.

There hadn't been much opportunity for conversation because the storm and the seasickness had prevented them from spending time together, but Katarina had hoped they would become good friends. So she was disappointed to learn that Greta and Istvan weren't going to a same city as they were.

Leo glanced at his wife's sad face. "You can talk to her tomorrow," he suggested.

"I guess you're right. Let's go to sleep now," Katarina said with a pout and stood up from the chair.

"We are both still beat from the storm, especially you, darling. A good night's sleep will service us well," her husband replied, and they strolled down the steps slowly and carefully. Even though the storm had subsided, they were not taking any chance.

While they soundly slept the night away, the Atlantic waters settled as much as they do in the winter season and the ship was sailing peacefully across the dark cold ocean toward Canada.

The following morning when they came up to the dining saloon, Katarina stopped and looked suspiciously at the stewards rushing all over. "Something's going on," she said, fearing another storm was in sight.

"It can be bad, darling. They probably have a lot of work to catch up. Besides, they're all wearing smiles," Leo observed as they progressed through the dining saloon toward their table.

She looked closely and said, "You are right, but for a minute—"

"You thought they are preparing for another storm, didn't you?" Leo finished her sentence.

"Well, yes, I did," she answered and her eyes drifted around the dining saloon. "Look at these tables, they are as rich with food as they were for New Year holidays. Don't tell me nothing is going on," she chided as they sat at their table.

"If it is. I don't know anything about it." Leo shrugged and dug into the food.

Just then Istvan and Greta strolled in, as cheerful as ever. Greta's eyes too wandered across the tables, filled with questions. "What's happening, why is there all this food?" she chortled before she sat down.

Katarina looked at Greta. "We'd like to know that too."

"No. You want to know. I like the tables this way, full of food," Leo commented and kept picking at the hors d'oeuvres.

The dining saloon was buzzing, filled with passengers. Everyone was enjoying their special breakfast, including Istvan and Leo, while at table 21 discussion still continued between Greta and Katarina about the bottle of champagne. "I don't know what's going on. But one thing is sure. Something is up," Katarina said, staring at the bottle on the table.

"You must be right," Greta agreed. "Champagne isn't usually offered to passengers, especially not to us refugees."

Tired of listening of their squabbling over the bottle of champagne, Istvan turned toward them and smiled. "Come on, girls. The crew is probably preparing to celebrate their beloved ship's retirement. Remember, this is its last crossing. We were all told that in Naples. *Cristoforo Colombo* won't be taking any more journeys to Canada or anywhere else."

"Oh, that's all right!" they both shouted. They all sighed in relief, and once again, laughter and happy chattering were heard at table 21.

The morning couldn't be more perfect. There was no more violent bow pitching, dishes flying, or stomachs churning, and the sun was shining again. For Katarina, it was even brighter as she was basking in the glow of having her husband back.

Everyone was so busy indulging in their delicious food that they didn't notice the captain had stepped into the second-class saloon room, but his cheery voice got their attention. "Good morning, everyone! This is your captain speaking," he smiled widely. "I'm happy to announce that we've just entered Canadian waters."

The dining saloon erupted into cheers, applause, and merriment. The passengers chanted, "Hurrah! Hurrah!"

The captain waited for the noise to subside and then continued.

"Our estimated time of arrival at Halifax is this afternoon, around two o'clock. I want to thank you all personally for your patience and understanding during the storm. I know it was hard, and I regret you had to endure such suffering on my ship. But now, help us celebrate our beloved ship's last crossing. You've earned it as you helped us pull it through the worst storm we've seen in the last eight years," he finished and raised a glass of champagne in a toast. "Cheers!"

The refugees lifted their glass and shouted, "Cheers!" and expressed their gratitude with songs and laughter that echoed from bow to stern. The captain's announcement removed the last shrouds of anxiety and doubts, even Katarina's or at least she thought.

She cheered the captain from the top of her lungs, jumping with joy. Her urge to cry was almost overwhelming. None was more ecstatic to hear that they'd soon be standing on terra firma than Katarina.

The captain finished his glass of champagne and dashed out of the second-class saloon. Leo took his glass with one hand and gave the other to his wife. "Let's go sit there beside the window," he suggested. Katarina smiled and rose from her chair.

Leo glanced at Istvan and asked, "Are you two coming with us?"

"Sure," Istvan announced. The four of them sauntered over to the window table with the glasses of champagne in their hands. Instead of sitting down though, the men placed their glasses on the table and said, "We'll be right back," before dashing out the door.

Their wives sat down and turned their heads to stare out of the window at the ocean. Katarina's fear came crashing down on her. Nettlesome questions still remained on her mind despite the captain's speech. "There's no end in sight," Katarina complained suddenly.

"Don't worry, we'll get there," Greta tried to assure her.

"Oh, I'm not worried," she lied. The only thing she knew for sure was that she was on the ship in the freezing Atlantic, probably thousands of kilometers away from the nearest shore. Sailing to a foreign country, she had no clue about it and whose language she did not speak. What the future would hold for them once, or if, they arrived in Canada was something she could only guess. The sound of loud voices coming from the deck intruded upon her dream and brought Katarina back to reality with a thud. "The land!" she yelled and rushed out to the deck. Greta followed her unable to say a word.

Outside, the wind blew cold, making them both shiver. A group of passengers were leaning against the deck rail, including their husbands, chatting and shouting something that was lost on the wind.

The girls worked their way over to their husbands who were staring ahead into the ocean. "Is there land in sight?" Katarina asked.

Leo glanced at his wife. "No. There's still no land in sight, darling, but look over there, dolphins!" he said, pointing.

Katarina's and Greta's eyes followed Leo's pointing and scanned the water. Suddenly, two slick gray dolphins leaped to the water surface and began cavorting in the bow wave, arching above the water effortlessly, and then diving under. "They are playing with the ship!" the girls said, thrilled with their acrobatic performances.

"That means we'll have good luck from here on," Istvan said, staring at the dolphins as they dive under and disappeared from the surface.

"This time I believe you," Leo interceded.

The girls smiled gratefully through their chattering teeth and trembling bodies. "We better get out of this cold beating wind," Greta said.

"You're right," Katarina agreed and they ran inside.

"I guess we should go too before we turn into a popsicle," Istvan joked and they rushed after the girls.

"Can I get you coffee to warm up?" Leo asked his wife and Greta, looking at their blue faces.

"Yes please," they said in unison, barely able to get their words out, their teeth were chattering so hard and their lips were numb.

"Four hot coffees coming up," Leo said and rushed away.

As soon as the steaming coffees were placed on the table, the girls grabbed a hot cup and wrapped their hands around it. While they drank their coffee and warmed up, they watched the passengers on the deck, waiting to hear the shouts when land was finally spotted. They were all tense and excited; Katarina finished her last drop of coffee and said, "I can't sit still." She stood up and began pacing in and out of the dining saloon. Whenever they ventured on to the deck, they searched the horizon apprehensively for the sign of land.

As the *Cristoforo Colombo* inched closer to Canada, Katarina's thoughts ran in another direction as a new worry emerged. "Greta, do you speak English?" she asked.

"No, I don't."

"How are you going to communicate with the Canadian people?" Katarina asked desperately.

Leo grabbed his wife's hand. "I'm sure there'll be people who can speak Croatian as well as English, darling," he said, looking around for confirmation.

"You are right, Leo," Istvan agreed, trying to assure them and himself.

After several hours pacing in and out the deck, Katarina began losing faith. "Let's go in, it's cold. The ship will probably never reach the land," she said and turned to walk inside.

Then everyone began to shout, "LAND! LAND! AHEAD!"

Katarina turned and saw a land in the distance. Her face flashed and her smile widened. "That must be Canada!" she yelled and ran into her husband's arms.

A new round of laughter, singing, and shouting followed as the refugees cheered the ship's approaching the Canadian port of Halifax, with the happy tears running down their cheeks. There wasn't a dry eye on the deck, for that matter, on the ship.

To make things even more exciting, four dolphins emerged ahead of the ship, from the deep of the Atlantic, and began a show. "Dolphins!" Katarina yelled, pointing. "Look! They are those four slick gray dolphins that were showing off before."

"They are so beautiful!" Greta sighed, watching them.

The dolphins sprang from the water gracefully and dove back down several times before speeding ahead. "Look, they are welcoming us to Canada," someone shouted from the crowd.

People clapped and laughed, but despite their joy in watching the land spread across the horizon and the antics of the dolphins, they continued to walk in and out as none could stay out long, it was too cold. Yet the lure of the growing vision of land was great so as soon as they warmed up with a hot coffee, "Let's return to the deck," Leo said and headed to the door.

"Why not," Istvan replied jokingly. "Who cares if it's freezing out there?" They all laughed and followed Leo out to the deck.

The sky was clear and the sun shone, but its warmth never reached their freezing bodies. Still, nothing could keep the refugees away from the deck railing, everyone wanted to see the first gleams of their new country.

"Oh, wow! Look, Leo, that must be Halifax!" Katarina yelled, exhilaration sweeping over her as she watched the city rise from the ocean, tears were never far behind in her eyes. She could hardly wait to step on terra firma.

Leo wrapped his arms around her body. "It seems that way," he replied, and they both stared at the rows of small houses covered with a thick white blanket of snow.

"Different. Too many small houses and a lot of snow and ice" was Katarinas's first reaction to their new country. With an ache in her heart and mixed emotions, she stared at her husband. "Our new home is going to be in a strange ice land."

"We'll be fine, darling," her husband whispered and squeezed her closer.

"So much snow. How am I going to walk in these?" she commented and glanced down at her light summer shoes. Her body shivered and she ran inside. Leo and their friends joined her to stare at the city through the window, waiting in anticipation for the ship to inch its way through the narrow spoon-shaped channel and pass under McDonald's bridge. They went back to the deck as many others did to watch the ship dock in Halifax at the harbor pier 21.

The Canadian bone-chilling wind stung everyone's cheeks, and soon their noses were red and running. Everyone on the deck was shivering, especially those girls who weren't wearing the warm clothes given to them by the Red Cross in Italy. Katarina was among them. Her teeth chattered as she pulled her summer coat tightly around her body and cuddled closer to her husband to keep warm. "Maybe I should have taken that ugly army coat from the camp," she whispered, but she wasn't about to go inside.

"It would have come in handy now, darling," Leo agreed as he took off his coat and wrapped it around her shoulders.

She looked at him. "Thanks, my love," his wife said, bundling herself tighter against the freezing wind. Katarina hid her nose in the coat and joined others to watch the ship dock.

The great *Cristoforo Colombo* inched closer to pier 21 with the help of Canadian tugs that helped the ship reached its spot at the pier.

When the ship docked, more passengers crowded the deck and just in time to see a huge sign flashed in front of them. "WELCOME TO CANADA!"

The words meant nothing to most of them and surely not to Katarina for she didn't understand a word of English, but within seconds, someone yelled the meaning of the words. She smiled at Leo and boasted, "Of course, I knew that."

"Of course, you did. Just like I did," he laughed back, rubbing his palms against each other and walking in place to keep warm while Katarina was scanning the crowded pier, searching desperately for a familiar face. There were many faces, waving hands, and incomprehensible welcoming words.

As if he read her mind, Leo smiled and embraced her.
"You are not going to find a familiar face here, darling."

"I know. I suppose I should be thankful and happy for being accepted with open arms, and I am," Katarina admitted. "But I wish my parents could be here waiting to welcome us to our new home rather than a bunch of strangers speaking a different language which I don't understand."

"Of course, you do. I wish that too, but you know that's not possible," Leo replied.

"I know," Katarina said, thankful and happy she had her husband with her to share the task of adjusting to a new environment and home.

"Now, let's go inside. I'm freezing. It's cold," Leo said and rushed toward the door. Istvan, Greta, and Katarina followed him; she took the coat off and handed it to her husband.

"No wonder you are cold," she said and placed the coat over his shoulders. "Thank you."

"Greta and I will say good-bye to you now. When we disembark, who knows whether we'll have a chance to see each other in this crowd," Istvan said, extending his hand to Leo and added. "By the way, you never did tell me what city you and your wife are going to."

"To a city called Winnipeg," Leo applied. "You two are going to Toronto, right?"

"No, Kitchener," Istvan said and shook his hand. "Good-bye. It was nice to meet you. Who knows, maybe some day we might see each other again."

"It was our pleasure to meet you both. Katarina and I wished we'd have spent more time together. Who knows maybe some day," Leo said, still holding his hand. "Good-bye."

The women embraced and said good-bye to each other. Then came the moment they'd all been waiting for such a long time. "The passengers are all free to begin debarkation," the captain announced.

Emotions ran high.

"Hurrah! Hurrah! Thank you, Canada!" The words spread throughout the deck as the passengers gathered at the exit, including Katarina and the company. As Istvan predicted, they were pushed ahead.

"Good-bye," Katarina whispered as she watched them disappear in the crowd. "Will there ever come a time when I'll be saying hello to my friends and not good-bye all the time?"

Her face flooded with tears just as she and Leo stepped off the ship onto Canadian terra firma, He transferred their handbags to his left hand and, with his right hand, pulled his wife tightly against him and kissed her as they navigated through the crowd toward the entrance into the building. "Don't cry. We made it! We're home now, darling!" Leo boasted and smiled at his wife.

Katarina paused and glanced back at the ship. "I hope so," she said in a low tone, not too sure what to think yet. She was about to embark on a new life in a new land that welcomed Leo and her with open arms. But what a price Leo and she had paid to be here. Katarina glanced at Leo with a look of satisfaction, and they stepped forward into their new life.

Edwards Brothers Malloy
Thorofare, NJ USA
July 5, 2012